THE FAI

Behind iron bars stood Kerridis—beautiful, magical, a woman of the fairy folk . . . the Faerie Queen . . . beauty remembered from a dream. She reached out experimental fingers and touched the grillwork, but flinched away as if it burned her.

Fenton advanced from the shadows, the flamedigger glowing in his hand. "My Lady," he asked awkwardly, "can I—can I help?"

She gestured at the metal grille. "Can you unfasten the door? If I touched it, my hand would go up in smoke. And already . . ." With a rueful smile, she held out her fingers, which were blackened and bent into a painful curve.

Fenton put out his hand to unfasten the door —and his hand went through the metal!

Of course. Here he was insubstantial, shadowless—a 'tweenman!

THE
HOUSE
BETWEEN THE
WORLDS

Marion Zimmer Bradley

A Del Rey Book

BALLANTINE BOOKS • NEW YORK

A Del Rey Book
Published by Ballantine Books

Copyright © 1980, 1981 by Marion Zimmer Bradley

This is a revised and expanded edition of THE HOUSE
BETWEEN THE WORLDS by Marion Zimmer Bradley, origi-
nally published by Doubleday & Co., Inc.

Library of Congress Catalog Card Number: 79-7800

ISBN 0-345-28830-0

This edition published by arrangement with
Doubleday & Co., Inc.

Manufactured in the United States of America

First Ballantine Books Edition: August 1981

Cover art by Laurence Schwinger

To POUL ANDERSON, fantasy writer extraordinary, poet, and translator of Norse epics; for sharing with me several of his favorite legends, and introducing me to the Alfar—not to mention, for informing me that they were in common domain, belonging not to any one writer but to the Commonwealth of Literature.

Marion Zimmer Bradley

Author's Note

There is not, of course, on the campus of the University of California at Berkeley (or anywhere else) any such building as Smythe Hall. Nor is there any Department of Parapsychology, nor any such faculty, student body or instructors as are described here. The campus of the University is a real place, and I have, in general, followed the general geography of the city of Berkeley for this novel, taking the liberty of erecting Smythe Hall somewhere near where Barrows Hall actually stands. All this was a convenience, to eliminate the necessity for creating an imaginary campus with a real one on my doorstep.

If the name of any living person has been used, it is unavoidable: any name invented by a novelist will at some time have been given to one of the multitudes populating this crowded continent.

MARION ZIMMER BRADLEY

CHAPTER ONE

CAMERON FENTON was beginning to feel nervous. The room was so white and sterilized, like a hospital, and there was a vague nagging smell of disinfectants and drugs. The preparations were unnerving. He hadn't expected it to be quite like this—the white sterile room, the white coats, the high hard hospital bed. Dr. Garnock had his back turned, and Fenton looked around uneasily at the door.

He could still get up and walk out any minute.

How did I get myself into this, anyway?

Curiosity, he replied to himself. *Curiosity; the same old stuff that killed the cat.*

It had sounded so different when Garnock mentioned it downstairs. The neat, shabby old office, tucked away in a corner of the otherwise new-and-offensively-bright Smythe Hall. Full of books and piled-high papers and the intriguing charts on the wall. Garnock had seemed different then, too; his old tweed coat open at the neck, his tie undone, a cup of scummy coffee cooling forgotten on the edge of the littered desk. Cameron Fenton had forgotten his own coffee, in excitement, at what the professor was saying.

"It started out as just another of the hallucinogenic drugs," Garnock said, pointing to the open magazine in his lap. "We found it, first, in *Psychedelic Review.* There were a few of the street kids brought in, tripping on the stuff. You know, of course, that as fast as they discover and ban one psychedelic, the kids come up with a new one? Eventually we got around to testing it. Oh, the technical poop is all in here, if you care to read it. And it turned out to be the big breakthrough we've all been looking for. Tested again and again, under absolutely

1

impeccable clinical safeguards. We even did what they wanted them to do at Stanford when they did those tests on Uri Geller that everybody's been arguing about for years—we got in a stage magician and let *him* fix up our subjects so they couldn't fake the results."

"So, basically, it's a drug to raise the level of available ESP—extrasensory perception?"

"That's about the size of it," Garnock said. He was a tall, rangy man, with a permanent five-o'clock shadow and longish hair; Cameron Fenton wondered why *he* had never broken down and let the hair and beard grow. On the Berkeley campus nobody would have noticed. Lewis Garnock, Waite Professor of Parapsychology, was outstanding in any crowd, and Fenton wondered if *that* was why . . . he dragged his mind back to what Garnock was saying and asked, "What about safety?"

"No serious side effects in more than two hundred clinical trials, first on laboratory animals and then on humans."

"And the ESP effect is definitely established, then?"

Garnock nodded. "Definitely. Most drugs, as you know, affect ESP scores adversely. Drug a man, and his ability to call a deck of ESP cards goes way, way down, even before he shows any other effect. One or two drinks loosen the inhibitions and raise ESP scores a few points, but let the subject keep on drinking, and he'll lose the ESP even before he starts getting drunk."

"But this new stuff—"

"Antaril."

"Antaril—where did you get the name?"

"God knows; came up out of the computer, I guess. Anyhow, it raises the ESP scores—listen to this, Cam— never less than fifty per cent; sometimes four and five hundred per cent. Under median dosage of Antaril— we're still experimenting for the optimum dosage—four men at Duke did *eight* perfect runs consecutively. You can figure out the mathematical odds against that kind of results, yourself."

Fenton whistled. He had followed the Rhine experiments from the time he was old enough to read about them. In the first thirty years of Rhine's experiments, there had been only four perfect runs—and somebody had cast doubt on those.

Garnock watched his face, finally nodded slowly. "Yes," he said. "It's the breakthrough, all right. It's the kind of evidence that we've been sweating for, for years —the kind we can shove under the noses of the diehards who still insist that ESP just doesn't exist."

Fenton knew all about that. He quoted now, grimly, the most quoted comment ever made about parapsychology.

"On any other subject, one-tenth the evidence would already have convinced me. On this subject, ten times the evidence would not convince me."

Garnock said, "If this proves out the way I hope it will, it's going to make it all worthwhile; all the years I sat here taking the crap they hand out to any reputable psychologist who goes into parapsychology. The years I had to fight to establish a Department of Parapsychology inside the psych department. The way they hassled my students to quantify everything and run it through the computer before they'd accept it. The way they turned my best students into rat-runners by requiring four semesters of behavioral psych as a prerequisite. And even after that, they said they didn't believe in brainwashing." His face was set, distant, remembering. Then he shook himself a little and came back to today.

"Take this stuff home, Cam. Read it overnight, and let me know if you want in."

Fenton had taken home the thick folder of "technical poop" and had come back the next day with a few more questions.

"The ESP-effect—is it infallible? Everybody gets it?"

"Not quite. Six out of ten. Regular as clockwork— six out of ten."

"And the other four?"

"Some of them lose consciousness too fast to maintain contact with the researcher, so we don't know what result they get. They wake up reporting coherent dreams and hallucinations," Garnock told him. "Sally Lobeck— you remember her, she was a student when you were; now she's one of my assistants—is trying to set up a content analysis of the dreams and hallucinations for possible precognitive value. I don't think there's much in it, myself, but Sally thinks she might get a dissertation out of it, so I approved the project. The tenth case—well, really it's rarer than that—gets a temporary improved ESP state, then slips into the hallucinatory phase and comes back reporting severe pains and temporary loss of orientation. This is the nearest thing we've had to an undesirable side effect. And in every case, it's been transitory. But, of course, we are still calling it experimental. We've given it to a hundred and four human subjects, and that isn't really all that many. There could be some side effects we just haven't run up against yet."

But Cameron Fenton had had only one question: "When can I try it?"

But now that the preparations were complete, Fenton was getting nervous. He somehow hadn't guessed that it would all be so clinical.

In the department itself, up on the lab floor of Smythe, the ESP tests were informal. For all the rigid control kept over them, they were done in an informal, easy atmosphere. That was necessary; Cam Fenton wasn't much of a behaviorist, but he did know that the easiest way to extinguish a response was to provide no feedback at all. Early ESP tests at Duke University had suffered from that problem; it was boring—just plain *boring* to call deck after deck of ESP cards without any hint of what your score had been. And this, of course, accounted for the fact that many early, promising subjects, displaying measurable ESP to a high degree, had fizzled out. Early ESP tests, with the best intentions in the world, all in the interest of rigidly controlled scientific research, had been set up in such a way as to extinguish any ESP the research subject might possess, through boredom, fatigue or exhaustion.

The way you did it was simple. You sat behind an enormous plywood panel, with "blinkers" on each side of your face to eliminate vague sensory cues from the other side of the lab. Someone on the other side of the panel turned a deck of 25 ESP cards face up, one at a time. You concentrated on the vague "feel" you got from the cards—cross, star, wavy line, circle, square—and wrote down your choice. When you finished the run, you came around the plywood screen and compared your written list with the list the researcher had made, and that was all there was to it.

Pure chance meant that you would get four, five or six right. If you were tired, or out of sorts, or had had a late night, usually it was dead-level chance.

But you kept going, and when they started having the operator press a little green light to "reward" you after every right choice, your scores went up. There were those times when, following your vague "hunches" you had called twelve right, then fourteen, and one shattering day you had called nineteen cards right in a row. You still didn't know how you did it. You just saw the little pictures in your mind's eye somewhere, and you wrote them down that way. You couldn't do it if you *tried;* you could do it best when you were working with an alpha feedback machine and running as close as you could get to pure alpha waves on the EEG machine. You got used to doing our tests hooked up to an EEG. Everybody had his or her own favorite set of conditions. They had tested some students repeatedly under minimal dosages of LSD, and Garnock had been delighted when *that* experiment failed.

"That's all we need up here," he said grimly, the day Paul Lawford finally dropped out of the parapsychology department. "For the word to get around that I'm trying to make acid-heads out of the kids in the department."

You got used to people on campus making jokes about serious graduate students who dabbled in witchcraft. You learned to cope with departmental politics; the psychology department had never quite recovered from the shock of having the Waite Chair of Parapsychology endowed and staffed, and when parapsychology was made a separate department, no more under the direction of the psychology department than was educational psychology, three full professors of psychology had threatened to resign, on the grounds that the Department of Psychology at Berkeley would become a laughingstock.

You learned to brush off the jokers who insisted they wanted their fortune told, and you got used to defending the department against the hecklers who still believed that the Department of Parapsychology was all one big hoax, that Doctor Garnock, Ph.D., M.D., L.L.D., and all his assistants were in league to do all this boring work for some unexplained but sinister reason, and thus perpetuate the hoax of ESP. You got used to the students who insisted they were psychic, but couldn't call even one deck of ESP cards higher than chance in a hundred runs. They usually left convinced that you were part of the plot against them. And you got used to coping with the temperament, and the occasional swelled heads, of the students who really *were* psychic. . . .

No. *Those,* you never got used to.

And that was why you kept on doing it, in spite of the fact that you wondered—God, how you wondered! —why you cared if anybody had ESP or not. Because, every now and then, somebody turned up with the genuine article. The real, genuine article.

The wild talent.

Rare. Terribly, terribly rare. Cameron Fenton had a little of it—not enough to scare him, but he had it and could call a good set of cards at least once a day. But there were the kids who could do it regularly, once an hour. There were the kids who could roll forty sets of doubles—in a mechanical shaking machine, with nobody touching the dice—consecutively. Nobody knew how they did it, but even the professional magicians on the staff admitted that they had done it without fakery.

And that was what kept you going. . . .

That was what kept you doing the boring ESP cards, what kept you bullying your giggling students into taking the ESP tests, most of them skeptical, full of the jokes every freshman class thought they had invented about ESP.

And you read everything, and wondered how in the hell, in the final quarter of the Twentieth Century, people still managed to kid themselves into *not* believing in ESP. To Cameron Fenton, that was like the interview he'd heard when he was a teenager, the day man first landed on the Moon—the interview with a Flat-Earther. The Flat-Earther still insisted that the ship couldn't possibly have orbited the Earth, because the Earth wasn't round. "Oh, sure, that ship went somewhere," the Flat-Earther had admitted. "In a big circle on the surface.

But it didn't go to the moon, because it *couldn't*." And he had shrugged off the photographic evidence. "Faked. You can do anything with photography these days— just look at the movies they make."

Maybe, Fenton thought, watching Garnock making his preparations, that was why he had gotten into parapsychology. He just didn't like the idea of being a Flat-Earther of the mind, the kind of person who didn't want facts muddling up his prejudices.

Freud had never accumulated half this much evidence about the existence of the subconscious mind. Einstein hadn't done half so many statistical researches on the structure of the atom. In any other field, the mathematical evidence alone would have overwhelmed all dissent. But because it was parapsychology, they were still struggling with proof that the phenomena *existed,* instead of studying them and finding out how the world could be altered because of this new knowledge.

There were a few exceptions, of course. The great Rhine. Hoyt Ford in Texas, who had first started requiring a course in parapsychology to graduate in psychology. And among those with the courage to speak out, Ford's pupil, Lewis Wade Garnock, Waite Professor of Parapsychology at the University of California, Berkeley. And here he was, working with Garnock for proof, after all these years away from the campus.

Am I still skeptic? Is it myself I want to convince?

"How about it, Cam? Ready?"

Fenton nodded. "But do I have to get up on the couch?"

Garnock grinned on one side of his face. "Sounds as if I'd turned Freudian in my old age, doesn't it? It's just that eventually you lose consciousness and, frankly, it's easier to manage if you're already in bed."

Fenton took off his shoes and got up on the hospital bed. He shoved the pillow into a comfortable position, loosened his collar, rolled up his right sleeve above the elbow. He felt the pressure spray and was grateful; he'd always hated needles.

"You ought to start feeling drowsy in a few minutes," Garnock said. "I'll tell them, out there, to get the cards set up."

Fenton shut his eyes, fighting vague dizziness and disorientation. He wondered for a moment if the dizziness was real and physical, or the result of suggestion. Garnock had told him to expect drowsiness. *I'll mention that to Doc, he could control it better by not telling a subject what to expect.* Now he felt faintly sick and wondered for a moment if he were going to vomit. Through the growing queasiness, Garnock's voice was a vague annoyance.

"Ready to run a deck, Cam? It's all set up."

Oh, hell, why not, that's what this whole thing is all about.

Cameron Fenton got up off the hospital bed and walked over to the screen, where the operator, behind the strip of plywood that barred her off from view from the hospital bed, was laying out the cards. He felt faintly dizzy; as he stumbled, he felt his hand go *through* the plywood screen. Strangely, he felt no panic. He looked back to the hospital bed, and saw, without surprise, that he was still lying there. The body on the bed, inert and drowsy, said, "Any time you're ready, Doc."

Garnock was poised with paper and pencil. *I'm glad he's handling it,* Fenton thought, looking back at his inert body. *Neither of us is in any shape to handle paper and pencil.*

Neither of us? What am I, then? The ka, the astral double? He felt like giggling. He had never believed in those theories. Now it seemed a great joke. Was it really ESP, if he could stand over here and see the cards from behind the screen, red-haired Marjie Anderson laying them down, one at a time?

"Circle."

"Circle," Garnock wrote down.

"Star."

"Star."

"Wavy line."

"Wavy line."

One by one, Marjie laid down the cards and one by one, Cameron Fenton relayed the information to his semiconscious double on the bed, who repeated the words without interest.

I'd better get a few wrong or he'll suspect I'm cheating. Funny, I never wanted to cheat before. And then Fenton felt confused.

Am I cheating? Or is this real ESP? My ordinary senses, that body on the bed over there, it can't see anything, so I'm not really cheating. And yet I am standing here watching Marjie lay out the cards and so in a sense I'm cheating.

He said something like this, and Garnock soberly wrote it down. "So you know it is Marjie, do you? That's very interesting. Next card."

"Square."

"Square."

"Star."

"Star."

"Cross."

"Cross."

He continued through the twenty-five cards. Garnock rose to go around the screen.

"Don't bother," Fenton said, or rather the unconscious double on the bed said; Fenton "himself" was standing behind Marjie. "It's a perfect run. It couldn't be anything else."

Garnock got up and went behind the screen. Marjie, of course, could not hear anything Fenton had said. But Garnock's face changed appreciably as he glanced at the written list in Marjie's hand, showing the order in which she had laid down the cards, and the list in his own hand, and—*this was eerie!*—Fenton could *hear* him thinking.

"Perfect run—my God, how did he know?"

As Garnock came back Fenton said, "I told you so."

Garnock struggled to keep his face and voice perfectly expressionless. "Good work, Cam. Want to run through it again?"

Fenton said, "Sure. As many times as you like."

Garnock touched the buzzer that started Marjie patiently laying out the cards again.

"Star."

"Star."

"Wavy line."

"Wavy line . . ."

But it was harder this time. Not to see the cards—he could see them as well as ever—but to control the voice of the inert body on the bed. He suffered from a disturbing sensation that the world was thinning out around him, and vanishing. He did not answer when Marjie laid out a card, and Garnock prompted, "Fenton? Next card?"

"You think I'm lying here on the bed," Fenton said, and heard the thickening and fuzzing of his voice. "But really I'm standing right over here beside Marjie and watching her lay out the cards—"

"Interesting," Garnock said, scribbling down something. "Would you care to tell me a little more about that sensation, Fenton?"

"Damn it," he said, hearing his voice thin out and blur frighteningly, "don't try your nondirective psychology on me! I'm over here, I tell you!"

"Yes, yes, of course. Will you finish the run of cards, Cam?"

"Why? Want to prove I can get another perfect run? Okay, then. Star, circle, wavy line, square, square, circle, star—"

"Wait a minute, you're going too fast, Cam. Marjie doesn't have time—"

"She can lay them out afterward, I'm giving them the way they're stacked up," Fenton said, aware that he could see down *through* Marjie's deck. "Wavy line, star, circle, wavy line, square, cross, square . . ."

Garnock was scribbling frantically, and Fenton could hear him thinking again.

This is one we only had once before . . . Funny. I expected Fenton might be one of those who didn't react to Antaril at all . . .

"Want to try another run of the cards, Cam?"

Before we lose contact with him. . . .

"No," Fenton said, "it's too damn much trouble to hold myself together now." The room was thinning; yet his body felt reassuringly solid. His hands gripped one another, he could hear his heart beat, the small reassuring murmur of the blood in his veins.

He turned away from Marjie and walked out through the wall into the corridor. Behind him he saw the inert body on the bed go flaccid, saw Garnock move to his side, concerned.

"Cam?"

He didn't wait around to see what happened. He walked out and left Smythe Hall behind.

CHAPTER TWO

OUTSIDE SMYTHE HALL he felt better. There was something about the way the floor had seemed to fade away and turn grey and thin under his feet, to disappear and crumble, that had scared—well, no; it hadn't *scared* him. He didn't think anything could have scared him right now; he felt euphoric. But it had made him feel uneasy. With his feet—they felt solid to himself, but unsettlingly unsolid on any artificial surface—with his feet planted firmly on *terra firma,* he felt better.

But all around Fenton the solid brick buildings of the campus were dimming out and getting unreal. *It would be weird,* he thought, *to walk right through the walls and right through Dwinelle Hall.* But he didn't want to do it. The bodies of the students were insubstantial too, not quite real, and when, in his restless movement, he walked *through* one of them, he couldn't feel it. Unsettling. Yes, that was the word, it was unsettling.

But when he walked up against a tree, in a mood of experiment, he felt a hard, painful shock. Evidently his new world displayed laws; it wasn't just a dreamworld where anything went, but had its own very serious laws and regulations; one of them was that while man-made objects like buildings had no material existence, the ground he walked on, and such things as trees—and rocks, as he discovered by barking his shins against a small outcrop—were completely solid.

But why weren't the people solid? People were natural objects, weren't they? It didn't make sense.

Or could one apply any kind of rational laws to what was, after all, supposed to be a drug-induced hallucination?

He seemed to move over the campus lightly, his feet

12

hardly touching the ground. When he looked back, he discovered that Smythe Hall was long gone. He went down northward along the campus, noticing that the roadways and drives had vanished. It occurred to Fenton that he ought to watch where he was going. If he wandered all the way across the campus, and out on to North Campus and Euclid Avenue, he wouldn't see the street, or the traffic—but what if they couldn't see him and ran over him?

No; obviously, where ever he was, the traffic wouldn't have any more effect on him than when he had wandered through the bike rack in front of the library. His material body was back in Smythe Hall.

Am I simply in another dimension, then? He had read a considerable amount about the theory of parallel dimensions. Was he on the campus in another dimension, then—a world as it might have looked if the campus of the University of California had been built somewhere else—or where it had never been built at all?

Nonsense. This is a dream, a hallucination induced by Antaril. Garnock said this was one of the known effects —abnormally lucid hallucinations; and Sally Lobeck is doing a content analysis on them.

Maybe I'd better take notes. He laughed at himself as he said it—take notes with *what?* He didn't have any notebook or pencil and if he did, how would he take notes when they had been left with his body in Smythe Hall? And then something else occurred to him.

Why am I still wearing clothes?

If my body is back in Smythe Hall, why aren't my clothes back there with it?

Is it because I think of myself as basically wearing clothes when I go outdoors?

At one time—early in the study of psychology which had preceded specializing in parapsychology—he had studied the psychological interpretation of dreams, and how to alter dream perceptions. He hadn't had much luck with it, but he had learned how to change a nightmare into a dream about watching a horror movie, so that he could watch it without waking in fright. Now, deciding to apply the same technique, he made his clothes melt off him until he was naked.

This proves it. I'm not in another dimension, I'm dreaming . . .

Or does it? Maybe in another dimension, I'm wearing whatever I think I'm wearing, or what would be logical to wear in that dimension . . .

But he felt cold. Quickly he let his clothes form around him again and added a heavy mackinaw jacket to them. It looked vaguely fuzzy until he realized he had simply *thought* "heavy mackinaw jacket." He carefully visualized a *particular* one, one belonging to his Uncle Stan Cameron, in the Sierras. He'd borrowed it, during a chilly climb, up north of Mount Shasta. It was red-and-black checks, threadbare on the sleeves and patched at the elbows; when he thrust his hands into the pockets he even felt a small carefully-stitched patch inside one of the pockets.

It would be interesting to write Uncle Stan and find out if that mackinaw really does have a patch inside one of the pockets. I don't remember. Maybe my subconscious has a better memory than I do.

I'm beginning to get hungry. Wonder if I could think a slab of chocolate inside one of those pockets?

But the pockets remained obstinately empty. There were limits to the power of thought, even in a dream.

And why was it so cold? He looked up; the grey sky was beginning to sprinkle down snowflakes. Snow? In Berkeley? Had he come so far up into the hills? In the fifteen years he had lived in Berkeley, he had seen snow exactly twice, in the highest hills. But it was, unquestionably, snowing hard. Before long, the ground was covered with a light powdering of snow, which seemed to grow deeper as he walked; he could hear the snow crunching, softly, under the soles of the boots he discovered he was wearing.

And then he began to hear something else.

It sounded like sleigh bells, and it was very far away, and somehow seemed high up, coming to him through the air.

All I need, now, is to see Santa Claus fly by, complete with all eight of his silly little reindeer. No, damn it. Santa Claus is out. I absolutely refuse to spend time—to waste time—in an artificially induced experimental hallucination, dreaming about Santa Claus.

The sleigh bells went on ringing, and became clearer. Now they were mingled with the soft sound of hooves. The air was so quiet and so clear that the sound seemed to carry echoes. And now he realized that the last vestiges of the campus were gone.

He stood high up in a mountain pass; there was a gravelled roadway under his feet. The snow was still falling. And up the hill, toward him, was coming a long caravan of mounted men; the bells he had heard were small bells, hung on the bridles of their horses, ringing and jingling in the clear air.

Cameron Fenton drew back until he was off the road, standing in the shelter of the trees there. Maybe they couldn't see him either; but he wanted to get a good look at them.

Sally Lobeck is going to want a good description for her content analysis, he told himself.

Then he began to hear the singing.

Fenton could not at first distinguish any words. It was only a high clear trilling, more like women's voices, or a boy's choir, or even, he thought in confusion, birdsong. There was melody in it, but it was incredibly polyphonic and multistranded, without continuity; one voice or a group of voices would take up a fragment of melody, then another would catch it up, embroidering on the fragment of song, stranding it richly. All of this was woven into the jingling of the harness-bells on the horses. The air was filled with it; and then, as they drew nearer, approaching the rocky cleft where Fenton stood, he got a clear look at them, and his certainty vanished.

Now that he could see the singers clearly, he was not sure that they were men—or human. Nor was he, any longer, quite sure that what they rode were horses, though at first glance they *seemed* horselike enough, just as, at a distance, the riders had seemed human enough.

Oh, they had the right number of heads and limbs and eyes and ears and noses and things. They weren't grossly *in*human like something out of a science-fiction play on TV. On the other hand, if they *were* human, they weren't any race he was familiar with.

It was something subtler about them; a curious racial stamp, an elusive, curious hint of *difference*. It was like the beasts they rode; horselike, surely, pale buff-colored with reddish manes, but not quite horses as he knew horses.

Yet he liked the looks of the—men? They were tall and, by human standards, a great deal too thin for their height. Even in the cold of the mountain pass, they were thinly clad, bare brownish arms exposed to the weather. Strange weapons were strapped to jewelled belts. Their faces were thin and narrow, broad of forehead and triangular of chin. They were—strange. Not human.

And all of them, even though they looked male, had high clear voices, well into the soprano register, and their singing was sweet and musical. Fenton couldn't believe that people who made music like that could have anything dangerous about them.

He wondered if they would be able to see him. He didn't know all the rules of this place yet. And if they did see him, would they be hostile? Resolving to take precautions, he stepped behind one of the rocky outcrops.

There were four or five of the strange men. In their midst rode someone shrouded in a long, furry cloak—or was it only a pale, shaggy fabric that *looked* like fur? From the depths of the cloak a slender, pale-golden hand emerged, gripping the reins; an abnormally slender hand, bone-slim, the thin fingers covered with jewelled rings. As they came closer, the one riding at the center—now he saw that they were clustered around her, guarding her, deferential—shrugged back the hood of the cloak as if it were too warm, and Fenton saw long, frost-pale hair, bound into jewelled braids. A woman of the strange people. And beautiful.

Beautiful, beautiful beyond dreams. Magical, a woman of the fairy folk . . . Spenser's Faerie Queen . . . beauty remembered from a dream . . . Fenton thought, with a strange pain in his throat, that the woman, and the music too, were of the stuff of dreams.

Music you hear in dreams and wake still half hearing, on the very edge of tears, knowing you will never be content until you hear that music again. . . .

Magic. Sorcery. The Faerie Queen . . . was this what he saw? Was this the glimpse that some writers had, and

*later called the kingdom of Faerie . . . the passing of the
Elf-queen among the elven folk, the Queen of Air and
Darkness, Morgan le Fay. . . .*

Clutching at calm, Fenton wondered if he had simply
wandered into the world of Jungian archetypes, the collective subconscious where these images were stored? He
looked up again at the woman he had called the Faerie
Queen, and saw, riding beside her, another woman.

And *this* woman was unmistakably human. Just as the
first woman was a creature of magic and witchcraft, this
one was, just as definitely, a woman of flesh and blood.
She, too, wore a long cloak, deep earth-brown. Her hair
was coppery-red, escaping down her shoulders, and her
features, suntanned and looking somewhat out-of-place
among all the angular alien faces, were rounded and
faintly freckled. As if to put the seal on her humanity in
a way Fenton could clearly understand, she was warmly
dressed. The woman beside her, the Faerie Queen, was
wearing under her cloak the scantest of pale tunics; her
long brown arms were bare to the snow, and her feet
were almost bare in brief jewelled sandals. The red-
haired woman wore a thick woolen cloak and under it a
long-sleeved, long-skirted dress; she rode astride, with
the skirt hiked up, and under the dress were thick heavy
long leggings and heavy boots. Dress and cloak were
trimmed and lined with fur; and her hands, which looked
firm and muscular and human on the reins of her mount,
were thickly encased in heavy gloves. Yes, she was human all right, but what was she doing in their company?

He could hear her voice among all the high, sweet
ones of the aliens; she was singing the same strange
catchy syllables as the others, among which he could
not distinguish a single word. Nonsense syllables or an
unknown language? He thought of the old ballad where
a single human knight was carried off in the middle of
the cavalcade of the elf-people. This woman certainly
didn't look like a captive; she was laughing and singing
with them, and seemed perfectly contented.

So they weren't harmful to humans. Fenton was about
to step from behind the rocky outcrop and make himself known, when the singing and the jingling of bells
were horribly interrupted.

First there was a blare of horns, a harsh discordant honking, a horrible racket of yells and screeches. And one of the strange singing aliens fell almost at Fenton's feet, his head horribly hewn away. Fenton leaped back to keep from being splattered by the blood that went on gushing for a moment from the severed neck and, with a hideous suddenness, stopped.

The road was suddenly filled with swarming twisted dark things, yelling, brandishing long wicked knives, broad and sharpened to razor brightness. Fenton found himself automatically dodging back into his hiding place. This battle was none of his affair!

The attackers were twisted and hairy, with thick bullet-heads; that was all he could see of them at first, that and the way they *swarmed,* like some kind of insects . . . the comparison was inescapable; they seemed to scuttle rather than walk, as if they all suffered from some deformity, though Fenton, watching, could see none. He could not at once decide—they moved so quickly— whether they were naked and hairy, or wrapped in some kind of dark furry clothing, covered with long, coarse, straggling dark hairs.

The mounted aliens were trying to control their frightened, rearing mounts half a dozen of them had placed themselves in front of the women, the Faerie Queen and the human, red-haired woman, struggling to free their strange weapons from their belts. One of them thrust himself between the Queen and the swarming attackers, a green-glass dagger beginning to glow with coruscating light in his hand; but one of the small twisted attackers kicked it from his hand and hacked at him with a machete. He fell, writhing, stabbed through the heart. At the same time one of the ugly creatures called out, in a loud and strident voice.

"This is luck, brothers! It is Kerridis herself—it is the Lady! Good hunting!"

The escort fought with a fierceness Fenton, standing paralyzed behind the rocks, found frightening; it was so hopeless. There must have been hundreds of the ugly dark things. One after another, they tried desperately to shield the women, some of them with their own bodies, and one after another they were cut down, hacked to shreds. Cameron Fenton was sickened by the blood, the cries of agony in those high sweet voices, like dying birds, and above all by the silence of the attacking, swarming dark things. The whole mountainside was black with them.

The Lady at their center had caught up, from one of her murdered escort, one of the green-glass, glowing daggers. She was fighting, quietly and desperately, at the center of a ring of the hairy twisted things; but one of them rushed in and knocked it out of her hand, and she stood, backing away from them, a look of desperate horror on her face. Fenton could not see the pretty red-headed woman. Had she been cut down, hacked to bits like the Lady's escort? He found that the thought nauseated him; he stood struggling with it.

If this is a dream, it's a doozy . . .

The woman was surrounded, now, by a ring of the small twisted attackers. She kept backing away as they herded her toward the mountainside, and Fenton knew, from the look of horror on her slender face, that she was deathly afraid to touch them, or, worse, to be touched by them.

The hairy things were hacking away at the remnants of the fallen escort with their steel machetes; watching sickly, Fenton found it hard to believe what they were doing. They were slicing up the living, still-screaming horses—and cramming the bloody, dripping flesh into their mouths with their fists. Fenton felt that his whole body would turn inside-out with nausea; he bent over, retching, clinging to the rock behind him, squeezing his eyes shut.

Oh, God, this is too much. Let me wake up, let me wake up now . . .

The cramping nausea was awful, twisting his whole inside; how could he feel such pain in a dream? But he did not physically vomit. *How could I? My body isn't here at all . . .*

But *something* was here in this dimension, something that could feel sickness and pain . . . and suddenly his paralysis broke.

If I am really here in this dimension—if it isn't a dream—maybe I should try to do something to help them—

There was a horrible noise of screaming from the dying men and the dying horselike beasts. Fenton turned, stepped out from behind the rocks, hardly aware what, if anything, he might be able to do. Where was the red-headed woman? After a moment he saw her; she was being held motionless by half a dozen of the hairy creatures. Now that some of them were standing still long enough for Fenton to get a good look at them, he liked them even less. They had fangs and they were very white, corpse-white, beneath the straggly long hairs. Many of them, now, were covered with blood, fanged snouts smeared with it, their hands dripping.

The woman he thought of as the Queen was still trapped within the narrowing ring of the disgusting creatures, backing away as they closed in on her. She caught up a machete from the ground—one of her escort had managed to disarm one of the attackers—but quickly dropped it and stood shaking her narrow hands as if it had burned her, and Fenton had the strange, wildly irrelevant thought: *of course; the old stories always say that the people of Faerie can't touch cold iron . . .*

It would soon be all over. But the attackers seemed, in a curious way, as much afraid of the Lady as she was of them. As yet none of them had actually laid a hand on her. Now one darted forward and laid a thick bone-white claw on her dress, dragging her toward him. For the first time she cried out, a sound more of horror and disgust than of pain. She ducked away, and suddenly Fenton saw what they were doing. They were *herding* her; using her fear of touching them, to drive her along the path. At the same time, she seemed to see this and stood firm.

Then half a dozen of the strange creatures grabbed her. She cried out again at the touch, in pain and horror; one of them dragged at her hand, and Fenton saw the delicate fingers darkening, as if the touch had literally burnt her. Pulling and hauling, they dragged her toward a dark cave-mouth, ignoring her shrieks of pain.

Behind her the red-haired woman had struggled free and was fighting with her machete, which she seemed to hold without pain or trouble; she fought like a fiend, sweeping the knife in swishing arcs, stabbing the thick-bodied creatures, driving them back. But there were simply too many of them. One final rush, and they had the machete out of her hand and piled atop her, bearing her to the ground. Her cry of pain was desperately human, rousing Fenton to rage and resolve; he jumped out and ran toward them, not knowing if they would be able to see him, not even sure he could touch them. But it was too late. They hauled the red-haired woman to her feet, grabbing her around feet and legs—none of them were more than three and a half or four feet tall— and dragged her bodily, drowned in the creatures, toward the cave-mouth. They bundled her through, fighting and shrieking; then one of them struck her a fearful blow beside the head with the hilt of his machete. Her head lolled; they picked her up, unceremoniously, a dozen or so of them lifting her like a log over their heads, and ran, carrying her unconscious body—or her dead one—into the dark cave-mouth.

Fenton was never able to explain what he did next. Maybe, on some deeper level, he was ashamed of standing by, uninvolved, while the whole escort, men and beasts, were hacked to ribbons and eaten alive. Perhaps he still halfway believed that this was a dream, that he was immune from this world's laws. If it was, after all, a dream, then it didn't matter *what* he did, but he wanted to know what happened next.

Whatever the reason, Fenton didn't stop to think about what he did next. He simply did it; automatically, almost without thought. Most of the hairy things had disappeared into one or more of the cave-mouths; the dying bloody remnants of the escort were still littering the roadway. Fenton bent to snatch up one of the green-glowing weapons. They were lying there as if the hairy things had been afraid to touch them; remembering the way in which they had kicked the green dagger out of the woman's hand, he was sure they *were* afraid to touch them. Fenton closed his hand over it. It felt solid and real in his hand; he had been half afraid that his hand would go through it. But it seemed to be real to him in this dimension, as the trees and the rocks were real.

Holding the green-glow dagger in his hand, Fenton ran into the dark cave-mouth.

CHAPTER THREE

INSIDE HE STOPPED. He had to. He literally couldn't see his hand before his face. It was black inside; blacker than blackness . . . velvet dark, invisible, blind, like the darkness of interstellar space without stars. And *cold*. Icy cold, freezing, with a cold blast of air that seemed to come right up from the depths of some iced-over frozen Norse hell. He blundered into a rock wall, and bent over his bruised knee, moaning in agony. For the rock, too, was cold, the cold of the iron pump-handle on a frosty Minnesota morning when, if you touched it with wet fingers, the fingers stuck and you had to pull skin away to get loose. Leaning against the wall, he felt that it would suck all the heat out from under his clothing, out of the very marrow of his bones, leaving him a cold stripped skeleton in the cold of an airless moon. He wrapped his arms around his body, but it didn't help.

In the first agonized shock of blundering into the rock wall, he had dropped the glow-dagger; now, faintly, he could make out the pale shape of its green light. He reached down and took it in his hand again. To his astonishment, it felt warm; he cupped it between his hands, feeling the warmth in it, like a live thing between his frozen fingers, slowly bringing the concept of warmth into his personal universe again. He wasn't warm, no. But he could believe in and imagine what it felt like to be warm. The dagger gave out a faintish green light which gradually, as it warmed his hands, began to glow more strongly.

Evidently something about holding it charges it with the energy that makes it glow.

That set him back a little. He thought one of the rules of this strange world was that his body was not really here. *But if I were completely without a body, could I be quite so cold?* There was enough energy remaining in the glow-weapon that holding it made it light up and glow with warmth. It was hot now; not hot enough to be uncomfortable, but hot enough that his hands were no longer agonized with the cold. And remembering how he had thought himself into the red-and-black plaid mackinaw jacket he was still wearing, he decided: if it had worked once, it would work again. Slowly, holding the glowing dagger between his hands, concentrating, he managed to change the red-and-black plaid mackinaw jacket to the down parka he had worn on a Sierra climbing expedition. He remembered reading the label on that one—that it would keep the wearer safely warm in temperatures down to sixty below freezing.

It must be just about that here.

And that brought him up sharp, too. He was certainly no longer on the Berkeley campus, nor in the hills behind Berkeley, which contained no such caves as this. The nearest caves he knew anything about were a couple of hundred miles north of the city, up past Redding, near Lake Shasta Dam.

So it wasn't simply an alternate dimension of the Berkeley campus.

He could see his hands now, and the rock walls, in the increasing glow of the green-glowing dagger. The walls were close in, and covered with a hoary rime of frost. And now that he could see and was no longer paralyzed with cold, he remembered, with shock, that he had come in here for a reason—to see where they were taking the red-haired woman and the captured Kerridis—the one he had dubbed the Faerie Queen.

Behind him, dimly—a long way off, further than he remembered coming from the cave-mouth—he could see the entrance, and it appeared to be receding, though Fenton himself was not conscious of movement. Was this, too, one of the rules of this place, or this dream —that you couldn't stay in one place? He wasn't sure, but he *was* moving further into the cave. If he wanted to get out while he could still see daylight—it seemed to be getting smaller and smaller, and dimmer and dim-

mer, while he watched——he had better turn around and
head for the entrance while it was still visible.

He hesitated, indecisive. He was warm enough now,
in the down parka, with the green flame of the dagger
warming his fingers. But what could he do if he did
find the woman or Kerridis?

As he was actually on the point of turning and heading for the entrance, he heard a woman scream.

That made up his mind for him. Clutching the dagger
tight between both hands, he turned his back on the entrance and ran down along the rocky path further into
the cave.

He watched his step this time, so that he would not
repeat the blundering into an exposed rocky outcrop that
still made his knee throb with pain. The path was steep,
and soon he had to slow and stumble down a series of
rocky steps. As he rounded a turn in the rocky steps, he
began to see a smoky glow of torchlight below him, and
to hear yells and screeches, and the honking blare of
those ugly horns again. And that almost made Fenton
turn and grope his way toward the entrance once more.

Was he going to blunder, again, into watching those——
those *things*——slice up the girl and eat her alive? He definitely didn't want to watch *that*. But what could he do to
stop it?

*If this is a dream, I must have a sicker, more morbid
imagination than I ever believed I had. . . .*

*No. Whatever this is, it's not a dream. I know enough
about the psychology of dreams to know that. You don't
inquire, in dreams, about your state of mind. If you begin not to accept what's happening, or to do reality testing on it, you wake up. That's what lies beyond the old
cliche of "pinch me, I'm dreaming." If you do reality
testing in a dream, the dream goes away or changes.*

So it isn't a dream.

The concomitant of that, Fenton thought, was obvious. *If it's not a dream, those things could do the slicing-
up-and-eating-alive trick on me, too. So I had better get
the hell out of here.*

He turned around and made for the entrance.

Abruptly the green glow of the dagger in his hand
ebbed and went out. Fenton was alone in the blind, ter-

rible dark of the underground cave, with only the smoky glow somewhere behind him. Panic gripped him. He would never find his way out, he would wander forever in these caves until he died . . .

Slowly, indecisively he turned, trying to orient himself by the faraway torchlight, now that the daggerlight had failed him. And as he set his foot again on the rocky downward steps he noticed that the daggerlight had begun to glow in his hands. Very faintly; but it was glowing.

Experimentally, he took a downward step; the glow brightened.

Again, experimentally, he took a step up toward the disappearing spark of the entrance.

The daggerlight went out.

It wants me to go down. . . .

That, of course, was ridiculous.

Or was it, by this world's unknown rules? Anyway, Fenton realized he had no choice. Without the warmth and light of the flamedagger, he would wander alone in the freezing dark until he died—*or,* he thought in a fragment of bewildered double consciousness, *until the drug wore off and he got back to his body . . .*

While, if he followed this world's unknown rules and what the flamedagger wanted of him, he had light and, after a fashion, warmth.

Talk about an offer I can't refuse!

He went on down the steps toward the distant torchlight, the dagger glowing and warming in his hands as he came. As he stumbled down it seemed to grow warmer. Was it only the heat of the green flame between his hands? No; the walls of the cave seemed less frosty, and here, rather than being rimed with cold frost, they seemed to be hand-hewn and decorated, somehow, with carvings Fenton did not really want to see; beyond the edge of consciousness he could see vaguely that they were gross beyond imagining. Well, if those hairy little horrors had made them, that was no surprise either.

Abruptly he came up with the jolt that comes when you land on the bottom step of a flight of stairs, thinking there were more, and found himself in an open, spacious cavern.

It was empty and bare, but the floor was level and even polished. Overhead, from some kind of a metal chain arrangement, swung a metal lantern with fire inside, casting a dim glow, flickering as it swung making eerie monstrous shadows along the walls. Fenton looked for his own shadow and found, not really surprised, that he had none.

Of course not. In this dimension I am only partly real. I'm here, I can feel cold, and pain, and fear . . . but I haven't any shadow, and I'll bet a nickel, if they have nickels here, which they probably don't, that if I ran up against a mirror I wouldn't have a reflection either. Those old yarns must come from someplace.

He paused, irresolute. Where was the woman who had screamed? Was it the girl, or the Faerie Queen? As he paused, the flamedagger seemed to pulse and flicker as if it was on the verge of going out again.

Does it respond to my own will and sense of purpose? That's ridiculous.

All around the great cavern, appearing and disappearing among the shadows that flickered as the overhead lantern swung, were black gaping mouths and entries. The hairy nasties could have carried girl and woman through any of them.

Come on, girl, scream again. I don't want you to get hurt, but I can't find you if you don't make some kind of noise!

But there were only distant sounds which could have been the horns again, or echoes, or Fenton's own imagination. He had no sense of direction about them; they could have come from any of the open cave-mouths around the big central cavern.

A flicker of motion at the edge of his visual field arrested his eyes, and he saw two of the ugly hairy monsters slipping along the cave-walls. He shrank into the shadows, his first thought to conceal the flamedagger so that it would not attract their attention. But they saw, raising their heads. He braced himself, hopelessly, to be rushed.

He was not prepared for what happened next. The ugly goblins yelled, covering their eyes with pain, and dived blindly for one of the cave-mouths and disappeared.

So they were afraid of these weapons. It didn't stop them when there were hundreds of them to a half dozen of the escort. But two of them wouldn't face one man with a flamedagger in his hand. They turned around and ran.

That gave him the first confidence he had had since he had found himself in this world. Had they run back to where their disgusting brothers were tormenting the women they had abducted? He couldn't count on that. He had better use a little system about this. Now that he knew he could count on the flaming green dagger for some protection, however limited, he was no longer too frightened to think clearly.

Slowly he walked around the huge cavern; at each cave-mouth he paused and listened.

The first two were dark and silent, without a gleam of light or a sound coming up from the depths. From the third he could hear a dull roaring, like distant fires, and see a reddish glow. Were there volcanic depths to these caverns? There was something ominous about that fiery glow; Fenton didn't want any part of it.

He was a little afraid that, if he turned his back on it, the green-glowing flamedagger would do that going-out trick on him again, but it didn't. He thought, irrationally, that maybe the flamedagger didn't want any part of the volcanic glow either.

He listened at two more of the tunnel mouths before he heard faint and far-off sounds that could have been shouts or cries, and the distant horn-honkings and gabblings. Fenton did not stop to find out if he were still afraid or not; he plunged directly into the dark tunnel mouth, before he had time to lose his nerve.

As he ran downward, he knew that it was definitely growing warmer. The distant shouts and gabblings grew louder. He stumbled on an unseen step or two, but mostly the tunneled corridor was level and smoothly sloping underfoot, and he could see clearly from the growing flare of the flamedagger in his hand. The loud sounds grew to a climax. Fenton heard a stifled cry and knew he had found at least one of the victims.

It was the Faerie Queen. Kerridis. She was standing in a ring of the little horrors, and they were pushing and driving her toward a niche in the rock. She kept backing away, unwilling to touch or to be touched by the ugly creatures; they were evidently aware of her fear, and made a point of grabbing her, twisting and pinching her hands, darting in and nipping at her flesh with their long clawlike fingers. Fenton wondered, if he rushed out among them, whether the light of his flamedagger would frighten them away from her even for a moment; but before he had time to do it, he saw a tall man walking out among the ugly-wuglies.

A man.

A *real* man, like Fenton, not one of Kerridis' unknown race. He was tall and dark and well-muscled; he was wearing long leggings, high boots with metal studs, a long-sleeved jacket and a shaggy dark cloak whose color could not be seen clearly in the shifting light of the swaying lantern above.

The man walked through the hairy horrors, and they drew back, receding like a wave at low tide. Fenton saw the relief in Kerridis' face as the goblinlike things drew back and away from her. Then the man spoke, and the loathing came back into her face.

"Kerridis," the man said, "come with me. There is no reason for you to be tormented this way. Give me your hand."

For a moment, moving almost automatically, Kerridis put out her hand; then, before the man could touch it with his own, she drew it back, her face twisted with distaste. The man shrugged. His voice was indifferent; but Fenton sensed that he was angry and wounded.

"As you like," he said. "I have none of your healstones, anyway. But remember, Kerridis, it was not my will that you should be tormented; I gave the strictest orders that you were not to be harmed."

"Did you give orders, also, that my faithful men were to be murdered?"

"They are nothing to me," he said, his voice hard. "You know why it is war between us, Kerridis. It was your doing, not mine."

She turned her back on him; he reached out and gripped her shoulder in his, turning her around and forcing her to look at him.

"Come with me, and you will not be hurt."

She flung his hand off, angrily. He said, "If you would rather, then, I can call them and they will make you come. I preferred, still, to offer you a choice. But I owe you no courtesy. Shall I leave you to them, then?"

Kerridis' face collapsed and seemed to fall apart. She covered her face with her slender hands. It seemed to Fenton that behind her hands she was weeping. Then she raised her head, arrogantly, tearless, and followed the man.

Fenton, in the shadows, came quietly after, hiding the flamedagger in a fold of his parka. He half expected that, since the parka was only thought-stuff, the glow would shine through, but it did not. Kerridis and the cloaked man passed through several deserted caverns; at the far end of the last one, Fenton could see again the red glow of fire, and it twisted his gut with strange apprehension. As the unknown man passed behind the shrinking Kerridis, Fenton could clearly see his shadow, huge and distorted on the cavern wall. So it wasn't a general rule in this world that people cast no shadows. Fenton didn't; but that was because he wasn't really here; or, at least, his body wasn't.

More of the ugly goblins were swarming out of tunnel-mouths into the cavern. They surrounded Kerridis, shouting at her in their honking speech. And the woman's arrogance broke. She shrank against the rock wall, flinched as if the burning cold bit her, and tried to keep a fold of her slashed cloak between her and the rock wall. The cloaked man spoke her name several times in a soothing tone.

"Kerridis. Kerridis, listen to me. Lady, I will not allow them to hurt you. You know what I want, but you will not be harmed. In simple justice—"

"Justice?" Kerridis turned to him, her face betraying that she was at the breaking point. "*You* speak of justice?" Her voice was very high and clear and musical, even when distorted with terror and rage.

"Justice! And I will have it. But I swear that you can trust—"

"Trust! There was a time when we trusted you.

Never again!" She spat the words at him and turned her face away.

He looked at her with an angry scowl. "Do you prefer my friends?" He gestured at the honking, gobbling creatures swarming into the cavern.

"Yes," Kerridis said, her hands clenched. "They are cruel because it is their nature to be cruel! You—" She raised her hand to strike the man, but he saw her intention and stepped back. He gripped her wrist, twisting it cruelly; Kerridis bit her lip, but she did not cry out as the man thrust her into a side tunnel in the rock. He swung a metal-grilled door closed behind her. One of the hairy things came and threw the bolt. Then the man gestured to the swarming blackish things and they followed him, pouring along down a tunnel and out of sight.

Fenton stood, concealed in the shadows, until they had gone. Kerridis stood behind the metal grillwork. She reached out an experimental hand and touched it, but flinched away as if it burned her. She looked at her fingers, and Fenton could see that the slender digits were blackened and burned. She stared at them in dismay, then sank down as if her last strength had deserted her and covered her face again with her hands.

Fenton stood watching her, troubled, struck by her beauty. Inhuman though she was, she was a woman and beautiful, a living creature in distress and torment, and she was weeping in pain. It seemed to him that she was like something he had seen in dreams; not a woman to be desired, not to be loved as a man loves, but to be treated with reverence and even worship, never to be touched with a rude hand or a rude thought. The Faerie Queen . . .

He started to move toward her prison, and hesitated. Maybe she would shrink from him, too, and angrily reject any offered hand—though Cameron Fenton had no idea what he could do that would be helpful.

But he knew he had to try.

And where was the redheaded woman? He was sure, now, that it was she he had heard screaming. Kerridis—he had *seen* this—simply wasn't the screaming kind, although he could still see that the hand crushed by one of the goblin-things was blackened and crisped. She had wrapped it in a fold of the torn dress. It must have been hurting her horribly.

Slowly, Fenton advanced, the flamedagger glowing in his hand.

He wondered, suddenly, if his voice would even be audible in this dimension. It seemed to stick in his throat. Even broken like this, weeping, huddled on a fold of a torn dress so that she need not touch the icy cold of the stone, the woman was so awe-inspiring that he could not simply say "Kerridis," as the booted man had done. The man had done it—it seemed to Fenton—out of deliberate disrespect. Fenton cleared his throat, making a small sound; to his relief, the woman heard. Pushing her long, pale hair back from her face, she raised her head a little, and looked straight at him.

For a moment Fenton wondered if she could see him, though the eyes seemed almost too large for the face; but then the great pupils—they were gold-colored, he noticed in amazement, with a strange inner glow like a cat's in the night—focused on him. With a small flinching of dread, she scrambled to her feet, backing away against the very wall of the rocky cell.

Fenton said awkwardly, "My Lady—" It did not seem strange at all to speak that way to her; it sounded like the most natural thing in the world. "My Lady, I won't hurt you."

She looked at him; and he could see the dread slowly leaving her face. She said after a moment, "Why, now I can see that you are not Pentarn; though you are like him. But no one of those who would harm me would carry a vrillsword." She pointed to the green-glowing flamedagger in Fenton's hand. "And your voice is not Pentarn's voice. How, then, did you come here?"

"I saw the attack—I followed you. Can I—can I do anything to help?"

She gestured at the doorway and the metal grille. "You are of the—of Pentarn's race, you can touch this. Can you unfasten the door? They need no locks to fasten our people inside—if I touched it, my hand would go up in smoke. And already as you can see—" With a rueful smile she held out her blackened fingers.

Fenton put his hand out to unfasten the door.

And his hand went through it.

Of course. It's a man-made object—if those creatures are men, which I doubt. Anyway, an artifact, not a natural object like a rock or a tree. And it isn't there for me.

How, then, can I hold this flamedigger?

"I am sorry, my Lady. I can't even *touch* the door, let alone unfasten it for you. I can walk through it—" He demonstrated by doing so. "But that's no help, I'm afraid. I am sorry—I'd help you if I could."

She smiled. Even with her face contorted in fear and weeping, she had been beautiful; her smile was pure enchantment. At that moment Fenton understood the old tale of men drawn away into the enchantments of Faerie. And she laughed; in the midst of danger and terror, with her hand burned to blackness by the evil creatures, she laughed, like a pure chiming of magic. Fenton was standing now, inside the metal door. She said, "Then you are not one of Pentarn's men?"

He shook his head. "Whoever Pentarn may be, I'm not."

"No, of course not," she said, "I can see you cast no shadow; you are not a worldwalker, but a 'tweenman. Let me hold the vrillsword." She stretched out her hand to the green-glowing dagger.

Fenton put it into her fingers. They felt insubstantial, like mist; but, as he had half expected, he *could* feel them; he did not go through them, as he had done through the metal grille. She laid her burned fingers against the glow of the dagger, and the green fire seemed to shine *through* her fingers; the pain-lines drawn in her face seemed to relax somewhat. She drew a long, shuddering sigh, which horrified Fenton with its restraint.

"It is not a healstone, but it does help," she said, her voice shaking a little. "Perhaps, now that I am not in pain, I can robe myself in a more seemly style . . ."

Slowly, she drew the dagger down the lines of her shredded cloak. Fenton had half thought that it would mold together by thought, as he had altered the light shirt he was wearing into the red-and-black plaid mackinaw,

and later into the down parka; but it was not so. He
watched, and slowly, slowly, as she held the flamedagger
over the rents, the torn strands moved, crawled together, seemed to—to reweave themselves, to reunite
somehow.

Fenton blurted, "How did you do that?"

She said indifferently, "When something like this—
a cloak, a gown—has once been given an imposed shape,
the shape remains. It can be torn apart by such folk as
the *irighi*—" That was what it sounded like. "Such
wounds do not heal, for they are made of the same substance as these bars—" She gestured gingerly at the
metal grilles. "A wound they make in our fabrics—or
our flesh—takes too much healing even for the vrill.
Yet the vrill can remove, a little, the heat and the burning, and I can again impose the true shape of my garments."

Perfectly clear, Fenton thought in confusion. *And he
didn't understand a word of it.* He did know that her
cloak, though it still *looked* slashed and torn, had come
together and covered her warmly, and her tunic was
whole and decent. She wadded the cloak around her to
protect her bare limbs from the rock. "Stranger 'tweenman, I thank you for this comfort. Tell me one thing
more; were all my people killed?"

Fenton lowered his head. "I'm afraid they were—"
He hesitated, but she seemed almost to read his thoughts.

"I know how the ironfolk treat those they take from
our people," she said sadly. "And yours too, at times.
Did you see what befell my companion Irielle? She is
one of your people, with hair like the lantern light—"

Fenton realized, with shock, that he had stopped thinking about the red-haired woman, in the enchantment of
listening to Kerridis' voice.

"Lady, I heard her scream; but I saw her carried away
unharmed and—and unwounded."

"You must go—" Kerridis stopped short.

"You must leave these caverns at once," she said.
"You are a 'tweenman, and it is not safe for you to be
beneath the ground for very long. They will be coming
in search of me. Go back—" She hesitated, then, re-

luctantly, she handed him the vrill, the green flamedagger.

"It tears my heart to part with it," she said, "but you must have it to find your way out of these caverns; without its light, you could wander here forever, and be trapped when the time came for you to return to your own world. It would not be so dangerous if you were a true worldwalker, but a 'tweenman can be trapped . . ."

"Lady, take it. You can use it to frighten them away from you. They're afraid of it, I saw that; they could see me carrying it—" Fenton added, ruefully, "It won't be any good to me, trying to get out. Every time I turned around to leave, it went out—its light stopped—"

Again the enchanting laugh. "It will not do that when your true purpose is to leave here," she said. "And truly, you can be of more help to me using it to find your way out and guide rescuers to me. I alone cannot reach them even in thought, through all these rocks heavy with the ironfolk's metal. Go, my friend."

She gave him the green dagger. Fenton took it with reluctance, seeing the lines of pain move again across her face as her hand left it.

"I wish I could have done more for you, Lady—"

"You have done what you could," she said, "and more than I would have expected of a 'tweenman. And now you must make what haste you can out of these caverns."

She touched his face. Her fingers felt insubstantial, ghostlike.

"I would you could have brought me tidings of Irielle. My heart is weighted with fear for her. Yet you must not stay here. Go, stranger." Again the ghostlike touch, like swansdown. "My thanks and blessings go with you. . . ."

He looked back, once, and saw that she had drawn her cloak about her, had seated herself, with a sorrowful patience, on it, carefully arranged so that she could sit on her cloak and need not touch rock or metal grilles.

At least I could do that much for her. It isn't everyone who gets to help the Faerie Queen . . .

And of course she isn't the Faerie Queen at all. It's ridiculous to think of her that way, when I know her name is simply Kerridis . . . But still Fenton suspected

that he would go on thinking of her as the Faerie Queen
for a long time.

The flamedagger in his hands brightened as he retraced his steps; he went back through the tunnel, into
the first of the large caverns, now deserted, then to the
mouth of the cave. He had dreaded the long climb up the
seemingly needless stairs, but to his surprise, it seemed he
was moving *downhill* toward the entrance. Was space,
too, an illusion in this world, and up and down mere ar-
rangements without material reality? Fenton's head
ached, and he felt confused. He was glad to emerge into
the snowfilled greyness of the mountain pass.

Snow was still falling. And it was growing dark, a
deepening twilight which made Fenton shiver and clutch
the down parka about him.

"Here he is," a voice shouted behind him, a high light
voice—one of Kerridis' folk, certainly. "And he is one of
Pentarn's accurst kind!" Rough hands seized him from
behind. Fenton shook his head, twisted, sensing—though
the hands *felt* firm—that in his present insubstantial
form in this world, he could slip between them if he
wished; through them if he must, as he had done through
the iron grilles. But the voice was the voice of one of
Kerridis' people, clear countertenor and musical; as he
looked up into the face of his captor, he could see the
almost-racial resemblance. The newcomer was not like
Kerridis, no; his hair was chestnut, where hers had been
long and ashen pale; his shoulders were broad, and he
was not much taller than Fenton's self. But the eyes, and
the brownish paleness of the face, were the same.

"Don't move," said the beautiful, threatening voice.
"There is a vrillsword at your throat, and even if you
are a worldwalker, it will kill you as readily as one of the
ironfolk."

Fenton felt the prick at the base of his throat. Perhaps
he was immune to metal, could walk through an iron bar
—but the unknown stuff of which the flamedaggers were
made was real to him in this dimension.

He said, keeping very still lest it slip, "I have come
from Kerridis. She is safe, and asked me to lead you to
her—"

"It's a trick, Erril," said a voice behind his captor. "Do

you think Kerridis would send a message by anyone from the caverns?"

He fumbled in his cloak, brought out the greenglass dagger he had carried all through the caves. His captor swooped, grasped it, after a short struggle wrenched it from him.

"Where got you that? And how is it that you bear it unscathed?"

"Let him go, Erril," said another voice, a voice with authority. "He has carried a vrill unharmed from the caverns. Loose him. Look—" A light was held high over Fenton's head. "Can't you tell a 'tweenman when you see one? How could such a one do anything to help or hurt Kerridis?"

"But where did he get a vrillsword?" Erril obediently let Fenton go, lowering the knife from his throat. Fenton looked up at the newcomer, another of Kerridis' race, with an indefinable air of authority and command. He said to Fenton, "Quick, tell us; where did you get it?"

"If this is what you're talking about—" Fenton gestured with the glowing flamedagger, and they stepped back a little, in an automatic, wary gesture. "I picked it up here when I saw Kerridis'—escort—dying. I thought it might protect me from the—the other things, I don't know what you call them." At the edge of his visual field he saw that the gruesome remnants of the dead men and beasts had been gathered together and that the strange people were piling up wood about them. For a funeral pyre of some sort? Dimly, on a deep level, he was glad to know they would have some kind of decent burial; they had met a dreadful end.

The newcomer said, "But how did you come here?"

Suddenly Fenton was angry. "While you stand here arguing about who and what I am and how I got here, Kerridis is in the caves down there, and she's hurt. I tried to let her out but my hand went right through the metal. And they have another woman, too, who was still alive when I last saw her! Instead of arguing about me, why not try getting them out, and *then* ask me questions?"

"He's right, Lebbrin," the one called Erril said, and the tall, commanding newcomer—was his name Lebbrin?—nodded. "There is no use in all of us trying to go in; bring what vrillswords still live, and you, Erril, you, Findhal—" He hesitated. "I think that will be enough, if we can slip in unseen and release her; but about a dozen of you—" Quickly, he pointed out one after another. "—come in behind us, in case we have to fight our way out."

Fenton could see that the abandoned weapons of the murdered escort were lying piled in a heap at one side; a few were still faintly glowing. Some of the others had turned cold and transparent, their flames extinguished. Lebbrin was gathering his men, but he turned to Fenton again.

"You—what is your name, 'tweenman?"

"Fenton."

"Fenton, then—do you dare come with us into the caverns again? How much time have you?"

Fenton said, "I don't know anything about it." Suddenly he was afraid. Man-made artifacts did not exist for him, out of his body this way. But rocks, trees, caverns —evidently they *did*. If he were trapped beneath the ground when the time came for him to return to his body —would he be able to get back at all? Dimly he realized that it was the first time in what seemed like hours that he had thought of his body, back in Smythe Hall. That was another world. . . . Did he dare go back down into those caverns? Suddenly he began to shake all over, thinking of the ugly hairy monsters Kerridis had called ironfolk, of their grim knives, of the way they had sliced up the horses and crammed them, living, by fistfuls into their great fanged mouths. . .

Lebbrin was watching him with compassion. "Probably we should not ask it of you, but if we can get Kerridis away—you say she is hurt? How badly? Could you tell?"

"One of her hands was blackened and burnt where one of the—the things grabbed her. And she had been pinched and dragged—but the hand was worst," Fenton said, trying to control his voice.

Erril held out the green flamedagger. "Try to clasp your hands on the vrillsword." As Fenton's fingers closed on the hilt, he said, "I think you have time, if we are quick. If you find you cannot hold it, tell one of us at

once, and we will try to get you away in safety. It is a
risk; we have no right to ask you. But for the Lady Kerridis—"

Fenton knew he was going to risk it, and Lebbrin
looked at him with approval. He said, "Come then,
quickly; the less time we lose, the less risk you must run.
Erril! Findhal! Come! You others—give our fallen com-
rades to the fire."

Between Erril and Lebbrin, Fenton moved toward the
cave-mouth a second time. He was paralyzed with fear,
despite the vrillsword in his hands. Yet it was easier, with
the two tall, armed men to either side, guarded; he
knew he should be confident, less afraid.

*How long have I been here, anyway? Hours . . . I
have no way of measuring time, and anyway, I have no
way of knowing whether time is the same here as
there . . .*

Plunged into the darkness of the entering tunnel, by
the light of the glowing flamediggers, Fenton found himself compulsively searching for his shadow, frightened
not to see it; its absence was disquieting, abnormal. Why
this sudden terror that gripped him? His feet stumbled on
the stairs; the bruise where his knee had smashed against
the rocky wall on his first entrance throbbed painfully.
He clutched at the vrillsword, feeling its hardness in his
hands as a reassurance. *It was real. Nothing else was
real . . .*

Behind them came Findhal, taller even than Lebbrin,
armed with two swords; the vrillsword or glowing flamedagger in his left hand, and in his right a long broad-
sword of some reddish metal with gleaming jewels set
into the hilt. His features were stern and pale, his big
eyes glowing like sapphires in the darkness, his hair
ashen-blonde like Kerridis', bound in a metal band and
streaming like a Viking's over his shoulders. Erril and
Lebbrin wore only the tunics which left arms and legs
bare to the cold. Fenton noticed that they both kept from
touching the icy burning cold of the rimed rock to either
side of the downward staircase. The giant Findhal was
clad like a warrior, in metal breastplate and greaves of
the same reddish material that bound his head, and on
his narrow hands were thick gauntlets.

I wouldn't care to meet him in a dark alley—and if I were one of those things Kerridis called ironfolk, I'd run like hell if I saw him coming!

He's not real either. . . . Suddenly, disquietingly, he could see *through* Findhal, and it terrified him. But the vrillsword was hard and definite in his hands, and for a moment that calmed his fears.

They had reached the bottom of the long stairway down into the first cavern. Above it the lantern of pierced metal swung, its fire burning low. The cavern was dark and full of monstrous shadows. Fenton heard his voice like a thin thread in the huge and empty shadows. "I will try to find the proper tunnel. I may have to listen at all of them." He began, slowly, to skirt around the walls. But he could no longer be sure where he had started to search. It had been the distant screaming of Irielle which had guided him before. *Irielle!* She was a woman like himself, yet he had never seen nor spoken to her; he had let Kerridis' fate, the glamoring enchantment of a Faerie Queen, make him forget her. Had she been eaten alive by the ironfolk, was she imprisoned somewhere like Kerridis in the cold and the dark, wounded, burnt, terrified? Was she, even now, screaming in pain and terror, tormented by the monstrous things? Dread gripped him and he stopped, insecure, listening helplessly at each of the tunnels in turn.

"Which way, Fenton? Which way?" Erril urged.

"I don't know—one of the tunnels seemed to have fire below—" Fenton wavered, going from tunnelmouth to tunnelmouth, searching for the one with fire below. He remembered that the shadow of the swinging lantern above had covered the first tunnel, where the two ironfolk had run away from the light of his vrillsword. Lebbrin's face, by the eerie swinging lanternlight, looked strained and dread-filled.

"I cannot reach her mind in a cavern so filled with the metal of the ironfolk. I can tell that she is here, but I can get no sense of direction. If Fenton cannot help us, we are finished . . ."

Slowly, with groping feet, Fenton moved to opening after opening in the rocky walls. *Here is the dark one where the ironfolk fled. Yes, this way—here is the one with firelight coming up through. Was it to left or to right . . . ?* He stumbled over a rocky outcrop, put out his hand to steady himself, cried out with pain as his hand went flat against the icy burning of the rock. He looked at his fingers by the light of the dim swinging lantern, half expecting to see them blackened like Kerridis' fingers. Lebbrin reached to his throat and pulled at a golden-colored chain hanging there. Inside his tunic, on the end of the chain, was a great white jewel, giving off a soft sparkling light. He took Fenton's fingers in his, not urgently, but with an irritable sense of haste, and pressed them for a moment to the jewel. The pain was gone. His voice betrayed fear and disquiet. "Fenton, make haste, *anything* could be happening to her down there. . . ."

"I think it is this one—" But Fenton was not sure. Had the entryway been to left or to right of the one with fire below? Was he lost in the caverns, after all?

"Hurry," Lebbrin urged.

"This way—I think—"

"We must risk it," Findhal said, and plunged ahead of them into the tunnel.

Only a little way inside, Fenton stopped, sure it was wrong. The steps seemed steeper, slimed with something which made his feet slip unpleasantly, something new and not familiar. He heard Findhal grunt in disgust, and hung back, suddenly unsure. Then from behind there was a blare of horns, and Findhal leaped back, toward the main cavern, shoving through Erril and Lebbrin, pushing Fenton unregarded against the wall. Findhal's longsword was bared in his hand, the vrillsword clutched for light between his teeth. He leaped out into the cavern and there was a great clashing of swords, a cry, a hideous barking noise. Erril and Lebbrin drew the swords belted at their waists and ran, fighting their way through the huge fanged beasts which had begun to flood into the cavern.

Fenton stood in the tunnelmouth, forgotten, out of the way. Keeping out of the way seemed the best thing he could do; though when one of the wolflike things leaped toward him he sank the vrillsword up to the hilt into its throat; with a suffocating sense of terror and relief, he

saw it fall. At first it had seemed that the cavern was full
of the creatures, snapping and howling as Findhal swung
his great sword; but Fenton, standing well out of the way,
realized that there were only half a dozen or so. Findhal
quickly killed two; Lebbrin and Erril, back to back, were
fighting off another, but when a second and then a third
rushed in, they were hard pressed; Erril's foot slipped in
the blood from one of the dead wolves and he went down.
Fenton rushed to his aid, thrusting with the vrilldagger.
The animal snarled and snapped and he felt the great
fangs worrying at his clothing and at his leg. Lebbrin
was bleeding from another bite. Overcome with horror,
Fenton thrust the vrill up to the hilt into the beast. It
felt strangely insubstantial, as if he were thrusting the
dagger into a pillow, but the wolf fell, snapping at the
air, kicking and twisting; and then lay still. The two remaining animals drew off, looking at the men with eyes
that seemed to Fenton too intelligent for mere animals.

Findhal sheathed his sword. "Quickly! If Pentarn is
desperate enough to loose banewolves on us, there's no
telling what else may be waiting down here! This way!"

Fenton was feeling sick now that the excitement of
battle had subsided. How could the wolves have managed to bite him? His body wasn't here at all! Yet his
trousers were hanging in strips, and he turned his eyes
from the bloody and lacerated flesh. It hurt, too, with a
sick, throbbing ache. Findhal bent and looked at it
briefly. "It will fade when you do. Come, quickly!"

Halfway down the tunnel, Fenton began to see the
flickers of light from the open cavern where he had first
seen the hairy creatures pinching and tormenting Kerridis. At first it seemed empty; Findhal turned angrily on
Fenton, demanding, "If this is a trap, I'll—" But Lebbrin stopped him, pointing to the rock niche, the metal
grille; they could all see the huddled, cloaked figure,
curled in a disconsolate heap on the rock floor.

Findhal shouted, "Kerridis! Lady!" He began to run.
The heap lay unstirring. They crowded around the metal
grille; they hung warily back from the iron bars, but Fenton slid through.

"She's not here," he said, shocked. "It is only her
cloak—"

Erril and Lebbrin cried out in dismay, but Findhal said, "Don't panic, any of you. It may be just as well; none of us could open the metal grille. If they have taken her elsewhere, we may still have a chance to rescue her."

Lebbrin took the white jewel from his tunic again, gazing into it fixedly; after a moment he said, "This way." He began to run toward one of the side tunnels, plunging into the darkness. Fenton heard Lebbrin cry out in surprise or pain as he vanished; Erril, shouting, ran after him. Fenton, following more slowly with Findhal, noted that the big warrior was beginning to limp heavily on the leg torn by the banewolves; Fenton, too, was conscious of pain, though not as much as he would have expected from such a wound. He stopped before entering the tunnel and went in carefully; even so, his feet slipped from under him and he slid down, bumping painfully, to land in a heap atop the others. Findhal's huge weight came down on top of them all, squashing them together into a great heap at the bottom.

Slowly, they sorted themselves out. Fenton had had the breath knocked out of him, and Erril had been bruised by Findhal's sword striking him athwart the ribs, but in general they were not much the worse. Down the corridor were torches fixed in brackets, giving a smoky light and a thick, sickening smell. At the end of the tunnel was a glaring reddish light, and they could see the figure of one of the ironfolk, his back to them, seated against the wall, chewing on something—Fenton, after what he had observed of the ironfolk's habits, did not like to think about what it must have been. Findhal, gesturing them back, crept silently along the corridor, vrillsword naked in one hand, metal sword in the other. The *irighi* heard him and sprang up, swinging his great machete, but Findhal's sword lopped his head from his shoulders; the corpse spouted blood and toppled sideways.

Findhal sprang back, shaking his hand, which had been splattered with the blood; his face was contorted with agony.

"Lebbrin, your healstone—" he began, but Lebbrin did not hear, hurrying past him into the rock-niche the dead monster had been guarding.

"Irielle! Praise to Air and Fire," he gasped. "Where have they taken Kerridis?"

"I don't know." Fenton, advancing, could see that the speaker was the redheaded woman he had seen in Kerridis' company. "They brought her through here a few moments ago, honking and chattering, and Pentarn was with them; I thought perhaps you people were already after them."

"Is she hurt?" Erril demanded, his face twisting.

"I do not know, my Lord. But they were dragging her along as such folk do, so I imagine she must be, at the least, badly bruised and burned," Irielle said. Fenton could get a good look at her now. She too had been thrust behind one of the metal grilles, but this one was locked with hasp and padlock, probably in recognition of the fact that, unlike Kerridis, she had no fear of touching the metal.

Irielle looked exhausted, draggled, drawn with horror; but she was struggling to compose herself. She said, "If you can free me from this place—you," she said, gesturing to Fenton. "There is a key on that creature's belt—"

"He is a 'tweenman," said Findhal. "He could touch the metal of the key if he were *here* but now he cannot—"

She laughed, an almost hysterical sound. "Must we then get Pentarn to open it for us? I shall be here till the rocks crumble, in that case—"

"I think we can do better than that," Findhal said, shielding his hands with gauntlets, and dragging the corpse of the dead *irighi* toward the grille. "Can you reach the key, child?"

Irielle got down on her hands and knees, reaching through the grille, scrabbling toward it. "Turn him a little—I am sorry, foster-father, I know it is an unpleasant task. *There!*" She had her slim fingers on the key, was thrusting her hand through the lock; but the padlock stuck, out of reach.

"This is provoking," she said, after a struggle to manipulate the key through the grille from inside, "I cannot reach it—cannot one of you—"

"Wait," Fenton said. The vrillsword was still in his hand and he suddenly remembered that this was solid to him and to things in that dimension too. He lifted the padlock, on the end of the vrillsword, turning and manipulating it so that the keyhole was toward Irielle. It was tricky work, since time and again the padlock fell off the end of the green-glowing flamedagger, neither of them having been shaped for such maniupuations. But finally he managed to maneuver it so that he could hold it by a crack in the metal, and Irielle managed to get the key through.

She turned it with a rasp and the lock came free; she wrenched the door open with a rusty screeching of hinges long unoiled. She favored Fenton with a breathtaking smile.

"Clever! Clever, for a 'tweenman!"

"Not so clever," Fenton said glumly, "or I would have thought of doing that with the cage where they had Kerridis confined, that one was not even locked—"

"There is no sense fretting after last season's snowfall," Lebbrin said. "Are you hurt, Irielle? Did those creatures harm you?"

She shook her head. She was still breathing heavily. "No, although Pentarn favored me with some choice words about his plans for me, and I sank my teeth in his wrist, so he is in a foul humor. I would not have angered him, had I realized that Kerridis was still alive in his hands; he may vent his spite on her . . ." Her face twisted in dread. "They took her down that way, toward the fires . . ."

"Come, quickly," Findhal said. "We must follow, as fast as we can." He began to lead the way, running with his quick graceful lope—not human, Fenton thought, watching him run, not *quite* human—and the others followed.

At the end of the corridor he began to see firelight; and once, passing a tunnelmouth, it seemed that he could see cracks in the floor and fire below, as if they walked above a rock floor leading down into a volcano.

Irielle, hurrying along at Fenton's side, asked, "How did you come here? Did you go through the World-house?"

"I don't know what you mean."

"No, of course not, otherwise you would be a worldwalker and not a 'tweenman. But you surely did not come in Pentarn's Gate—"

This was all Greek to Fenton, and he shook his head. "I am not sure. I—I woke up and found myself here. For a long time I thought I was dreaming—Is it *your* world? You look as human as I do! You're not one of those people—" he pointed to the figures of Lebbrin, Erril, and the giant Findhal striding before them.

"One of the Alfar? No," she said with a sigh, "I can never be truly one of them, though Kerridis is as kind to me as if I were her own changeling. What of you? Where are you from? What world do you walk when you are yourself?"

"I came here from Berkeley, California—"

She shook her head. "I have no idea where that may be. It is not any world I have seen from the World-house." She broke off, with a cry, and began to run. "Look! Look, I think they have found—"

The three men—Irielle had called them Alfar—were clustered together at the far end of the tunnel, looking down on a nightmare scene below. The cavern was black with the hairy, thickening bodies of the ironfolk, honking and screeching in their ugly voices. One of them was shouting what sounded like a speech—Fenton was unpleasantly reminded of old newsclips of Hitler—but none of his people were paying the slightest attention. At the far end of the cavern steam was coming up through cracks in the floor, and there was a sulphurous stink. Irielle pointed, and Fenton could see Kerridis, thrust unregarded into a corner, surrounded by ironfolk; only, at this distance, a shimmer of brown flesh and streaming hair.

Lebbrin said grimly, "We must fight our way through to her. We have vrillswords; fighting at such close quarters, they will be more help than in the open. I never thought to die in the maw of an *irighi,* but there seems no help for it . . ."

Erril held him back. "No, my Lord!" he said urgently. "You must not, not even for Kerridis! Others are coming behind us! They will follow soon, and then we may have a chance; otherwise you will simply throw your life away!" He turned to Findhal and said urgently, "Go back, hurry, guide them down here. They must be on their way by now! Tell them the ironfolk are here. If they come we will have a chance—" He looked quickly around. "Fenton! Take the vrillsword, and slip along the edge of the cavern toward Kerridis. Perhaps they will think you only a shadow, if you keep the vrillsword concealed under your garments till you are very close to her. Then, perhaps, you can be some protection to her; at least you can whisper to her that help is on the way, very quickly."

Fenton thought, *Who, me, go down there among all those ugly-wuglies?* But he could see the sense of Erril's plan. The ironfolk had not been able to see him before. It had been the sight of the vrillsword in an apparently invisible hand that had frightened them away.

He nodded, though he was paralyzed with fright. Only the knowledge that Kerridis must be even more frightened, alone and surrounded by the ugly monstrosities who had cut up and eaten her escort alive, kept him from refusing. Keeping close to the wall, he began to slip along the edge of the cavern, clutching the vrillsword in his hands under the down parka he was still wearing.

It was hot in here, with the fire below and the thick, sulphurous steam. *I ought to think myself into something not quite so warm.* But he was too busy for that now.

He tiptoed along the wall, through the flickering shadows, trying to move like the shadow they thought he was, past the screeching, capering ironfolk. Their speech sounded like the gabbling of wild seafowl. Once Fenton's heart stopped; one of the *irighi* was looking straight at him. Fenton froze motionless, and the *irighi* finally turned his eyes away, without interest. Fenton was afraid he would sneeze from the smelly smoke that was coming up now in billows through the floor.

Volcanic caves. Where in hell am I? Yeah, in hell; it's a good imitation. No wonder the occasional old churchman who got a good look at the country of the Faerie folk, in the medieval legends, thought they were from the devil. Pointy ears. And the stink of sulphur and brimstone from fire down below. And those damned—things! —sneaking around!

And then Fenton got the shock of his life.

He was looking straight at one of the *irighi*, who was capering and yelling like a damned soul on the grid, and suddenly the thing—vanished. In its place, Fenton suddenly saw metal pipes, a squared-off wall, a pair of doors that said clearly, ELEVATOR . . .

Fenton blinked and was back in the cavern again.

I am somewhere in the basement of some building on campus!

He clutched at the vrillsword in his hand, and had a second unpleasant shock. His fingers began to sink through it. He could just manage to hold it—though the sensation was enormously unpleasant, like sinking his hands up to the wrists in wet cold mush.

That was the danger signal. I am beginning to fade, I should be out in the open air . . . if that elevator appears again I should run like hell and get into it . . .

No. My finger would go right through the elevator button, too. But I might find a set of stairs and be able to get up them. . . .

Panicky, he turned round and round, clutching at the vrillsword, and then he saw Kerridis. He was very close to her now, only a little way, a few steps, to where she was surrounded by the ring of ironfolk.

Devilishly ingenious; they know she is afraid to touch them, so they need only surround her and she is imprisoned.

I've got to get out of here. But at least I can tell her that help is on the way . . .

But how could he get through the ironfolk to her? He did not think they could see him. But he was afraid to take the chance. The big steel machetes they were carrying looked unpleasantly tangible.

And how am I going to be able to get out afterward? I'm well and truly lost, and they're all going to have their hands full rescuing Kerridis . . .

Once again the cavern winked out of existence. This time his hands slithered on the vrillsword, and it fell to the floor with a green-glassy sounding *clink*. One of the ironfolk saw it and came leaping toward him; stopped, confused, looking around. They *couldn't* see him! Fenton bent and managed to scoop up the vrillsword. He leaped across the crevasse, thrust his way through the ironfolk—

they felt like thick fog—and shouldered his way to Kerridis' side.

"Lady Kerridis—" he whispered, wondering if she could hear him.

She looked around, her great golden eyes searching for him in the gloom.

"Where—is it you, stranger 'tweenman?"

"Help's coming," he whispered. "Irielle is back there, and Erril and Lebbrin, and Findhal bringing reinforcements." He struggled to hold on to the vrillsword; she reached out and took it from him.

She said, her lovely voice throbbing with concern, "But—you are beginning to fade—you are endangered here—"

The ironfolk, evidently suspicious of what they could not see, were milling around; Kerridis swung the vrillsword in a circle, and they fell back a little, muttering and honking suspiciously. Then from the far end of the cavern came a great ringing shout.

"O ho hi hei Alfar! Kerridis! Kerridis!"

Findhal and another warrior, armed like him, came leaping through the floor that was crowded with ironfolk, lopping off heads with every great sweep of their swords.

"Look! Look!" she cried in excitement. "It *is* Findhal and my brother's men—" She turned and cried out in her high, bell-like voice, "O ho hi hei Alfar! To me, to me—I am here!"

The booted, bearded man they called Pentarn shoved hastily through the ring of ironfolk, shouldering to Kerridis' side. He shouted, "We must get her away before the fight or we will lose everything! Come, quickly—"

He tried to grab Kerridis by the shoulder. Fenton grabbed the vrillsword from Kerridis and shoved it at him. It went in through Pentarn's cloak, but had such a mushy feel that Fenton could not keep hold of it; it seemed to push back with an equal force, and simultaneously the cavern faded out again.

Oh, no! Not now!

Fenton blinked, looking wildly around the basement assembly of pipes, furnaces, lumber. Then he was back in the sulphurous cave, among the stink, and Pentarn was

grappling with him, hands at his throat—which went
through like mist.

He can see me. But he can't touch me. . . .

"Damned 'tweenman," Pentarn grated, shouting to his
ironfolk; but Findhal had fought his way across the floor,
swinging his metal sword in a great arc. He cut off heads
of the ring around Kerridis and the rest scattered. And
then Irielle and Lebbrin were kneeling beside Kerridis,
gathering her up, Irielle gently draping her in her cloak,
Lebbrin took up Kerridis' blistered blackened hand. He
drew out the white jewel from round his neck; clasped
Kerridis' blackened fingers over it, and the light began to
shine through the fingers. Kerridis cried out in agony, but
Lebbrin, with gentle force, held her hand clasped over
the stone. After a moment, her face convulsing, she sank
motionless into his arms.

Below them on the floor, the ironfolk were dying by
hundreds. Irielle turned quickly to Fenton, who was still
trying to hold the vrillsword, and her face immediately
told Fenton that she recognized his predicament. She
tugged at Lebbrin's cloak.

"Lebbrin, the 'tweenman who helped us, he is fading,
we must get him above ground quickly—"

"Don't prate to me of 'tweenmen, child, the Lady
Kerridis is hurt—come quickly, look to her—the healstone is not enough—"

Irielle looked, dismayed, from Fenton to the fainting
Kerridis. She was distressed, but her voice was stubborn.

"Is this Alfar honor? He endangered himself for Kerridis, and you know it! Will none of you guide him above
ground, or must I do it?"

Erril's voice shouted suddenly behind them, "Pentarn!
Don't let *him* get away—"

Fenton looked. The bearded man had turned and was
striding through scattering ironfolk, and then Fenton saw
through the blinking, thinning caverns a strange greying
oval. Pentarn hurried toward it, Erril hard on his heels.

"It's a Gateway! Hurry, don't let him—"

But Pentarn reached the greying oval, stepped into it
as if it were a doorway, slid through and disappeared.
There was no other word for it. Behind him the oval narrowed to a slit, turned and was gone.

He stepped into a hole and pulled the hole in behind him! That was simply the only way to describe what had happened!

Findhal's reinforcements were chasing down the iron-folk, killing most of them, the others fleeing into side caves and tunnelmouths. One of them slipped through a widening crevasse, and Fenton saw him fall, screaming all the way, to the fire below. Findhal caught up Kerridis in his arms.

"We must get out of here! There's fire down below, and they may have some way to let us down through. Come!"

He beat a hasty retreat across the floor and up through the long tunnel. Irielle, gesturing to Fenton to follow, hurried after him, but as he was about to climb with Kerridis in his arms up the long tunnel down which they had fallen, she tugged at his cloak.

"No, there is another way—I saw him come through here—" she said urgently. She turned down a side tunnel and began to run. After a moment Findhal followed. Kerridis had begun to stir in his arms. Fenton hurried along at Irielle's side, keeping pace with the girl, though again and again the dark tunnel blinked out around him and he could no longer hold the vrillsword; after it had fallen twice, Irielle turned around and scooped it up, waving him on with desperate haste. Erril and Lebbrin crowded into the new tunnel behind them.

And then—although the tunnel was now flickering around him so that Fenton could hardly see it—they were outside, in daylight, on a rocky ledge, sleet-covered, with wind and rain blowing hard around it, wet on Fenton's face. The Alfar bent over Kerridis, trying to shelter her with their bodies against the rain.

But through the rain Fenton could see flickering sunshine now, smog-ridden yellow sunshine and the circle of tall trees. . . .

He was in the eucalyptus grove on the Berkeley campus, stumbling over the circle of fallen logs . . . once more the flickering came, and the rain on the ledge was beating down on him, and he saw Irielle's face, wet with rain, her long red hair streaming wildly in the wind, looking

after him in surprise and dismay, and then she was gone.
Gone for good, this time.

Gone. All of it gone. . . .

Fenton became aware that he was very tired and hungry, that his leg ached horribly where he had bruised it
on the rocks, that his down parka hung in shreds around
him. There was a painful pull at his midsection. He
looked and saw something grey there, streaming out—he
could not touch it, but he could not resist the pull either.
He went along with it, and after a moment became aware
that it was hauling him along in the direction of Smythe
Hall.

It was very late, and the campus was deserted, except
for a rare student bicycling across Sproul Plaza. He could
see lights in the student center building, and brilliantly
from Telegraph Avenue. But the urgency of the pull
hurried him along, into Smythe Hall, up the stairs. He
drifted through a mopbucket where a solitary janitor was
mopping the stairs, through the wall were the ESP lab
office was situated. He saw a folder lying open where
Marjie had sat earlier, laying out ESP cards, but now
he could clearly see his body on the high couch, Garnock
bending over it, taking his pulse.

And now he could see the greyish thing clearly. leading
from his own midsection to the midsection—actually, he
knew without seeing, he could *feel*, to the navel—of the
body on the bed.

Which of them is me? he wondered in confusion. *Is
this the* silver cord *they talk about?* He drifted now,
above the bed; suddenly with a hard shock he slid downward into his body.

His head throbbed. His leg ached with a hard agony
that made Fenton realize that everything he had suffered
while he was out of his body was only the shadow, the
echo of real pain.

"Good God," Garnock said, looking into his open eyes,
"I was beginning to be worried about you. How do you
feel?"

Fenton blinked, shaking his head. Dream? Had it all
been a drug-induced hallucination after all? Kerridis,
Irielle, Lebbrin, Findhal, had none of them ever existed

in reality? He bent—he couldn't help it, the pain was terrible—and rolled up one pants leg.

The stone-bruise where he had taken the fall against the icy rock ledge was darkening to black, with purple bloody swellings at intervals.

"That must have been some hallucination," Garnock said, looking down at the swollen leg. "That happens sometimes—remember the freshman experiment with hypnosis and the ice-cube? I remember you developed a dilly of a burn, a second-degree one, blisters and all, because we told you it was a red-hot poker."

But Fenton was not listening.

Below the stone-bruise, in the calf of his leg, he could clearly see toothmarks.

Toothmarks!

More accurately, fang-marks. The fangs of a banewolf, which had met in his flesh.

Garnock was rubbing his hands in glee.

"I'll set you up with an appointment with Sally for tonight," he said. "She'll want a complete content analysis before it fades out—you know how dreams fade. You'd better start making notes right away, before you forget. I have a tape cassette here—want to dictate while it's fresh in your mind?"

But Fenton was hardly listening. He was still looking at the fang-marks of the banewolf, red and ugly on his leg.

CHAPTER FOUR

THE NEXT MORNING, Cameron Fenton walked slowly toward Smythe Hall for his appointment with Sally Lobeck.

He had dutifully dictated his memories of the dream experience into a taped cassette before leaving the lab, knowing how even the most vivid dreams had a tendency to deteriorate into a mishmash of half memories and confabulations. When he had finished, dusk had fallen outside and Garnock dismissed him.

"I'll set up an appointment with Sally for ten tomorrow; she has a section of freshmen in Introductory Parapsychology Readings at eight," he volunteered, and Cameron Fenton chuckled.

"Better her than me!" He had never particularly liked teaching freshmen.

"Shall we say Thursday for your second session? We schedule them in groups of ten sessions, and we've found out that it works better to have at least three days between sessions."

"Fine with me."

"Now you'd better go and get something to eat," Garnock dismissed him, almost paternally. "You may find your appetite is up somewhat—a couple of the subjects reported that, though I don't know how much of it is objective yet. We don't know all that much about the biological side effects of Antaril—of course rats can't report their subjective sensations—and students seem unable to report much of anything else."

Fenton had indeed had a voracious appetite for supper, which had been a pleasant surprise; his major objection to the series of experiments he had made as a student with LSD was the way in which they sensitized his palate and virtually destroyed his appetite. He had lost almost ten pounds, and didn't have it to lose. On the contrary, he had heard that some of the women students, who were or believed they were overweight, had welcomed that particular side effect.

Now, as he crossed the campus, he found himself unconsciously looking for landmarks which might correspond to his sojourn in the dream. *I came out of Smythe Hall right about there, through the wall by the bike rack. And I'll bet the sign I saw marked ELEVATOR was somewhere in the basement of Barrows . . .* he had forcibly to restrain himself from going to see for himself. There were no caves, certainly no volcanic caves, beneath Berkeley campus.

But if I saw the stairs and the marked elevator in Barrows, and they are really there, wouldn't that be extra validation of an extrasensory perception?

He decided not to search. He was not, after all, sure that he had never been down in the basement of Barrows Hall, and subconscious memory was the bane of ESP; the time to verify the existence of the stairway and elevator was after the experiment was over, though he should make a note of it now, while reporting the content of his dream to Sally.

He remembered Sally Lobeck as a lanky intense undergraduate, all eyes and teeth, with dank masses of sable hair, which she had then worn uncombed and waist-length; big glasses, bulky skirts and sandals. He was startled to find that she had grown up to match the eyes, which were now fringed in heavy dark lashes and framed in smart silver frames. She was a tall, handsome young woman, well-dressed in a highly individual manner. A dark braid, as thick as her wrist, hung over one shoulder.

"Did you bring along the cassette, Mr. Fenton? Please sit down. Want some coffee?"

"Please," he said, glancing gratefully at the pot. "Ten is early for me, in civilian life."

She chuckled, busying herself with paper cups.

"Sugar?"

"Black, thanks." He accepted the cup, noticing that she had slender, graceful hands and that her gestures

were delicate. Something about the long fingers made
him think suddenly of Kerridis, with her blackened hand
and fingers; crying out in pain as Lebbrin had clamped
her hands over the glowing healstone. He wondered
where Kerridis was, and if her hand had gotten all right
again, then angrily dismissed the thought.

*Kerridis was just a woman in a dream. And Irielle.
None of them were real. . . .*

"You can put the cup right over there, Mr. Fenton.
And please feel free to help yourself to more if you want
it."

"Cameron, please. Or just Cam."

Her chuckle was low in her throat. "Sorry. I still think
of you as a teacher. Where I grew up, you just *don't* call
teachers by their first names."

"Where was that?"

"Over in the Valley; small town near Fresno," she
said. "They haven't fully decided whether or not they'll
extend diplomatic recognition to the twentieth century."

Cam thought that probably explained the unwashed
"hippie" period she had gone through—and fortunately
out of again. "What do they think of your choice of parapsychology for a specialty?"

"I don't know," she said coolly, "I haven't asked them.
I don't think I really care to know. Shall we get started?"

Knowing he had been warned off personal territory,
Cam reached for the cassette into which he had, at
Garnock's behest, dictated the episode. "Will this fit your
machine?" He watched her slim dark fingers opening the
mechanism, dropping in the cassette, and again had the
flashing memory of Kerridis' fingers.

"Now, if you don't mind, I think I'd like to have you
tell me again; listen to the cassette as we replay it and
add in anything you've missed. And I'll want to stop it
every few minutes and ask questions; is that all right
with you?"

"It's your project," he said. "But I don't think I quite
understand what you're doing here, Sally."

She leaned back in the swivel chair behind her desk,
tucking her arms behind her head.

"I'm not quite sure, myself, that I know where it's going to lead," she said. "I thought I did when I started, and

now it's turning into something else. I got the idea from a paper they did over in psych, on religious motifs in the hallucinatory processes of LSD experiments; there were enormous numbers of people who had some kind of religious experiences under LSD. Do you follow that?"

Fenton nodded.

"Well, the question raised there was whether it was unconscious expectation, or some general quality of the experience itself, that colored the attitude toward a religious phenomenon. In short, was it an objective or a subjective experience; and if it was subjective, were we tapping into the collective unconscious of humanity? Basically, did the quality of the religious experience correlate positively with basic mental set and individual emotional history, did it correlate negatively, or was there no correlation at all?"

"What conclusions did he reach?"

"Well, there were the usual exceptions—pious Jews and devout Protestants getting visions of the Virgin Mary, or atheists having a religious experience—enormous numbers of them had some kind of vision of Buddha, for some reason—but in general there was a positive correlation with childhood religious imaginations as brought out under hypnotic regressions. So I thought I would try a similar content analysis of dreams under Antaril. How the dreams correlate with previous expectations, etc. And, once again, are we working with the collective unconscious, or with individual mental set and previous experience?"

"Garnock thinks it's individual," Fenton said. "When I dictated the experience, Garnock said, 'Sounds as if you were reading too much Tolkien.' "

Sally grinned. Her mouth was a little too wide for beauty, but he had remembered her smile as toothier and snaggled, which it wasn't. "And were you?"

Fenton shook his head. "I read the Tolkien books when I was a kid, but I don't remember them much."

"Still, if your experience under Antaril keyed into *that*," Sally said, "I'd say that the books might have made more of an impression on you than you realized at the time."

"Hmmm, maybe," Fenton said. "But once again, if

it's the collective unconscious, maybe I'm just keying into whatever it was that Tolkien saw. Anyway, these people didn't look that much like I always pictured his elves."

"Well, let's listen to it," Sally said, turning on the cassette, and fiddling with the controls of her own machine, which was a large one and obviously of professional quality. "Now, Cam, if you don't mind I'm going to tape the whole thing; take it off your cassette, along with whatever comments I make and whatever you have to add. All right with you?"

"Sure, fine."

"All right then." She dictated his name, the date, month and year into the microphone. "Two cc. of Antaril by pressure-spray injection; loss of consciousness preceded by three perfect runs of Zener cards; subject not in same room with cards but separated by standard screening." She shut off the mike. "Now what happened immediately after you ceased to talk to Garnock, Cam?"

"I never actually lost consciousness," Fenton said. "It just got to be too much trouble to talk."

Sally switched on the cassette, and Fenton heard his own voice: ". . . was aware of increasing difficulty in making what seemed to be the separate body on the bed talk coherently. So I walked out through the wall."

"Wait," said Sally, flipping the *stop* switch and turning to *record*. "You're sure about that? You definitely had an impression of walking through the wall, and not the doorway?"

"Yes, through the wall. It felt like it wasn't there at all. Like going through fog."

"Can you describe precisely what was in the corridor at that time?"

"There were a lot of students. I remember—" He frowned. "There was a big tall chap with glasses and a bulky white sweater, redheaded. I walked right *through* him—"

"Sounds like Buddy Ormsby," Sally said, making a note. "He's in my freshman section; I'll try to find out if he was in the hall about then. Anything else?"

"Outside, a girl on a blue bike . . ." Fenton went on, meticulously describing what he had seen, and the way in which the campus had slowly faded out around him.

"Let's get that on the tape again," Sally said, and snapped it on again, to hear Fenton's voice describing:

"There was a young woman, with blonde hair and jeans, riding a blue bike. She had a baby in a backpack —a red-and-blue striped backpack, and when I bumped into the bike I was worried about upsetting the baby—"

"I know her too," Sally said, making another scribbled note. "Jessica takes her kid to all her classes. I can verify if she was outside Smythe Hall just then. Clairvoyance could account for you seeing her there. Go on—" She returned to Fenton's taped account of his journey, listening in silence as he described the vanishing and thinning of the campus, the appearance of the red-and-black mackinaw jacket, the singing in the distance.

As he listened, Fenton realized that the dream hadn't faded, as dreams do. It was clear in his mind, in the way that any other strange adventure is clear in recent memory. This intensive debriefing only seemed to make it clearer. As he listened to his own voice describing the first attack of the ugly creatures, he found himself thinking of Garnock's comment that it sounded as if he had been reading too much Tolkien.

There is a kind of correspondence at that, Tolkien's elves and the orcs. But I don't remember ever thinking of the elves as looking like that. . . .

He heard his own voice on the tape saying, "I heard them speak of her as *Kerridis*—"

"Wait," Sally said again, and stopped the forward flow of the tape. "Are you sure of that name? Say it again, will you?" Fenton obliged and she repeated, thoughtfully, writing it down in quick scribbled symbols that he assumed were phonetic. "Like this, *Kair*-eed-iss?"

"Like that. Only not quite such a strong accent on the first syllable. Why?"

"You're sure it wasn't Keridwen?"

"Positive. The thing yelled it out at the top of his lungs, and some other people repeated it later. Why?"

"Keridwen was a Welsh goddess, a kind of world-mother figure," Sally said. "Don't you remember your comparative mythologies?" She started the tape again, and Fenton felt deflated. He was, after all, quite familiar with the theory that the subconscious never forgot anything at all, and to have the name of his Faerie Queen turn out to be almost identical with a goddess from mythology was something of a comedown. Later when, on the tape, he referred to her as the Faerie Queen, she stopped him again.

"Have you read Spenser's *Faerie Queen?*"

"No. I know there *is* such a—is it a poem or a play?"

"How did you happen to think of the term Faerie Queen for her, then?"

"I'm not sure," Fenton said, "it just happened to come into my mind. Maybe I was thinking of the Child Ballad—you know the one about Tam Lane and the Faery Queen?"

"But you weren't any *part* of the action, then?" Sally asked, and she seemed disappointed.

As she started the tape again, Fenton thought that it was rather strange. He wouldn't have been surprised to find himself on the white horse, in such a dream, being ransomed by a courageous woman *from* the Faerie Queen. But to find the Queen herself in need of rescue— that was indeed a switch on the old ballad, and probably told something about Fenton's psychology. He wasn't sure what.

And why—if it's a dream, and we get rid of our frustrations in dreams—didn't I take a more active part in the rescue myself, instead of behaving like a helpless bystander? That business of having my hands go right through the metal—

He heard his own voice again, on the tape. "The man was big, and had long sideburns and a short dark beard. The Queen called him Pentarn—"

"Oh!" Sally's exclamation was low but unmistakable, "You got Pentarn too—"

"What?" Fenton demanded.

But Sally hastily motioned him into silence. "Nothing, nothing . . ."

Later when he spoke of Kerridis and her fear of iron, she interrupted him again.

"Had you heard the story of the elf-people not being able to touch cold iron?"

"I'm not sure," Fenton said. "I must have heard it somewhere." He was ransacking his memory for what he had heard of superstitions. "I can't remember where.

Maybe I read it in—wasn't there one of Kipling's stories
called 'Cold Iron?' I'm not sure. And isn't it in—let me
see—Lady Charlotte Guest—no, in Yeats, *Irish Fairy
and Folk Tales*—that a piece of cold iron laid in a cradle
will prevent the fairies from stealing an unbaptized baby,
or something like that. But I really don't remember
where I heard it."

She stopped him only once more, to have him repeat
a name or two.

"Ariel?"

"Irielle," he corrected. "Longer than *Ariel*, and a more
liquid sound at the beginning. A lovely sound."

At the end she went back, summarizing, making sure
she had it all written down correctly.

"Do you take this much care with all the dreams,
Sally? As I remember, content analyses on ordinary
dreams turned out to be a fairly blind alley. Has there
been any evidence to prove that there is that kind of collective unconscious—like people having similar dreams?"

She smiled good-naturedly. "You mustn't ask me to
tell you that, Cam," she said. "It's called leading the witness. I don't want to suggest anything at all to you. I'll
see you after your next session."

Just the same, he remembered the one unguarded
phrase that had escaped her. *You got Pentarn too.* Did
that mean that someone else had seen the sinister Pentarn
in a dream?

Sally was labelling the notes of the session, taking a
reel of tape from her machine, and stowing it in a box.
His eyes followed her as she put it into a file drawer. He
would like to hear some of them and compare dreams.
Had someone else dreamed Pentarn?

*Damn it, the name sounds familiar at that. Is he some
character in a kid's book I read sometime and forgot?*

"Want another cup of coffee?"

"No, thanks," he said, glancing at the clock. Could
it really have taken three hours? "But it's late enough
that I can buy you a drink at the Rathskeller."

She laughed and shook her head. "Thanks, Cam, but I
have a seminar at one."

"Another time, then?"

"That might be nice," she said, noncommittally. "But

just now I really have to run to my class. Thanks for your time." She gave him her hand, in a friendly, matter-of-fact way, "When is your next session?"

"Thursday at three."

"I'll see you Friday at ten then, shall I? And don't forget to tape what happens afterward, before you forget any details." She went out with him, firmly locking the door behind her. As they walked down the hall, she said, "The problem we have in parapsychology—aside from the problem that we still have to justify our existence—is that, in spite of enormous masses of raw data, we have virtually no conclusions. We don't know whether the phenomena belong to biochemistry, to neurological pathology, or to individual psychiatric or psychological gifts."

"I never thought of it that way," Fenton said.

"The trouble is," Sally said, "there is some support for each of these positions. The work Garnock's doing on Antaril, of course, tends to indicate that ESP is a function of disturbed biochemistry of the forebrain; stir it up with a psychedelic drug, and you get ESP—simple as that. And then there is the case for a neurological explanation. Were you here when Ellen Ransford was being tested?"

Fenton nodded. It had been the same year he had Sally in his undergraduate psych section, though he didn't say so—he found he was very much reluctant to remember that gauche and unattractive young woman or to associate her with the smartly dressed and sophisticated teacher at his side.

"Ellen, as I remember, tested incredibly high—but only during the period of scotoma before those ghastly migraine headaches she used to have," he said. "And only when she held off taking ergot to control the migraines. The control drugs aborted the migraine—but they aborted the ESP too." In his mind was a picture of the small blonde Ellen, tears rolling down her face with pain, her eyes squeezed shut against the acute photophobia of the episode, calling off the one perfect run of cards he had heard that year. "What finally happened to Ellen? I was drafted that June; did she come back to school again in September?"

Sally nodded. "She did," she said. "For a while, as you can imagine, she was something of a pet of the department, and I remember one day when Stefanson, from the medical school, was over here doing an EEG on her, while Mortwell, from psych, was holding forth about migraine being merely a manifestation of a personality defect, and obviously psychosomatic. They practically came to blows, while Ellen sat there with electrodes pasted on her skull, crying. And then she developed *petit mal* epilepsy, and had to go on Dilantin full time, and the ESP went away as long as she was on Dilantin. Which gives some life to the neurological-phenomenon explanation, too."

"Where is she now?" Fenton asked.

Sally chuckled again. She said, "Over in the psych department. She had an affair with one of old Mortwell's teaching assistants. I think she was shacked up with him for a while, switched her major, took up behavioral psych, and the last I heard she was contentedly running rats around mazes." She glanced at her watch in consternation. "Cam, I'm going to be late for my seminar! See you Friday." She fled up the stairs, not looking back.

CHAPTER FIVE

THIS TIME FENTON KNEW WHAT TO EXPECT; and, knowing, he managed to complete five perfect runs of the cards before it became too difficult to control his voice. But when Garnock asked him to attempt control of the PK dice machine, he refused.

"You think it's ESP," he managed to say, "but it isn't. It's bilocation."

"Would you like to explain that?" Garnock asked, in the carefully neutral tones that annoyed Fenton so much in this state of consciousness.

Fenton said churlishly, "No. I wouldn't like to at all. Too hard to talk now . . ." And he walked out through the wall again.

He was beginning to feel nervous, conscious that it wasn't really fair to blame Garnock for his irritability. The fact was, he was beginning to feel the world fade around him, to be aware that if he stayed there much longer he would go right through the floor.

Outside, the campus was already so dim that it was difficult to find landmarks. He turned north again, hurrying toward the eucalyptus grove which had been there in both worlds, looking for the characteristic arrangement of the trees. The trees were there, as they had been; but already they were no longer eucalyptus. They rose upward, with narrow silvery stems and some kind of feathery white flowers; and there was no sign of the mountain pass where he had first seen the Alfar attacked by the ironfolk.

This stopped him short. Somehow he had never doubted that he would be able to return to exactly the same place he had left this world last time.

But by the time he had reached the landmark euca-

*lyptus grove last time, the world of the Alfar was begin-
ning to fade, and the campus was already around him
again. . . .*

It was a grove, or anyway a circle of trees, in both
dimensions, then. But only in his world, the campus of
Berkeley, was it a grove of eucalyptus.

Experimentally he touched a tree. Yes, it was hard and
solid here, too; with sharp thorns which pricked his finger
painfully. He wondered if back on the couch in Smythe
Hall, his finger was bleeding. Well, he certainly wasn't
going back to see!

Next question. He had established that the fading of
man-made objects from his world, and the persistence, at
least in early stages, of natural ones, was consistent from
trip to trip—or at least had been so for both his trips so
far. But did he go back to the *same* dream, or dream-
dimension, or alien world? Was he back in the world of
the Alfar at all? Or did some totally new dream-
adventure await him this time?

This brought him a sudden sharp sense of disappointment. He realized that secretly, at the back of his mind,
he had been expecting, looking forward, to returning to
the world where he had seen the Alfar—and Irielle. He
wanted to see Irielle again.

If this followed dream-rules he could *force* it to be
that world . . .

No. He would play fair. He would move through this
new experience without expectations or prejudgments
that could bias the results. He was a scientist, not a kid
enjoying dream-adventures and peopling his chosen
world with fairy queens and wicked goblins. He would
take whatever came, and accept it.

And that decision, he realized, made him less happy
than he had been before. Had it really meant that much
to him? Because he found himself rationalizing, *if it's
only a dream, an hallucination, does it matter? It's my
dream, I ought to be able to choose what's in it!*

Wryly, he thought: *that should tell me something
about myself. I'm a psychologist, I ought to be able to
understand what it says about me—that I actively want
to go back to the world of the Alfar!*

But he wasn't the focus of the experiment. He would

play fair and take whatever came. Slowly, he began to walk northward, trying, as nearly as he could, to follow his previous path toward the north side of the campus.

There were no familiar landmarks; and there was no snowfall, although hard crusted snow lay deep underfoot and again the first sound of which he was really conscious was the crunching of hardened snow under his boots. He had clothed himself again, without thinking, in the warmth of the down mountain parka, and was not particularly conscious of cold. But there was no sign of the mountain pass. Was he in a different world? Did he cover the ground at a different rate of speed? There was the same grey twilight. He realized that in this world, as yet, he had seen neither moon nor sun. Nor was there any sound of human or near-human occupancy, though once, as he moved through the woods, some small animal broke cover and scuttled from tree to tree. Fenton got a brief look at it, long enough to realize that it was neither rabbit, squirrel nor any other small climbing or burrowing wild life which he knew. Remembering the oddly sinuous movement, Fenton wished he could have gotten a real look at it; then, irrationally, was relieved that he hadn't.

The woods seemed to be getting thicker, and Fenton hesitated, wondering if he should retrace his steps before he became hopelessly lost and look for the road he had seen last time. There were disadvantages to that choice —for one, it led past the caverns of the *irighi*, and he had really seen all he cared to see of them. On the other hand, if Kerridis and her escort had been travelling on it, it must lead to somewhere that the Alfar were likely to go. Fenton realized he was still taking it for granted, with quite unscientific persistence, that he really *was* in the land of the Alfar.

Anyway, wherever he was, *this* time he damned well wasn't going into any caves! Quite apart from his rejection of the obvious Freudian symbolism involved, he felt he had had a lucky escape last time; and he didn't even have one of those flamedaggers, this time, for light.

All right, so that was settled. No caves, this time. But if he didn't get somewhere fairly soon, he wasn't likely to have anything much to explore.

The woods were still getting thicker. There were more of the trees which had been in the not-quite-eucalpytus grove, and evergreens with dark, bluish needles. And there was underbrush, too, mostly a kind of thick green bush with bright red berries growing in profusion. Fenton was tempted to taste the berries—if his body wasn't really here he couldn't be poisoned by anything he ate—but something held him back, and after a minute he identified what it was; a vague memory from comparative folklore.

You never eat anything, or drink anything, in Fairyland. . . .

Oh, nonsense! Defiantly he plucked a spray of the berries, put it to his lips, then hesitantly crushed one between his teeth. After a moment he spat it out. It had a sharp minty taste and smell, but wasn't tempting enough to encourage him to break the remembered taboo; it smelled and tasted faintly like toothpaste.

Following the trajectory of the spat-out berries with his eyes, he began to discern what looked like a path among the trees. Not anything you could call a road, hardly even a footpath; more like a rabbit-run. Still, it was the first thing he had seen which indicated that the forest was not, after all, entirely untrodden. He might as well go along the rabbit-run path as any other way.

When he actually set his feet on the path, he realized that it was fainter than he had imagined, only lines in the dirt, surrounded by heavy bushes and thick underbrush. Ahead it seemed to dead-end in thick briers; when he tried to force his way through, they caught and held his clothing. He saw what seemed a small path to one side of the thicket and went to explore it, but it too seemed smaller than when he had first seen it. After hunting without success for a third path, he realized that it was true; the paths were closing before him, as if the road itself, the trees themselves, were rejecting him and forcing him out. That, of course, didn't make sense.

But this is a dream-world. Where did I get the idea that it ought to make sense?

"This is idiotic," he said aloud, and heard his own words hanging heavy in the air, almost echoing. He saw what looked like a small clear path leading through the underbrush and walked quickly toward it, but by the time he got there it was no more than a thick tangle of thorns.

Then Fenton got mad. He said out loud, "Look, you can't do this to me. I'm coming through, like it or not. If every path here is going to hide itself as soon as I set foot on it, I'll *make* a path!" He started down the small rabbit-run he had first started to travel. At first he had to force his way through the heavy underbrush; then, gradually, it seemed to transmute into a well-marked track and then into a real path, with the marks of feet clearly visible under him. He said aloud, "That's more like it." Now, as he walked, it seemed more and more like a road, as if the very act of travelling it made it more definite and real.

He wondered if roads in this world followed the Heisenberg Principle—that was the principle, he remembered, which meant that the act of observing a process altered the process. Come to think of it, Fenton thought, if the Heisenberg Principle actually operated anywhere, parapsychology would be a reasonable field for its operation.

Now, ahead of him the crowding bushes actually withdrew slightly, like women drawing their skirts aside to give him room to pass. Far ahead, through the thick trees, he could see a light.

He began to walk toward it, half wondering if the light would tease him by receding like a will-o'-the-wisp. But the light stayed in one place, and Fenton made for it. It grew a little clearer, but it was still a faint, will-o'-the-whisp glimmer; it was definitely not electric light. Neither was it torchlight, candlelight, or any other light he could identify; he began to wonder if it were simply some stray gleam from natural causes, reflected light on water, something of that sort.

Then a darkness loomed before him. It was not precisely blocking his way; it was too indefinite and tenuous for that, not *solid* enough for that. It wasn't a building, for instance. He wasn't sure what it was, but he was quite, quite sure that it wasn't a solid structure of any kind. It didn't, for instance, have the faint echoing quality that an actual building would have had under those circumstances. He could hardly have come so close to any building without knowing it, without seeing it. Besides, he could faintly see twilight and dim starlight through it.

He paused, not wanting to blunder into that obstructing darkness without first having a pretty good idea of what it was. It might prove as dangerous as the caves of the *irighi*.

He stood studying it. No, it wasn't a building. Yet it did, somehow, give the impression of a building, with two enormous trees like pillared portals. Beyond, through the darkness, he could see that it was a grove of trees, arranged in a way that seemed to simulate some kind of structure, with a vast hall, and small floating internal lights too distant to see clearly. Under his feet, the roadway seemed to have vanished, or rather to have reverted to its original status of a barely discernible rabbit-run; had he only imagined that it was a roadlike path?

Or, having brought him here, had it ceased to have any reason to be a road?

And now, between the huge pillarlike portal-trees, he saw two slender-bodied forms and realized, with an almost childlike sense of recognition and delight, that he was once again in the land of the Alfar.

No other race of humankind had ever been so slender, so delicately made, with such strange triangular faces. They wore vrillswords at their belts, glowing faintly greenish. They were talking softly, in that high singing speech of theirs; and one of them suddenly broke off, swinging his great golden eyes in Fenton's direction, peering into the thick underbrush.

"Thought I heard something," he said.

"Shadow. Are you jumping at shadows now? The ironfolk or their kind couldn't come so close to any place guarded the way this one's guarded," his companion said. "Or what do you think Erril and the Lady were doing all last night? A band of ironfolk could walk by within a bowshot of this place, and never even see it, it's spelled so carefully!"

"Just the same, you can't be too careful," the first speaker said, "or why did Findhal bother to set a guard at all? And nobody knows what's moving on the planes these days. I don't care what you say, Rimal, there is *something* gone wrong. When I was a tad, the ironfolk broke through maybe once, twice in a Change. Now they've been coming through when they choose, not only at the equinoxes when the Gates are open, but anytime they seem to choose. What's letting them through? What's happened to the Seals and Wards? Worldwalkers, 'tweenmen, ironfolk, coming and going as they please in this world. Who's minding the Worldhouse, that there's this kind of leakage?"

"You ask too many questions," the other said. "The great folk know what they're doing, and it's no concern of our kind; our business is to do the bidding of the Lady as we've always done."

"No, now, there I can't agree with you," said the grumbler. "It's my business, all right, if somebody's been meddling with the Seals and Wards and as a result I end up in the maw of an *irighi* or caught out when things start shifting and the landmarks won't stay put. I tell you, Rimal, just the other day—"

"Wait," said Rimal, breaking off.

Fenton, realizing that in his eagerness to listen, he had drawn too near, turned to flee; but too late. A branch slid under his foot, he slipped and the next moment Rimal had him by the arm.

"Here, you, what are you doing here? Sneaking around in the darkness to spy—come here under the light so I can get a good look at you!"

Fenton let them drag him along without protest. He realized that their grip on him was tenuous at best, and if he really chose he could slip right through their hands and escape; but he held still, partly because both Alfar were carrying vrillswords which *could* harm him, and partly because, in spite of their rough words, he was not really afraid of the Alfar.

"One of Pentarn's accursed kind," said Rimal in disgust, hauling Fenton into the light. "There were some of them around when the ironfolk caverns started breaking up through, last time; when the Lady was hurt."

"This one can't hurt anyone," the other said. "No shadow; look, he's a 'tweenman. What's this world coming to, with this kind of scum cluttering up the planes?

You!" he said to Fenton, emphasizing his words with a small shake. "What are you doing here?"

"I saw a path, and I followed it here," Fenton said, and they both stared at him.

"Could he follow the hidden path? Then there must be some reason for his being here," Rimal said.

But the other one shook his head. "You can't tell. There could be spies anywhere."

Fenton said, "Take me to the Lady Kerridis. Or to Findhal. They know me—"

"No doubt," Rimal said. "But the likes of Findhal or the Lady don't come and go for such as *you*."

"Then," Fenton said, "take me to the Lady Irielle—"

"Huh!" the second man said. "I thought so. I don't trust any of Pentarn's kind, even though the Lady's too soft-hearted to turn out the changelings."

Fenton said, "The Lady Irielle can tell you I'm no spy and I don't mean you any harm. I helped rescue her—"

"A likely story," Rimal scoffed.

But the other one said, "No, Rimal, it's true; I heard from Findhal, there was a 'tweenman helped them. I'll go fetch him."

"Do that. If he's one of Pentarn's folk, Findhal will make short work of him. You!" Rimal said to Fenton. "Move over here real slow, and don't try anything."

Fenton did as he was told. After a time of waiting, while the darkness thickened around them, the huge form of the warrior Findhal appeared with the guard.

"You," he said. "The 'tweenman. I wondered what had happened to you, and if you got back safely." He stood, hands on hips, looking down at Fenton. Cameron Fenton was a good height, but before the giant armed figure of Findhal he felt like a schoolboy. "Irielle said, though, if you did manage to slip back, after all the Seals and Wards they put on here, you were to be brought to the Lady Kerridis at once; so come along."

"Careful, Lord Findhal," Rimal warned. "He still might be a spy for one of Pentarn's people—"

Findhal's ringing laughter raised echoes in the grove. "Not likely. No, Rimal, he risked his own life to carry a vrillsword to the Lady when she was trapped underground on a level where there was fire; I don't think we have to worry about him."

Rimal grumbled, "That might be a clever trick to win your confidence, so he could carry tales spying for Pentarn, maybe. I never trust a 'tweenman. I like folk to be in one world or t'other, not shilly-shallying about betwixt and between."

Findhal ignored him, saying to Fenton, "Come along, the Lady is waiting for you."

Fenton followed the giant warrior. As he moved inside the loom of the trees, once again he began to wonder if, after all, he was inside some kind of enormous building which he simply could not see—either because it had been, in Rimal's colorful but not very informative phrase, "spelled," or for some other reason.

The illusion persisted, growing stronger by the moment, that around him were not trees, curtains of moss, thickets and groves, but pillared halls, elaborate corridors, side chambers hung with faint colorful drapery. Was anything on this level what it looked like? Could he trust any of his senses at all?

After a time he began to hear music, fragments of melody, caught up and strangely embroidered by another singer, passing quickly to another voice, tossed lightly upward to another melodic fragment, filled with trills and careless high notes. Behind it he could hear the trilling of a flutelike instrument—panpipes, he thought, without the slightest idea what panpipes might actually be—and beyond that, the light soft chording of plucked strings.

Light burst abruptly on his eyes—moons, stars, suns of light in the greyness. Fenton automatically flung up his hands to protect his eyes, so brilliant was the light. After a moment it dimmed to a tolerable level—or had his eyes simply grown adjusted to it? He lowered his hands, and through the lights, tolerable now but still brilliant, he saw Kerridis.

Robed, jewelled, crowned with starlike gems, she sat on a throne draped with festoons of green and gold. At her feet knelt a young girl of the Alfar, playing on the panpipe; at the other side someone softly touched the strings of a harp. And behind it all was the singing, flung from voice to voice in incredible counterpoint. Was this simply the way the Alfar talked among themselves?

Kerridis gestured. The singing died away; but the pipe and harp-chords continued, through all that followed, and after. Later Fenton realized that at no time in his stay in this illusory dwelling had the air been wholly free of music.

"Come here—" she said, beckoning him forward. "You are the brave 'tweenman; I am glad to know you got out unharmed. Come here and sit down before me, Fentarn —Fentrin—" she grimaced. "I know your name is something like to Pentarn, but it is not."

"Fenton," he said, and her laughter had the remembered sound of enchanted bells, high in midair.

"Fenn-trin. Well, it is no matter." She motioned to Fenton to sit on the ground before her, between the child with the panpipes and the woman who plucked the harp. Awkwardly he sank down, sitting cross-legged there.

"I hope all your hurts are healed, Lady Kerridis."

She extended one slim hand toward him. The fingers still bore faint blackened traces. She said, "As near as may be; such wounds never wholly heal. Yet I am fortunate it was no worse. In the days of my mother—but that is neither here nor there."

"Do such things happen often?"

"It is not unknown," she said, "though truly, it seems to me that they happen oftener now. In the past, the iron-folk could not break through except at certain times; and now, it seems, they can come whenever they will, and I cannot help feeling that folk of your kind and Pentarn's have brought about this change. Do you, then, come from Pentarn's world?"

Fenton shook his head. Then, slowly, he amended his denial, not quite sure. He said, "It's true this Pentarn person looks human enough. But he doesn't dress the way they do in the world I come from, and the way he wears his hair and beard and so forth . . ." Having said it, he was not sure. Berkeley was still a Mecca for eccentrics, and in the North Campus area, almost anything might go unnoticed. Hair, beard, even boots and cloak like Pentarn's would not be unremarked, but would attract attention only as another of many peculiarities.

"Anyway," he finished weakly, but truthfully, "he's nobody I ever saw before."

Kerridis was studying him. She said, "It is true that your garb and his are in no way similar. And surely if Pentarn had sent you here to work us harm, he would have allowed you to walk in this world with solidity and a shadow. Yet some of our people are suspicious, and who can blame them, after the ironfolk slew so many of my faithful companions. Even Irielle has not been immune to the suspicion." She fell silent, musing.

Fenton, emboldened by hearing Irielle's name, said, "I hope Irielle has recovered from her experiences at the hands of the ironfolk."

"She was not truly hurt, only frightened," Kerridis said. Raising her slender hand, she called, "Irielle? Child, come and speak to him—"

Irielle was dressed, now, in a long brown dress trimmed with fur—it faintly resembled the clothing of the Alfar women but was much warmer, and somehow this again reassured Fenton. These people were careful of the well-being of the humans who lived among them; they had gone to the trouble of giving Irielle warm clothes, recognizing her essential difference from them. Her hair was braided and looped up with some twinkly stuff that glittered almost like the jewels in Kerridis' hair. She smiled shyly at Fenton. "I am so glad you could come back to us. Most 'tweenmen come into our world only once, astray perhaps in a dream, and never find their way back. How did you manage it? Did you find a Gateway?"

He shook his head. "No, it was part of an experiment," he said, but both Irielle and the Queen turned eyes of polite incomprehension on him. Well, perhaps it wasn't surprising that in this world where what looked like magic was commonplace, nothing should be known of the scientific method or of ordinary experimentation.

Kerridis beckoned one of her attendants close. "Will you drink with us, Fenn-tarn?"

He hesitated. "If I can."

Kerridis frowned faintly and Fenton wondered if he had committed some dreadful breach of manners—he was, after all, being presented at Court and he had quibbled about what amounted to a Royal Command. Irielle bent and whispered to her, and she laughed, the frown vanishing.

"I had forgotten; yes, some of the worldwalkers and 'tweenworlders have some such illusion, that if you eat or drink here you will be trapped and cannot return. Under some conditions, if you are here in the body—a worldwalker—it might be dangerous to eat certain things; I suppose you will learn that later." She took the jewelled cup which was handed to her, touched it lightly to her own lips, then handed it to him. She said, hesitating, the cup between their joined hands, "Do you understand—it will give you the *illusion* of refreshment; if you truly suffer from thirst or hunger it will not allay it."

Fenton took the cup in his hands. For a moment he wondered if his hand would go through it, as the metal grillwork had done; but it stayed in his hands, feeling solid and cold against his lip. He bowed and drank, studying the cup covertly. The drink inside tasted cold and refreshing; it was neither sweet nor noticeably tart, and certainly was not alcoholic. The cup itself—what a shame, he thought, that there wasn't some way to take it back, as verification for his story.

But if I did—don't they say fairy gold turns to a handful of dead leaves or something, if you look at it by daylight? And if this world is real, a parallel universe or extra dimension of our own, where is the sun? For that matter, where is the moon?

Anyway, he held the cup, empty, in his hands for an extra moment, trying to memorize and trace the design so that he could draw it for Sally. Then he returned it to Irielle. Kerridis, smiling kindly at them both, said, "Lebbrin is coming, children, and no doubt he has some weighty matters for my settling; so I must send you away. Take him out into the grove, Irielle, and entertain him for us." She nodded to them in kind dismissal. As Irielle led him away, he heard the fragments of song-speech begin again, melodies and fragments of harmony tossed from voice to voice, a curious obbligato.

He followed Irielle along the curiously enclosed walls of this strange dwelling, which both *was* and *was not* enclosed in tenuous walls; to this moment he was not sure whether they were indoors or out. Did definitions have any reality here?

Reality? he wondered, with a shock, *what is reality?*

"You are quiet," she said.

"I was listening to the music. When you are alone with them—can you talk that way?"

She laughed. "A little, like a young child; mostly they are careful to speak slowly when they speak to me. Not as slowly as the Lady did with you, but more slowly than she would speak to her own women of the Alfar."

They had come out into brighter light and he sensed that they were outdoors, though the trees still enclosed them. She asked, "Do you mind the cold?"

"Not really. I should think you would, though," he said.

She shook her head. "I am accustomed to it now; though I remember when first I came here I was always cold; I cried with the cold night and day." She dropped to the ground and gestured to him to sit beside her. "That seems a very long time ago now, and as long as I have warm clothing I do not mind the cold at all, though when I was in the caves of the ironfolk that was a different thing, a different kind of cold."

"How did you get here, Irielle?" *She's human; as human as I am . . .*

She looked at him in faint surprise. "I am a changeling, of course."

Of course. I am a changeling, of course. Well, what had he expected? One thing he could say for this dream, or this dimension, or whatever it was, it made sense by its own rules. So what had he expected? She was a changeling, what else? When you found a human being in fairyland, what should she be except a changeling?

But what in the world—*this* world—is a changeling, anyhow?

He asked, "And this—Pentarn—is he a changeling too?"

Her mobile face contracted in scorn. "Pentarn? He a changeling? Who among the Alfar would bargain for such as *he*? No, Pentarn, I think, must have come somehow through one of the Worldhouses, or through a Gateway, for he is a true worldwalker; he casts a shadow and has

substance, and I have seen him eat and drink here.
Like me, he can handle cold iron. But he cannot be an
Alfar fosterling; he does not know enough of our ways.
And he has no fear of the ironfolk. I think he has made
compact with them, which no Alfar fosterling would dare
to do."

"Just what is a changeling, Irielle?"

She looked at him, startled. She was human, all human, she had none of the chilly elegance of the Alfar; she
was warm, breathing, but one thing she had of theirs,
Fenton thought; her face was mobile, swiftly reflecting
every changing mood and thought. "How came you here,
knowing so little? The Alfar bear few children, fewer—
so the Lady has told me—as the seasons come and go,
turn upon turn. And so they must sometimes take children
from other worlds. Findhal and his lady, who fostered me,
have no children; nor has Kerridis, nor Erril; and Lebbrin's only son was slain by ironfolk before I was born."

"They—steal children?"

"You can call it that," she said, with a flash of anger,
"but they take only such babes as are ill-used in their
cradles and will die . . . Kerridis took her other fosterling
from a great asylum, so she told me, where unwanted
children were abandoned to paid hirelings and left un-
tended, so that half of them died before their second year,
and the rest grew up simpletons, for sheer lack of a mother's care. Should the Alfar leave those children to die un-
mourned and unwept, when they long for children and
have none?"

Fenton thought this sounded like what he had read of
dreadful Victorian orphanages, where children died of
what came to be called *marasmus;* but now that it was
known, it was prevented by loving care and gentle
handling. Yet he was sure there were, even now, homes
for retarded or abandoned children where the children
were still neglected this way and death, when it came, re-
garded only as a merciful release. "How do they get the
children without anyone knowing they are gone?"

"They leave an image in the child's place," Irielle said
matter-of-factly. "It does not live very long, but that does
not matter, since those who care for it are only waiting for
the child to die; and it is buried, and no one knows the

difference. But I did not come here that way; I was old enough to remember . . . I was thrown from a carriage, and my mother and father must have been killed, for when I cried out to them there was no answer." Her face contracted with remembered pain and terror. "I remember lying there, bleeding everywhere, and the carriage pole crushing my back . . . and then Findhal was there, and he lifted me out of the wreck—I do not know how he did it without breaking me in pieces—and he told me that if he left me there I would be crippled always, but that he could take me to a place where I could be healed and could run and play again. I asked—" Her mobile features slipped into a brooding calm. "I asked if my father and mother could come, and he said no, they were already dead; but that he and his Lady would be mother and father to me in their place as long as I lived. I saw— I didn't *quite* see what he left in the wreck, but he said it would last long enough to be buried with my mother and father; and then he lifted me out of the wreck of the carriage, and I was here—look," she said ingenuously, raising her long thick skirt to reveal a slim, untanned long leg. "You can see my leg was smashed through to the bone; it took a long time to heal, and it was long, long before I could walk again, but they were very good to me."

Fenton looked with horror at the frightful scars; how had they ever managed to rebuild such injuries? The shin and calf were only a twisted ropy mass of scar tissue. She pulled the dress down and said, "It is ugly, I know—my back is worse; that is why I always wear these clothes, even though now I do not mind the cold and could wear what the Alfar ladies do. But I hate ugliness as they do."

Good God, what a mess! It would have taxed medical science in our world to repair that; she'd probably have lost the leg. If that's what they saved her from, it's probably a mercy they brought her here!

At the same time he suddenly felt a tremendous tenderness for Irielle. She was not, after all, a perfect fairy-tale princess, but a scarred survivor of God-knows-what ghastly accident in some world which might, or might not, be his own. "And you were brought up here?"

She nodded. "As Findhal's fosterling; I lived with them till I was grown, and he is still a father to me . . . but when I was grown, Kerridis asked me to come here and be one of their singers and handlers." She raised her face, asking, "Now tell me, how did *you* come here?"

Fenton tried to explain something about the experiment, but her fluid features twisted in distaste.

"I hope your wise man, your *professor,* is not one of those who for idle curiosity would put strain on the fabric of the Worldgates, so that the ironfolk may break in when they will, and not only when the sun and moon are right and we can be prepared against them! Or is he in league with Pentarn's people to destroy the Gates?"

"Good lord, no!"

"Then what reasons could he have for this?"

Fenton tried to explain, but was aware that his explanation sounded lame. How could you explain the nature of parapsychology in a world with rules as different as all this? Irielle shrugged off the explanation.

"It would be better if you could come here through the Worldhouse. I will try to find it for you, but I do not know if it can be found just now—" She was silent, her face a study in puzzlement, and Fenton sat watching the play of emotions on her vivid features, the fine transparent skin so delicate that it seemed he could actually see the blood bluish in the veins at her temples. She seemed so vividly alive; next to her every woman he had ever known seemed dull, lumpish, heavy, dead by contrast.

She's only a woman in my dream, she's not a real woman, I mustn't start thinking of her as if she were real.

Not real! Next to her every woman I have ever known seems like someone I dreamed about a long time ago . . .

Her small chin rested in the curve of her hand, she was very still, but nevertheless she seemed very vital, delicate lights and shadows coming and going in her eyes. At last she raised her head and said to him, "We could go and look for the Worldhouse; perhaps you could learn to recognize it when you see it . . ."

"Go and *look* for it? Irielle, don't you know where it is?"

"It is not aways in the same place," she said seriously.

"It shifts about—or, perhaps, *it* is always in the same place; sometimes, I think, it does not want to be found—"

Fenton burst out—he couldn't help it—"I think that's the most ridiculous thing I ever heard!" Once again his emotions threatened to reverse themselves. And he had been thinking this world had enough logical consistency that it might be real!

His dismay and disappointment came through to Irielle as anger; she flushed in turn and her quick movement, scrambling to her feet, was like a bird gathering in its wings to take flight, her whole body quivering with resentment.

"What do you know about it, *'tweenman!*"

Quickly Fenton put out a placating hand.

"Irielle, Irielle, don't be angry. I am sorry, I do not understand—how can you say that it—that a solid thing, a —a house, you called it a Worldhouse, does not *want* to be found?"

She looked at him, troubled, sobered. She said slowly, "I do not know—I have been through the Worldhouse more than once, and it is never twice the same, nor twice in the same place. Or perhaps *it* is always the same, and the other worlds shift around it, though it is the Worldhouse that seems to move. Ignorant folk used to believe that the sun went around the world, and now all but the little children know better than that."

Against his resolve he glanced at the sky. "Does the sun shine here?"

"Not often, it is true . . . it is for that reason that Melnia, who was Findhal's Lady, used to give me leave now and again to walk in the other worlds; she said I, who was born under the sun, would sicken if I did not see it oftener than it shines here. It was Melnia who showed me that the Worldhouse cannot often be found if you are actually looking for it; it is easiest found by accident. Didn't you ever find a place as if by accident, and when you were looking for it by intention, you could not find it again?"

Fenton frowned, remembering the queer little bookshop in North Beach, whose windows had been a bibliographer's dream; but although he had found it twice and looked into the windows when the shop was shut, he had quartered all the streets of San Francisco, it seemed, and had never been able even to find the proper street-corner when the place was open.

He told her about it, and she nodded. "The World-house is like that. You might even have seen it in one of its disguises. I think possibly when you search for it, it activates some—some kind of key, some defense; your *thoughts* do. It is not supposed to be found, you know, except by those who have business there; though Findhal can come and go as he will, and now it seems that Pen-tarn has access when he wishes." She was silent, thinking. Then she raised her head, quickly, with a breathtaking smile, and Fenton felt a curious constriction in his chest.

Oh no! I mustn't start feeling this way about Irielle— about a woman in a dream—

She stretched out her narrow fingers to him. She said, with that flash of a smile again which seemed, like the flame of a candle shining through, to illuminate her whole face with a delicate interior light, "I will ask Findhal; he is my foster-father and he has never denied me anything. I will ask him how to find the Worldhouse so that you can come when you will."

The touch of her hand was ghostly on his, barely per-ceptible, yet it stirred Fenton—mind, body, emotions—to an incredible pitch. He heard his voice crack. "Do you want me to come back, Irielle?"

"Of course I do," she said softly. "The Alfar are kind, but I am so often alone among them, and I cannot talk to them as I do to you. I am alone so much, and you are like me. Please promise me you will come back, Fenn-tarn?"

It was an ache, an agony; nothing in his whole life, it seemed, had ever been quite so painful as that innocent plea. *You will come back?* How did he know? How did he know if he could ever come back here, how did he know—this was, he realized, the crux of his anguish—if there *was* any such place as *here?*

"Fen-trin? What is it?" She was looking at him, deeply troubled, close to him, her vital lovely face upturned to his. Strangling with grief, Fenton turned away from her.

"Oh—please—" she begged. "Can't you tell me what

is the matter, Fen-tarn? Why are you so—so sorrowful? You come like a shadow, you go like a wraith—why are you so sad?"

He managed to say, getting the words out through shaking despair, "I don't know if I can come here again. I want to, but—I have no control over my coming, over my going—I cannot even be sure—" His voice caught, and he had to force the words out, "I cannot be certain that it is not a dream, that *you* are not a dream—that I did not invent you in my dream—" To his own dismay and wretchedness, Fenton felt his words catch in an audible sob.

Irielle looked up at him, her face reflecting the despair he felt. "Oh, what sorrow," she whispered. "Who has done this to you, and why? Fenn-trin—" Even her very mispronunciation of his name sounded poignant, forlorn. She flung her arms impulsively around him. She felt insubstantial, feather-light; he could not even seem to feel her breathing, but she was there, her arms clasped around him. "Fen-tarn, do not weep. I am real. How can I prove it to you? How can you know that *you* are real, that all of this life is not a long dream while we are waiting for something else?" She flung back her head and looked up at him, throbbing with intensity. "I wish there might be some way to show you—I wish I had some comfort for you. I can only say—" She suddenly became aware that she was clasping him, and he saw her face slowly redden, turn crimson, embarrassed, all intensity, and yet all frightened modesty again.

Modesty. That's a word we don't think about for women in our world . . . but it fits. . . .

She looked away, struggling to recover her calm, and he saw her mouth move once or twice before she could speak. At last she said, almost in a whisper, "I can only tell you something Kerridis said once to me, when I was very small, and new-come here; I could not walk, and I was in pain a great deal, and crying with the cold, and still grieving for my mother and father, though Melnia was very kind, and Findhal sat beside me for days at a time and sang to me so that I would forget the pain of the healstones. Kerridis came to speak with me, and she asked how it was with me, and I said it still seemed to me

like some strange and frightful dream. And she pointed
to a bird singing in a tree, and she said, 'Life itself is a
dream, little one. For all we know, you and I might be a
dream of that bird; dreaming he has someone to listen to
his song. Perhaps this life is a dream, or perhaps your
other life was a dream and now you have wakened to the
truth you should always have known; or perhaps you
are only in my dream, after all; or in Melnia's dream, a
dream where she has the child she longed for and could
not bear.' " Irielle's voice was distant, faraway.

Fenton said, "There is an old philosopher's story: I
dreamed I was a butterfly; am I dreaming I am a butterfly or is the butterfly now dreaming that he is me?"

Irielle nodded, and he heard the long, shaking sigh she
drew.

*What came over me? To break up like that and frighten
her?*

She drew his hand to her. She said very softly, "You
must come again, truly. I will ask Findhal for leave to take
you to the Worldhouse. But meanwhile—do you know
of a place which is the same in your world and in mine?
If so we will make it our rendezvous, so that if you cannot come to me, perhaps I may come to you."

Fenton thought, holding her delicate fingers like frail
shadows between his own. *I will never believe Irielle is
not real!* Somehow, somewhere, she existed, in a reality
as genuine as his own.

*What kind of parapsychologist would I be, to reject a
reality because I couldn't measure it by my own criteria?*

And the scientist in him was surfacing again through
his grief and sudden dismay. He said, frowning in thought,
"There is a circle of trees. In my world they are near—
near the place where I study. And in your world they are
a circle of trees too, a circle of white feathery flowers. . . ."

"I know the place," she said. "It is a good place, or was
until recently; now there are ironfolk sometimes breaking
through, but perhaps the goodness of the place will keep
the ironfolk out from under those trees." She was thinking deeply. "Come, I will take you there, it would be a
good place to return to your own world. And you must go

soon, or you will be beginning to fade, and that is unpleasant, I know. . . ."

She stretched her hand to him again, and he felt the light clasp of the insubstantial fingers. She said, "We must return through the Great Hall. I am not a child and I come and go as I please, but Findhal has been troubled since I was taken by ironfolk, and has bidden me not to go unguarded outside the spelled places where the ironfolk cannot come, even if they bear talismans for the Gates. He has always been a kind father to me, and so I will not defy his rules."

Fenton was not displeased. Much as he longed to be alone with Irielle, the thought that she should fall again into the hands of the ironfolk was something he did not want to think about.

Again she led him through the bewildering maze of the Great Hall. Automatically Fenton looked for ways to orient himself, but he saw nothing even remotely like the parts of the—dwelling? castle? enclosure?—which he had seen before. Was Irielle taking him through a different part of the place? Or, as he had begun to suspect, did it shift and change so that it was no longer quite the same? Stable landmarks were not, so he had surmised, anything one could find easily in this dimension. The talk of the two Alfar guards at the entryway had told him that.

Irielle found Findhal in a part of the enclosure which, if it had looked a bit more solid, Fenton would have tagged as a kind of armory and weapons depository; there were vrillswords carefully wrapped in some shimmering stuff not unlike the twinkling cloth bound into Irielle's bright hair, there were shields and bits of bright armor and odd weapons. Irielle rushed to him and Fenton, watching from a distance, followed her request by measuring the quick shifting of her mobile features. They were talking in the Alfar speech, which Fenton could not follow. Findhal seemed to demur at what she was saying, and he looked two or three times at Fenton, as if he were displeased; but at last he nodded, saying slowly enough so that Fenton could hear and understand, "Carry a vrillsword upon you, Irielle, at all times when you go beyond the spelled places, and certainly anywhere you go in the company of this 'tweenman." He gestured to two of the Alfar to accompany her.

She came back to him, looking sulky. "My father does not trust you," she said at last, "and not the least because you have come back; most 'tweenmen cannot return, and he feels you must somehow be allied with Pentarn's world. And so he would not listen when I asked him to show you to the Worldhouse, or to give you a talisman so that you could find it whenever you wished. Nor would he trust me with one, now, though he has always done so before."

"What have I done that Findhal should not trust me?" This struck Fenton as irrational and unfair. He had, after all, taken considerable risks on his first visit here to lead them to the imprisoned Kerridis, and to help Irielle out of her cell.

Irielle nodded, slowly, reluctant to say it. At last she said, "He fears, still, that you are a spy from Pentarn's world, come to win our confidence because none of us— now—trust Pentarn. If I were younger, I think he would try to forbid me to go anywhere with you at all, or to make any rendezvous with you. You cannot blame him," she added, painfully. "Remember, it was his Lady, Melnia, my foster-mother, who was slain in the very first raid of the ironfolk when they came through when we were not expecting them. And he had trusted Pentarn and even grown fond of him, so that he has never ceased to blame himself. . . . It is not a happy thing," she added, and her sensitive features were drawn, "to think of someone you—you love, dying at the hands of the ironfolk, so dreadfully."

Fenton wished he could comfort her, take her in his arms and shelter her against the emotions that moved so freely over her face. He asked, "You loved her too?"

"She was the only mother I can really remember. She loved me; she could bear no child, though they had lived together for long and long, and this is why Findhal risked going into the light of the sun to take me from the wreck of our carriage, though it is dangerous for the Alfar. His eyes gave him much pain for long seasons after, and he thought for a time he would be blinded; most of the Alfar will never risk it, except by light of a waning moon,"

Irielle said, "or when the Gates are open at Sunreturn or Sundarkening. He must have loved her more than even I can guess in my short years. And now I am all that he has for memory of her, so that he is always in dread fearing he should lose me too. So many of his kin have died since Pentarn brought this upon us. . . ."

"Why?" Fenton burst out, shocked. "Why should Pentarn have brought this upon you?" *What kind of man would make common cause with the ironfolk against the Alfar?*

Irielle sighed and shook her head. "Why does any traitor betray his friends?"

With that Fenton had to be content.

As they retraced the path from the Great Hall to the circular grove of what were, in his world, eucalyptus trees, Fenton came to the conclusion that the landmarks *did* shift, that the landscape *did* change. He recognized a few familiar things—a rock with a projection like a bird's beak, a pair of the bushes with the minty berries, set at a curious angle across the path that widened before them, the grove of trees itself—but the landscape itself was not familiar. He mentioned this to Irielle and she said, surprised and curious, "But of course, all this land around here is open, not spelled. Is it different in your world? How dull that would be, to live in a never-changing landscape."

Fenton was very conscious of the presence of Findhal's two men following him and Irielle just out of earshot—if they talked softly—but weaponed and carrying vrillswords. Irielle, too, at Findhal's urging, had tied one around her waist on a kind of narrow, embroidered leather girdle.

I wish I could take one of these back and see if it is still solid on my plane! He hesitated to ask, knowing how highly prized they were, how valued a defense against the ironfolk. *Maybe sometime later, if I can come back, I can arrange to borrow one and have it examined on my plane.* That would, he thought, certainly be proof enough for anyone, even Garnock, that this dimension is real.

Real. Even though it changes, as dream-landscapes do?

Possibly it does have something in common with wherever it is that we go in our dreams, he thought, and caught himself in shock: *Dreams, after all, are just periods of REM sleep, characterized by the rapid eye movements that had given the name to that type of brain activity....*

Or are they, really?

"Is this the grove which is present in your world, Fenntarn?"

Fenton nodded. Abruptly her continuing mispronunciation of his name began to get on his nerves. He repeated it twice, then said, "Does it really suggest *Pentarn* so much to you?"

"It does," she said with a shiver. "So much that I am reluctant to speak it. Is there no other name by which we can know you, 'tweenman?"

"My other name is Cam—or Cameron," he said.

"Cameron!" Her eyes suddenly dimmed with a strange emotion.

"Irielle, what is it?"

She said, her hands going swiftly to her breast as if in great agitation, "That was—that was one of *my* names, when I was—when I lived in the sunworld. Cam-eron." She said it slowly, reflectively. "Cam-eron, Cameron— now indeed I begin to feel it is *meant* that you have come here. Or is this another trick to lure me into trust?"

"*Your* name was Cameron?" Was she, then, really from his own world? *Cameron* was a common enough surname; though as a given name, a Christian name, it was unusual, he supposed. It had been a family name somewhere in his mother's family; she was of Scottish descent, several generations back.

Irielle nodded, her face fluid with emotion, and she seemed to be struggling with a memory. "*Irielle* was the name Melnia gave me. She said my name was harsh and not pleasant to her ears. I have not heard the sound of my —my sunworld name since I was very small, but I think it was—Emma—Emma Aurelia Cameron—" she said, hesitating. "I seem to remember, in that other world, learning to write it on a—a kind of slaty rock with a white crumbling stone—let me think," she said, and her face contorted with the struggle of memory. She knelt in the circle of trees; Findhal's men drew near, and when Fenton laid a hand on her arm they moved closer, swift, suspicious.

Irielle tried to draw with her finger in the dirt, but the ground was frozen hard; after a moment she drew the vrillsword from her girdle and with the tip, her face drawn with effort, began to make strokes in the hard ground.

She said, preoccupied, her face twisting with the effort, "It is hard to remember. Hard. I have not done this for so many, many seasons, I have forgotten, and I do not think I was big enough to—to write well even then. But my name was like this."

Fenton looked down at the childish, kindergarten printing:

EMMA CAMRON

He stared at it, with wonder and wild surmise. Had she, as a child—*How long ago? What was time in her world, and where?*—learned to write that on a slate with chalk? Certainly she moved her hands as if she did not, quite, know how to hold pen or pencil. But the words and letters were ordinary English letters, the name an American— or at least European—name.

Changeling?

Suddenly the guards cried out in warning; Irielle sprang up, the vrillsword thrust out before her. Findhal's guards closed in on either side of Irielle.

One of the ironfolk ran through the grove, a warrior of the Alfar in hot pursuit. Behind, Fenton caught a glimpse of Pentarn through the trees; and simultaneously he realized that above him the trees were wavering, now eucalyptus, now pale with feathery white blooms.

"Irielle—"

"Get away from her, you!" One of Findhal's guards swept him contemptuously aside. He no longer felt the blow; he was beginning to fade; but he felt the stinging rage in the voice of the Alfar guard. "Again you have led her into a trap! Get hence and if you come here again, I swear Findhal shall have your head!"

"No! It's not true, I swear—Irielle—Irielle—"

Her face swam before him, drawn entreating, fright-

ened. The Alfar were fighting; he heard the clash of the
vrillsword against the brutal knife in the hands of the
goblinlike creature. Something struck him on the back of
the head and the world exploded into darkness and did
not return.

He was lying in the eucalptus grove; it was growing
dark above him. How long had he been unconscious?
Around him, his own world wavered, and there was an
insistent tug. . . .

I must get back to my body. . . .

What would happen if I stayed away too long?

Irielle! Did she escape, did Findhal's guards manage to
keep her safe? He stared wildly around the grove, as if he
could manage to force, somehow, from the unyielding
stuff of trees and grove some answer about her where-
abouts.

*She could still be here, lying dead, or fighting for her
life, and I couldn't see her . . .*

Fenton felt spasmodic anguish. Once again, at a crucial
moment, he had been exiled from the world which was
growing so real to him.

How could he get back? *Could* he get back?

Was there anything real to get back to?

Then, on the ground between the trees, he saw something. Half obliterated by scuffed footmarks, probably
rubbed away in the fight, but still, graved deep by the
vrillsword in the ground that was frozen in her world, he
saw the marks:

$$EMMA \ CAM \ N$$

The rest had been rubbed away. Yet these survived;
here in his world. Proof.

Realization cut through his jubilation. He was still outside his body; in the dream, or whatever it was.

*I must come back here, as soon as I can, check these
marks, take pictures of them if I can. . . .*

Then, since he knew he must, he rose and let himself
drift with the sharpening, dragging tug on the shining cord
that led him back to Smythe Hall and to where his body
lay.

CHAPTER SIX

THERE was a card tacked to the door of the parapsychology office.

MISS LOBECK
will not meet her classes this week.
Appointments and Emergencies: call
WA56-77312

Sally Lobeck's voice on the phone sounded angry and trapped. "I seem to have dislocated my knee. By next week I'll manage to swap cars with my ex-husband—he has an automatic transmission—but I can't drive my own car. I suppose you'd better come here—I have a pretty good tape setup. And I can't afford to lose a whole week of appointments; by next week you'd have forgotten most of it."

She cut his expressions of sympathy short, giving him directions to her apartment.

"Is there anything I can pick up on the way? Since you're trapped in the house."

She cut him off with a brusque, "No, thanks, I don't need anything. Just don't forget to bring the tape cassette you made for Garnock."

Cameron Fenton wondered, as he walked across the campus toward Euclid Avenue, whether Sally really disliked him that much. Or was it simply that she resented the necessity of bringing work home to her apartment, instead of using the cool impersonal setup of her office in Smythe Hall? Sally's moods weren't relevant, but he disliked this kind of personal resentment in work that was, or ought to be, a genuinely shared endeavor.

The path he took led him near the eucalyptus grove

and, on impulse, he turned aside. He had come here last night, after leaving Garnock's office; but he had been delayed by making the immediate tape cassette, the hasty debriefing lest he forget details; by the time he had reached the grove it was too dark to see, with the energy cutbacks. He had debated going back with a flashlight; but after several rapes on the campus this year, security on campus had been tightened, and he was not sure how he could explain digging around in the eucalyptus grove, looking for marks which had, or had not, been left by someone in another world.

Even by daylight, he wasn't looking forward to it.

Berkeley gets bigger every year. When I was an undergraduate it was still a small city, some students still left their apartments unlocked sometimes, and robberies were fairly rare. Anyone who left an apartment unlocked now, even to take down the garbage, would have to be crazy.

The grove was virtually deserted: a small group of undergraduates was sitting at one of the redwood benches and tables, with a notebook, small figures of men, and mutifaceted dice spread out in front of them, playing Dungeons and Dragons, or something of that sort. *That's a campus fad that's really lasted. I used to play it a lot when I was going to school here. I suppose it could have come and gone two or three times, like skateboards or frisbees, as a campus fad, since then.* The thought depressed him, made him feel somehow older and more tired than the students in their bright costumelike clothes, bending over the little figurines of brightly painted swordsmen and wizards and warrior-elves.

Damn it, I wonder. He was enough of a trained psychologist to realize, suddenly, that the milieu of his two Antaril hallucinations were not unlike an episode, a long game, of Dungeons and Dragons.

I'd forgotten, I was always playing it, my freshman and sophomore years. I remember once we got up a game that went on, off and on, for the best part of two weeks. That wasn't a record—some kids in Newman Hall kept a game going, I heard, all semester—but it was quite a game, and must have left some impression! Is that where the Alfar-images came from?

The thought left confused depression behind. *Damn it, I want it to be real!* It was wrenching pain to realize that perhaps Irielle was a dream out of vague half memories of the Tolkien novels, out of the Dungeons and Dragons games of his undergraduate days!

He looked down at the scuffed earth of the eucalyptus grove. Nothing left, of course. Students' feet on their way to morning classes had trampled it, even if last night some young couple in search of privacy for whatever the mating rites of undergraduates were these days, had not obliterated the last remaining trace. There would certainly be nothing to see, and he had no taste for getting down on the ground and hunting, in front of the clustered undergraduates gathered around their boards and figurines, for a mark which might have been left—or so he had dreamed in what was probably an Antaril hallucination—by a magic sword from some other dimension.

Or am I rationalizing a good excuse for not looking, not making sure?

Angrily, with determination, he looked for the tree under which he and Irielle had been kneeling before the breakthrough of the ironfolk creature. There were random scuffmarks in the ground, footprints, coming and going in such profusion that he doubted if Sherlock Holmes himself could have made much sense of them.

"Man, what's your problem?" asked one of the players from the bench. "Lost a contact lens or something?"

"Not sure," Fenton said, feeling like a fool. "I might have left something here last night, but I'm not sure."

"Must have been some little party," said the student, chuckling. They were passing around whiffs of a narrow brown cigarette; Fenton grimaced at the sweetish smoke, but the marijuana laws, though still on the books—a ten dollar fine for more than an ounce—were unenforceable and largely a dead letter nowadays; anti-tobacco laws were much more rigid. Fenton, who didn't much care for either, and didn't much care what anybody smoked as long as he didn't have to breathe it secondhand, tried to get downwind of the drifting smoke, and there he saw the scratches that could have been an E, a crooked M, another partly rubbed-away M leaning in another direction like Irielle's lopsided uneven childish printing.

Wishful thinking? Or the proof I want so much?
If they are really there, really letters, Irielle is real.

But he wasn't sure. He couldn't be sure. Any thought of
asking the Dungeons and Dragons players to step over
and verify what he had seen, to ask if they thought these
looked like letters, he quickly put aside. Witnesses? Five
undergraduates stoned out of their minds on what must
be, from the smell, the very finest homegrown air-dried
marijuana? He could imagine what any trained investigator would make of that kind of evidence, what he himself
would make of it if anyone else tried to present it.

Just the same, he felt that the crooked letters had wiped
out the worst of his depression. Possibility, hope, was still
alive. Irielle might be real, after all. Or, should he say,
Emma Cameron?

Sally Lobeck lived in an old brown-shingle house, one
of the very few in the Arch Street area which had not
been torn down to build student high rises on the beehive
model. In the small lobby, an old entrance hall with a
parquetry floor that had been remodelled to add name-
plates, letterboxes, TV monitors and the other security
paraphernalia of the day, he looked in vain at first for
any LOBECK on letterbox or nameplate. Then, pencilled
in on a card under TANNER, he saw LOBECK, S. Yes,
she had mentioned an ex-husband with whom she was
still on good terms—at least good enough to be on car-
borrowing terms—and it was possible she was still wearing his name, or had been when she rented the apartment.

He pressed the button, and after a moment Sally's voice
came, mechanically distorted, out of the speaker. "Up the
stairs and to the left, Cam." The buzzer rang; he pushed
the latch and went upstairs.

Sally opened the door. Her leg was heavily bandaged,
and she looked drawn and haggard; she hadn't done anything with her hair except to comb it after a fashion, and
she was wearing a faded housecoat with a couple of but-
tons missing. She sketched an apologetic shrug around
her. "You can see why everything is in a mess. Come in,
Cam. If you want some coffee, you'll have to get it for
yourself. I can stay on this leg about two minutes at a

time." She limped heavily to a sofa piled with books, papers and reference materials.

"I don't need anything, Sally, but can I get you anything?"

"Coffee," she said, with a dry grin. "I found it was too much hassle to stay on my feet long enough to fix it."

"Oh, in *that* case——"

She had a small electric coffeemaker; under her directions he found coffee in a canister in the kitchen—it was just as chaotic as everything else in the apartment—and plugged it in. When the coffee was ready, he brought her a cup, and she lifted it to her lips with an appreciative laugh.

"I managed toast and a boiled egg, but I do miss my morning fix," he said, sipping it gratefully.

"You ought to be in the hospital. Why haven't they put you in Cowell?" he asked. "How did you manage to do it anyhow?"

"This?" She gestured at the bandaged knee. "Pure stupidity. I did something I'd have spanked any kid for trying. I do ballet exercises every day for the benefit of my waistline, and for once I tried doing them without changing into an exercise suit or leotard first. I slipped and fell; instead of the skirt tearing, something tore in my knee. I collected quite a crowd—they had to take me down the stairs on a stretcher. But I couldn't stay in the hospital, I have too many appointments."

"Is it broken?"

She shook her head. "They say not. Kneecap dislocated and the muscle torn up. It's a hell of a lot more painful than a break." She set the coffee cup down, to lift the leg with both hands on to the sofa. "Anyhow, I can manage, after a fashion."

"It must be hard on you, living alone, though."

"About the only thing I can't do is to get in and out of the shower," Sally said. "For the hygienic rudiments—well, I grew up on a fairly primitive farm, and bathing in the kitchen sink doesn't really bother me all that much provided it's temporary. Better that than being in the hospital, worrying about all I'm not getting done here!" She sounded grim and angry. "Anyhow, my ex-husband promised to swap cars with me—I could drive his car even if I didn't have a left leg; it has automatic controls and only one foot-pedal, no clutch to mess with. So I'll probably be back at classes day after tomorrow."

"How long have you been divorced?"

She shrugged. "Legally, three months to go on the decree. Effectively, about a year and a half. I did the whole Liberated Woman bit at first—even lived in a women's commune for a while. It was a valuable experience—I found out that group living isn't for me, either. The way I put it was that I liked my privacy and couldn't get any work done in groups with other people around all the time. The way *they* put it was that I was really a middle-class housewife at heart. I found out I could tolerate really being alone better than being alone in a horde of other people."

Fenton nodded, understanding that. "I found that out in the army," he said. "Before that, I liked the idea of group living. Afterwards I realized I'd practically kill for the privilege of having a room to myself and a door with a lock on the inside."

She shrugged. "I didn't mind being married," she said. "It was just that Tom wasn't the person I wanted around for the rest of my life. When you marry to get away from home, you don't stop to pick a husband on those terms."

"You're lucky," he said, "you could have had a kid to raise."

Her face hardened into a tight line. "Yes," she said, "I tried to tell myself that when Susanna died. She was three." Her taut face forbade him to show the slightest sympathy.

God, did I put my foot in it that time!

She saw his shocked face and took pity on him. "You couldn't have known. Let's get down to work, shall we? Did you bring the cassette you made for Garnock? Slip it into the slot there, and push the red button marked *play*."

Her stereo system was enormous and, unlike anything else in the apartment, it looked meticulously dusted and kept in order, with records and tapes carefully filed by composer. There was a lot of classical music, and some good jazz and folk music, though nothing newer. He stood looking, losing track of his own voice on the tapes, until he reached the point where Irielle had offered to ask Findhal to help him find the Worldhouse so that he could come and go as he pleased. He heard his own voice quaver as he said, "And then I had a kind of emotional outburst—"

Sally reached out and stopped the tape. Her voice was chill and clinical again. "Can you describe the emotions?"

The clinical tone repelled him. He felt like saying, "Yes, I can, but I'd rather not." He reminded himself he was a scientist, taking part in a research project, not a subject for personal psychological analysis of his own dreams and fantasies. He said, as dryly as he could, "At that point I felt I wanted very much for it all to be real. To be objective, you could say, rather than subjective."

"That happens," she said absent-mindedly, as if for once he had caught her off guard. "I know the feeling." Then she seemed to catch herself. "Go on, Cam. Interrupt the tape any time there's anything you want to expand on."

But he didn't interrupt again, listening to his own voice and watching Sally's hands as she made notes on her clipboard. They were long narrow hands, with thin delicate wrists, slender pale fingers, and tapered nails, varnished but uncolored. Sally was a plain woman, he thought, especially now, bundled in the shapeless housecoat. But she had beautiful hands, and something in them, something in the way she used them and moved them, made him think of Kerridis handing him the delicately-chased metal cup. Thus reminded, he took the pencil she offered and tried to sketch the cup, the patterns round its edge. But when he handed it to her she did not look at it, merely put it aside and listened to the end of the tape.

Then, after a long silence, she said, "Cam, I think you ought to ask Garnock to take you off the project."

His first reaction was shock: *I'd never see Irielle again. . . .*

God! Doesn't that prove what Sally's saying?

"I'm a psychologist," she said, with that cold smile. "At least, I'm qualified for an A.P.A. license, for what that's worth. I don't want to lose a good subject, and you're one of the best; the content analysis on this is clear and interesting, and you're a lot more articulate than the freshmen in this group. But as I say, I am a psychologist. A shrink, if you prefer. For your own good, I think I ought to recommend that Garnock drop you from the project. It's getting too real to you."

Fenton was enough of a psychologist himself to know that there was some validity in what Sally said. He was sufficiently versed in psychology for that—a researcher in parapsychology must be sufficiently knowledgeable to screen out his own neurotic needs and fantasies. It was just this objectivity, he knew, which divided the research parapsychologist from the True Believer: the search for truth without emotional commitment to one theory as opposed to any other.

Yet he told himself that this too was valid, a desire to know factually whether these things he had experienced were subjective or objective. All he said was, "I see what you're driving at, Sally. I'll watch out for that. After all, I *did* report my own emotional response as part of my experience, a part like any other."

"That's true," she admitted.

"I'd like to see this through."

She shrugged. "The danger's for you, not for me," she said and picked up the drawing he had made of the cup. "I'd like to keep this and file it with the rest, if I may. Are you familiar with Warlock's *Signs and Symbols of the Celtic Faith in Ireland?*"

After considering a moment, Fenton shook his head. "I don't think so. Comparative folklore wasn't really my thing. I can't swear I haven't glanced through a copy in passing, though—there's no way to prove that kind of negative. Why?"

She shook her head. "Just asking," she said and slid the drawing into a folder. "That's all I need, I guess."

He hesitated on the way out. "How are you managing about shopping and cooking and so forth?"

She shrugged. "All right. For such housekeeping as I do. As you can see from a quick look around, I don't really do much. I do fine, if I don't mind living out of cans—I don't feel much like staying on my feet long enough to do a lot of cooking."

He could see that there were lines of pain drawn deep in her face. He said impulsively, "Why don't I go out to the Chinese place down the street and bring in some Chinese food?"

She said sharply, "I wasn't hinting."

"It never occurred to me that you were," he said, with a touch of annoyance. "Get the chip off your shoulder, Sally. Is it so unthinkable to you that a man could make a gesture of simple human kindness without ulterior motives? I happen to like Chinese food and I get sick of eating alone. Or do you prefer fish and chips, or fried chicken?"

She laughed, shaking her head. "God forbid; I've had too much of that, the last year I lived with Tom. One of the reasons we broke up was that I stopped cooking. I couldn't see why, when we were both holding down a full teaching load, I should come home and cook supper, and he should come home and put his feet up and read professional journals. So I quit cooking, and did my own laundry and left his, and he didn't like it. In theory he was perfectly willing to do his share, but when it came right down to practice, his attitude was: why in hell should I have a wife if she can't do my share of the world's cooking and laundry? As it was in Fresno, is now and forever more shall be, *in saecula saeculorum, amen*. Well, anyway—I love Chinese food. Especially wonton. Almost anything but fried squid. I'm too much Fresno, I guess, to cope with those squirmy little tentacles, even fried."

Fenton shrugged into his coat. "Personally, I'm partial to duck. Duck anything, roast duck, duck wonton, fried duck, duck with almonds—"

"In that case, I'll trust your judgment."

Over a selection of cartons from the Hop Lee Chinese takeout, they began to talk more easily; Sally's suspiciousness relaxed, and she told him something of how she had happened to choose parapsychology.

"My mother was a spiritualist," she said, "always getting involved with psychics and mediums, each one worse than the last. But she used to go to psychic healers too, and she was never sick. It intrigued me—could her belief in it keep her well? So I got into psychology, and then I began to realize they were cutting out a good half of the human psyche. Growing up in Fresno, all I ever heard of religion was the Bible, and I couldn't swallow that; and right alongside lip service to the Bible, dead worship of scientific materialism and a belief in a kind of science which was outmoded in 1960, with the new breakthroughs into modern physics. So I realized that their view of science was just as irrational as their lip service to the Bible—praising the afterlife on one hand, and on the other, doing anything they could to put off going to Heaven for even one additional day; worshipping their beloved science, and not even seeing that it made monkeys out of their ministers and played hell with their religious views. For a while I stopped having any religion at all, but I found out I couldn't put science there either, which most atheists do. So I started looking for a new model of the universe. When I started college I discovered that the new physics led right into the new psychology and the parapsychological model. And—" she shrugged. "Here I am. And what about you?"

"I studied some wild talents," he said, "and got fascinated by the idea of knowing how they do what they do. In freshman psych I saw a man hooked up to an EEG alter his electro-encephalic pattern on a biofeedback machine, and I also saw a Yogi alter his heartbeat and blood pressure in meditation. Took a class or two with Garnock, and got hooked."

"One could make a very good case," Sally said, "for explaining any student's interest in parapsychology as what the psychologists and shrinks said it was all along— an attempt to compensate for our own neurotic needs. I want a model of the universe that will allow me to reject the narrow one I had during a deprived childhood out in Fresno. You want an explanation for powers which you find desirable in the human body and mind, in order to justify believing you possess them. It would be interesting —and scientifically valid, I'm convinced—to do a psychiatric profile of everyone in the parapsychology department, to see to what extent his own research fills his own neurotic needs." Her smile was suddenly lovely, fluid. Again, with that sharp awarness, Fenton thought of Kerridis. She was dark where Kerridis was fair; but her voice, when she was off guard, and the bitterness was out of it, was lovely and musical, and her hands were graceful; he could well imagine that she had had ballet training.

She would be beautiful if she relaxed. It's tension that makes her look plain, almost ugly. He found himself wondering if, in fantasizing Kerridis—if he had—he had subconsciously used something about Sally. He said very gently, "What neurotic need are you filling, Sally?"

"Oh—" She shrugged, relaxed still and smiling. "Maybe a need to prove to myself that other people have neurotic hangups too. That I'm not all alone with my neurosis, everybody else isn't all nice and normal the way they seemed to think everybody was—everybody but me —in Fresno." She stretched, like a cat, winced, the pain moving across her face visibly, and tensed, moving her hands to her knee. Fenton said quickly, "Have you got something to take for that?"

"The doctor at Cowell gave me some stuff; it's in the bathroom cabinet," she said, and did not protest when he went to fetch it. Rummaging in the untidy medicine chest, he found a phial of pills with Sally's name and a date three days before, and the instructions: *Two as needed, for pain.* He brought her two of the pills with a glass of water and waited while she swallowed them, took the glass away, set it aside, leaned down and, suddenly, on an impulse, kissed her.

She flinched a little, starting away, and Fenton, abruptly recalling himself, drew back.

"Sorry, Sally. That was—a mean advantage to take."

She shook her head. Her neck was long, her throat very white and pale, and he found himself wanting to kiss it again. "No, I invited it, Cam. I'm not a tease." Stirring on the couch, she added uneasily, "If you have any other ideas, though—and I wouldn't mind if you did—they'll have to wait till I have something on the nature of a functioning knee joint again. Right now I'm afraid the only sensations I'm capable of are fairly unpleasant ones in the knee region."

This was so blatantly self-evident that Fenton had no sense of being put off. He leaned forward and kissed the white throat, realizing, with an odd sense of despair, what he was doing.

Compensating, with a real girl, for my fears that Irielle

may not be real . . . and this *was,* in a sense, a mean advantage to take of Sally. Was it because of a chance, accidental resemblance with the unattainable Kerridis?

But as her arms went around his neck, he knew the question was completely academic. Sally was here, and he wanted her—although he knew and accepted that, in her present physical state, there wasn't going to be any lovemaking more strenuous than this until Sally's knee was all right again. It wasn't a casual seduction thing; he *cared* what happened to her. He wanted to see the taut bitterness leave her face and the lovely, relaxed smile come back, to see Sally as he had seen her for a little while, not the hard, closed-in, independent face she showed to her classes and her students. Once having seen the flash of the hidden Sally behind the facade, he knew he would never be content until he drew it forth again for himself.

She drew her fingertips gently down his cheek. "I was jealous," she said in a low voice. "Jealous that you could get all worked up over a girl in a dream. I wanted you, even last time. It was hard not to—to show it. There's no reason nowadays for a woman not to show it." She gave the little helpless laugh again. "Fresno dies hard. You can take the girl out of the boondocks, but you can't take the boondocks out of the girl, and in Fresno women didn't show it. Oh, Cam, Cam, I shouldn't talk this way. . . ."

"No," he said, silencing her words again with a kiss, "you shouldn't."

But even through the upsurge of tenderness, he felt disquieted, wretched.

Was he being unfaithful to Irielle with Sally?

Or to Sally . . . with Irielle?

CHAPTER SEVEN

THE ACCIDENT to Sally's knee was just the first wave in a series of minor disasters that laid the parapsychology department low that winter. First Marjie, Garnock's assistant, then Garnock himself, went down with what they were calling, that winter, Teheran flu. Fenton's next two sessions in the ESP lab with Antaril were cancelled, and Fenton found himself at loose ends and fretting, wondering if Irielle would think he had lost interest—or that he had feared Findhal's threats and was afraid to return.

I wonder if there is any way I could get into that dimension as Pentarn does—as a solid entity? What was it Irielle called it—a worldwalker and not a 'tweenman? Pentarn casts a shadow there, and can touch things.

And when he had gone this far, Fenton would stop and bring himself up short. The last thing he should do was to take it for granted that this unknown realm he had visited was *real*, with objective reality.

Had he lost sight of the purpose of Garnock's original experiment—to test a drug which enormously enlarged the ESP or psi facility? Secretly Fenton knew that in a very real sense he had lost interest in Garnock's experiment. He felt like a traitor, but he knew it was true—he didn't actually care that much. What did it matter if he could, under the bilocational ability of Antaril, walk disembodied over to Marjie and see what cards she had laid out in an area beyond the sense limitations of his eyes? Nobody was going to believe it anyway. He remembered something in his childhood Sunday-school going days, where someone had said: *Yea, even if one came from the dead they would not believe.* By and large, he was enough of a psychologist to know that people believed what they wanted to believe and rearranged facts to suit themselves. Was he going to have to spend the rest of his life arguing with the Flat-Earthers of the mind? Did the space program spend a lot of time trying to convince the True Believers who were absolutely convinced that we had never gone to the moon and the whole government and the scientific community of four countries were engaged in a gigantic conspiracy to pretend that we had?

What would it matter, then, if we did prove that some people can hear things believed to be out of earshot and see things out of the range of their eyes? Most of us have known all along that clairvoyance and clairaudience are facts; why should we spend all this effort trying to prove these things to ignoramuses who have told us they wouldn't believe them with ten times the evidence, anyhow?

And having gone that far Fenton was forced to stop and wonder; what was a fact anyhow?

If Irielle had actually managed to scrawl her name with the vrillsword in the earth of the eucalyptus grove, *Emma Camron*, that was a fact the most skeptical would have to believe. Why, then, had he not insisted, the very moment he got back to his body, on going there with Garnock and perhaps a few independent witnesses from the parapsychology department?

Did I want to prove it, after all, or was I afraid to prove it?

Because, after all, if Irielle or Emma Cameron had actually done that, then the whole nature of reality was so different from what Fenton believed it to be, that he could no longer believe in even the most solid facts. Clairvoyance and clairaudience would be irrelevant, with the whole nature of reality at stake.

Is this why most people are scared to death about ESP and simply won't listen to the facts? Fenton himself, then, had done a criminal thing for a scientist; he had ignored, and failed to check up on, a fact. Inexcusable, not to check it until the next day, and then to ignore what few small marks were left.

But in any case it was too late now. Rain had wiped out the last possible remaining trace. Now, when it was too late, he went back to the eucalyptus grove and stared at the dirt in the circle, where Irielle, if there had ever

been a real Irielle, had scrawled the name EMMA CA-
MRON. There had been no excuse for ignoring that; he
should have dragged Garnock there by the hair if necessary . . . Why hadn't he?

Sally. Sally, who was real; he had been afraid of her
disbelief, of her accusation that he was formulating imaginary women for himself. Sally was real, and he didn't
want to believe that he could set aside a very real
woman in his arms for a woman who might not have any
existence outside a drug dream. And if he had insisted to
Sally that Irielle was real, there would have been no way
to silence her secret scorn, her contempt for a man who
refused involvement with real women to dream of imaginary ones. Fairy Queens, changelings! On the surface it
sounded completely mad. Okay, he'd play it Sally's way;
she was analyzing dream-symbology under Antaril and
he would play the game by her rules.

Sally. Slowly, day by day, he felt he had been slipping under Sally's guard. Seldom now did she turn that
savage cold withdrawal on him. They had fallen into a
habit, almost, of having dinner together; a few times he
had spent the night at her place and once had persuaded
her to come back to his. Whatever it was with Sally, it
was not casual; she was not a woman for casual affairs,
and she seemed very much afraid that he would make
any demands on her, more than this.

When for the third week there was a card on Garnock's
door saying that the regularly scheduled appointments in
the parapsychology lab would not be held, due to continuing absenteeism in the department, Fenton was sunk in
gloom. The semester was moving toward Easter vacation
and there was little chance of completing the project this
quarter. He called Sally's apartment, and received no answer, then rang her office on campus. When she answered, she sounded distant, harsh, abstracted.

"Garnock's had a relapse. You know how the flu is,
and you know he doesn't take care of himself. I'm practically minding the store all by myself down here. Personally I think we should just shut up shop for this quarter,
give all the students an incomplete without prejudice, and
let them repeat their courses next quarter. But I suppose

the Board of Regents would raise Cain—they could never do anything so sensible."

"It would be hard on scholarship students and people graduating this June."

"Yes, I suppose so."

"Anything I can do to help, Sally?"

"No, I'm catching up on paperwork and I have thirty-four freshman papers to read this weekend. How would you like to read and grade the damned things for me?"

He hedged. "Do you require typed papers?"

"Damn right. The way they teach—or rather, the way they *don't* teach—handwriting in high schools, I'm not likely to be able to read a handwritten paper, even if there were any freshman here who could *write* more than half a page. Thank God for required typing courses in the grade schools. Seriously, Cam, are you game for that?"

"Why not? Do you grade on a curve?"

"No way," Sally said. "I told the freshmen that I would willingly give thirty-four A's if thirty-four of them learned ninety percent of what I expected them to learn and proved it to me; but on the other hand, I would equally willingly give thirty-four F's if nobody learned more than thirty per cent of what I expected them to learn. If I decide for myself that I should give out three A's, nine B's and no more than six failures, I am laying myself open to all kinds of subjective evaluations of who's at the top and bottom of the class and who's just average. So I measure them up against how much they've actually learned of what I want them to absorb about parapsychology. The only question on their paper is: Describe what this course has taught you. If they just copy a lot of clichés out of the textbook, well, I assume they haven't learned anything much. I look for evidence of the ability to judge and evaluate. And of course that is sacrilege these days, but to me grading on a curve is just rewarding conformity instead of original thought. They think I'm tough—most freshmen like to get into Joe's section. He grades on a curve and gives nothing but IBM-scored multiple-choice tests."

Fenton laughed. "That's why I don't teach," he said. "I'd be hacked to pieces between those two rival theories."

"What *are* you going to do, if you don't teach, Cam?"

"God knows." Suddenly he felt uncomfortable. "Thank heaven I don't have to worry about it for a few more months and then I'll have to face up to it. Not right now, though. Look, Sally, shall I bring some supper along?"

"No, my turn to provide supper," she said. "I got some salad stuff, and I'll pick up something on the way home. But what you could do if you wanted to, and I'd appreciate it, is to stop and bring along some extra blank tape cassettes."

"I'll be there by seven," he said. He dropped his voice and added, "Love you."

"Love *you*," she said softly into the phone and hung up.

In the shop where they sold tape cassettes, batteries and cheap recordings, he was waiting for the order Sally had telephoned when a young woman standing close to him spoke, and he listened. Nothing is so clear in a strange place as the sound of your own name, unexpectedly spoken.

"No," she said. "That order is for *Cameron;* my name is *Dameron*, with a D. Look under the D's, as for David, and you'll find it."

"Is that Frances Dameron?" the clerk asked, riffling through a file, and the woman took the package and paid for it; but this had brought Fenton back to memory of Irielle.

Cameron was not an uncommon name. It was Cam's own Christian name, or one of them. His mother had named him Michael Cameron Fenton, after her own father, and since there had been, that year, four Michaels in his first grade class, he had become Cam, and had used it ever since. But he supposed Cameron was the family name of pagefuls of people in every telephone book in the country. If he tried to locate an Emma Cameron who had, perhaps, been killed with her parents in some kind of horse-and-buggy accident, generations ago, in an unknown town in an unknown state—no, the task of locating a needle in a haystack would be elementary by contrast. So much for factual validation. Irielle herself had probably been too young to know the year, the town or perhaps even the state. The task of scientific validation resembled locating, with the naked eye, one specific star in the distant Andromeda Nebula!

He pocketed the cassettes and walked slowly across Telegraph Avenue. It was late afternoon of a sunny spring day and the avenue was alive with students, neo-hippies, street people of all kinds, stands selling jewelry, tarot readings, homemade cookies and homemade leather goods, batik-dyed T-shirts and cigarette papers.

A shabby youngster, student age—but Cam had never seen him on campus—confronted Fenton; he was shaven bald in the latest fashion, his ears pierced with three holes and containing three rings. Fenton had heard on campus that this had some private or esoteric significance about the person's sexual tastes, but he didn't know what or especially care.

"Hey, man, how about buying some good, legal homegrown and air-dried grass? None of that import stuff from Mexico with chemical fertilizers on it—real organic stuff from San Diego county."

Fenton shook his head. "Sorry, fella. Don't use it."

"You a Jesus-freak or something?"

Fenton shook his head. "Nope. Stuff hurts my throat, that's all. Sorry, man."

But the neo-hippie tagged after him as he started to walk on. "Look, man, this is good stuff. Try a water pipe with ice in the water to cool it down and you'll be surprised how mild it is, it'll really send you outside the moon in no time at all!"

Fenton laughed. "Sorry. Why go to all that trouble? I just don't like the stuff, that's all."

The student looked dejected. "Come on, man, I got to make my room rent, or I'll be hocking my electronic organ again this month! Try a present for your girl, then. I got some special stuff flavored with musk, really turns the women on. Makes them forget all about their inhibitions, if you know what I mean, man."

Fenton smiled. Whatever Sally's problems might be, inhibitions weren't among them. "Sorry, don't need it."

"No girl?"

"No inhibitions."

"But I bet she'd enjoy this stuff. Come on, man, just smell it," the young man coaxed. Then he lowered his voice. "Or if you don't go for legal jolts, I can probably get you some tobacco. Good clean stuff smuggled in from Ecuador. Or I could get you Owsley or Sandoz acid, but that comes kind of high. Or any other jolts you want."

On a sudden impulse Fenton said, "How about Antaril?"

The hippie stepped back. "That takes some doing," he said, "and most of what you get is acid mixed with a little datura; not many people can tell the difference. But I know a guy says his stuff is real. I could meet you here about eleven," he suggested, and Fenton hesitated, then said, offhandedly, "Okay, maybe I'll look you up."

"I'll be here," the bald student promised, and went off.

Fenton went across the avenue, passing many small shops selling tacos, ties, printed scarves, homemade candy and art prints. In one he saw a set of Rackham prints of elves and goblins which reminded him, with sudden intensity, of Kerridis among the ironfolk. He was tempted to go in and buy it, but the shop was closed and barred, and he thought: *I'll come back and get that one, Sally might like to see what they look like.* And then he realized that the elf-woman in the print reminded him less of Kerridis than, subtly, of Sally herself.

"I wonder," he thought. "Did I see this picture as a kid, maybe?" During Cam's childhood, Rackham-illustrated books of fairy tales had probably been commonplace, even if he had no conscious memory of them. Sally had suggested something like that.

He went on, crossing the campus, striding through the eucalyptus grove without yielding to the temptation to stop and examine the ground again—any traces would have been washed out by the recent rain.

If the project wasn't started again in a few days—he scowled at the thought of the Antaril, and resolved to stand up the hippie. He took a very dim view of recreational drugs. Even at the height of the "hippie" years he had refused to get involved in casual "tripping" for the fun of it.

He rang Sally's bell and she greeted him with a kiss; she looked relaxed, less withdrawn or suspicious than usual.

"Let me take your coat. I brought in some chicken, and

all I have to do is make the salad. Want to come and peel an avocado for me?"

While he was slicing avocadoes and tomatoes he glanced up at the picture of a small, fair-haired child, hair drawn into two wispy pony-tails. He didn't say anything, but she followed his glance.

"That's Susanna," she said. "I wanted to remember her like that. Tom wanted me to put everything out of sight. Pictures, toys, everything, just as if she'd never lived at all. And to have another baby right away. Only I—I couldn't. I didn't want another baby to be Susanna for me. I wanted to wait, and then—then I was struck with this awful guilt. Because now that Susanna was dead I realized I didn't have to stay with Tom any more, and it was as if I'd wanted her to die to get away from Tom—so I could be free. I know it was neurotic; I couldn't live with it, though. Now I realize that even if Susanna had lived I would probably have left Tom sooner or later, so it doesn't hurt so much." She bent over the lettuce, tearing it with those long, slender hands that so much reminded him of those of Kerridis. . . .

"Here," she said, putting the bowl of salad into his hands, "carry it in for me, will you?"

He set it into the middle of the table and they sat down, Sally handing him the carton of chicken. "Not elegant, but filling," she commented.

There was a thick file of papers on one edge of the table; Sally picked it up just before the gravy tilted over it. "Here, set these things on the desk, will you, Cam? I have to transcribe them on to tapes again tonight—"

The topmost one bore his own name, M.C. Fenton. He started to thumb it open and she frowned and shook her head.

"No fair, Cam, I trust you."

Reluctantly he put the file on the desk and bit into a piece of chicken. "Come on, now, I ought to have a right to see my own file."

"I explained that, Cam."

"Okay, okay. I got your tape cassettes. They're in the pocket of my coat."

"I'll get them after supper," she said. "Was it very far out of your way?"

"Not really. But it's a hell of a nuisance coming over here; one of us ought to move in with the other."

It had been a mistake. Sally's mouth tightened and she said, in the old harsh voice, "I don't have the faintest intention of either choice. If it's too much trouble coming over here, we can set up the next session in my office in Smythe."

"Sally, Sally!" He put his arms around her across the table, "I was joking, darling! Don't go all cold on me that way, for God's sake!"

She said, angry and shaken, "Men do that. Taking advantage. The very minute a woman makes the least concession—"

"Sally, for God's sake, I'm not men, I'm *me,* and you're not a woman, you're Sally! I love you, I like making jokes with you!" He stared at her in such dismay that she dropped her eyes.

"Cam, I'm sorry. I know I'm too touchy. But let's not talk about it, all right? Just now I need my independence. I don't want to think that just because we—we get along this well, right away you want to start talking about—about moving in together. I'm not ready for that yet and I don't know if I ever will be. Let's leave it a while, all right?"

"All right," he said, reaching for a second helping of salad. Sally's sudden cold withdrawals had begun to hurt him.

"Did they make any trouble about giving you the cassettes on my account?"

"None at all."

"I appreciate it, Cam. I don't like to walk down Telegraph these days; it's too full of freaks and street people. I know most of them are harmless, but I still feel weird."

"Weird is what some of them are, all right," Cam agreed, glad of a neutral topic. "One of the dealers, chap with three rings in his ear, whatever that means, came up and offered me some special grass flavored with musk—said it would turn my girl on, make her lose her inhibitions."

She laughed. "Do you really think I need that?"

"No; that was what I told him, that was the last thing I needed to bring you," he said playfully baring his teeth.

She stretched her hand to him and squeezed it, then said, still laughing, "Down, boy. We have all those papers to grade and read. Sometime when there isn't so much work to do, I'll show you how much I need stuff like that! Anyhow, I don't like the smell of musk."

"I'm not crazy about it myself," Cam said. "But this chap was really eager to make a sale. He even offered me Antaril."

"Has that turned up on the streets again? Well, come to think of it, it's easy to make, and relatively nontoxic," Sally said. "Probably better to sell that than something lethal like methedrine crystals. As far as I know, Antaril has no bad side effects, but of course nobody really knows. There hasn't been that much experimentation."

"And it seems that there never will be. I'd be tempted, unless Garnock gets back and we can go on with the project."

"Are you in a hurry, Cam? Actually, I'm glad to have the time to catch up my paperwork and correlate the elements in the dream-symbolism. I'm way behind on professional reading too. What's the hurry?"

He made the mistake of saying, "I'd like to know what's happened to Irielle and all the rest of them."

"Make up the rest of it yourself, Cam. You can, you know; just turn your involuntary fantasy into a conscious one, make up any end for it that you want to."

He said, very quietly, "You don't believe in any of it, do you, Sally?"

"No, I don't. I've listened to too many of these fantasies. I think it's telling you a lot about yourself, that's all—that you want a fairy queen, a changeling, because a real woman is too threatening. She might have needs of her own, real needs in a real world. It's a very common male fantasy, after all."

Fenton kept back the anger he felt at the casual scorn in that. "What about the lines in the eucalyptus grove?"

"Did anyone else see them?"

"Damn it all, Sally, *I* saw them!"

"Come *on,* Cam. You're enough of a psychologist to know that people see what they want to see. Eyewitness testimony is notoriously worthless. People are still seeing flying saucers. If you had been sure of them, you would have made sure that someone else had a chance to see them, too."

"That's a long way below the belt, Sally."

"You won't see that you're deceiving yourself, will you, Cam? That you've created an emotionally perfect woman for yourself, one who will make no demands on you."

"Perfect, hell," he said angrily. "Irielle isn't perfect! I told you about the scars, that she'd been in an accident, that they fixed it to look as if she'd died in an accident—"

Sally's face was cold and pale. She asked, "Who told you about Susanna?"

"I don't know what you're talking about!"

"Do you expect me to believe that? It was all over the department. Some of the people gave blood for her. The accident. And—" Her voice faltered, broke. "And what happened to her leg. They said if she'd lived, she would have been completely crippled. Horribly crippled. I didn't blame you when I heard it on the tape. I thought you probably didn't even remember it was me, *my* kid they were talking about—"

"Sally, Sally," he said in consternation. "It must have happened while I was overseas, I never heard a word about it."

But she was not mollified. "Your own unconscious needs made the whole story into what you needed it to be. Even the fact that you couldn't touch anything, so you didn't have to give anything to anyone, you weren't responsible for anything that happened, you could withdraw and not be responsible—"

He flared out at her. "What about your own emotional needs to disbelieve, to make me into the kind of a man who could do a shabby thing like that? What about your emotional need to believe that every man you get involved with is a shithead, so you can have a good excuse to cut him into ribbons?"

She sat very still, not moving. Her face was dead white and he was shocked. Had she really allowed him close enough that he could hurt her so much? Then she said, with a long, shaking breath, "Point well taken, Cam. I did do that, didn't I? I'm sorry. I don't mean to be—to be unreasonable. Let's try to look at this rationally—"

"*Your* way, you mean," he said, still angry.

"Cam, I'm a scientist and a parapsychologist, and you know and I know that wishful thinking and working on unvalidated data have been the curse of every parapsychologist who ever lived. Give me one piece of hard evidence, Cam, and I'll listen. But on the surface of it, it's too fantastic, it shakes up too many realities."

"Are you saying, my mind is made up, don't confuse me with facts?"

"No. I haven't seen any facts yet, just wild theories. About multiple universes and alternate realities."

He said slowly, "When I was first telling you about it, you said something—I had the idea somebody else had mentioned it to you independently. You said: *Oh, you got Pentarn too.* Did somebody else get it, or a whole raft of somebodies?"

"Cam, you know I can't tell you that. It would invalidate everything. Maybe when the project is over—Anyhow, names don't mean anything. It might be a name from some book. I'm checking."

She stopped and looked at him. "Cam, I said this before and I'm going to say it again. I think you should drop the project. It's too real to you. How will you feel if you discover that it is completely imagination?"

"Not half as bad as I'd feel never knowing whether it was or not," he retorted. "Sally, you make a big thing about being a scientist. Give me credit for the same thing. I want to validate this, sure, but at least half of that is being able to be sure whether it is or whether it *isn't*. Can't you understand that much?"

She reached her slender fingers across the table again and took his hand. She said, "All right, Cam. But try to keep a little perspective, too?" Her smile was wan. "All right, I'll admit it, I worry, damn it. I worry about *you*, Cam . . . oh, damn it, damn *you*, do you think I *wanted* to get in a state where some damn man means something to me?" She pushed back her chair, then leaned her head on the table and covered her face with her hands. "I know I'm on the defensive. I can't help it, Cam. I've been through too much," she said, thickly, through her hands. "I'm no good to you. I'm no good to anyone. I'm no good to myself. If you had half a brain you'd walk out of here and down those stairs and never come back!"

He came around the table and knelt beside her, holding her while she cried; he didn't try to talk. At last he took her chin with one hand and held her face up to him.

"Want me to get lost, Sally? I'm not trying to threaten your independence. But I don't want to complicate your life, either. You mean a lot to me. I think you could mean a lot more. But I'm not just looking for an easy lay. Give me a chance."

She said, her eyes turned away from his, "Oh, God, I've done it again, haven't I? It's what you said, I guess. My own need to prove that every man I meet is just out to exploit me, that men are no good, to protect myself against—against getting hurt again. I don't want to, Cam. I know you're not like that, but I start acting—well, damn near paranoid, don't I? I want to trust you, Cam, I like you, but I—I'm not ready to commit myself any further, not yet. Can we go on for a while without a lot of pressure? Just see how things work out?"

He nodded, his arm tight around her. "All right, Sally, no pressure. No commitments. We'll play it the way it comes up and see what happens. Here, let's get started on those freshman term papers?"

She sniffled a little, getting up to clear the table of the chicken. "You say you aren't trying to exploit me. Look at me, using you to grade term papers!"

"That," he said, laughing, "is a fate worse than death, isn't it? Here, give me the damned things before I lose my nerve."

They worked to nearly midnight on the term papers, and Sally was drooping over the table by the time they had finished reading and grading them. "At least they're finished," she said, yawning, rubbing her eyes. "It would have taken me another couple of days, trying to read them in the slots between classes. Cam, how can I thank you?"

"That's okay; it was interesting to see parapsychology again through a freshman's eyes," he said. "I hope I didn't grade them a lot tougher than you would, though."

She shook her head. "I don't think so. Probably about the same. At least, that kid who thought parapsychology was a good way to develop occult powers—we can tactfully weed him out of the department, or make him repeat the course so he'll get the message." She yawned.

He said, "Go to bed, Sally. You're asleep on your feet. I'll let myself out."

"Cam, if you want to stay, it's okay, but I'm so whacked—"

"That's all right, sweetheart. There'll be other times." He kissed her, gently, not lingering.

"Snap the lock on the door, will you, when you go?" She went toward the bedroom, and Fenton picked up his raincoat. To get at it he had to pick up the stack of file folders, and one slid out. He bent to retrieve it, and it seemed to stare up at him, mocking.

M.C. FENTON.

He put his thumb to the edge. One quick look, and he could verify what she said about him. Or had she said anything at all, discarding what he had told her as an emotionally induced vision?

No. She had trusted him. He couldn't snoop in her files.

Damn it, Fenton thought, there had even been court decisions upholding the right of students to see what was written in confidential files about them . . .

Then he admonished himself to be honest. That applied to labels which might retard a student's work for the rest of his life, not to files maintained for the duration of a scientific experiment. Okay, he would play it straight. He set down the file and let himself out, carefully locking the door behind him.

It was well past eleven, and he had not expected to see any sign of the bald-shaven hippie, but the man was there on the corner, looking cold and cramped, and rather resentful. When he saw Fenton, he said, "Hey, man, I'd just about given you up! Another ten minutes and I'd have split. I got you the Antaril, though. Four jolts. Guaranteed pure stuff, no cutting, no contaminants, no jimsonweed or datura in it. No sugar. Twenty-four."

"That's high!"

The hippie shrugged. "What it costs. I'm not making but five. Look, this is pure stuff, I guarantee it. If it doesn't work you can find me on this corner four days a week and I'll give you your money back. Hey," he asked, as Cam dug out the money, "aren't you Professor Fenton?"

"I'm no professor."

The hippie didn't care. He said, "You look a lot like one

of the professors over at Cal, in the spook department, you know, the one where they chase ghosts and flying saucers and people who can read your mind. They got money for all that, and not enough to pay my scholarship on time, so I have to peddle jolts on the street. See you around, man," he added, pocketing the folded bills without counting them, and faded into the thinning throng on the street.

Fenton put the envelope of four blue tablets into his pocket and walked slowly along Telegraph. The crowds of students and street people had thinned—they would not completely clear away until well after midnight. He thought about going into one of the coffee houses for a cup of espresso, but instead he kept walking along the avenue. Now that he had the Antaril, he would probably never use it. He knew nothing about the effectiveness of Antaril as taken by mouth, as compared with the intravenously injected and clinically pure variety.

Yet it was a temptation. Swallow one of the small blue tablets and a few minutes later he would be in the world of the Alfar, free to communicate with Irielle—and with Kerridis.

No. The experiment had been scientifically laid out. He shouldn't mess it around by throwing in the unknown factor of street drugs. He was a scientist, and had heavily emphasized that fact with Sally.

But he wished—*how* he wished—that he knew what she had meant when she said: *Oh, you got Pentarn too!*

Now he wished that foolish scruples had not kept him from looking into his folder. It was obvious that Sally didn't have the faintest idea what this experiment meant to him.

It could mean that nothing in this world was what people believed it to be, that even the parapsychologists, cautiously dipping one toe into the perimeter of standard scientific materialism, didn't have the faintest notion of the true nature of reality. He had heard some students in the new physics department say something like that once, that perhaps we had no notion of reality, that our senses were probably inadequate to have the faintest notion of reality.

Another hippie, this one wrapped in a drab and faded blanket, approached him and whined the ritual, "Spare any change, man?"

Fenton said an equally automatic, "Sorry," and realized that in the doorways ahead, half a dozen of the street people were lined up and he would have to run the gauntlet of them. He looked across the street. Two or three of the small shop windows were still lighted, including the small shop where he had seen the Rackham prints; he'd go over and buy that one for Sally.

He started to cross the street, then was held motionless by the sight of a tall, thin man, walking swiftly along the opposite side of the street—a bearded man, in high boots and a long, dark green cape wrapped around him. Fenton's first thought that it was one of the Anachronists who affected medieval trappings was driven away by sudden awareness of just *where* he had seen that particular long green cape, that particular arrogant cast of the head before.

"Pentarn!" he bellowed, and broke into a run across the street.

The man's head whipped up and he looked all round him with a quick, swivelling motion. Fenton saw him bare his teeth, briefly, in a strange gesture; then Pentarn too began to run, straight toward the small shop of prints. Fenton was on Pentarn's heels by the time he reached it, but on the very threshold he collided hard with one of the street people playing a guitar, spilling the man's collected hatful of coins all over the threshold. He had his hand on Pentarn's shoulder; the tall man wrenched away and the hippie yelled with outrage as the guitar collided with the edge of the doorway,

"Hey! Man, can't you damned Anachronists keep your fights for the tournament ground, huh? If you broke my guitar string, man, I'm going to—"

Fenton muttered hasty apologies and thrust on through the doorway. On the threshold he reeled, a sudden black and sparkling giddiness crossing his eyes. He felt himself falling sidewise. . . .

Falling. Falling. Space twisting, reeling. . . .

He blinked, feeling his feet solid on the flooring of the little shop. Dazed, he blinked and stared. The shop was gone. There were no Rackham prints; no sign of the bearded and caped Pentarn. Instead only the bland whiteness of a laundromat and dry-cleaning place, and the proprietor, a withered small man, was looking at him belligerently, saying, "No time for a load of wash; we close midnight sharp."

Fenton blinked, saying some dazed apology whose words he never remembered. The wrong door; he had come in the wrong door, after all that. Pentarn was gone, if it had ever been Pentarn at all, and not some anonymous campus Anachronist on his way home from a tourney or gaming-revel. Yet he had to try. He *couldn't* believe the man had vanished into thin air, not *that* fast.

"Was there a man who came in before me? A tall man, in a cape?"

"No cape," said the man indifferently. "Just a guy with a raincoat to clean. You been jolting, mister?"

Fenton shook his head and stumbled out.

Pentarn. Had it been Pentarn at all?

Or had he hallucinated that too?

No, he told himself firmly. I came in the wrong door, that's all. He turned and looked to either side, hunting the little shop where he had seen the Rackham prints behind steel-gated windows earlier that day—where Pentarn had gone.

But next to the dry-cleaner, on one side, was a doughnut shop; on the other side, a bookstore with a prosaic placard reminding students that the last day to turn in required-course textbooks for full refund was April second. Fenton strode up and then down the block, but there was no small print-shop on that block at all. It simply was not there. He checked every door and even checked the street numbers of every shop, wondering if his eyes were playing him tricks. After that, he checked the next block and the next, working his way back, door by door, to the edge of Bancroft Way and the campus; then he started to work his way back down the other side. When he finally heard the campanile clock strike one, he gave up, frowning, beginning to doubt his sanity.

The shop had been *there!* Damn it, it had been there, and he had seen a Rackham print with goblins and a tall elf-queen who looked a little like Kerridis, and even more like Sally.

A grim thought stole through Fenton's mind as he clutched his raincoat around his chilled body and began to walk back, slowly, toward his room. Had he hallucinated the whole thing out of a desperate need for validation? He had needed to believe the whole thing was real; so he had invented an episode that would make it real.

But he had seen the print before he went to Sally's, he reminded himself, and was struck with an immediate rationalization of that too.

It must have been in one of the other bookstores. Rackham prints were fairly common. And the proprietor could have taken it out of the window and sold it.

But why wasn't the little shop there? Why was it, when he went into it, nothing but a dry-cleaning shop? And why couldn't he find the little print-shop?

Unbidden, the thought came: *it's as if the damned place were hiding from me.* Fenton sat down on his shabby couch and thought about that.

A place that doesn't want to be found.

A place you can't find when you're looking for it.

The queer dizziness that had come over him as he stepped inside was not unlike the peculiar dizziness he had had when he entered the alien dimension on Antaril.

There was a prickling all along Cameron Fenton's spine, as if all the tiny hairs on his back and neck were bristling like a frightened cat's, standing up erect.

Was it possible that he had seen, encountered, what Irielle had called the Worldhouse?

CHAPTER EIGHT

THE NEXT DAY Fenton searched again, all up and down the whole length of Telegraph Avenue, from Bancroft until the character of the avenue was lost in the banks, gas stations and ballet studios south of the new freeway. Then he went back, checked the whole length again, both sides of the avenue, and was finally convinced that there was no small print-shop, with or without Rackham prints in the window.

Which meant one of two things: either he had hallucinated Pentarn, after previously hallucinating a disappearing print-shop into which the man could vanish. Or else . . .

Or else . . . *what?* Irielle's stories about the World-house?

He couldn't tell Sally about this. Certainly Sally would think he had invented the whole thing. He reexamined his own notes about the first Añtaril experience, then remembered the mackinaw jacket, belonging to his Uncle Stan, which he had seen, and the questions in his mind. Well, *that* he could check.

There was nothing he could do on campus now, with the department shut down. Nothing, except glance through professional journals and look at the want ads. He noticed that there was an assistant professor's opening at Cornell University. He didn't have much chance—he was a white male and with affirmative action they would probably prefer a black, Mexican or a woman—but he sent off the application anyhow, wondering if Sally would be willing to live in upstate New York. It was a long way from California and she had relatives here. On the other hand it didn't seem that she was very close to them.

And Irielle?

He told himself angrily to forget about Irielle. She probably had never existed. Sally was real, Sally was a human being, and furthermore Sally needed him. This was insane anyhow, seriously hesitating between a real woman and one in a dream. Maybe he had deserved everything Sally said about him!

Anyhow he hadn't visited his relatives upstate for a long time and Uncle Stan would be glad to see him.

As he drove northward, turning off just before Sacramento to take Highway Five, he thought of what Irielle had told him about the Worldhouse. You can't find it when you are looking for it, she had said. Well, that certainly was true of the little print-shop. And yet, why should a print-shop be the Worldhouse? Camouflage— could it be camouflaged in such a rational manner, like anything so prosaic?

Since there wasn't any such thing in his reality, did it matter what it looked like?

All right. Assume for a moment that there was such a thing as a Gateway between dimensions, a house that somehow stood between worlds. Think it out on its own realities. What would such a thing look like?

It seemed to Cameron Fenton that it ought to resemble a computer center. He thought, wryly, that he was mixing worlds. Of course, if there was a science-fiction movie where a Gateway between dimensions could function, it would have to be done with computers—computers were the modern-day equivalent of magic, which, after all, just meant something you couldn't understand. Most people who made science-fiction movies, or went to see them, didn't understand computers but knew that computers did strange, difficult and supposedly impossible things; ergo, their equivalent of the god from the machine was a computer control center.

But there was no reason to assume that a Worldhouse, a Gateway between dimensions, would look like anything that was rational to him, or that his senses could measure. *Ergo,* it probably didn't. Maybe it looked like nothing his senses could resolve into sanity at all, and so his mind rationalized the experience into seeing something else that did make sense. Like a print-shop.

Or a dry-cleaning place? Maybe, if I'd just gone on

through the dry-cleaning shop, I would have got—wherever Pentarn was going. That was what I should have done! Grabbed him and hung on hard and gone with him wherever he escaped to . . .

That queer dizziness that had come over him as he stood poised on the threshold of the little print-shop . . . Pentarn had gone through that dizziness into someplace else. And the Worldhouse had gone with Pentarn, leaving Fenton standing in the ordinary laundromat in his own dimension.

But, Fenton thought, looking abstractedly at the road ahead and the tip of Mount Shasta, which was beginning to play hide-and-seek on the twisting highway, *I saw the print-shop on the avenue before I even went to Sally's . . .*

You saw it locked and barred. You saw it where you could not get into it.

But he had seen it open . . . once. Just as Pentarn dodged into it. And then it had twisted into some other dimension. . . .

This is bughouse. If I keep on thinking this way I'll wind up in a padded cell up at Napa.

And Fenton tried to pull away from it, dismissing the whole thing as a curious hallucination brought on by obsessive worry about the Antaril project. He couldn't discuss it with Sally. She would just use it as further evidence that he had lost his scientific objectivity about the test and ought to withdraw from it right away.

And then he would never see Irielle again. . . .

Which very emotion, he supposed, meant she was right and he ought to withdraw. . . .

By the time he reached the small, Sierra town north of Shasta, he was sick and tired of hashing it over.

He found the little side road, turned aside, rattled over a small wooden bridge and drew his car up in the yard. A couple of inquisitive goats shouldered and butted their way toward him, and he shoved them away, good-humoredly. He had to elbow them aside as he went toward the farmhouse door.

"Uncle Stan?" he called. "It's Cam!"

There was no answer; the shabby kitchen was clean and deserted. His uncle must be working around the ranch; or, if Fenton wasn't lucky, might be guiding a group of young climbers into the Sierras on a backpacking trip.

There was a pot of coffee on the back of the stove. It was stone cold, but that didn't mean anything. Fenton turned on the gas under the coffee. While it heated he checked to see if his uncle's camping equipment was in place. His sleeping bag hung on a rack in the bedroom, stretched to air; his down parka was behind the door. Therefore he wasn't far away. The coffee began to boil, and Fenton poured himself a cup black and sat at the oilcloth-covered table, sipping it. Then he went into the spare bedroom and hunted in the closet.

The red-and-black mackinaw that his uncle kept for him to wear on hikes was there. He felt in the pocket, and again his spine prickled as he felt the small rough patch, unevenly stitched.

Confirmation?

No. Not necessarily. It might just mean that his sub-conscious had a better memory than he did. He felt literally sick with frustration. How do you prove you *didn't* know something, *hadn't* read something or seen it? Everybody, from Oscar Wilde on down, knew the futility of trying to prove a negative. The defendant didn't have to prove he *hadn't* done it; the prosecution had to prove that *had*.

Only in scientific research into parapsychology, Fenton thought with a surging sense of the injustice of it, the re-searcher had to prove all kinds of negatives. Instead of the outsiders proving that he was lying, he had to prove that he wasn't. He had to prove even that he wasn't yield-ing to subconscious fakery. How did anyone ever prove that many negatives? How could he possibly prove he had never seen or read anything like his experience with the Alfar and the ironfolk?

Was it any wonder that so many parapsychologists just got tired of the inhumanly rigorous strictures which as-sumed that you were automatically a liar, a cheat, a hoaxer, intellectually dishonest? He sat discouraged at the table, swallowing down the cooling bitter coffee. What was the use? He could never convince Sally. Even if he did convince Sally and Garnock, what good would it do? No-body else would ever believe him, and if he wrote a book about it, what would it prove? Just another crackpot from the parapsychology department . . .

I ought to throw it all up and go back to running rats through mazes.

Recognizing that he was on the very verge of slipping back into the depression he had driven up here to escape, he shrugged on the mackinaw jacket and went out into the cold, crisp air of the Sierras. The goats shouldered around him with growing aggressiveness; he pushed them away and was oddly reminded of Pentarn striding through the ironfolk.

Only, the goats were harmless. Curious, maybe, and pesky, but essentially harmless.

He walked along a narrow path, overgrown with liveoak and mountain juniper, toward the hill behind the house. In the clear echoing air, he heard the ring of rhythmic blows and knew that somewhere his uncle was chopping wood.

This high in the Sierras, the snow had not yet melted; a few miles away, snow lay heavy, glistening on the peaks above him. The air was cold and frosty, the edges of the paths rimed with snow. Fenton walked along the path, thinking of the track he had followed in the Alfar country. But this one was solid under his feet.

Had he visited in dream a country familiar to his mind?

The axe-echoes were closer now; Fenton began to climb up the steep path leading toward the sound. There was still a perceptible pause between stroke and echo.

"Uncle Stan?" Fenton called.

The distant sound of chopping quieted for a moment, and Fenton called again.

"Uncle Stan, are you up here? It's Cam!" He came around the edge of a fallen log into a small cleared space. At the edge of the clearing a tall, lean man, in a faded flannel work shirt, was chopping away at a tree. He ceased, waved and yelled, "Through in a minute—let me finish this here!"

After a moment the tree toppled and came crashing into the underbrush. It wasn't a very big tree. After a moment, Stanley Cameron set the axe upright on its head and came toward his nephew, mopping at his forehead with the tail of the plaid shirt. "Hi, Cam, good to see you. Did you drive up from Berkeley today?"

He stuck out his hand; Fenton gripped the hand of his mother's brother, shook it hard. Stan Cameron was a lean old man, his hair greyed-over rusty brown, his eyes set deep in the sun-wrinkles of a man who has spent a great deal of his life outdoors.

"I thought it was a pack of kids I promised to take climbing on Shasta tomorrow," he said. "I figured one, two of them might turn up today, spend some time climbing around here, getting ready for the real climb tomorrow." He dropped down on a fallen log. "Minute or so, I'll have to get that tree chopped up for firewood. Takes all I can do to keep the brush cleared out here, keep the woods from crowding in again. The goats keep the lower leaves down some, but this stuff grows fast. Used to burn it over every five, ten years, used to have lightning storms come along and give you a good burn, but too many folks live in here now, and they're scared of a burn, and of course you can't have it where folks are living; it's not like this country was all wild. A good fire does wonders for a brush tract, but not in settled country. Well, Cam, how come you drove up here right in the middle of the school term? Not teaching this season?"

"Department's shut down with the flu." He could hardly say to Stan Cameron that he had driven up here to inspect a hole in the pocket of a plaid mackinaw jacket!

"Don't know how you stand it, down yonder in the city with all the smog," Uncle Stan said. "You ought to move up here."

Fenton grinned. "Too lonely for me, Uncle Stan."

"Get you a nice girl, then," Stan Cameron said. "Marry her and move up here and raise you a houseful of young ones and you won't have time to be lonely. I'll give you a couple of goats."

Fenton chuckled. His uncle had made this offer periodically since Cam got out of the army. "Might just take you up on that some day."

"Don't tell me you've got a girl?"

"Kind of," Fenton said. "She's not ready to get married yet, though."

"Give her time. That's what all the girls want, no matter what they say."

"Maybe in your day," Fenton protested, and the old man grinned.

"Any day at all. Can't argue with biology."

Fenton said, "I think maybe we've reached a state where women don't like thinking about biology as their only destiny, Uncle Stan."

"Maybe not," the old man said, unimpressed. "But thinking one way or other doesn't make any difference to the biology, either. You show me a vegetarian lion some day and I'll admit that maybe biology isn't destiny. Otherwise, I'll stick with nature. I been around too many goats to start arguing with biology."

Fenton chuckled. "I don't know how Sally would like being compared to a goat."

"That her name? Sally? Bring her up here sometime," Stan Cameron said. "I promise not to compare her to any goat, but she might like being out here where the air is clear and nice. If she's into climbing, I'll take you both out on Shasta."

"She just hurt her knee, but maybe when it gets better." He found there was a distinct pleasure in thinking about introducing Sally to what remained of his family.

"What does she do?"

"She's in my department. Parapsychology."

The older man shrugged. "Good enough; you understand each other's work and that's a help."

There was a rustle in the leaves. "Raccoon," Stan Cameron said, as Cam Fenton jerked around.

One of the ironfolk, bizarre, scrawny and gnarled, ran directly across the clearing, picked up Stan Cameron's axe, and vanished into the underbrush.

Fenton yelled, wordlessly, and began to run. He found himself crashing through thick underbrush, shouting.

"Hi! Cam! Cam! Come back! What happened?" his uncle shouted, and Cam shook his head, dazed, looking around.

"It took your axe—"

"Don't be silly," the old man said practically. "No raccoon could drag off an axe."

"It wasn't a raccoon."

"What in tunket was it, then?" Stan Cameron demanded, looking around at the foot of the fallen tree. "Good lord, looks like the axe *did* get drug off, at that! Must be raccoon tracks here."

He came back, scowling. "Beats me," he said. "Nothing in these woods big enough to drag off an axe, short of a bear, and bears don't usually drag off nothing but food, maybe. Raccoons, now, they steal everything, goats' food —take the cover right off the feed pail and dive in. I found one there eat enough, he like to bust, laying in the food pail so stuffed he could hardly move. But no raccoon could drag off an axe, and bears don't like the smell of things men have handled . . . Cam, you're white as a sheet! Sit down!" The old man's hands pressed him down on the log. "Look, son, even if a bear did come by, they don't bother you 'less you bother them they're lots more scared of you than you are. He made off, he's gone now."

"It wasn't a bear, Uncle Stan. Nor a raccoon either. I saw it."

"What was it, then?"

"Looked like a—a little man. A dwarf. Short. Gnarled. Hairy." He got up, moving toward the tracks. "Are you going to tell me those are raccoon tracks?"

In spite of all, he had not believed they could leave tracks. That meant they were solid, they were actually on this plane. They had not come on this world as he had come into the world of the Alfar, as a shadow without substance, unable to touch solid material objects. They could cast a shadow, leave tracks, drag off a cold iron axe . . .

He knelt to examine the tracks on the earth: narrow, with sole and long toes, not the paws of any animal.

"No," Stan Cameron said over his shoulder. "They certainly aren't bear tracks, or the tracks of any animal *I* ever saw. I'd almost say they were human, but why in the hell any human would come up here and run around barefoot where there's thornbushes and rattlesnakes and poison oak, maybe—"

"No. Whatever they are, they're not human," Fenton said.

His uncle looked at him sharply. "You sound like you know what they are."

"Yes." Then Fenton looked helplessly at the older man and said, "But you won't believe me."

"Why not? You're not going to lie to me, are you? You've always been truthful before. I guess I'd believe just about anything you wanted to tell me, even if it did sound a little unlikely, unless I thought you were pitching me a yarn for the fun of it. You saw what took my axe?"

"I saw it. I've seen it—I mean them—before. I don't know what to call it. Or them. The only name I ever heard was ironfolk. Maybe it's like sheep, one sheep, lots of sheep, one ironfolk, lots of—hell, I'm babbling."

"You said you saw it, you'd seen it before. Come on, tell me what it was like."

"Small. About three feet, I guess. Hairy. Horrible. They smell bad. I—" Fenton realized he was shaking, that his knees would not hold him up, and he let himself slide down to sit on the log again, his hands shaking.

"To see one of them. *Here.*" It had been bad enough when he knew they couldn't get to him, because he wasn't really there, but was only dreaming, hallucinating. But they were here, they were solid, they could cast shadows, drag off an axe . . . *cold iron* . . . leave tracks.

"I saw—I saw a pack of them, once, slice up a—a horse and eat it, alive. Alive and screaming. Oh, God, I *told* you that you wouldn't believe me . . ."

"I can tell from the way you're shaking that you saw something threw a real scare into you, Cam," said the older man. "I've seen things in these woods, sometimes. Things I couldn't explain. There was a crew of scientists up here one summer hunting for what they called Bigfoot, and a pack of reporters hoorawing them and chasing them around like they were looking for Martians, but I remember folks thought the gorilla was a myth up to two hundred years ago, and they discovered the orangutan in my own lifetime. There could be animals on this planet we don't know anything about. There's one hell of a lot of wild country out in the Sierras."

And if they come and go, if they aren't always even on this dimension . . . but he hesitated to say that to his uncle.

"Listen," said the older man, "I want to have a good look round for that axe. *Something* dragged it off, that's for sure, and it wasn't me, and it wasn't you, and it wasn't a bear—we can start with that much. Let's see if they dropped it anywhere close by. If it's gone, it's gone. I've missed tools before this, but I always figured it was raccoons took the small stuff. Like monkeys, they are. Only I never saw the raccoon could drag off a full-sized axe. Let's follow those tracks a ways, and see what happens."

Fenton was not shaking now, but he felt unwilling to walk into the brushwood, where there might be one of the ironfolk, or more . . .

"Wait," Stan Cameron said. "Let me get my gun. If there is some unknown animal, or humanlike ape, we don't know about hiding in back there, and it's dangerous, I don't want to shoot it, but I don't want to get mauled, either. Better to take it off to some zoo or animal study place, but it would be damn foolishness to walk in on top of it. And you say these things are intelligent enough to use knives."

"They use knives." Fenton's voice was grim.

The older man went back to the house and returned with a rifle and a shotgun. He handed the shotgun to Fenton.

"I don't shoot much," he said. "Load of rocksalt, now and then, to discourage the raccoons when they get too pesky. Once a year I get a deer—about the only meat I ever eat any more, and if you don't shoot out some deer they overgraze and starve winters, since people got so careful about the deer that they shot all the cougars. A bear won't bother you none unless he's sick or scared real bad, but I don't want to walk into one on a rampage either, and a load of buckshot won't hurt him much, but it'll chase him off . . . they don't like loud noises. But if there's something out there I never met, I'm not going to walk up on it empty handed."

Fenton took the shotgun without arguing. He had no intention of walking up on a single ironfolk, much less a tribe of them unarmed.

I wonder if a gun would hurt them any? Yes; they're solid enough to leave tracks . . .

But they followed the tracks for several hours—tracks which finally faded into hard ground and no amount of circling would pick up the trail. Finally, Stan Cameron sighed.

"Well, so much for that," he said, and they started back.

"Do you have a camera, Uncle Stan?"

The man nodded. He said, "I was thinking about that myself. Like to have some kind of proof that we didn't spend the whole day chasing a wild goose."

They took the pictures; but the light was fading, and Fenton realized that these poorly exposed, poorly lighted, blurred tracks were not what anyone in his department would ever think of as scientific validation of the existence of ironfolk on this plane.

Would even Sally believe in them? And suddenly Fenton was angry again. In every other field except this one, a relatively honest witness, or at least a witness with a reputation for truth, was believed honest until proven guilty.

My God, even Freud didn't have to prove the existence of the id, the libido and the superego, he only had to get results . . . some people say he didn't even get results, he just alleged that he got results!

No wonder parapsychologists got sick of the whole thing or gave up and spent the rest of their lives on the lecture circuit instead of in the lab! Suppose Einstein had had to prove the existence of the atomic nucleus? Suppose people who didn't understand his math had been deadset on exposing him as a fraud, and insisted that he made up the math to suit himself and the whole department of mathematics at Princeton had been going along with the hoax for fun?

Inside the shabby kitchen of the mountain cabin, Stan Cameron put on some beans to reheat, moved around making salad, and shoved a panful of biscuits into the oven. Curtly, he refused Fenton's offer to help, saying he knew where everything was, and the kitchen wasn't big enough to have two people getting under each other's feet. He made up a fresh brew of coffee, and asked if his nephew would rather have a beer, "I bought a few bottles when I was in town last time."

Fenton refused, and finally sat down at the table.

"Come and eat, Cam. Here, take a napkin, I don't

like those paper things." He bent his head momentarily and murmured: "Lord, in the name of Him who said, Give us this day our daily bread, bless this food to our use and my life to Thy service, Amen."

Fenton, who was not in any sense religious, wondered briefly if this was one reason why his uncle was somewhat readier to believe in the unseen. A different kind of validation system, perhaps? Different kinds of results than you could get on a laboratory scale?

"Coffee? There's tea if you'd rather have it, Cam."

"Coffee's fine, thanks. These are good beans, Uncle Stan."

"Can your girl make biscuits like these?"

Fenton chuckled. "I don't know; Sally doesn't cook a whole lot." He picked up the unspoken cue; during the meal they would relax and keep off the subject. He told Stan something about Sally—that she was from Fresno, that she had a degree in parapsychology and worked as a teaching assistant, that she was married and divorced and had had a child who died.

"Have you asked her to marry you yet?"

"Not yet. I made a joke about it and she didn't think she was ready to think about it yet."

"They used to say that if a man married again, his first wife made him happy, but if a woman married again, exactly the opposite," Stan said. "It doesn't always go that way. God knows, I was happy enough with your Aunt Louise, but after she died—sorry if the word bothers you, I never could get used to that stupid habit of saying 'passed on' or 'went to her eternal rest.' The dead are dead and their souls are with God and I see no reason not to say dead!"

"Okay by me." He had seen enough dead men in Viet Nam that he had no wish to use euphemisms about the ugliness of the thing. "You do believe in the soul, Uncle Stan?"

"Got no reason not to," said the old man tranquilly. "If it turns out there isn't one, I haven't lost anything, because it's made my life a lot happier, and if death's nothing but eternal silence, I'll never know the difference or have a chance to laugh at myself for being a fool. And if there is one, well, I've got eternity to be glad I didn't listen to the debunkers. Not that I can believe very much in a God who'd send people to hell for not believing in him, with no better proof than he passed out for his existence. I figure you must feel like that sometimes, or you'd be in some line of work where proof was easier and people not so ready to sit back and hooraw you and make bad jokes about it. So maybe some day I'll see Louise again, and that's a pretty good idea. And maybe not, and I can live with that, too. Only I figure you're a lot like me, spending your life not worrying if people believe in what you're doing or not, if it makes sense to *you*."

Fenton drew a long, deep breath. He said, "Uncle Stan, I think I'd like to tell you all about this, if you don't mind. When I came up here, I didn't come to tell you about that, but—"

"Come to think of it, son, you never did tell me what you *did* come for."

"I came to look at a mackinaw jacket. Or maybe at the hole in the pocket of a mackinaw jacket. But now I think I'd like to tell you about the whole thing."

The telling took a considerable time. Stan Cameron did not interrupt, listening quietly as Fenton told the details of his two experiences in the world of the Alfar. But when his nephew moved on to his attempts at validation, he frowned somewhat, and when Fenton told of seeing Pentarn on Telegraph Avenue, he leaned his chin on his hands and stared intently at the pattern on the tablecloth.

At last he said, "When you were a kid, of course— and hear what I've got to say all the way through before you decide I'm on the debunking side, Cam, you've got to listen to all the evidence, not just the part that suits you. When you were a kid, you could have heard about Emma. On the other hand, no reason you should have, and I'm sure you never saw the old album."

Fenton reached with shaking hands for the thick coffee mug. "You mean there is—or was—an Emma Cameron? I mean, there are hundreds of them, I suppose, but—"

"Well, probably not today," Stan Cameron said. "Emma's one of those names you don't hear an awful lot any more, but when my mother was a girl, it was real popular. But here's the thing. My father told me about his favorite cousin—back before the turn of the century, it was, back in the eighteen nineties, so of course round here it was in the horse and buggy days. My father said his favorite cousin was an Emma Cameron, and she was killed, with his aunt and uncle, in a buggy accident when she was six, seven years old. Now I don't think I ever mentioned her to you, just someone my father knew when he was a small boy, and it's for sure Louise never did, because I don't think my Pa ever mentioned her to Louise. But he had his picture taken with her when they were little tykes —my Pa and his cousin Emma, that is. One of those oldtime family portraits, kind where everybody's all stiff and done up like wax, I guess because with the kind of cameras they had then, you had to hold still so long. The old album's still put away somewheres, if I can root it out. I suppose you could have seen it when you were a little kid, somehow."

Fenton could not open his throat to speak. He didn't know whether he was excited by this knowledge that Emma Cameron might have been a real person after all . . . or that it was one more bit of flotsam from the unforgetting subconscious. *Changelings*. But how strange that he had chosen the name of a real person, and described the accident in which she had been killed!

Or, perhaps, not killed but whisked into a world where she could survive her terrible injuries . . .

He said, trying to suppress the tremble of excitement in his voice, "Uncle Stan, will you hunt up that album, right now?"

"Sure. I was figuring to do just that," the older man said. "How's about you clear the dishes off the table?"

Fenton was glad to have something to occupy his hands and his mind while Stan Cameron rooted around in the other rooms, opening old boxes and trunks. He cleared the kitchen, washed dishes, put away the food, made fresh coffee, and finally, shouting a word or two to his uncle, went out to attend to the goats and bed them down for the night. Forking fodder into their pen, a task long familiar from previous visits, rubbing friendly polls that were thrust up against his knees and thighs, scratching a frisky, friendly kid behind the budding horns, he found himself suddenly shivering at the thought of one of the ironfolk let loose among these friendly, trusting animals.

That, after all, settled one of his questions. If an ironfolk was solid enough in this dimension to carry off an axe in broad daylight, it was certainly solid enough to eat a goat. The question was why the ironfolk, who after all were living creatures and not some kind of fairy tale monster bent on evil, should go to the trouble of coming through to other dimensions at all. If the matter could be explained by simple hunger, it did a lot to remove them from the monster-movie horror category and give motive and reason to their actions.

After all, the basic tenet of psychology was that no living thing did anything without some reason. It might not be a reason he would personally think good, or comprehensible, but it would be a reason that made sense to the living thing doing it.

And hunger was, after all, a very basic reason . . . and after the way they had behaved to the Alfar horses, not at all a surprising one. He fastened the hasp on the goat shed with extra care, but realized it would probably not keep out determined ironfolk.

Now he was seeing the bogeymen in the goat shed, of all places!

When he came back inside, his uncle was sitting at the kitchen table, a faded album lying on the oilcloth before him.

"You got the goats all bedded down? Thanks, son."

"It's all right, I like doing it. Uncle Stan, did you ever lose any goats you couldn't account for by natural causes?"

"This close to wild country? Of course," the older man said. "Lose one, two every year. I figured a cougar got them. I'd rather lose a couple that way than move in closer to town." Then his eyes narrowed. "You're thinking about that varmint got my axe? Could be, I suppose. I never examined the bodies all that careful. But that's why I bring them in, nights, and fasten them up in the shed. Some farmers around here, they leave their goats out at night, and sit up shooting cougars and coyotes. I figure the wild animals got a right to eat, too, and if I don't want them eating my goats, it's up to me to keep the goats out of their territory while they're hunting. Only the other farmers, they can't see it that way."

He shoved the faded old album at Fenton, opening it at an early page. "I haven't looked through all this stuff since Louise died. And this one I never paid much attention to. Maybe it ought to go to some museum some day about early California. Here." He pointed a stubby stained finger at one page.

Two families stood stiffly posed, two women in the high-collared shirtwaists and sweeping skirts of that generation, two bewhiskered men . . . one of whom had a strong family likeness to Stanley Cameron and to Cam Fenton himself . . . and in front of them, two small boys, one collared and necktied and looking uncomfortable, the other small and pudgy in a sailor suit and black stockings. Beside them was a tiny, prim girl with light corkscrew curls falling on the collar of her plaid dress . . . Cam Fenton felt his breath go out in a jolt. This was not Irielle as he had seen her, her bright hair loose, singing among the Alfar. But the set of the small chin, the levelled eyebrows . . . yes. This was Irielle.

Stan Cameron pointed to the small boy in the sailor suit. "This was my Pa," he said, "your grandfather. Your mother's Pa, too, of course. The other boy there, that was my Uncle Jerome, he got himself killed in Flanders. Before I was born, just by a year or two, but I heard about it, of course. Mustard gas, that was the atrocity weapon those days; we heard as much about it when I was a kid as you hear now about napalm. Uncle Jerome's buried over in Flanders Fields, the place they sell all the Armistice Day poppies about every year. Every generation comes along, they think *they* invented atrocity warfare. I guess they were saying that when they threw boiling pitch down from castle walls in the Middle Ages. Anyhow, that's Emma, my father's cousin. Her folks were . . . well, never mind, no sense in going into all those family trees. She was killed just one, two months after that picture was taken, along with father's uncle and aunt."

Fenton looked again at the small, daintily prim face, the curly-haired Victorian child in the fading sepia photograph. Irielle. Emma Cameron. Killed in a buggy accident sometime in the eighteen nineties—or whisked into an alien dimension where time was somehow different, and she was still a young girl in her twenties. How old would Emma Cameron be now? Somewhere upward of ninety, if she were still alive at all.

If I brought her into this world, would she do the Lost Horizon *trick, and suddenly turn into an old, old lady, or crumble away to dust?* Uncontrollably; he shuddered.

Stan Cameron was carefully removing the page from the old album and hunting up a used catalogue envelope to wrap it in. "I suppose you'd like to keep this," he said, "and better you should have it than me. No sense in the thing sitting around until somebody throws it out with the trash after I'm dead, and I sure won't want it afterward, whatever happens to me. And anyhow, no reason to be sentimental about a picture of my Pa in a sailor suit when he was six years old. He's your grandfather too, anyhow. You can keep it, Cam. Only I wouldn't expect it to convince anybody, if I were you. People who make up their minds not to believe something are just about as stubborn as the ones who make their minds up to believe it."

Fenton nodded in agreement, but he did take the wrapped envelope and the portrait and put it into his car. He hadn't exactly been intending to shove it under Sally's nose and say, "See, Irielle is a real girl." But it was good to know there had actually been such a person.

But that night, bedded down on a sofa in the living room of the shabby farmhouse, he lay awake, every small rustle and sound magnified, and it seemed that he could hear the steps of prowling ironfolk. If there were any danger that the ironfolk could actually intrude into this dimension, to eat goats and horses—and he didn't suppose they would stop at people, either—he would much, much rather that the whole thing had been a bizarre dream.

Only he didn't suppose there was a choice. Either the ironfolk were real or they weren't, and what he, Cam Fenton, thought about the reality wasn't going to make a damn bit of difference to the ironfolk.

Cam groaned aloud and got up to rummage in his uncle's bathroom for some aspirin. If the ironfolk were real, he might not really have the right to keep quiet about them. He had the duty, then, to warn people of a very real menace—he didn't even like to think about ironfolk loose on the Berkeley campus.

He felt like the flying-saucer contactees, sent back to earth to give what they seemed to believe were warnings about a very real earthly menace.

I can see it now, he thought. Dismissal from the faculty as a serious lunatic was the least he could expect, if he started warning people that they ought to look out for ironfolk in the eucalyptus grove!

CHAPTER NINE

ALL THE WAY BACK to Berkeley on the highway, Fenton accused himself of moral cowardice.

The ironfolk were real. That was the long and short of it. And that being so, he had a duty to warn people.

Warn them of what, for heaven's sake? he demanded of himself indignantly. *That there are hairy little ugly-wugly monsters who could suddenly pop into existence out of nowhere, and haul you off to be sliced up and eaten alive? They wouldn't believe me anyhow! All that would happen is that I would be hauled off, very promptly, to the closest ninny-bin, there to live on tranquilizers forever after, and it wouldn't do the Department of Parapsychology any good, either.*

In the end he said nothing at all, but he discovered that whenever he walked across the campus, he was casting wary looks over his shoulder at the eucalyptus trees. He haunted Telegraph Avenue, trying to catch a glance of the small shop where he had seen the Rackham prints, and made a nuisance of himself in bookstores, asking if they had had any Rackham prints in their window on the day in question; but if they had, no sales clerk in any of the stores could remember it, or would admit it—and when Cam reached this point in his thoughts he began to understand why parapsychology was considered a direct road to paranoia.

Maybe I ought to get out of the field. Maybe I'm cracking up.

Is this why they get so hung up on proof, to prove to themselves that they can live with the knowledge of something which doesn't fit into ordinary currently-believed scientific principles?

It was one thing to believe that all parapsychological

phenomena had to conform to natural laws—natural laws still unknown, but still natural laws. After all, anything which actually occurred, any phenomenon, must by the very fact of that occurrence be possible.

But suppose the laws by which it occurred were so unknown that by their very knowledge, once accepted, they would make hash of the whole body of scientific knowledge, so-called, and expose the blunt fact that humans knew no more about the universe in which they lived, than the rat in his laboratory cage knows about theoretical psychology?

Is it any wonder the whole scientific establishment is determined that not even ten times the evidence would convince them to believe?

Fenton came to the conclusion that whether it was true or whether it wasn't, he was damned scared, and that was the long and short of it.

He knew afterward that if the uncertainty had gone on even a few days more, he would have cracked beneath it. One night he found himself taking out the bootleg Antaril he had bought from the shaven hippie and looking at it for a long time, wondering if swallowing it would resolve his doubts once and for all—or would it simply renew them? Finally he wrapped the stuff in an envelope again and put it away, fighting a conviction that he ought to flush it down the toilet and forget about it.

By enormous effort he said nothing to Sally about what had happened to him in the Sierras. He did not feel equal to the task of convincing her. It made their relations strained, and at one point he considered breaking off with her. But she was already embittered, distrusting men; it occurred to Cam that if, without explanation, he simply withdrew from her life, the effect on her would be disastrous; and if he tried to give an explanation, the effect would be the very thing he wanted to avoid, another long wrangle about how badly the Antaril experiment had affected his mind. So he took her to the San Francisco Zoo and to several of the noon concerts of music in Hertz Hall, and to dinner at one of his favorite Japanese restaurants, and one night when she was asleep after they had made love, he seriously considered sneaking her keys off the ring and sneaking out to an all-night key place and having them duplicated; he knew that sooner or later he had to get a look at her files.

Finally, hating himself, he slid the drawer open quietly and took out the file that said *M.C. Fenton*. He glanced swiftly inside; there was a typewritten, bald, objective account of his description of the Alfar and his trip through the caves of the ironfolk. He did not look at the handwritten notes she had made in the margin. *Yeah,* he thought sourly, *real ethical, aren't you?* But at the first mention of Pentarn, she had made two notes. The first was simple:

Archetype villain, devil figure? collective unconscious?

And the second was: *Ref Amy Brittman for PENTARN.*

He started to rummage through the files for mention of any Amy Brittman, then stopped in a cold sweat. He could not, he *would* not, do this. He slid the drawer shut and went back and slipped into bed beside the sleeping Sally, holding her remorsefully tight.

Sally, Sally, how can I make it up to you? I'm a louse.

But even from himself he could not disguise that he was turning the name Amy Brittman over and over in his mind. He knew he had heard it somewhere. And Sally had said: *Oh, you got Pentarn too.*

Was Amy Brittman one of those who had turned up, on Antaril, to have keyed into the collective unconscious and discovered that it threw out the name of Pentarn?

The next day a visit to Sproul Hall, where names and addresses of students were filed, turned up the information that Amy Brittman was a first-year student, majoring in educational psychology and volunteering for occasional experiments in parapsychology. The address given for Amy Brittman was one of the campus residence halls, but a telephone call there informed him that Miss Brittman had moved out three weeks ago and left no address.

He went far enough to check the records of students involved in the research projects of the department. But the department records said only that Miss Brittman had, freshman-like, failed to notify the department of any change of address; she was still listed as living in her residence hall. Fenton thought fretfully that there might be some merit in the customs of dorms in his own student days, where woman students were required to check in and out at certain hours, as if sin and sex could occur only after eleven at night, and were not allowed to change their address without notice. He recognized that as irrational, and laughed at himself, but still wondered how he could locate the missing Amy Brittman and ask her what she knew about Pentarn.

Then on Wednesday night, Garnock called.

"Cam, I know this is short notice, but we're trying to get the Antaril project back on schedule. Can you be here at eleven tomorrow morning?"

This, Fenton thought with detachment, is what Sally was talking about when she said I ought to withdraw from the project; it's getting too important to me. He noted with clinical awareness that his pulse was racing and that there was an odd sick emptiness in the pit of his stomach. But he said into the phone, quite calmly, "Sure thing, Doc. I'll see you then."

He turned up a little before eleven, and while he was rolling up his sleeve and getting ready for the shot of the drug, he said to Garnock, "You said that some of the participants reported vivid dreams and hallucinations. Did anyone describe them more fully than that?"

Garnock shrugged. "People always like to tell their dreams. I never pay any attention."

Garnock checked his wrist as he applied the ligature. "Have you had the flu, Cam? Your pulse is a little high."

Fenton said, "No, it's missed me. I'm fine. Nervous, maybe."

"It's within normal limits anyhow," Garnock said, readying the shot. "Try to hang on to yourself long enough, this time, to do three perfect runs for me, will you? We have the information that you can do it, but you lose control of yourself a little too fast to be a really good subject."

Fenton realized, despite Garnock's enthusiasm, that he had lost interest in perfect runs of cards. The implications were fascinating, of course. But the further implications, that Antaril acted as a Gateway giving access to other dimensions and alien realities—this, to him, was now the main focus of the experiment, and the way in which it made hash of all their previous suppositions about the structure of the physical universe.

And Garnock wasn't even interested in that side of the experiment!

He felt the brief blast of the spray hypo, and waited for the effects to begin.

"Ready to start calling this run, Cam?"

"Okay," he said, leaving his body behind on the table and walking around the screen to inspect Marjie's layout of cards. "Cross. Wavy line. Cross. Circle. Square. Wavy line . . ."

He managed to complete three perfect runs and to get halfway through a fourth before he felt himself beginning to sink through the floor of the lab, and knew he must get outside. Probably, in this state, a fall through the floor wouldn't hurt him, but he wasn't interested in finding out. He had wondered, sometimes, about those old stories of ghosts and so forth, walking through walls, and wondered why they didn't fall through the floor, too.

By the time he got outside, the campus was almost completely faded, and he could not see any familiar landmark. He had to wander in circles a long time to find the white and feathery circle of strange trees which, in the world of the campus, was a grove of eucalyptus trees. He did not understand the strange telescoping of space and time which had on his first trip landed him somewhere in the Sierras, and now seemed to locate him in the area of the campus eucalyptus grove. He supposed it was subject to some kind of natural law . . . *everything* was subject to some kind of natural law. But he didn't understand the laws at all.

He finally found the grove of feathery trees, but the landscape was strange and shifting, and it was already growing dark. He did not feel as if he had been there long enough for that—it had been eleven in the morning when he left the campus, and he had certainly not spent more than one or two hours of subjective time hunting for the eucalyptus grove—but it was growing dark, and the moon was rising, white and cold and full, above the trees, a dazzling light. Cam could see clearly by its light, clearly enough to keep from stumbling over rocks and logs and thornbushes, but he could not see clearly enough to hunt for roads or find the pathway he had taken from the strange palacelike tree-structure where Kerridis had held court.

He found himself wondering what Kerridis' court would look like if he had substance in this world . . .

He thought, once, that he had found the path; but almost as he stepped into it, it seemed to close, perversely, and be nothing but a clump of thornbushes, from which he had painfully to extricate himself; natural objects like thornbushes were real to him, even if man-made objects in his own world weren't. With a chill, he thought that he could now be walking around on the new freeway, with the traffic passing over and through him.

And suppose I materialize back there. . . .

No. He clung to the knowledge that his body was safe in Smythe Hall, no matter where he might find this shadow of himself, his 'tweenman's body, returning to his own world.

He began to hunt again for a path. Damn it, there *must* be roads here. Irielle said this was a frequented and known area; she referred to it as a good spot in her world too. But at any point where he left the circle of trees, there were tight thornbushes, through which he could not walk, and any gap in the bushes closed as he tried to approach it.

He remembered, against his will, something one of the guards of the Alfar had said last time—something about having the roads spelled against strangers. Perhaps Findhal, having discovered an ironman in this refuge of their people, had closed off this place and created some illusion for those who arrived in it from other worlds. Considering the way the little print-shop had spun itself on some invisible axis and disappeared, taking Pentarn with it, how could he say that anything was impossible?

If he had substance in this world, he could force himself through the trees. Or, if the thornbushes were illusions, he could somehow get past them . . .

Then he heard a sound that made his blood ice over; the strange gobbling speech of the ironfolk, somewhere outside the circle of the white feathery trees.

He remembered with shock what Irielle had said; there had been a time when they could only come through when the moon and sun were right. From time immemorial, in folklore, strange things had happened under a full moon. Perhaps the time spoken of, considering the fact that time ran differently in the different universes, meant that when the moon was full in both worlds, the worlds could overlap ... but of course full moons were not synchronized.

That doesn't make sense! If it's the same earth, the orbits of earth and moon would be the same ...

But time may pass differently, or be experienced differently, in the different worlds ...

Fenton admitted that he didn't understand it. But it was happening and he could theorize about it later. He dived into a thornbush, just as a small party of ironfolk—maybe four or five—came trotting into the circle.

By moonlight, he decided, they were even more repulsive.

They went round the circle, and Fenton realized that they had been trapped, like him, in the spell of the white trees and thornbushes. One after another would dive toward an apparently opening path and find himself caught, held and torn on the thorns. He couldn't understand all they said, but he knew they were swearing horribly in their clucking, gobbling language. And slowly, by the curious rules of this world—was telepathy one of the ESP powers brought on by Antaril or was it something else? —he began to understand them as he had understood the Alfar.

"Curses!" said one, who carried a cruel hook-edged weapon. "They've put spells on it! Damn these thorns! Even my hide can't stand up against them! It will take us half the night to find the counterspell!"

"Patience," another said, a big crude-looking one with a broken fang. "The moon will be high for a long time yet, and once we get through to Kerridis' palace—" He licked his hairy chops suggestively.

"Yes, and there will be yrillswords waiting for us," the first speaker said dismally. "But it's what Pentarn wanted when he brought us through; we're to keep Kerridis and all of them busy while he finds the place where the changelings are lodged ..."

"We're just doing *his* dirty work," Broken Fang said morosely, untangling himself from a thorn which had torn his scanty skin garment, but a third one shrugged. He carried a hatchet which might have come from any hardware store and made Cam think of the axe carried off from his uncle's farm. Evidently they picked up their iron tools ready-made wherever they could find them.

"I'll do Pentarn's dirty work or anyone else's, for a chance at a good meal, and perhaps a chance at one of the changeling women," he said. "The Alfar women are no fun. Who wants a woman who crisps up and blackens when you touch her? But the changelings are something else, and maybe when Pentarn's finished with the one he wants, he'll turn us loose on the rest of them. He'll owe us something, if he gets that brat back!"

Fenton, lying hidden in his hiding place among the thorns, shuddered at the thought of the ironfolk turned loose among the changelings—Irielle was among them.

"Not fair, anyhow," Broken Fang grimaced. "Pentarn's the cause of all our troubles anyhow. Used to be, we could come in at full moon and if we'd calculated the time right the Alfar would be dancing in the moonlight and we could grab their horses and run without any trouble. Only now, every time the full moon shines they manage to keep their main entry Gates spelled against us, and it all happened when Pentarn turned against them. I think we did better without his help."

"Oh, I don't know—he brought us here tonight, and I'm going to enjoy myself—providing I can ever get free of these accursed thorns!" The one with the hatchet wiped streaming blood from a gnarled arm. He swung the hatchet at the thornbush.

"There, curse them, not even their bushes enjoy cold iron, and their spells can't hold against it," Broken Fang said. "Go all round the circle with our knives. It will take time, but we should have thought of it before instead of trying to shove through the thorns. Let's get started here; Pentarn wants us there when the Red Star rises so we can divert them while he gets through to the changelings, and this is going to take some time."

One after another the ironfolk started to travel methodically round the circle, muttering, and Fenton, lying hidden, iced over.

I've got to warn the Alfar, he thought. Warn them that

they've broken through the spell of the circle with cold iron . . .

Natural objects were solid to him in this world. He could not pass through their rocks; he could be caught and held by their thorns. Still, as a 'tweenman, without substance in this world, he had some small advantage over the ironfolk, all of whom were now bleeding from vicious scratches. Fenton had only to disentangle himself carefully—and quietly, lest they hear the rustling of his struggle against the thorns—and then he was outside the circle of the spell, and running down the path which magically appeared before him.

And then, as if he moved with the swiftness of thought, he could see the darkening gap, the illusion of tall pillars and spires, the castle of the Alfar, and the tall Alfar guards pacing at the entrance. He rushed up against one of them in his eagerness and the Alfar guard, vrillsword in hand, turned on him.

"Stars and comets! It's that 'tweenman, the one Findhal said wasn't to be trusted," one of them said.

"Look, man, don't worry about me," Fenton said. "There are ironfolk in the—in the spelled circle, breaking the spell with cold iron! There are five of them, I think, and I heard them talking—"

"Here, here, slow down," said the Alfar guard, "You'll tell your story to Findhal; I'm not taking the word of any spy from Pentarn's world. And meanwhile—" He glanced at his companion and shook his head.

"You can't imprison a 'tweenman; he can just walk out between your bars. Here, you," he said, gesturing with the vrillsword. "Make one suspicious move and we'll run you through. Can't trust anybody when the moon's full, and Findhal says tonight it's full in at least four of the worlds. Make one false move and you'll find yourself dead in all four of them!"

He forced Fenton along ahead of them. The other guard said, "I think we should run him through anyhow. He looks too much like Pentarn to suit my taste."

"Oh, all people from the changelings' world look alike to me," the first Alfar said. "I suppose they have good ones and bad ones just like everywhere else. The changelings are pretty decent, and if they were all evil in that world, the changelings wouldn't grow up to be decent folk. And they do. Here, you—" He prodded Fenton with the tip of the vrillsword. "In here."

The Alfar shouted in his high, ringing voice. After a moment Findhal came out and stared at Fenton without enthusiasm.

"You," he said. "How did you get through the spelled circle? I thought we had managed it to keep you out at least, though Lebbrin warned me it was killing dragonflies with dragonswords."

"And it's a good thing you did," Fenton said, "because while you were keeping me out you also trapped four, or maybe it was five, ironfolk; they're still there, if they haven't broken through the circle. I heard them talking; they're supposed to keep you people busy while Pentarn's crew come after the changelings."

"Fire and deviltry!" Findhal said. Although in Fenton's world the words were harmless, he knew that Findhal was swearing horribly. "You're trying to tell me they could get through that circle! You did this," he accused. "You brought them through; that used to be one of the places where the ironfolk could not come, and I never saw one there until the day you led one to Irielle in that circle!"

"Don't trust me, then, damn it," Fenton said, outraged. "I don't know why I bother to warn you people at all! Let them come through, what the hell do I care? But you'd better get Irielle to a place where she's safe or they'll be going after her. They were saying nasty things about what they liked to do to changeling women!"

The tall Alfar paled. "True. I have no time to waste on 'tweenmen, but if you should get out to take a message to Pentarn—"

"As a matter of curiosity," Fenton said, "how are you going to hold me? I can walk right through even the ironfolk's bars."

"You won't go through the Rockhold," Findhal said, and gestured to the Alfar guards.

"Take him to the Rockhold; I must go to Kerridis with this, and I must be sure Irielle is in a place of safety," he said and hurried off.

The Alfar gestured with his vrillsword. Fenton began to be afraid.

"In here." It was a cave, and Fenton shuddered, thinking of the caves of the ironfolk. An Alfar guard gestured him into something like a cell, a natural niche in the living rock. The door was glowing faintly green.

"You will not escape from Rockhold," the Alfar guard said. "It is reinforced with vrill and with our strongest spells."

Left alone there, Fenton discovered that indeed the rock barriers were solid to him. He was well and truly imprisoned, shadow that he was.

And suppose he should materialize again into his own world . . . and find himself somewhere below ground, in the solid rock or earth? Sooner or later, when the drug wore off, if his shadow-self was imprisoned here and he could not return to his body—what would happen to his body, conscious but without the element of personality that made that body Cam Fenton? He shuddered. He didn't even like to think about that. He had, in his work in psychology, seen mental patients who were completely in a vacuum, without any indwelling awareness of being human.

He might soon be one of them. . . .

He made a few futile efforts to get through the vrill-strengthened wooden door but only managed to bruise himself badly. He had grown so accustomed in this state to walking straight through the walls in Smythe Hall or even the ironfolk's bars that he simply could not believe they had imprisoned him.

Rockhold. Clever. They must have had occasion to deal with 'tweenmen before—and that somehow made him shudder worse than ever.

He examined the walls and bars of Rockhold as much as he could. Then, angry and bored, he sat down to wait. There was nothing else he could do. But he was angry, with a growing anger. He had worked so hard to get back here, and what happened was that he found himself in the local equivalent of the slammer!

He thought, almost triumphantly that at least this validated the reality of the experience. By the very nature of the brain-activity called dreaming, it did not generate inactivity and boredom; on the contrary, it led to vivid action, if only in neural synapses.

But he could hear what Sally would say if he adduced this as an argument for the reality of what was happening to him. "As a trained pyschologist," he parroted the appropriate psychological cliché, "surely you must know that your mind is simply reacting to your own anxiety about the state of hallucination; therefore you postulate a dream of imprisonment as a way of expressing that you feel trapped." Talk about circular reasoning!

And that, Fenton thought, was probably why he had left the field of psychotherapy and the psychology of the unconscious. Whatever happened, it had to be twisted to fit theories about the unconscious mind and the ego. Twisting facts to fit theories wasn't even as scientific as parapsychology, which at least made some attempt to validate its fantastic hypotheses.

Yet Sally accused *him* of not being sufficiently scientific!

He reminded himself that all this was pointless. There was no sense in anger at Sally; if he was going to be angry, he might as well save his anger for Findhal, or for the ironfolk.

A soft voice said behind him, "Stranger 'tweeman—" Fenton jumped to his feet. Kerridis stood outside the Rockhold, wrapped in her pale cloak.

"My lady Kerridis—"

"Indeed, indeed, I am sorry for your imprisonment," she said. "Believe me, I have made my anger known to Findhal; but he had no time to explain what he has done. I do not believe it is you who have led the ironfolk to us."

"Hell no," Fenton exploded. "If I were going to do that, would I tear myself all up on your confounded thorns to get out of the circle ahead of the ironfolk and come and warn you people?"

"You told me you know nothing of Pentarn," Kerridis said, "and it is true that you have done us nothing but good; this is not worthy of Findhal, and I hope a day will come when he will know that he has done you an injustice."

Cam Fenton said bitterly, "I should live so long!"

"You must not blame Findhal," Kerridis admonished, stretching out her long slender hand to him, and he was struck again with the delicacy of it. Not really a woman, not even really human, still there was that faint and indefinable resemblance to Sally.

Kerridis said, "Findhal, too, once trusted Pentarn, and he blames himself for the tragedies that trust brought upon us."

"But Irielle is a grown woman, isn't she? Can you let her decide for herself? Will you let me go to her?"

Kerridis' smile clouded. "For myself, I would be tempted to do so," she said. "But I also owe Findhal loyalty, and I do not want to anger him this way, either. I do owe you a service, 'tweenman, and even if Findhal should be right, you cannot hurt me here."

"I wouldn't anyway," he said and that made Kerridis smile at him, the smile which reminded him of Sally at her best, when she was neither angry nor suspicious, when she had relaxed the fierce guard she kept on her emotions, that smile he could never see without wanting to see it again.

"It is true I owe you a service," she said, "and it is true that Irielle has come to years of discretion; I am her mistress, but she is my friend and foster-daughter, not my slave; otherwise all Pentarn's evil tales of us are justified. I will let Irielle make her own choice. I will send her to you, 'tweenman." Kerridis hesitated. "Tell me, 'tweenman. Are you in love with Irielle? Do you mean to win her away from us?"

"I don't know," Fenton said honestly. "I have reason to think she may be a—a—a young relative of mine." Young relative? He thought, with absurd hilarity, that she was, if the picture Stan Cameron had showed him were accurate, his grandfather's cousin. He said to Kerridis, "I don't know what you know about time, but it seems to pass differently here then elsewhere. Irielle is still young, here; but time has gone on and our world has changed greatly. If she were to return to our world—would it be safe, would she suddenly become an old, old woman, would she—" His throat locked. "She wouldn't—wouldn't die or crumble into dust or anything, would she?"

Kerridis said quickly, "No, no! It is true we do not age as other people, but once grown to manhood or woman-

hood, stay much the same till we die; and we are longer-
lived than your folk. Irielle has been much the same
since she outgrew her childhood; but if she changed
worlds she would simply begin to age again at their
rate of aging. That is all. Change and decay are terrible to
us, and I would not be happy to see their hand on Irielle's lovely face, but that is for her to say. If her world
has changed so greatly, and many that she knew are
dead, such a return might be more sorrow than she could
bear. She could die of grief . . . but again, that is between the two of you. She is not our slave, and she is kept
here from love, not necessity."

"I believe you."

Kerridis said gently, "And I believe you. If you wished
us ill, you could not be so concerned for Irielle. Would
that Pentarn had believed us when we told him this.
No—" She held up her slender hand. "That is a long
story, and very sad to the hearing. I will not tell you
now."

"Will you let me out of this damnable place?"

"I cannot," she said. "Findhal won a promise from me
that I would not, and I never break my word. But Irielle
is under no such promise; I will send Irielle to you."

CHAPTER TEN

WHEN KERRIDIS HAD GONE, Fenton sat down, with what patience he could manage, inside the Rockhold, and waited for Irielle. He wondered if the guards outside, who after all were Findhal's men and might think themselves bound to obey his orders even over those of Kerridis, would let her in when she came.

Which in turn caused him to speculate about this world in which he found himself. He had seen only the merest surface of the world of the Alfar. He was intrigued and fascinated by that surface—but what was it really like? What did the Alfar do with themselves when they were not fighting off ironfolk—assuming that it was not a full-time occupation?

Then he wondered what would happen if it should be proven that all these interlocking worlds he heard about from Irielle were real—not subjective, but objective. Not only would it change the nature of his own world beyond recall, demanding acceptance of things long believed to be superstition or worse, but it would immediately demand the reforming of all sciences and branches of knowledge. Not only that, he thought with a touch of humor, but it would open up a whole new world—literally, *many* new worlds—for the sociologists and specialists in alien cultures. Not to mention what it might do to the field of psychology.

Fenton stopped short at trying to consider the international implications of this. He would have to leave that to the politicians. But considering how much trouble the Alfar were having, trying to guard their Gates against ironfolk, the political repercussions would be substantial. Imagine the military might of the nation, protecting itself not only against enemies on this planet, but against a multitude of alien worlds which might offer some danger? He thought, rather wryly, that he could predict the reaction of some congressmen—to ask for larger military spending! He didn't even want to think about the probable increase in the departments of military intelligence and spying!

Fenton was aware that he was thirsty and beginning to feel some hunger. Of course, since time apparently moved at a different rate in the world of the Alfar, he had no way of knowing how much time had elapsed in his own world. He assumed—since subjectively in the world of the Alfar it could not have been more than three or four hours—that what he felt now was a repercussion from his semiconscious body in Smythe Hall that it was getting near dinnertime. But the thought troubled and frightened him. Suppose he should materialize inside solid rock? Even the Alfar had admitted that was dangerous for a 'tweenman, which is what he seemed to be in this world.

Time passed. At last he heard a small sound of bells outside the Rockhold, and raised his head to see Irielle standing just outside the bars.

"Fenton," she said, with a shy smile. "I am happy to see that you have come back, and I apologize for my foster-father. He does not know you as well as I do, and a time will come when he is ashamed of what he has done to you. But we must not wait for that. Are you beginning to fade? If so, we must get you outside, at once!"

"I don't think I'm fading yet," Fenton said. "I haven't noticed it."

"Well, we must watch you carefully. How long have you been here?"

"I haven't the least idea."

"However it may be, we must get you above ground at once," she said, unfastening the bars. One of the tall Alfar guards saw what she was doing and came over to her in dismay.

"Lady Irielle, your father gave orders—"

"But I have direct orders from the Lady," she said, and showed the Alfar something in her hand. "Kerridis sent me here; complain to her, if you wish."

Grumbling, the guard withdrew. Irielle finished whatever she was doing with the fastenings of the vrill-

reinforced bars of the Rockhold, and Fenton stepped out.
He found that he was cramped, with shooting pains in
his legs that made him stumble. This surprised and distressed him; he thought, *this simply doesn't make sense,
my body isn't really here at all; how can I be cramped?
My body is immobile in Smythe Hall. . . .*

He bent to rub the pains from his legs; Irielle looked
at him in sympathy.

"You are not very warmly dressed for this world," she
said. "Are you cold?"

"Cramped, rather."

"The best remedy for that is to move about," Irielle
said. "Come."

She stretched her hand to him; limping a little from
his long confinement, he followed her, out through the
armory of the Alfar and through a series of long corridors
into the open air.

It was very dark now, and the moon soared, brilliant
and white and cold, larger than any moon he could remember seeing in his own world, above the alien tree-
tops.

With an effort, he managed to summon up the clear
picture of Uncle Stan's mackinaw jacket—the one with
the mended hole in the pocket—and found that it was
about his shoulders. As he subsided gratefully into its
warmth, he wondered what would have happened if Stan
Cameron were actually wearing this jacket in the other
world, the real world—no, he wouldn't say that—in the
world he had come from?

*Nothing, probably. Because this is only an imagi-
nary analogue, a thought-form if you will, of the real
jacket . . .*

If I can be in two places at once, why can't my Uncle
Stan's plaid mackinaw jacket?

"Come," Irielle said, pulling on his hand. "Only one
place is safe for you now; among the changelings. We
have separate quarters, where fires are kept, because we
feel the cold more than the Alfar, and you will be more
comfortable there."

Fenton said, as they moved through the trees, "I
thought that was where Pentarn was heading with his
ironfolk."

"But now that we are warned," Irielle said, "my foster-father will be at the circle, to deal with the iron-folk. And there are enough of the changelings willing to defend themselves, even against ironfolk. I have no wish to be captured by them." She shuddered and held out her hand; Fenton quickly clasped it. She seemed like a child, curiously in need of comfort. He wondered if it were the strange life of the Alfar which had made her so young and vulnerable; a girl even of her apparent age usually seemed older than Irielle. Yet what among the Alfar would give her the kind of thing usually thought of as wordly wisdom, sophistication?

And how old was she really? He found that he was shuddering too.

"Are you still cold? I am afraid to take you underground again, lest you should fade there," Irielle said. "But I have something for you which may ease it a little." Around the belt of the warm woolen dress she was wearing, a couple of little bags were tied, like the kind Anachronists wore with their medieval outfits. Suddenly it occurred to Cam that this was, actually, the origin of *pockets.* She rummaged in them, frowning, and finally brought out something solid, wrapped in a thin square of the silky material which the Alfar wore.

"Spidersilk is pretty," she said, "but I will not wear it, for it does not keep out the cold, although Findhal could dress me in nothing else if I wished for it; it is rare and hard to come by, but my foster-father denies me nothing. But I have this for you; I begged it from— from one of the other changelings." Carefully she unwrapped the piece of what she called spidersilk.

Fenton drew his breath in an audible gasp as he saw it, for what Irielle held in her hand was gold; glittering, exquisitely carven with symbols.

"Take it," she urged. "It is a talisman for the Gateways."

"But Irielle, how can I take this? This is a precious thing—priceless—" he said, but she only looked at him without understanding.

"I do not know if you can take it into your world," she said. "I do not know much of the laws under which 'tweenmen live. If you were a worldwalker, you could take it with you into any world, and when you were carrying it, it would move between worlds with you, for it is different in every world. But I do not know if, when you fade in this world, it will go to your own with you. But you can try to take it, at least."

Fenton pursed his lips, trying to imagine Garnock's face if he turned up back in the lab carrying this thing. That, at least, would be proof of the reality of the world of the Alfar. Irielle put it into his hand. It felt comfortingly solid, hard as nothing except the vrillswords or the rock had felt to him.

"I do not go into the sunworlds much any more, not since I was grown," Irielle said. "Though I like thinking that I can, if I must; I am not imprisoned here. This is what Pentarn cannot understand—" She led the way toward one of those strange and sketchy dwellings which gave, from the arrangement of the trees, the appearance of pillars and a door; and when they had passed among the trees Fenton realized that it was really a door. The walls seemed somewhat insubstantial to Fenton—he had no idea what they were made of, or if they were really there at all, but he felt a little less cold. Still he bent to rub the cramps from his legs; they had now been joined by stabbing pains in his arms, and he rubbed and rubbed at them, painfully. This was new; this had not happened on any of his previous visits to the Alfar! For a moment the pain was so agonizing that he had to stoop and rub at his legs; the pain was like knives thrusting into him. Rationally he knew that this was only a resonance, a repercussion, of the cramping of his body where it lay in Smythe Hall, and he knew that he should begin to think about returning. He was tortured by thirst.

But I don't want to go back, who knows when I would get here again? I don't even know if I can take Irielle's talisman with me—what do they say about fairy gold, that it wilts away to a handful of dead leaves by the light of our sun?

Irielle was watching him with sympathy. "You are in pain?"

With difficulty Fenton managed to master his limbs. "It's all right," he said, and stood up. "Only I'm thirsty. Is there anything to drink here?" Water, he was thinking, would be the same in all worlds, being a natural object like rock . . .

"What have you there, Irielle?" A woman's voice laughed. "Have you taken to bringing in changelings for your lovers, when the moon is right?"

Irielle laughed. "Ah, no," she said. "This is a 'tween-man who risked the spelled circle to bring us warnings that Pentarn had sent ironfolk there. Fenton, this is Cecily, my friend and foster-sister."

Cecily was blonde, round and rosy, wearing much the same sort of rust-colored woolen dress as Irielle—he began wondering if the Alfar were partially colorblind; they seemed to use so few colors in their clothing. He would like to ask Irielle about that.

There were so many things he wanted to ask Irielle and he wondered if he would ever have enough time. He was sweating with the pains, which had returned full force, and Irielle looked at him with sympathy.

"Bring him a drink, Cecily. I do not want to leave him. . . . Has there been trouble here?"

Cecily went and returned with a goblet, handing it to Fenton. Irielle said as he took it, "Remember, Fenton, it will not truly quench your thirst, for your body is not here; but perhaps it will give the illusion of doing so."

Fenton nodded, took the cup and drank. The liquid was cool and refreshing, balm to his parched throat. When he had drunk it, somehow, although in a part of his mind he knew the thirst was still there, he felt wonderfully refreshed.

Is this why the fairy worlds are so dangerous? Because the food and drink in an alien world do not truly nourish or refresh and the one who tries to live on them pines away and wastes away . . .

Well, at least it made him feel less thirsty for the moment.

Cecily said, "There are guards everywhere; Findhal and Lebbrin came themselves, to warn us not to stir outside here. Findhal was looking for you, Irielle, and was wonderfully angry when he did not find you!" She laughed. "I did not want him to come and vent his anger on you, so I told him you had gone into one of the sunworlds to look for spidersilk for Kerridis . . . Was that wrong?"

"Not wrong," Irielle said. "But perhaps ill-advised; he will worry about me there. Yet it is something I have done before and will do again. She says no one else is so quick to recognize it in the sunworld."

Fenton asked, remembering the shiny square of spidersilk in which Irielle had wrapped the talisman, "What does it look like in the sunworld?"

Irielle wrinkled her face in distaste. "Grey and ugly," she said, "and it tears almost at a breath; but when you bring it back into this world, it is strong and tough and very beautiful. In one of the sunworlds it is everywhere in woods and dark caves, and ugly."

Cobweb. Of course, it would look different in this world . . .

What the hell is reality anyhow?

But Irielle had turned back to Cecily. She asked, "What did Joe Tarnsson do when the word came?"

"What could he do?" Cecily demanded. "He took a vrillsword and vowed he would rush off to defend his foster-father and the Alfar, if he died for it; it was all Lebbrin could do to restrain him, saying he could not live with the guilt if he shed kinsmen's blood. So now he is sulking, under guard in the changelings' quarters . . ."

"Ah, that is so like him," Irielle said softly. "I wish I had been here to see."

"So do I," Cecily said, "for none of us could make him see reason."

Abruptly there was a commotion outside, what sounded like a clashing of swords, cries, the sound of fighting. Irielle cried out in dismay, and suddenly the door swung wide and Pentarn stepped into the room.

He still wore a green cloak, but a half visor was lowered over his face; Fenton knew him by the characteristic height, carriage, the flaming red beard. He was unarmed, except for a small vrill dagger in his hands.

To Fenton's amazement, Pentarn ignored the women, and spoke directly to him.

"Lurking here among the women? I might have expected that," he said in a tone of contempt. "Make haste now and we can get away without more fighting, if that is what you really want. The guards do not know I am here; they are busy with the ironfolk. I care nothing what happens to the Alfar, but these women are human, and even if they are the depraved slaves of the Alfar, you do not, I suppose, want to see them ravaged by the dark people. Come with me at once, and I will not let them be hurt."

Irielle laughed, a merry, contemptuous laugh. "Look again, Pentarn!" she mocked.

The tall man started and put the visor back from his face, and in that moment Cameron Fenton received a shock.

Pentarn was long-haired and bearded. But otherwise it was like looking into a mirror; Pentarn's face was his own. And now Fenton could see the reason for the distrust the Alfar had shown him.

"Fire and death!" Pentarn swore. "Who are you?" He turned fiercely on the women. "Is this some shape-changing sorcery? Where is he?"

Cecily said, "He is where you cannot come at him, Pentarn—by his own desire!"

"You lie!"

Cecily said angrily, "I lie, then, to spare your feelings, Pentarn, false friend, though I really do not know why I should! What he really wished was to take sword and defend the Alfar against your own vicious kind, those *things* you have let loose on us—"

"Shut your lying mouth!" Pentarn raised his gauntleted hand and struck Cecily a blow that sent her reeling; she fell, stunned, and Irielle rushed to her defense, kneeling on the floor beside her friend.

Fenton rushed at him. "Where I come from, we don't hit women, you bastard," he shouted, and received a blow from the edge of the vrill dagger that sent him, too, reeling, as Pentarn, with a savage movement that sent the green cloak spinning out like smoke, leaped at Irielle.

"Changeling for changeling!" he shouted. "If I have *you*, Irielle, Findhal must give me what I want!" He grasped Irielle in his arms; Fenton reached out and tore at him.

"Do you think any 'tweenman can hold me—*shadow?*"

Pentarn taunted, manhandling Irielle to her feet. She was fighting between his hands like a cat; the worldwalker was solid to her, while Fenton could not get a solid grip on the man. But his determined rush made Pentarn step back. Irielle clawed viciously at the unvisored face, and he let her go for a moment, wiping blood from his cheeks.

Cecily shrieked; and suddenly the door burst open and two Alfar guards rushed in. They flew at Pentarn, vrill-swords out; the man drew back quickly, let Irielle go, and spun. He glimmered a moment in the light and at that moment Fenton shouted, "No, damn it, you're not going to do that trick again! This time, wherever you're going, I'm going with you!"

He felt Pentarn's form evaporate under his hands, felt a moment of thick reeling darkness that enfolded them; then there was a curious little snap, his feet hit solid ground, and he was standing in the center of Sproul Plaza, his arms still clutching at Pentarn. Again the world reeled and pivoted, the sky blazed dark and light, and suddenly Fenton was standing beside Pentarn in a flagged courtyard, a dark and lowering storm-cloud sky overhead, the sky lit with the glare of lightning. There was no sign of the Alfar, or of Irielle or Cecily.

Pentarn lifted his eyebrows and surveyed Fenton with an ironical glare.

"Now how did that happen?" he inquired. "I thought you were a 'tweenman; I thought at least I would have lost you in the Middle World. Don't tell me you have a Gateway talisman in your pocket!"

Startled, Fenton clutched at the golden thing he carried in his pocket. Somehow its texture had changed; it was no longer chill and metallic, but warm, with an almost soapy texture. It felt like jade. But it was reassuringly solid, and he could feel the deep carvings, unchanged.

Behind them a building rose, almost a palace. Flags —Fenton couldn't see the details in the darkness—were flying from the posts, and guards, in dark uniforms, with a good deal of what looked like gold braid, were standing at the entrance of the pillars. None of them had taken the slightest notice of the precipitate arrival of Pentarn and Fenton in their midst. Was this kind of travel a commonplace, then, in Pentarn's world?

Pentarn shook his head. He said, "You're no good to me; you're not who I thought you were. I don't suppose you know what you have done, do you?" He wiped his forehead. He looked tired, and older than he was—Fenton supposed the man was about his own age, thirty-five or so, although the beard made him look considerably older.

"I suppose you're like all 'tweenmen, you don't have the slightest idea what this is all about, do you?"

Fenton said, "I know I don't like the look of the ironfolk, and the idea of letting them loose on helpless women—and I've seen you do that twice—"

Pentarn shrugged. "The ironfolk look worse than they are," he said, "and necessity can't choose its own tools. I am a humane man; you were there, you saw I didn't let them hurt Kerridis. Not much, anyway; and she deserved worse. I suppose you have fallen for the Alfar nonsense, you think they are shining and bright and beautiful, you can't see the other side of it—and why should I explain myself to a 'tweenman?"

One of the gold-braided, uniformed guards was walking slowly across the square. He thrust out his hand in a breast-high salute.

"Leader, is this person—" He raised an indefinable weapon at his hip; it looked ugly, like a blaster from some space-opera movie. Pentarn gestured to the man to put it away, and Fenton knew that this world's weapons, unless they were made of vrill, could not hurt him.

"He can't hurt anybody; he's only a 'tweenman," Pentarn said. "Come along, 'tweenman, you won't be here long enough to do any harm. In case you're wondering what this is, this is the War Palace."

He led Fenton through the long halls, taking no other notice of him. There were weapons of all kinds, not the simple weapons of the Alfar armory, but monstrous machines which made Fenton gasp with their unknown menace; huge, towering, pointing obscenely blunt muzzles which looked as if they could project unknown rays of death, something like a tank with great spikes which, rolled forward over the earth, would tear everything living to bits. . . . Pentarn smiled a strange self-satisfied smile at Fenton's dismay.

Hanging on the walls, in the monstrous War Palace, every thirty or forty feet, were huge pictures, far bigger than life, of Pentarn himself; and Fenton noticed that the guard walking behind Pentarn saluted every one of the pictures with the same outthrust Roman salute as he had done to Pentarn himself. He did not do it ostentatiously; in fact, Pentarn didn't see him do it at all and the guard didn't seem to notice whether Fenton noticed it or not; he just did it, with a strange look which Fenton finally understood as worship.

This guy is a dictator who puts Hitler to shame! No wonder the Alfar despise him!

Finally, after what felt like half an hour of walking—Fenton's legs were hurting terribly, and again and again he stopped and bent over, in a futile attempt to ease the cramps in them—they came to a small modest door.

"Come in," Pentarn said. "These are my private apartments."

The guard demurred, "See here, Lord Leader, this is likely to be some trick of those spooks to get you off your guard! I wish you'd let me deal with this fellow!" He laid hands on Fenton's shoulder, but the hands went right through Fenton's shoulder, and Pentarn laughed, his mocking, contemptuous laugh.

"Deal with him? How? He's a 'tweenman, a shadow," Pentarn said. "But I'm interested in how he got here." He hesitated. "I suppose you have some kind of a name. I can't keep on calling you 'fellow' like a dog!"

"Fenton."

"Fenton." Pentarn gave him a long, appraising look. "Yes, I suppose so; we're probably analogues." At Fenton's confused look, he explained impatiently. "The person I would have been, in your world, whatever it might be. The key decisions alienating the worlds were made so long ago that we have no other relevance; but there are analogues. I suppose in your own world you're nobody important; it doesn't usually work that way. Come in."

"No, nobody important." Considering what Pentarn's world considered important, he didn't suppose a research worker in parapsychology would impress Pentarn at all.

"Maybe we can come to some agreement. I might be able to use a double," Pentarn mused. He led the way inside. The apartments were spartan, bare and featureless, with no decorations on the plain walls. He said to the guard, "Tell the woman of the Middle World that I would like to see her."

"At once, Lord Leader." The guard went away and Pentarn gestured Fenton into a chair, where he bent again to massage his aching legs. The thirst, momentarily appeased by the draught Irielle had given him, was raging again, an agony. Pentarn watched him with a detached look which Fenton interpreted, surprisingly, as sympathy.

"How did you get here?"

"I came with a drug," Fenton said, between spasms.

"I don't suppose offering you a drink would do any good, would it? I've been a 'tweenman myself, before I found the Worldhouse, and I know how it works. But it might make you feel better. Here." He offered him a tankard that looked like silver. Fenton gulped thirstily; it seemed to help a little. At least he could speak again.

Pentarn said, "I'd heard about that drug." He broke off as a woman came into the room. She was dressed in elaborate robes, her hair done in a high comb. Her eyes were vacant, adoring, fixed mutely on Pentarn.

"How can I serve you, Lord Leader?"

"Is this man from any part of your world you know about?"

The woman nodded. "He's one of them in the department," she said. "He has access to the drug I was telling you about."

"That would be useful," Pentarn said. "I could send spies into the Alfar country—'tweenmen, who couldn't be held by the Alfar but who could tell me what they're up to and perhaps get some kind of picture of the way the land changes there. Think how useful it would have been if I could have switched the Gateway right into the changelings' quarters for Joel, before they had time to spirit him away again. They were hiding him, as usual."

"How disgusting," the woman said, her eyes still fixed adoringly on Pentarn.

Pentarn took the tankard. He asked, "Feeling a little

better? Good. Now we can talk. Can you get me some of that drug of yours? I can get you access to the World-house, so you can bring it here. That way you could come and go between worlds as a worldwalker, not having to come as a 'tweenman, a shadow. You'd have substance, you could eat and drink and take a woman or whatever else you wanted to do. But I *have* to have some of that drug."

Fenton said bluntly, "I don't like the idea of helping you spy on the Alfar."

"Hellfire!" Pentarn said angrily. "They've fooled you, too, with all that peace and song and beauty nonsense they give out? You don't know what a scummy lot they are! They steal children—they can't touch cold iron, they need people who can handle it to fight their battles for them, now that vrill is getting so hard to find; people they can train as warriors to fight for them and get killed. They take children from their parents—"

"Children who would die anyway," Fenton said. "And they give them a good life."

Pentarn shook his head, impatient. "Of course that's what they told you. They're holding my son, do you understand? And they have him brainwashed so he thinks he doesn't want to come back! I've got to get him away from them long enough so that he can use his reason again, not have his mind blown away by their singing and dancing and all that ecstatic stuff! Look!" He gestured at the armory beyond the doors of the spartan little apartment. "That's what's waiting for him! He's my son, my only son. He's old enough, now, that I could train him to be Lord Leader of all these people!" He struck the table with his fist, in a rage. "And those people have got him! *My* son! Would any normal boy prefer that to what I can give him here? Damnation, my son is no mollycoddle, no singing whelp, he's my son! He's *the Lord Leader's son,* and he has to come back. I can convince him, if I can get him away from them long enough! But they won't let me talk to him; they're afraid the glamor they put on him will wear off and I'll make him see good sense!"

Pentarn sounded angry, but reasonable. Or was it the thin edge of paranoia, the paranoia of a dictator drunk

on power? Fenton didn't know. He said bluntly, "I'm
not so sure. Between a dictatorship and what the Alfar
have, I think I'd prefer the Alfar too."

Pentarn ignored that. "People in the Middle World
are all stupid. I've had to go through their world often
enough."

"Why?" Fenton asked.

"Because it *is* the Middle World, the pivot from my
world to the world of the Alfar," Pentarn explained, as
if he were explaining something elementary to someone
very stupid. "And since I have to go through it, I have
made it my business to know a little about it. Come, let's
do business. I could use a double, and I could give
you access to the Worldhouse. This is a good life," he
said, with one of those gestures which took in the War
Palace. "It's a good life for a man. Your world has
weeded that out, and your people are so starved for action and warfare, they even submerge themselves in
elaborate games about it—haven't I seen the streets of
Berkeley full of your Anachronists, wearing swords and
playing at fighting because there's no work fit for a
man in your world! You can't change human nature with
a lot of sentimental nonsense about peace! When you see
the lion and the lamb lying down side by side without
one of them thinking about dinner, then your sentimental
rubbish will make some sense. Until then, war is a man's
business, and I brought up my son to face realities—and
now the Alfar have brainwashed him!"

But Fenton was not listening; suddenly, and in shock,
he froze as a car rushed by, roaring along a lighted
street . . . he could not see his own body; and then he
was back again in Pentarn's austere rooms in the War
Palace.

"You are fading at last," Pentarn said. "You have
stayed too long; don't you know that if you stay too long
out of your body, you can die of hunger and thirst?
Where can I reach you? I can come to your world and
talk with you about this. . . ."

Fenton, in agony, was not conscious of the words; he
was incapable of speech. The world kept flicking in and
out around him. His arms and legs ached with white-
hot needles of pain; agonizing spasms had seized his

throat. Abruptly the War Palace and Pentarn were gone. Around him was all the bustle and crowd of Telegraph Avenue, cars rushing by on the street, one narrowly missing him by inches. He stumbled, reached the safety of the curb before he realized it did not matter, his body was not here, he could safely pass right through cars and sidewalk . . . he walked through a sidewalk stall displaying brilliantly formed glass mugs. The talisman Irielle had given him was still clenched in his pocket.

The pains were blinding. Staggering, he made his way along the avenue toward Smythe Hall. Only one thought was in his mind, to get back to his body, to still this agony . . . Nothing like this had ever happened before. What had gone wrong? He was aware that it was very dark, and the dim fading spire of the campanile showed the hour of eleven-thirty at night. Near midnight? He had never stayed so long before! Had Garnock given him an overdose of the drug, or had the Gateway talisman—he clenched his fists on it in his pocket—somehow affected his fading and the return?

He stumbled into Smythe Hall, along the corridor, up to the deserted lab. Garnock should be keeping watch by his body. But there was no one in the lab. Marjie's notes were neatly laid out on the table; but Garnock was gone.

And his body was gone.

CHAPTER ELEVEN

FENTON'S FIRST REACTION was pure panic.

His body was gone, had been taken away—*dead?* Years ago he had read a horror story in which a man, dead and buried, did not know he was dead, and wandered for years among the living, unable to make them hear his voice, unable to touch anything. . . . It had been the author's version of hell. But a moment's thought brought him back to sanity. He had, after all, been away a long time, and when Garnock found that he did not come back to consciousness in the usual time, he had him taken to a hospital. Reason told him it would be the hospital on campus, Cowell Hospital. It would not be the first time a laboratory experiment had gone wrong . . .

But he was so tired, so racked with recurrent pain . . . Fenton let himself collapse into Garnock's chair. Predictably he went through it, landed on the floor and began to sink frighteningly through that too. Hastily he recollected himself . . . he could walk on the floor, or appear to, in whatever insubstantial physical form his body had now, if he kept concentrating on it. But he was so tired, it was such an effort to concentrate. . . .

Fenton made a very serious attempt to collect his thoughts. He was really beginning to be frightened now. He was not sure what would happen to him in this present form if he was trapped outside his body too long, but he was very, very sure he didn't want to find out!

The first thing, obviously, was to get back to his body. *Next time,* he thought, clutching the talisman in his pocket, *next time when I go into that world I am going to take my body with me! I've had enough of being a 'tweenman!*

166

As he stumbled painfully down out of Smythe Hall, he thought with longing of the world of the Alfar, with the landscape that shifted and flowed, and could be travelled more quickly with will and concentrating on your destination. Now he was aware that his body—now flickering and wavering to his conscious sight, and feeling far less substantial—was tugging at him by means of the cord connecting him to it. The cord was a fine greyish substance which seemed to extend from somewhere about the middle of his body—he didn't know just where it was fastened, but he thought it was about his navel, and it felt like it—and which extended off in the distance. Fenton was beginning to feel almost delirious; he wondered whether it could get snagged on anything and what would happen to it if it did.

Down the stairs of Smythe Hall, stumbling, recurrently racked with spasms of pain. Across the deserted campus, stumbling in desperate haste, once taking a shortcut through the corner of a building because it was quicker than going around. The building felt rough and grainy, painful to his insubstantial skin. Stabbing pains seized him and he had to fall to his knees repeatedly, ignoring the insistent tugging, like an itch inside his belly, from the cord, and try to massage the pain out of his calves and feet. He found it was easier to slide down stairs than to climb down them. The painful tug and itch became more extreme as he neared the hospital. He had wondered, vaguely, how he would find his body in all the rooms of Cowell Hospital. Now he was left in no doubt, because he could feel the pull, the demand and tug of his body. He didn't try to resist it but let himself be pulled along.

But he had Irielle's talisman, he kept reminding himself. It was probably not carven filigree gold, here; in Pentarn's world it had been green jadelike precious stone. He wondered suddenly if the medieval tales of alchemy had had some such interworld transmutation as this in mind. Certainly there was no way to change base metals into gold in *this* world. But changing worlds might change them . . .

In a small waiting room on the second floor, Garnock slumped half asleep in a chair. Fenton discovered that he was touched. So Garnock would stay close to him, instead of delivering him over to the hospital and going home peacefully to sleep. Or was it only scientific curiosity? Garnock was unshaven, rumpled, his clothes disarranged.

Fenton said, "Doc, it's okay—" but Garnock did not hear him and dozed on, oblivious. Of course Garnock could neither see nor hear him in this insubstantial body; in this form he was a ghost. . . .

The tug now was excruciating. He let it pull him into the other room where he lay on a hospital bed, in a hospital nightgown. Appalled, he realized that tubes were in his throat and nose, that needles were in his arm and vein, some kind of intravenous drip . . . *what the hell* . . . As he watched, a nurse came and wound a blood-pressure cuff around his arm, inert, and started to pump it up. He heard her say, "His blood pressure's going down. We'd better have some . . ."

Oh no, Fenton thought. *The last thing I need is some kind of heroic resuscitation procedures!* He let himself drift back toward his body, making sure Irielle's talisman was firmly clutched in his hand.

Irielle herself had been uncertain whether, as a 'tweenman, he could carry it back to his solid body. Well, he would try. The tugging was harder and harder; he surrendered to it.

Agonizing pain shot through mouth and nose, arm, legs. He shouted with the impact of it. He sat up, wildly flailing his arms. The nurse stepped back a pace in consternation, staring down at Fenton with the blood-pressure cuff in her hand.

"You're conscious!" she said. It was like an accusation.

Fenton said, "Damn right. Don't you think it's about time?" But he found he couldn't speak through the nasal tube and put a protesting hand to it.

The nurse said, "It's all right, Mr. Fenton. You've been unconscious quite a while . . . here, let me."

Removing the tube, even carefully, as she did it, was painful, but when it was out, Fenton sat up and said, "I'm all right, I tell you. What's going on here?"

"Just lie down there and let me take your blood pressure," the nurse said. "Clench your fist . . ."

Fenton clenched his fist, obediently. With a soaring triumph which let him ignore the biting pains all through his body, he realized that Irielle's talisman was still in his hand.

He had done it, he had done it! Garnock could not ignore this proof of the reality of his experience!

"Well, I don't understand it," the nurse said. "A few seconds ago your blood pressure was so low I couldn't even find it, and now it seems to be quite normal."

"Tell Garnock," Fenton said. "Call Doctor Garnock right away."

"He's right outside," the nurse said, and hurried to get him. Fenton lay back, dizzied, cramped, exhausted. He felt sick and weak, but otherwise, he knew, he was normal enough.

Garnock hurried in, his face troubled, a smile breaking through as he saw Fenton lying with his eyes wide open. "Thank God! Cam, are you all right?"

"Of course," Fenton said, touched. "You shouldn't have worried, Doc. I wanted to stay as long as I could this time, and see all there was to be seen."

Garnock shook his head in dismay. "Cam," he said, "you've been lying there, unconscious, for thirty-six hours! And you sit there and say you're okay?"

"But I *am* okay," Fenton said. Inside, though, he felt dismay as great as Garnock's. *Thirty-six hours!* No wonder the effort of remaining away from his body had come close to killing him! He had not the slightest doubt that if he had remained away much longer, he would have died from the slow failure of all vital systems. Hunger and dehydration could be handled by intravenous drip—as they had done, he realized, feeling the sharp pains in his arms—but there were other, subtler failures.

"But this time I've brought back proof. Doc, it's real. The other dimensions are real, objectively real. Irielle gave me a talisman which will let me pass the gates. Look."

He opened his clenched fist, feeling the weight of the talisman in his solid, substantial fingers.

Garnock reached out to take it from him. He said in a

pleasantly neutral voice, "So you brought back an apport, Cam. That's very interesting. I always suspected you had some telekinetic ability, though you don't measure very high on the dice machines. But of course here there's no possibility of any fiddling, you have been in that bed under the eyes of special nurses for the past twenty-four hours. Nurse—he didn't have anything in his hand when you brought him in, did you?"

The nurse said, "Definitely not. Certainly not when the doctor came down to start the IV drip."

Garnock grinned. "They'll never believe it," he said. "I'll never be able to prove that I didn't do some sleight-of-hand and shove it into your fist. Not even if the nurses testified under oath. But I *know,* that's what's important to me now. I saw it with my own eyes." And with a cold chill running up and down his spine, Cam Fenton realized that even Garnock himself, professor of parapsychology, had not really believed. All of his search for proof had been a desire to convince himself, to transcend his own disbelief.

When you spend your whole life operating on *one* set of postulates, with the lines of the possible and impossible rigidly defined, there is no way—*no way*—you can transcend them. No amount of proof will convince you, because on this subject you have been conditioned not to believe even the evidence of your own senses.

And no matter how much you may think you want to believe, you can't.

Fenton had never seen a flying saucer. He didn't believe in flying saucers. And if he saw one, even if one lit on the lawn of Sproul Hall, he wouldn't believe it, because he *knew,* deep inside of himself, that such space-faring was impossible. If he saw it with his own eyes, he would call it a hallucination, and this he would call sanity, and reality testing.

That was why the primitives in Africa and Asia had died. Not because the white men physically damaged their tribal environment. But because the culture of the white man destroyed their postulates and their sanity.

It was hopeless, probably.

But he said, "Apport, Doc?"

"Yes. At some of the old séances I saw them—flowers, jewels. I always believed the mediums had been very, very clever, so clever even the stage magicians we set to monitor them couldn't catch them, about smuggling them in." He sank down weakly into a chair by the bed. "But I *know* you didn't smuggle this one in. Cam, for God's sake, after ten years in the parapsychology department, to get this kind of solid hard evidence about telekinesis, teleporting that hunk of rock—"

"Wait, wait," Fenton said. "I didn't teleport it in. Irielle, the girl I told you about in the world of the Alfar, gave it to me—"

Garnock waved that aside. "I don't know how you rationalized it in your hallucinations. The important thing is that it was important enough to you to teleport a hunk of rock from outside the campus into the hospital and into your hand—"

Fenton said, "I can't believe this! The talisman—just *look* at it, Doc, look at the carvings, look—"

"No," said Garnock. "*You* look at it." He held it out to Fenton.

It was a flat, featureless piece of rock.

CHAPTER TWELVE

"I'M SORRY, Cam," Garnock said at last. "Can't you see that everything you say is just making it worse? You've had the first really serious side effect we've found with Antaril, and until we know whether this is a personal idiosyncrasy to the drug, or something the statistics just haven't come up with yet, we still can't take the risk of letting you go on with the experiment. Look, Cam," he added, and he sounded sincerely regretful, "I'm sorry to disappoint you; I know you're very deeply interested in what this experiment is doing. But I admit, even before this happened, I was at the point of cancelling your participation. Drugs are always tricky. You didn't get too involved with LSD, I remember, but we had one or two, even during the very short time we were experimenting with that, who got too involved in the drug itself. I had to cancel the Brittman girl because when we started on Antaril she became psychologically dependent on it in the same way you've started to do—"

Fenton interrupted angrily, "Damn it, I am not psychologically dependent—"

"You would be the last to know," Garnock said brutally. "She started talking just the way you've been doing, about the reality of the other world, and wanting to spend more and more time in what she insisted was a genuine alternate reality. I've heard that she's dropped out of school and gone to drug-tripping with the street people, and there's nothing we can do about that—they couldn't find any way to ban the drug; it's virtually nontoxic even to mice, let alone humans."

Cam said bitterly, "Oh, can't you fake something, the way they used to do with LSD and grass? The old pious lies about grass just being an inevitable first step to heroin addiction?"

Garnock looked offended. He said, "Look, we saw, in California, what happens to the law-abiding citizen when you try to prohibit something he knows to be harmless and which he wants to use. The case of alcohol during prohibition, LSD and marijuana through the sixties and seventies, and legitimate prostitution right up to the last few years. Well, vice squads are notoriously corrupt and cynical, because they know they're only trying to collect fines for the tax authorities. But what happened to Amy Brittman and what's happening to you can give some statistics; if we can certify Antaril as being a serious psychological danger to certain types of people, we can get its use restricted to supervised laboratory research, as they did with LSD. And we've had a whisper already that the government might be funding the next Antaril experiments through the parapsychology foundations. The department is up for a grant right now; just imagine the military uses. You know as well as I do that the whole Communist bloc has been experimenting with psychic research—sort of the ultimate spy weapon; with no need to send their people within reach of our agencies at all—physical reach, that is. The government in Washington is finally getting wise to the fact that we ought to be equal with the Russians in psi research, at least, and preferably ahead of them. And so there could be some good government contracts to do research here on the campus, for possible military uses of ESP and psi powers. And you ought to know what that means to the department. We've never had enough funding, and now we're within a step of getting it."

"Good God," Fenton said. "I thought parapsychology was one department which couldn't be twisted to military uses!"

"Look, it could be the new military frontier. Imagine all the lives that would be saved if we never had to send spies physically into any other country at all!"

"And all you care about is getting funding for the department? You aren't interested in the ramifications of what this research could mean? Suppose we had genuine access to other dimensions. Not interested in basic research into the nature of reality?"

Garnock looked honestly distressed. "I wish you wouldn't talk that way. Once your system is really clear of the drug, you'll understand what happened to you. Look, shall I set up a couple of interviews with the psychiatric counseling service? Would you like to talk to somebody really objective about this?"

Fenton drew his long legs together and rose. "No, thanks. I know just how objective they are," he said, with a wry twist of his mouth. "So objective that they'd start by inquiring into my Freudian conflicts and why I needed the sense of power that comes with work in parapsychology, and end by deciding I was an escapist. Thanks, Doc, but—no thanks. Give me my talisman—excuse me—my 'hunk of rock'—and I'll be on my way."

"I hate to see you sound so bitter! I thought you were seriously interested in research!"

"Funny. The reason I'm bitter is because I sort of had the same notion about you, Doc. But when it's a toss-up between research and department funding, department funding is going to win every time, isn't it?"

Garnock's fat chin tightened. "You'd better drop it, Cam, before we say something we'll both regret."

"You already said it. Let me have my talisman, and I'll go."

Garnock shook his head. "Sorry, Cam. That piece of rock is the one genuine apport we have ever received here in fifteen years of experiments, and it belongs in the department's exhibits."

"If you're so damn sure it's just a hunk of rock," Fenton said, "just go out in the plaza and pick one up anywhere. They're all the same to you. I happen to need that particular one; it was given personally to me, and you can't keep it."

"As a matter of fact," Garnock said, and now his mouth looked ugly, "I can. Materials developed during a department experiment belong legally to the department. I never enforced it before, but this is serious enough that I'm going to. That piece of rock stays locked in the department safe, and that's all there is to it."

"Look, if you'd only *listen* to me! With the talisman, I

have a key to other dimensions. I can find the World-house, and maybe I can even take you through—"

But Garnock's face made it obvious that he was listening to the ravings of a lunatic, and Cam stopped himself.

He quoted, "Yea, even if one came from the dead they would not believe." He felt his grin twist his mouth. "Sometimes I wonder what Lazarus found to say to people. I wonder how many tried to convince him he'd never been dead at all?"

Garnock spoke with considerable gentleness. "There's no way we can inquire into the miracles in the Bible, Cam. Nobody knows whether any of them ever happened, or whether the faithful just believed that they did. Don't get trapped in that one. It's the trap all parapsychologists have to look out for—believing that we've found special exceptions to the laws of nature. When this wears off, and you're feeling more rational, come back and talk to me about it again, Cam. Until then, I don't see much point in going on."

"No," Fenton said, "there isn't."

At the door, Garnock hesitated. "Be sure and give Sally your final report," he said. "She's still working on content analysis."

"Okay," Cam said, with a grim shrug. "I'll go." He guessed he owed that to Garnock. And it was possible Sally might be induced to believe him. But now that they had deftly stripped him of the talisman Irielle had given him . . .

He stopped himself. He mustn't resort to the paranoid "they." Possibly he could induce Garnock, or Sally, to return the "apport" to him for a little while, and he could substitute some similar piece of stone. He could imagine just about how far he'd get, trying to sue the department for confiscating a piece of personal property, namely and to wit, one piece of apparent grey alluvial stone, approximately three inches in diameter, circular in form and approximately one inch in thickness, which defendant alleges to be, in some other dimension, a golden talisman incised with mystic runes, and in another dimension, a piece of green jade similarly carven. Fenton had enough sense of proportion left to be able to grin at himself as he went down the stairs and outside Smythe Hall. Actually, when you put it like that, he couldn't blame Garnock for not believing him. There were times when he didn't believe himself.

Maybe I ought to go and talk to the people at psych, after all. . . .

After being released, he called Sally and invited her to dinner.

While he was waiting for Sally to finish her last conference, he dropped around at the undergraduate residence hall, and discovered that when Amy Brittman left the hall she had given a forwarding address down where Telegraph merged into the grubbiness of North Oakland. With a glance at his watch, he set off down the avenue.

It was midafternoon, a sunny day in late fall, and the avenue was alive with the street people. He saw the shaven hippie with three rings in one ear and several Anachronists in high boots and swirling cloaks. Were they actually looking for a leader like Pentarn because this world gave no scope for war and battles? On the surface, their play-acting masqueraded as a game; but did it have the sinister undercurrent Pentarn believed?

And as that brought his thoughts round again to Pentarn, he saw the shutters of the small print-shop where he had seen the Rackham prints. He crossed the street to look at it.

In the window was a picture of a tall elf-queen beset by small crowding gnomes who did, indeed, bear a frightening resemblance to the ironfolk. *Kerridis among the ironfolk, as he had first seen her . . .* There were other prints in the window, one of a tall and featureless building with banners fluttering, which somehow reminded him of Pentarn's War Palace, some strange structures which he had always dismissed as science fiction or fantasy art. Now he wondered if, instead of being fantasy art, they were intended to alert people who *knew* to a situation where worlds crossed . . .

But, he thought in dismay, *I walked all along this block, twice. There was a laundromat and dry-cleaning shop, here, between this bookstore and that Greek restaurant . . .*

He hunted on the front of the building for the house

number; but there wasn't one. Of course, that was nothing unusual, probably even the postal service didn't think of the buildings along here by their street numbers. Well, there was one way to find out. He pushed the door and went in. At least this time it hadn't turned into a dry-cleaning shop.

"May I help you?" The clerk was a youngish woman, in a hippie-like floor-length gown, flowered and swirling, in the Pre-Raphaelite style affected by some Anachronist women for street wear.

"The picture in the window. The elf-queen and the—what-do-you-call'ems—gnomes. Goblins."

"That's a Rackham illustration for Rossetti's poem *Goblin Market*," the girl said. "Lovely, isn't it?"

Fenton agreed that Rackham had been a talented illustrator. "Do you have it in a larger size?"

"I'll see," she said, and began to look in hanging files of drawings and prints, while Fenton looked around the room. "Yes, I have a nine-by-twelve print, and a six-by-eight mounted on a redwood panel for hanging."

"I'll take the print," Fenton said. He didn't want to be bothered with the heavy panel, though he supposed Sally might like to have it. While the girl was wrapping the package he pointed to one of the goblins and said, "Good thing we don't have any of those people around here."

She gave him a mischievous grin. "I'd certainly hate to meet one of them in a dark alley."

He said, carefully choosing his words, "I'd hate to meet any of the ironfolk anywhere, wouldn't you?"

For a moment he thought something flickered behind her eyes, but she only said, "Will there be anything else, sir?"

"Yes," he said. "What hours are you usually open? I have come by here often, and I have a hard time finding this place. In fact, once I thought I'd found you open, and instead I found myself walking into a dry-cleaning shop."

"Well," she said, looking around, "I don't *think* we look that much like a dry-cleaning shop, do we?"

Looking at the brightly colored illustrations posted on the wall, Fenton thought that anything less like a dry-cleaning shop would be hard to find.

"And then," he added, "I came back and I simply couldn't find this place at all."

"Well," she said, "we are a little hard to find—open, that is. We're a little tucked away here. I guess we're like anything else, you just have to know where to look for us, and when. And why. That's very important," she added, and Fenton had the maddening sense that she was waiting for him to say the right thing, the important thing, some password. He wondered what he would have found in here if he had indeed had Irielle's talisman in his pocket. Was this indeed the house between the Worlds, the place where the pivot Gateway was, and Pentarn could come and go?

She repeated again, "Will there be anything else, sir?"

"No," Fenton said, discouraged, knowing that he could never hope to stumble on the password by accident. "Not this time."

"Please come again," she said. As a young Anachronist in boots and cloak came in, she smiled. "You can go right through." She waved him through a door at the back.

Fenton asked, "What's back there?"

"Dungeons and Dragons club," the girl said. "I'm sorry. Members only."

"Not even a look for outsiders?" Fenton asked, knowing that somehow this was what he had missed, and she smiled and shook her head. "No harm in looking," she said blandly, and opened the door. Very briefly, so briefly that Fenton never knew whether he had imagined it, there was that odd swirling sensation; then the door swung, and he saw a table and chairs and a couple of young Anachronists sitting in their chairs, bent over the board spread out, an unusually large and elaborate board, with large figures. But still only a gameboard . . .

"See?" the young woman said. "Just a game room."

"Can anyone join? I mean, I'm a bit of a Dungeons and Dragons buff myself, and to play in a place like this, with all these different worlds on the wall—" Fenton said, trying to sound as if there was some deeper meaning behind his words.

But her face was unrevealing. "I'm sorry, sir. You have to be recommended by a member. Don't forget your package, sir. Here, I'll let you out and lock the door."

Not knowing quite how to protest, Fenton found himself on the threshold. He made one final try.

"Is Pentarn a member? Does he come in here very often? I thought I saw him come in here the other day—"

"I'm sorry, sir. I don't know all the members," she said, and Fenton was outside in the street and the door was locked.

At least now I can find the place again. Right between that bookshop with green awnings and the Greek restaurant.

And he had the Rackham drawing. But as he strode on down Telegraph Avenue, he had the maddening sensation that he had somehow missed a very important clue.

Well, perhaps Amy Brittman could provide another one, if she had had, somewhere in her Antaril experience, an encounter with Pentarn.

At least Pentarn was not a mythical monster, warring with the Alfar for no reason at all. He had a sort of reason for what he did, even if his reason was wrongheaded and stupid. The Alfar had taken his son. Fenton wasn't surprised that the boy preferred the Alfar—he did, himself, to Pentarn's military dictatorship. He'd had a lifetime bellyful of the military.

This far from campus, Telegraph Avenue dwindled into banks, gas stations, real-estate offices; and across the freeway, ballet studios, roominghouses and small religious bookshops. In one of the side streets he found the address he had been given for Amy Brittman.

He pressed the button beside the small card that said *Brittman* and after a moment heard a crackly metal voice.

"The vid's not working. Who is it?"

"My name's Fenton, I'm from the parapsychology department," he said, and the buzzer sounded. Fenton went through into a ground-floor apartment, and rapped at the door; a young woman peered carefully out at him.

She was very young, her face round and plump; some day she would be fat. She was wrapped to the chin in a frowsy housecoat, her hair straggled uncombed about her face. She looked slatternly and used, and for a moment Fenton did not recognize her.

She said uncertainly, "Look, I don't know what you want—" In that moment Fenton recognized her.

She was the woman from the Middle World, the one who had stood at Pentarn's side and stared at him with so much adoration. The Lord Leader's woman.

And the recognition was mutual. She blinked and said in a small squeaky voice, "It's you! The 'tweenman!"

And slammed the door in his face.

"It ought to be obvious to any reasonable person," Sally said, "that Amy Brittman is deranged. She's dropped out of school, she's head-over-heels into the street culture, drug-tripping on acid, psychedelics, Antaril, all kinds of mind-burners—"

"You don't know that, Sally, you're guessing. All I know is—"

"You saw her in a dream. And you fasten on the fact that she allegedly saw you—"

"You still claim it was a dream, Sally?"

"I don't *claim* anything; I am speaking of facts. You were lying up in Cowell Hospital, under constant observation. You claim to have seen a girl who resembled Amy Brittman—"

"I didn't know then who she was; I never saw her around the department."

"Nevertheless. You claim to have seen a girl resembling Amy Brittman—Cam, for God's sake let me finish one sentence without interrupting!—and that she alleges to have seen you in that same dream—"

"Sally, damn it, you sound like a lawyer I knew. He stood over three bleeding corpses and said, 'Now, about this alleged accident . . .'"

"I am *trying*," Sally said, in a dangerously quiet tone of voice, "to maintain something remotely approaching scientific objectivity about the statements you are making."

"How do you explain the fact that she spoke of me in the same words the Alfar, and Pentarn, had used—'tweenman?"

"I don't explain it. I didn't hear her say it."

"Sally, will you do me the simple justice to admit I might, just possibly, be telling the truth to you? You're talking like some rat-running debunker sent in to expose the department as a twenty-year hoax!"

"I'm a psychologist, not a True Believer! I'm a researcher, and that means I'm not going to argue with facts and make them fit your theories!"

"No—you're going to ignore the facts unless they fit *your* theories!" Fenton said, angrily. He glared at her over the table in the small, dim restaurant where they were sitting.

"I find that statement offensive, Cam. It's a reflection on my integrity, both as a woman and as a scientist!"

"And I suppose the statements *you* have been making all evening aren't a reflection on mine? You've as much as said that I'm a liar, I'm deluded, and every supposed fact that I give you, you dismiss as a hallucination or a flat lie!"

"Facts, for heaven's sake!" Sally looked at him in the light of the candle. It cast strange, wavering lights on her face, hollowing her cheeks, accentuating that strange resemblance he had seen, or fancied, before this. "What facts? You drag me along Telegraph Avenue with a story about some print-shop that isn't there—"

"It *is* there," he said, "or where did I buy that print I gave you?"

"Are you trying to tell me that is the only shop on Telegraph Avenue which handles Arthur Rackham prints?"

"But this particular print," Fenton argued, "came from a small shop with no name, but a huge number of prints in the window, right between a bookshop and a Greek restaurant—"

"Cam, what do you want me to say to you? That a dry-cleaning shop can suddenly become a print-shop or vice-versa? I *know* that dry-cleaning shop. I take my cleaning there every other week, and they know me. Are you trying to tell me that sometimes it won't be there and I'll find some sort of magical shop which is the headquarters of a Dungeons and Dragons club which is really a cover-up for something sinister?"

"It happened to me."

"I heard you say so. But I have to go on evidence, Cam. I didn't see it. As for the fact that you and Amy happened to come into one another's dreams, even using the same somewhat unusual term, 'tweénman, well—one of the few things we *have* proved in the parapsychology labs is that telepathy *does* exist, and it wouldn't surprise me at all if you had been in contact with Amy Brittman. In fact, since Amy is obviously a very disturbed young lady, these are precisely the kind of fantasies I'd expect her to have. The only thing I'm curious about is why she picked on you to share her fantasies when she's in a disturbed state. I'm only concerned that her mental disturbance might—might influence—"

"What you're trying to say is that it might be contagious?"

"Yes," Sally said. "I've begun to hypothesize that some people do project their fantasies by way of telepathy. It would explain one of the biggest riddles in standard psychology—the *folie à deux,* where two people share a delusion. It could also explain some of the extraordinary popular delusions, the crowd madness, mob psychology —remember when Hitler infected a whole country with the belief that Jewish people were dangerous and had to be exterminated in self-preservation? He was, perhaps an abnormally strong projector of his fantasies—perhaps that would explain the astonishing charisma some crowd leaders have."

"Now who's talking about pet theories?"

"Certainly not I," Sally said. "I'm simply stating that it's possible to explain your experiences in terms of facts already known, such as telepathy, without multiplying hypotheses to take in such complex theories as multiple interlocking parallel worlds or whatever it is that you call them."

Cam said quietly, "If any simple theory fit *all* the facts of my experiences, Sally, I would accept it. But it fits only because you are ignoring all the facts except the ones that fit *your* theory." He ticked them off on his fingers. "The name Emma Camron scratched in the dirt at the eucalyptus grove. The shop where I bought this print of *Goblin Market.* The fact—and do me the justice, Sally, to admit I was telling the truth—that it was not there when I went back; I showed you—"

"You showed me a site which I have known, for more than a year, as the spot where I take my personal dry-cleaning. I'm not saying you were lying to me, Cam—"

"But you don't believe me."

"I think you were confused. I think you are still having a very severe side reaction to Antaril, and that sometimes you confuse the internally-generated fantasies of the drug with the external input from the environment. This, of course, is why the so-called psychedelic drugs have been a dangerous blind alley in parapsychological research, even under controlled conditions; both you and Amy Brittman are casualties of this. Will you please understand that I am not making a value judgment about this, Cam? I don't think you will ever be able to tell what was real and what was not, during the time you were on the drug. I know Garnock is just sick about it; he was so sure —we were all so sure—that Antaril was what we were looking for, the ESP-enhancing drug with no dangerous side effects. Do you think I wanted you to be the one exception? Or one of the two, counting Amy? I could have discounted her; I suspected from the first day of the term that she was potentially unstable, and her freakout might have been due to her own basic instability rather than to the drug. But for you, Cam—you, who are so stable— no, it's got to be the side effect of the drug."

"So you are just discarding all my evidence as the result of drug side effects?"

Sally hesitated, reached across the table and touched his hand. "That's putting it a little more harshly than I would, Cam. Let's just say that I haven't seen any objective proof, and all of these things which you experienced *did* take place while you were more or less under the effects of Antaril. Cam, I'm going to make an appointment with you to see a regular psychotherapist at Cowell. Maybe if you could talk about this, you could get a—a little more objective viewpoint on this."

Fenton stared at her, his brows drawing together in dismay.

"So you're just saying I'm crazy."

Sally frowned back at him and said, "Now you are

reacting like any untrained layman! I suggest you see a psychotherapist and you just react with an automatic, *You think I'm crazy!*"

"What you're saying," Fenton said, at white heat, "is that I'm having uncomfortable ideas which don't fit your preconceptions so you want to send me to a psychotherapist to be talked right out of them again and convinced that any ideas which don't fit into yours are nothing but delusions!"

Her mouth was open in a dismay that reflected his own.

"Do you even know how paranoid that sounds, Cam? It sounds like a sophisticated version of, *it's all a plot against me!*"

"Of course! Anything which sounds a little scary can be defused! Call him paranoid and he'll shut up and stop talking about what makes us all so uncomfortable!"

Sally picked up the glass of wine on the table before her, and sipped at it. The glass was shaking in her hand. "You are determined to make a fight out of this, on personal grounds, aren't you, Cam?"

"I admit I resent it! I come to you as a person, trying to tell you what I saw and experienced, and you turn into a psychologist and explain it all away as my delusions!"

"That's why I want you to see another psychologist, Cam. I'm too emotionally involved." He saw the candlelight glistening on the long streak of a tear down her cheek. For a moment she looked frail, vulnerable, the woman in the Rackham painting pressed against the rocky wall by the crowding goblins, Kerridis besieged by the ironfolk. With a sudden, overflowing tenderness, he pressed her slender fingers in his own.

"I don't want to quarrel with you, Sally. God knows, that's the last thing I want to do."

She caught her breath, nodded. "I know. And I don't want to sound the way I know I do. Maybe I'm arguing with myself as much as with you." Her fingers trembled under his. "Oh, Cam, I *want* to believe you! I want to believe that you're right, that it all happened the way you tell it, no matter how fantastic it is. And sometimes, I almost do. You sound so sure, you're so darned *consis-*

tent! But don't you see, that's the danger? If it's infectious . . ."

Fenton wanted to pursue the topic, to explore any doubts she might have. Instead, he changed the subject to something safer.

"When I was up in the mountains, I was talking to my Uncle Stan about you. He wants to meet you. He's a fabulous old man, in his seventies, but he still takes young people out on backpacking trips in the Sierras, chops his own wood, raises a herd of goats and makes his own cheese, sells it to an organic-foods shop. He said you sounded just like what I needed. He asked me to bring you up to talk to him. Will you come?"

"I'd love to," she said, with her quick smile. "He does sound like a marvelous old fellow. There aren't so many of that kind of old men around as there used to be when we were kids, are there? Would he approve of my being a psychologist? Or is he old enough to think a woman's place is in the home?"

Fenton chuckled. "I don't know; I don't intend to consult him on the subject, but you can ask him yourself, if you think it matters."

She shook her head. "Not really. Only I guess I wanted to reassure myself that I wasn't the only person in the world with freaky narrow-minded relatives right out of the Stone Age, and your Uncle Stan sounded so perfect I was jealous. *My* relatives—really, Cam—they belong in a Gothic novel. American Gothic. My first husband thought they were wonderful, of course. He would."

Her face grew distant and bitter, as always when she spoke of her marriage, but Fenton noticed, in a random corner of his mind, that she had said her *first* husband, which meant that somewhere inside her, the concept of a *second* had begun to take shape. It filled him with tenderness. He didn't have much use for the ordinary concepts of marriage, but the idea of a life shared with Sally was beginning to assume more and more attractiveness.

And then he remembered something else.

"Look, this could be your independent witness. You keep saying that all the facts which I regard as objective proof were all subjective, that they just happened to take place when there were no witnesses. But my Uncle Stan saw one of the ironfolk. It carried off his axe."

"He actually saw it? Saw it clearly enough that he could testify on oath about it? Not that eyewitness testimony is worth all that much—look at all the people who testified to seeing little green spacemen—but he actually saw it clearly?"

Fenton's heart sank. "He saw its tracks, where it hauled off his axe."

"Not good enough," Sally said with a frown. "Cam, how old is your Uncle Stan? What's his eyesight like? Any history of eyesight failure, of mild aphasia, of minimal stroke damage—"

"He isn't senile, if that's what you mean," Fenton said angrily. "And if you talked to him yourself, you'd know it."

"But again—I haven't talked to him, Cam. Look, can we leave it at that? This conversation isn't going anywhere, and I don't want to quarrel again. After you've seen that psychotherapist—"

"Are you off on *that* again? Sally, for God's sake, do you really think I need a shrink?"

"I find that term offensive," she said icily. "I see no reason a genuinely stable person should hesitate to talk with a reputable therapist. Are you afraid of jeopardizing your fantasy structure by subjecting it to rational inquiry?"

"Damn it, Sally!" he exploded, so loudly that the two undergraduates at the next table turned their heads to stare. "I'm fed up with the way you retreat into psychotherapeutic jargon every time you don't want to face the issues I bring up! Can't you admit you could be wrong?"

"Same question, right back to you!" she snapped.

"Will you come and meet my Uncle Stan?"

Her face softened for a moment. "I'll come, certainly, Cam. I'll come because he's your uncle, and because he sounds like a marvelous old character. I'd love to meet him."

"I'll pick you up Friday morning, and that will give us the weekend."

"I'd love it," she said, smiling. "But, Cam, please,

don't try and badger the old man into supporting some wild story you've cooked up to support your fantasies."

He stared at her, angry and shaken. "What you're saying is, don't confuse me with facts, I've already made up my mind!"

"And what you're saying is, love me, love my delusions. If you can ever show me some facts, I'll be happy to listen to them!"

He slammed his chair backward from the table, keeping a grip on himself with both hands. He said, carefully, "All right. I'll pick you up at ten Friday morning."

He stalked away without looking back. He had to. He knew if he had stayed there one more minute he would have hit her. He threw some money at the cashier and slammed the door of the restaurant behind him.

CHAPTER THIRTEEN

THE DRY-CLEANING SHOP was still there, seeming to mock him. He thought angrily, *if I still had Irielle's talisman . . .* and rage surged up through him. That was *his*—by what right did Garnock keep it?

He stood looking at the bleak white front of the dry-cleaning shop as if by sheer effort of will he could metamorphose it into the little print-shop which he now suspected to be the Worldhouse which could carry him through without the drug. And now Garnock had cut him off from any access to the Alfar world, first by removing him from the Antaril experiment, then by taking away Irielle's talisman . . .

Who the hell does Garnock think he is?

Angry plans churned in his head, none of them making any sense. He could stay here, watching the doorway, until it changed back again into the print-shop. A watched pot never boils. Would a watched Worldhouse never shift its shape? Did it change only when no one was watching it? Could he stay there and watch until Pentarn came through? He suspected that no one would allow the ironfolk through. Or would they? What kind of laws were there governing who came through and who did not? He had tried to dive through after Pentarn, and in the very instant the Worldhouse was gone, and was an innocuous dry-cleaning shop again. Did it only *look* like a dry-cleaning shop? Behind some curious spatial interface he could not see, was it really the little print-shop/Worldhouse after all? But no. Sally said she had taken her dry-cleaning there. So somehow they were both real and shifted back and forth, one replacing the other. When the dry-cleaning shop was here on Telegraph Avenue, where was the Worldhouse? Was it anywhere at all, was it hiding in some other dimension? Was it somewhere at the other side of this world, masquerading as some innocuous business, shifting in space as it did between dimensions? Could it masquerade, say, as a flower shop, a market stall somewhere, hide itself in the gift shop of the British Museum? An art-film moviehouse? What was it really and where would it appear next? What of the small bookshop he could never find twice in San Francisco? Cam felt his head begin to ache.

Sally didn't believe there was a Worldhouse. Damn the woman, did he care?

Yes. He cared. Facing the knowledge that Sally was alienated, he felt the same aching emptiness he had felt when Garnock took him off the project, and he realized the world of the Alfar was barred to him.

Forever. . . .

No, Cam thought in a rage. I won't accept that. Irielle, a child of two worlds, who was like himself. Kerridis . . . Kerridis forever beyond his reach. His friends there, Findhal who in spite of his rage had been his friend. . . . There had to be a way back, even if he had to sit here all day and all night waiting for the Worldhouse to appear again.

But could he get through it without Irielle's talisman?

Well, he thought wryly, if all else fails I can always burglarize Garnock's office and take it back. What the hell, Garnock called it a piece of rock. I could stick any chunk of granite from the campus into his office, and he wouldn't know the difference!

Standing here on the street, staring morosely at the little dry-cleaning shop, wasn't going to do him any good. If he actually tried sitting here day and night till the Worldhouse appeared here again, he suspected the cops would have something to say about it. There were still vagrancy laws on the books in Berkeley. They probably weren't enforced very often, but they were there, and if he tried to sit there on that sidewalk for forty-eight hours or so without a break, he supposed he'd find out that they had teeth. Anyway, he thought with the first ripple of humor he had felt since storming out of the restaurant, if he tried to sit there for two or three days, he could hardly manage it. He could go without food if he had to, he could even duck into the Greek restaurant to get a quick glass of something to slake his thirst. But he'd have to go to the bathroom sooner or later, and with the way his luck was running, the Worldhouse could come and go while he was hidden away in the can!

He leaned back against the wall and pondered the options that were open to him.

He could go back to the restaurant, make it up with Sally, and take her up into the Sierras to talk with his Uncle Stan. Right now, the open spaces of the mountains would feel good to him. Maybe, there, he could convince her.

He could go back and bully his way into Amy Brittman's apartment and get a message through her to Pentarn. Pentarn had offered him a way to come and go through the Gates, and he could probably stall Pentarn on doing anything against the Alfar long enough to warn them.

No, that had to be a last resort. Pentarn had been affable enough to Fenton, but somehow Cam didn't think Pentarn could be trusted.

He could bully his way into Garnock's office and demand the talisman Garnock had insisted on calling an apport.

It was growing late on the street, and Fenton shivered a little. A young couple, coming out of Larry Blake's Rathskeller, stared superciliously at the street loafers, and Fenton realized that for the moment he was just another of them.

One of the street people, this one with long hair braided into the neo-Indian plait, tattooed cheeks gaunt and a long earring dangling nearly to his shoulders, moved toward Fenton. He murmured, "What you waiting for, man, what kind of connection you want? I got Cuban grass, the best, clean, guaranteed."

Automatically Fenton shook his head. "Can't use it, friend. Sorry."

"I don't deal in anything *really* illegal, but I can steer you to a fellow with good acid or downers."

Fenton shook his head again. "Sorry. Not my scene," he said, but realized that he had better move off. After all, this was one of the time-honored ways to deal with street pushers, simply wait until one of them approached you. What the hell, he wasn't there to make moral judgments about them, if that was the way they wanted to spend their lives. He thought rather wryly that when Garnock cut him off the project he had actually given a fair imitation of an addict deprived of his drug.

He set off at a brisk walk toward his apartment. In the mood Sally was in, she wouldn't be receptive to any calls. He'd give her time to cool down and call her in the morning. It was late, he could hardly get into the place where Amy Brittman lived, and if he tried to force his way into her room at midnight, somebody would probably call a cop. All he wanted was to talk to the woman, but he'd have a lot better luck convincing her of that in broad daylight.

That is, supposing she wasn't off in the alien world at Pentarn's side, his adoring sycophant, delighting in her position as the Lord Leader's woman . . . maybe she was there now. *Damn* Garnock, how dare the man take his talisman, Irielle's gift! If he had his talisman, he wouldn't have to wait around for the Worldhouse to come back to this plane, he could find the damn thing wherever it was hiding . . .

Twice more he walked the length of Telegraph. Dealers in recreational drugs approached him, slipping up to him and murmuring offers of various things. Fenton refused, but the last one to approach him had three rings in his ear which reminded him of the shaven hippie who had sold him the Antaril.

His apartment was cold and empty. He dug the envelope out, and sat staring at the little blue tablets.

Again, temptation. And now, since he was off the Antaril official project, he couldn't even say that it would disturb the final results. Swallow one of those little blue tablets and he could walk out of here through the wall, and before long he would be in Irielle's world and do his explaining to her. Irielle was reasonable, not a man-hating paranoid like Sally!

That brought him up sharp. Sally had accused him of exactly that, of wanting a dream woman because a real one was too much challenge. And if he fled to Irielle because of a disagreement with Sally, wasn't he proving what she had said? Self-doubt suddenly flooded him. Had Garnock been right, too, that he was using the drug for escape into a world more sympathetic than the one he was in now?

He could go round and round that dead-end, squirrel-cage mental trap all night. He was committed to believing that the world of the Alfar was real, that Pentarn's world was real. The ironfolk were real too, real enough to run off with an extremely solid steel axe, and he found he didn't like thinking about what they might be going to do with it. If they could chop up horses alive and eat them, he somehow didn't think they'd stop at doing the same to people.

And if the ironfolk are coming through now into the other worlds . . .

Pentarn had a legitimate grudge against the Alfar. But letting ironfolk loose on them was playing dirty, and once he started messing around, letting one world spill over into the other, how long was he going to be able to control it?

I've got to get to the Alfar and warn them. They know what Pentarn's doing, but they don't know why.

He thought about that too, sitting at his desk, the blue tablet on the table before him. Pentarn wasn't a fairy-tale villain, doing evil for no reason at all. He had a grudge against the Alfar and it hadn't been handled right at all. He believed that they were holding his son prisoner with magic and enchantments. If the Alfar could convince him that the boy didn't want to go back—no. Worse and worse. That would hurt Pentarn's pride unendurably.

I ought to take Pentarn's offer up, and try to make peace between the worlds. . . . He laughed sourly at that. He was treating this whole thing like a story, a fantasy which could have a nice pat happy ending. And he had cast himself in the role of hero, making peace between the warring worlds. Nice work if you can do it, he admonished himself, but he wasn't hero stuff at all.

The best thing to do was to get back in the world of the Alfar and try to make his peace with Findhal, who seemed to be their leader, after a fashion. Maybe Kerridis would help.

Now that he had resolved what to do, he started making serious plans. Could he take anything with him? No, probably not, not unless he had the talisman Garnock had taken from him.

Disembodied, he could walk through walls and the artifacts of this world could not stop him. But the talisman was solid in all worlds. Could he break into Garnock's office in his 'tweenman form, walk straight through the walls of the office and into the display of items there? That ought to be his first plan, to get the talisman back, and then to go straight to the Worldhouse . . .

With the tablet halfway to his lips, he stopped in dismay. He knew from experience—three sessions now under the influence of Antaril—that the world around him quickly dissolved into the forested world of the Alfar. How in the world—in any of the worlds—could he locate Garnock's office, or the talisman? Physically, he was about ten city blocks from the campus, and by the time he walked that far in his 'tweenman form, he would be hopelessly lost in the shifting landscape of the Alfar world.

Maybe if he swallowed the tablet just outside Garnock's office—but then what would happen to his body? He'd step out of it, and leave it lying unconscious on the stairs, and what would happen then? When they came in and found him lying, apparently in a drugged stupor, outside Garnock's office, he would just wind up in Cowell Hospital again, this time with "unauthorized drug use" written up on his chart. That wasn't going to do his reputation any good, and it would just reinforce Garnock's opinion of him, which was low enough already.

Out-of-the-body travel, he thought, *certainly has its limitations.* The same would apply if he followed his first impulse—to swallow the tablet on the very gates of the Worldhouse.

It wouldn't be the first time a comatose hippie, deep in his drug-dream, had been lying spaced-out somewhere on Telegraph Avenue. Find a nice soft doorway, where nobody would step on him, stretch quietly out and take his Antaril, go through the Worldhouse . . .

But he realized he could not visualize with equanimity the thought of Cameron Fenton, late of the parapsychol-

ogy department, lying around on the street with acid-
heads and street people stoned literally out of their minds
. . . in his case, out of his body. And what if they carted
him off to the drunk tank or—again—to a hospital? It
would be a black mark on his record he could never
erase.

Fenton scowled at the blue Antaril tablet, sitting there
mocking him. This wasn't going to be nearly as easy as
he had thought it would be.

There was only one safe place—aside from the parapsychology lab, which was now barred to him—for his
body while he was out on Antaril; and that was right
here, in his own apartment. This time he didn't have Doc
and the whole staff to monitor his body and take it to the
hospital if he stayed away too long. He'd simply have to
get back in time to keep his body from deteriorating.

Wasn't there anyone he could trust to stay by him
while he was experimenting?

The only person he could think of was his Uncle Stan,
up in the Sierras, and he couldn't go there. He didn't
know any of the landmarks between the worlds, there.
Here at least he had the awareness of Kerridis' palace,
the eucalyptus grove which was a "good place" in both
worlds, certain areas in space and location in both
worlds. He'd just have to go it alone.

He might as well be comfortable. He undressed, put on
a warm bathrobe, stretched out on the sofa, and looked
thoughtfully at the small blue square. He had no way of
knowing comparative strength; he did not know the
strength of what Garnock had given him, and he didn't
suppose he'd get a very favorable response if he called
up to ask! Should he take one or two of the small tablets,
or all four?

What would happen if he got an overdose? Would an
overdose do anything at all?

It would be easier to cope with the effects of an underdose than an overdose. He'd start with one tablet. If it
didn't work the way he expected it to, he could experiment again later, but for now he would play it safe.

He faced the knowledge, too, that there was no way of
knowing precisely how the drug would act by mouth, or
even if it was Antaril at all. The shaven hippie might

have given him anything from LSD to pure dextrose, colored blue.

Well, there was nothing to do but take the chance. If it was dextrose, the worst that could happen was nothing at all. If it was LSD—well, the worst he could expect was his very own light show, and a wasted night and day to show for it, provided he didn't get overconfident and try to drive a car under the influence; and he knew better than that.

If it was something really dangerous, like datura, jimsonweed—well, he could only hope that he would recognize the symptoms in time to get rid of the stuff. Methedrine wouldn't kill him, not one dose, but he was not certain how his metabolism would react to it; depending on its strength, he might be awake for the next three days, climbing the walls, or simply run around babbling inanely at the wind for a few hours.

What you're doing, he told himself grimly, *is stalling. You're scared.* He didn't bother to deny it, even to himself. He'd had a narrow enough escape, last time. The memory of seeing his body, tied and restrained in Cowell Hospital, tube-fed and unaware, terrified him.

He got up off the sofa, took pen and paper from his desk and sat down, firmly dating the paper, trying to collect all his scientific detachment. After a little thought he wrote: *I am engaging in an experiment with a pharmaceutical*—even in his mind he shied away from the connotations of *drug*—*which I believe to be Antaril. If I am discovered unconscious and display no signs of any recognizable toxicity*—any halfway competent doctor would know it right away if he was showing signs of jimsonweed poisoning—*it is necessary only to provide life support and guard against dehydration, by intravenous saline and glucose feeding, until I recover consciousness.*

That ought to protect him against almost any contingency.

He hesitated, the pen in his hand, took another sheet of paper. He wrote before he really thought about it:

Darling Sally; please believe I am only doing what I have to do. Don't worry about me—

He stared, incredulous, at the paper; scowled and tore it into unrecognizable fragments. He swept the pieces

into his wastebasket and propped the other note where
anyone coming into his apartment would see it. He put
the blue tablet into his mouth and washed it down with
a glass of water.

He wondered, grimly: *Underdose? Overdose? Or nothing at all?*

One of his questions was answered swiftly; a wave of
dizziness swept across him, making him stumble, putting
out a hand as he collapsed on the couch. Not dextrose or
some harmless placebo like aspirin or milk sugar, then.
Something, and something powerful. But even the purest
LSD did not act that swiftly; nor did any of the other
psychoactive drugs he was aware of. As he swiftly recovered himself, pulling himself upright, he realized that
his body lay below him, collapsed limply half on and half
off the couch. He had made a big mistake: he should
have arranged his body comfortably before swallowing
the stuff! But who would have imagined that it would
have acted more swiftly than the intravenous dose
Garnock had given him? Remembering that for the first
few moments under the drug before, he had been able to
speak, he tried hard to get back into his body long
enough to rearrange it in a safe position on the couch,
but his limbs were stubbornly unresponsive. Well, there
was nothing he could do about it and anyway, he now
knew that whatever it was, it was Antaril. And, judging
by results, a damned big dose of it.

The walls still appeared solid around him. If he could
manage to stay in the physical dimension of Berkeley
long enough, he might be able to reach Garnock's office,
or at least the Worldhouse/print-shop. Which meant that
the sooner he got out of here the better.

He walked toward the wall, put out an experimental
hand and walked through. Already the man-made artifacts of this dimension were fading around him. Hurrying, moving with the speed of thought—he wondered
briefly what the speed of thought *was*—he seemed to
himself to race along Telegraph Avenue, somehow
dressed in his normal street clothes. Now for Garnock's
office and the talisman—

But already the streets were thinning and disappearing.
For a block or two he could see the cars, the shops and

house-fronts, and wondered what would happen if he stepped into a shop. Nothing; they couldn't see him. *If this gets around,* he thought, *it would be very attractive to sneak thieves. Just walk in through the wall.* But, of course, the thief would not be able to lift up anything; he would be in the same shape as Fenton trying to unlock the iron door for Irielle and falling right through it instead.

But it could be used to case a place for a gang of thieves to come in later. And voyeurs could get a kick out of it, walk in and watch women undressing, or whatever their particular kick happened to be. Fenton told himself that he probably had a criminal mind and turned it back to the business at hand.

If the talisman, he thought, is real in all the worlds, and it's here now, when I get to Garnock's office will I find it hanging in midair without the display case around it? Somehow the thought made him uneasy. The vrill-swords were supposed to be real in all the worlds and yet he'd never found one just hanging around in his own world. Maybe they were real *in only one world at a time.* That must be it. And if so, once he was in the world of the Alfar he couldn't get to Garnock's office this time.

And already he could hardly see the cars in the street; around him only insubstantial ghosts loomed, shadows of streets and houses and shops. Under his feet was not stone, but a soft sandy soil, in which he could thinly see the shadow-shapes of strange bushes and trees.

Well, if he were in the world of the Alfar, the World-house ought to be somewhere around here . . . although he remembered what Irielle had said, that the World-house might not *want* to be found. He found himself wondering what the Worldhouse would look like in this dimension if he *did* find it, and if he would know it when he did. Maybe it would be disguised as another tree. What would the Worldhouse be like in its real aspect, anyhow? Would it look like a massive computer center, or a temple? Some odd combination of both, like the Lawrence Hall of Science in the Berkeley hills? If the palace of the Alfar queen Kerridis looked like the shadow of a ghostly cathedral made of trees, what made him think the Worldhouse would be any more recognizable?

I ought to have Irielle as a guide, he thought disconsolately. *I'll never find my way around unless I have somebody to guide me!*

Because he certainly was no longer in Berkeley. And he was not where he could see any familiar landmark in the country of the Alfar. Beneath his feet was a sandy soil, sparse grass growing thinly; and there was a strange, dull, growing light around him. It could not possibly be near dawn yet, in Fenton's world, and when he had come here it was about ten in the evening. Now an odd saffron-colored light, lurid and eye-hurting, was growing around him, not like the misty pale sunlight of the Alfar world, not at all.

He looked around for any landmark. Of course there were not many landmarks which he could recognize in the Alfar world, only the grove of the feathery white trees which corresponded to the eucalyptus grove on campus, and the cave-mouth into which the ironfolk had dragged Kerridis. And since in his own world he was about ten blocks south of the campus, he couldn't even estimate what distance in the unfamiliar Alfar landscape separated him from the grove, or even from the network of volcanic caves. He need not assume that, because the scenery looked different, he had ended up somewhere else this time.

After all, Irielle had said something about how boring it would be to live in an unchanging landscape. Maybe they had gotten bored, changed this one around a little bit, and he just hadn't caught up with it yet. He kept doggedly walking along in a direction which seemed to be north, to take him toward the eucalyptus grove, even though he faced the knowledge that it might take him to the volcanic caves, where ironfolk could walk out at any minute.

There seemed to be, in those caves, an eerie kind of overlap between the world of the ironfolk and the world of the Alfar. Maybe Pentarn had had something to do with that; Kerridis seemed to think so. It was obvious that Pentarn knew all about the world-overlap, the world gates and how to find his way around in them.

If I'm his analogue, I ought to know it too, shouldn't I? Then Fenton chuckled at that thought. He wasn't anything

like a Lord Leader in his own world either. If Pentarn
somehow made it into Berkeley, he'd be the governor of
California—or at least the head of the department—before anyone stopped to figure out what was happening!

Only Fenton really didn't find it all that funny. That
thought showed himself something about his own feelings
that he'd never been aware of before, and he didn't like
it.

Damn it, where were the trees? The one constant of his
three visits to the Alfar world had been trees, huge towering trees which dwarfed the redwoods! All he could see
here were low scrubby bushes and the sandy soil. Of
course, insisting that the shifting landscape of the Alfar
world must be always alike was thinking from his own
experience, and he already knew that kind of reasoning
made no sense. The beach at Malibu didn't look much
like the high Sierras, and they were both California. Only
this looked more like the Joshua-tree national park, with
those curious, twisty thornbushes, the dry sand underfoot,
and whereas another constant of the Alfar world was cold,
Fenton found himself wiping away sweat that dripped
down his body in great streams.

Wherever he was, he had probably better resign himself to the knowledge that he wasn't in Alfar country.

*Oh, great. That was all I needed, to find myself in a
completely unknown world.*

What had done it? The unexpected strength of the
street-made Antaril? Should he have set his will more
firmly on the world to which he intended to travel? He
didn't know. This world went by its own rules. But here
he was. He hadn't seen enough of Pentarn's world to
know whether he was there, or not. The one thing he
knew was that he wasn't where he had wanted and intended to be.

He kept on slogging drearily in what he felt was a
northerly direction, across the thick dry sand. Above him,
slowly, the light grew and a great, strange, burning orange
disk began to spread above the horizon. That, Fenton told
himself uselessly, certainly isn't the sun I expected, and it
isn't the sun of the Alfar world either. But if he kept on
going north, sooner or later he might find himself at the
point in this new world which corresponded to the euca-

lyptus grove. Irielle had said that was a good place in both worlds. Maybe it would be a good one in *this* world —though he found it hard to imagine that this world *had* any good places.

It looks, he told himself, just exactly like what the Bible called Gehenna, which was a scorching place in a howling desert.

Abruptly, as he slogged on, he stumbled. Then he fell full length, measuring himself against the ground with a bone-shaking impact. *Damn!* He remembered the freezing rock in the Alfar world, which had nearly taken the hide from his shin. Gasping with pain, the breath knocked from his body, he put out a hand and discovered that he had stumbled over a low edge of rock, a kind of natural wall which rose about a foot and a half in front of him.

Not man-made. One of the rules of these worlds was, or seemed to be, that you could not touch artificial objects. Except those valid in all worlds, like vrillswords and the shifting talismans. But Fenton stared down in amazement at this wall, wondering how anything so regular could possibly be a natural object. It stretched away across the otherwise featureless thorny desert, as far as he could see; perfectly straight, perfectly regular, about eighteen inches high, and quite square. Fenton stared at it and scowled, putting out a hand to touch its hot stony surface.

There weren't supposed to be any straight lines in nature.

Well, that was rubbish, of course. Crystals split off in straight lines; that was what made them crystals. The electrons in a lodestone or natural magnet were all lined up in a more regular display than anything that could be drawn with a ruler. And here in this alien world was something that looked like a man-made artifact, but the barked shins told him that it was something natural to this world.

Unless, of course, the rules were different here than they were in his own world or the world of the Alfar.

Only why hadn't he seen it until he fell over it? He would have sworn that there wasn't any straight line anywhere, when he was looking before. Had the wall suddenly poked its way up out of nowhere?

Fenton got to his feet, staring at the great orange disk in the sky—he hated to call it a sun—and at the glaring ochre light that was beginning to hurt his eyes. He put his palms over his eyes but fancied that the ochre light came through anyhow. The glare was dreadful. *Hell,* he thought. *I'm in hell. Anyhow it looks that way and feels like it and if I were a religious sort of guy I'd wonder if I were being punished for taking drugs. Maybe it serves me right. Sally would probably think so.*

The pain in his shins had abated enough so that he could walk again, and he tried, confused, to get his bearings. Which way was north, which way had he been going? And why bother anyway? All around him, in the terrible glowing blast-furnace glare, there was not a single object he could see, just this unholy flat desert, acres and acres of thorny low grass, and this ugly rock wall stretching itself from nowhere to nowhere, until it faded out into the dim distance in either direction.

It wasn't even high enough to give any good shade. Fenton looked at his feet and discovered, as he had surmised, that he himself cast no shadow. So he couldn't get out of the sun. But if this wall was a man-made object— and there didn't seem any way it could be natural—it would lead him from somewhere to somewhere.

Pick a direction, Fenton, he ordered himself grimly, *and start walking. Go somewhere!*

He walked.

And he walked.

The huge orange sun climbed the sky as he walked, and all around him there was a thick silence, overlaid with a small dry rustle, as if the thorny grass were muttering in the nonexistent breeze, or some kind of small insect's chirping. He followed the wall.

Which led, it seemed, from nothing to *more* nothing. As he walked it seemed that even the grass thinned out and grew more sparsely, and there was only the sand and that unending low hideous wall, which stretched as far as he could see into distance.

The street people, the ones who were really into LSD and similar drugs, said that sooner or later you were sure to get a bad trip. Well, as trips went, Fenton reflected, this was about as bad a bummer as he could imagine. On the other hand, people who had experimented legitimately with LSD said that most bad trips came from the experimenter's own unresolved neurotic conflicts, or from impure or contaminated acid. That would at least account for the difference between his "legitimate" trips in the laboratory, and this one on Antaril purchased from a dealer on the street and contaminated with God-knows-what.

Well, there was no point in griping about it. Nobody had forced him to come here. In fact, both Garnock and Sally had warned him.

Fenton felt a sudden, gripping fear. Was this proof that the Alfar world had never existed, that it was all inside his own head, and that now when he was doing "illegal" experimentation, his mind punished him with a bad trip and exile from the fantasy world he had built to be maximally satisfying to his own emotional needs?

He wouldn't accept that until he had to. Damn it, he was a scientist, not a hippie tripping out. If this was a way to prove whether or not it was real, he'd accept it. As far as he could see, the worst thing about this trip was that it was boring. It could be a lot worse. He could have landed in the volcanic caves of the ironfolk, for instance.

He slogged along under the orange sun, and even though he knew his body was safe on the floor in his apartment, he scratched with the heat and grumbled to himself; he stumbled along, doggedly following the wall which went further and further, with nothing to hear but the dry rustles and chirps in the grass. It seemed now that they rose and fell like distant half-heard speech, just over the limit of his hearing. Suddenly he felt a prickly sensation between his shoulders, a sensation he had known all his life, and had learned to understand only when he went into parapsychology. He knew what it meant.

Someone was watching him.

Fenton whirled, half expecting to see someone previously invisible standing there.

But there was nothing; in the penumbral light, the desert and the grass stretched featureless and blank, with nothing but the unending wall. Fenton saw a faint shred of movement at the very edge of his visual field, as if something had quickly scuttled out of sight. Feeling foolish, he asked, "Is there anyone there?"

No answer.

Of course there was no answer. There was nobody in this god-damned wilderness to answer, there was nobody there but himself. And it was a debatable point, he thought, remembering his body sprawled in his apartment, whether he was really there either!

He went on.

Why, he didn't quite know. He wasn't getting anywhere, and the wall went on and on without the slightest indication that it was getting anywhere or had come from anywhere. The Great Wall of China, Fenton thought, had nothing on this one. At least the one in China made some sense. The Chinese had too much sense to build a wall like this one, which went nowhere, ended nowhere, with the surrounding territory exactly the same on both sides. Fenton felt the prickling in his back again which meant that some one was watching him. He ignored it as long as he could—he felt like a fool to turn around and see nothing but the featureless desert again—but finally it became too much to ignore and he turned.

Nothing. Of course.

He said out loud, "There is nobody watching me."

Then where was nobody? It reminded him of the Greek legend of Ulysses, where the crafty hero told the Cyclops that his name was Nobody. So when Ulysses put out his eye, the Cyclops roared, "Nobody is murdering me," and his friends and relations shouted back, "If nobody is murdering you, why are you making such a dreadful noise?" and went on about their own business.

Well, nobody was watching him, all right, but he wished he could get a sight of nobody.

> Last night I met upon the stair
> The little man who wasn't there.
> He wasn't there again today,
> Gee, how I wish he'd go away!

Fenton slogged on, wondering if all through the hours and hours of what must have been an incredible overdose of Antaril, he would slog through this bare and dreadful nowhere, tormented by heat and the sense that somebody was watching him.

But there was nobody there to watch him except the wall; and while he had heard an old saying that walls sometimes had ears, he had never heard of a wall with eyes. He thought of giving the wall a good kick. If it *were* the wall that had eyes, maybe the wall, in true Alice-in-Wonderland fashion, would demand, "Why did you do that?" At least then he would have someone to talk to.

He actually drew back his foot to try out his theory. Then he set it down, and realized that he was shaking. He didn't know which scared him worst; the thought that the wall might actually answer him—or the fear that it might *not*.

Actually, I'd just as soon not know. He wondered vaguely why he didn't sit down—or lie down, to get what little shade the wall did cast—and wait out this thoroughly boring trip, until the Antaril wore off and he found himself back in his own body.

But he didn't. He walked doggedly on, telling himself that if he only went on long enough he would have to get somewhere.

Because right now, as the hippies say, I'm real nowhere!

As he walked he began to hear faintly, through the dull stridulous sound of the invisible crickets or insects in the thorny grass, a faint far-off sound. He couldn't distinguish it. Slowly it became a dull hammering sound, muffled, as if underground, the sound of a great engine. Fenton tripped and fell again, full length in the sand, and he had the definite impression that somehow the earth had buckled under him. Well, that was all he needed. He might have expected, here, that he would run into earthquakes. There was nothing else here; the very ground under his feet got bored and wanted to stretch a little . . .

He climbed to his feet. Well, there was definitely some sound now, and it was definitely a machinelike roar, but he still couldn't see anything but the desert and that damned wall!

He supposed it could be worse.

It got worse. Ahead of him, the earth buckled and rumbled again, and a great gaping cave-mouth opened in it.

Fenton shrank back, looking into the darkness, and abruptly a great horde of the ironfolk burst out of the cave-mouth and ran, screeching and gobbling, toward Fenton.

He stood, frozen, shaking, frightened to the point of paralysis. There was no escape. He might have known that in a landscape such as this, those repulsive little creatures would be right at home. And now they were going to run right over him, and he supposed the next thing he knew he would be rent alive by those horrible knives of theirs . . .

"Quick," said a harsh grating voice, "in here."

Under his feet the earth slid, moved, buckled and thundered and a gap widened beside the wall. A cave-mouth opened. Without stopping to think, Fenton ducked inside. After he was inside, he had sudden second thoughts; this one was probably filled to the brim with the ironfolk too. But as he whirled to get out faster than he had come in, the reddish-orange light was gone and he stood in total darkness.

The cave-mouth had closed behind him.

CHAPTER FOURTEEN

FENTON STOOD in the muggy heat, blinking, unable even to see his hand before his face, and suddenly submerged in panic. Underground, surrounded by natural rock—suppose that when he began to fade, he was trapped here?

Is this my personal neurosis, nightmares of being trapped? Last time, it was the Rockhold . . .

He said aloud, "Is anyone there?"

"One is here," said the harsh, grating voice that had bidden him to step into the cave-mouth. "Nothing rescuing from hairy swarmers among them, question? No good hiding from swarmers seeing, question? But this surrounding is a shadow, and so explaining why there is intrusion; permission not given for anyone else invading. Swarmers not asking permission, stating obviousness. And shadows from Middle World coming now without inviting . . . polite request, be standing still," the harsh voice grated, as Fenton shifted his feet. "One is knowing the intruding presence is shadow, but small things not knowing, fearing feet of intruder."

Fenton froze, wondering what kind of "small things" should fear his feet, what kind of small things might be concealed in the darkness. Was this the world of the ironfolk, from which they had come? No; in that curious speech, the invisible voice had indicated that "swarmers" had not asked permission. He supposed that what he had heard as a voice was actually a series of thoughts, incapable of translation into Fenton's own language, only a laboriously-transmitted series of concepts. But the alien presence, whatever it might be, seemed to mean him no harm—or would it have invited him out of the way of the ironfolk?

He said aloud, "Who are you?"

"One is here," the grating voice remarked in the darkness. "Not knowing answering, intruders of Middle World always calling this presence in sounds of identity."

Puzzling that out, Fenton was reminded of the Alice-in-Wonderland world where things had no names, and now he knew what had always struck him as being slightly wrong about that interchange; that the things mentioned knew the concept of *names* and were aware of not having them. Now he seemed to have encountered a presence which not only didn't have a name, but couldn't imagine what the concept of a name could be, so that the question, "Who are you?" conveyed only vague unease about the identity encountered.

How in the world—any world—could he communicate with a presence which had no sense of individual names? Well, he had heard once of a language without nouns; at least this one wasn't as alien as all that. The "swarmers" were pretty obvious; the ironfolk. He himself had been conceptualized as "intruder." He said, carefully trying to think himself into the way the invisible voice had spoken, "This intruder regrets intruding and was not intending to come here, but elsewhere. I don't know——" Hell, they didn't have a concept of personal identity either! "This intruder regrets disturbing any small things, was unaware of their presence. I didn't think——" Again he checked himself; habits of language certainly affected speech and even thought! "This intruder was not aware of any presence except wall, and of—of that one who speaks in the darkness."

Around his feet he heard a curious rustle, and quivered; it sounded for all the world like many tiny claws dragging on stone. But he stood still, aware that if he injured any of the small creepy things around him, the speaker, who seemed to have a certain amount of good will at this moment, could abruptly close up this suddenly-opened refuge around him and probably suffocate him. He stood still through the creaks and rustles, like half-heard conversation.

The harsh voice said, "One is not aware of intruder's differentiations. One is wall and also one is small things, but now aware of difference from intruder, and knowing intruder is not of self. Question: intruder is not part of hairy things?"

"No," Fenton said emphatically, "intruder is not."

"Question: then, intruder is other, will please be explaining otherness?"

Now *that*, Fenton thought, was reasonable—but also impossible. Forgetting his attempt to speak in terms comprehensible to the invisible voice in the darkness, he said, "Not possible. I don't know where I am, or how I got here instead of where I was intending to go. And I can't see you, so I don't know who you are."

There was a protracted silence, as if the presence in the dark was laboriously trying to puzzle out Fenton's alien concepts. *Well*, Fenton thought, *better that he should try to read my mind and know what I'm really thinking, than that I should try to speak his kind of thoughts and maybe give the wrong impression.*

Finally the harsh voice came again. It sounded plaintive and a little frustrated.

"Question: this intruder is more aware of surroundings with color of sun displaying same?"

Fenton realized, following that with some difficulty, that he was being asked if he could see better in the light.

"Emphatically yes," he replied. After a minute a crack widened somewhere and the dull-orange, penumbral light began to penetrate. Slowly, as the light grew, Fenton became aware of the cave walls around him, and beneath his feet an array of small scuttling many-legged things, like small orange hermit-crabs or armored spiders.

"Question: reason for intruder presenting self here when not intending?"

Fenton frowned, his brain flinching from the task of trying to explain the alien dimensions and multiple-worlds' theory to this invisible presence—he had begun to think it was the very rock cave itself which spoke to him. All he could say was, "Not knowing."

He supposed this made sense. He had been able to communicate with the Alfar because, while they were not human, they had humanlike speech organs. Pentarn, as far as he could see, *was* human. But why should he assume that *all* the worlds were inhabited by anything resembling humans? Here he was in a world which extended sapience to the very ground under his feet. Was this what was called an earth-elemental? Well, he supposed even that could be worse; suppose he'd run into a volcano and had to communicate with *that?* At least this presence was benign and rather slow of speech and thought—though it had been quick enough to open the cave-mouth to hide him from the ironfolk.

He said, "Question," and realized that in a sense he *was* picking up the way the other presence communicated, "the one I'm speaking to—you are not belonging to the hairy things?"

"Emphatically not belonging," the voice, which he now started to consider an earth-elemental, replied. "One feels anger and repugnance which intruder not meaning offense, supposing. Reassuring, hairy things not any part of identity, or of intruder, so otherness to both and agreeing on same. Question: intruder sharing sense of disgustingness to hairy things?"

"Definitely yes," Fenton said, and realized dimly that he had just managed the first definition of terms in communicating with an alien presence!

"Welcoming agreement with intruder, sensing wonder and asking, intruder wishing to arrive elsewhere and not in immediate surroundings?"

"What I was wanting," Fenton said, "was to get into the world of the Alfar." And after he had spoken he wondered if he had just blurred their communication again. I wish I could see the one I'm talking to, he thought, and after a moment realized he had spoken the words aloud.

"Being agreeable to intruder sensing confusion, making easier to exchanging thought," rumbled the voice, and after a moment, in the dull light, a piece of the rock wall began to bulge and move outward, rippling upward, creating something a little like the wall Fenton had been following across the desert. But now he wondered who had been following whom; had the ground under his feet, which was evidently part of the elemental, extended itself into that form to follow where Cam was walking? Did it experience time so differently that the whole long march along the wall had been simultaneous? Cam gripped his head, feeling it ache. He wondered if somehow he could conjure up an aspirin into his imaginary pocket? Slowly, the rock wall moved, stretched, formed itself into a low, stumpy creation with two short stubby legs, a small bulge where the head should be, knobby arms, and a sort of sketch of a face, eyes which glowed faintly—light-sensitive reflectors, perhaps?—and a set of thick lips. The elemental had forgotten a nose. Of course; it didn't need to breathe, or smell anything.

"Presenting intruder with familiar form identical to appearance presenting," remarked the small rock mouth with evident satisfaction, and Fenton, blinking, realized that this was probably what he, Fenton, looked like to the rock identity; self-contained, moving on two legs, with two arms, a mouth and eyes, contained in the head on top. To him, the rock-elemental looked like nothing on earth. But after all, they weren't on earth. Or were they? Anyhow, this was a humanoid illusion, and he supposed that it could be called—what was the name for earth-elementals? Gnomes. Yes; a gnome stood before him, in the form it apparently thought proper for confronting humans.

"Gnome," he said aloud, and the thing before him moved a stumpy leg; the whole ground seemed to tremble a little, as if moving part of itself.

"One so being called, time not now," the gnome said, "long remembering. Question: intruder is of place where self ceases and other rock not understanding speech?"

"That's right," Fenton said. "Where I come from, the rocks don't talk."

"Sympathizing," said the gnome. "Sorry for other from such unhappiness." It took another stubby step, all the army of small scurrying things below its feet moving like water, surging and managing to avoid the step; the gnome was part of them too, it seemed. "Suggesting, hairy ones now having removed disgustingnesses elsewhere, intruder preferring return to sun displaying?"

"Fine," Fenton said, and the gnome took a heavy step toward the crack of light, which widened as it moved toward. And then they were outside in the orange sunlight. Fenton noticed that the stubby grass did not bend under the weight of the gnome, but seemed to flow around its feet, as the small army of spidery things had done inside the cave-mouth. *Of course. The gnome's part of them and doesn't feel itself separate at all.*

The wall, Fenton noticed peripherally, was gone. That had been the gnome-entity too, evidently.

As they walked the gnome put out one of the stubby protrusions which it had where Fenton would have expected a hand, as if confidently expecting Fenton would take it. As Fenton watched, the hand took on something like fingers and a thumb, and Fenton, surprised at himself, took the dark stumpy little hand in his own. It did not feel cold, like rock, but sun-warmed and firm, rather like an animal's hard shell or horn. The gnome walked beside Fenton, subtly shifting the length of its step until their strides kept precise pace; this disconcerted Fenton at first, but then he realized that the gnome was accustomed to feeling everything in its world as literally part of itself and evidently was uncomfortable—if rock could feel discomfort—at what it called *otherness*. He felt very grateful for the gnome's friendliness. The rock-creature could, after all, have kept him in the dark indefinitely.

From the hard, warm, thick fingers in his own, Fenton began to *feel*, inside himself, the warmth of the sun, the flow of the small grasses under his feet, the far-off chirps and stridulations that were vaguely like half-heard speech. Only now it seemed that he could understand them, that they spoke of soothing warmth—Fenton realized that the heat no longer made him uncomfortable. Everything around him—now that the ironfolk had removed their disturbing element somewhere else—seemed to radiate slow and sluggish content.

The gnome muttered at him, "Question: why leaving this best-of-all-places, why wishing elsewhere than warmth and sun and happiness here?"

That, Fenton thought, was a damned good question. Why should he want to go anywhere else? The temptation was almost overwhelming, to sink down into the warmth, lie like a rock: in the sun, soaking up the heat and calm, with the soothing music of the cricket-chirps and all the small live things around him; why leaving, why discontent in warmth . . . He felt himself slowly sinking to his knees, as if melting into the rock surrounding. . . .

In shock, Fenton realized what was happening; he was

beginning to think like the rock, to make the gnome comfortable by melting into his comforting ambiance. To lie here comfortably like a rock, content with the passing of time, go no further. . . .

Shaking his head in sudden determination, he struggled up to his feet, pulling his hand loose from the gnome. The little rock-thing stood staring up at him with what looked, even to Fenton, like hurt on its amorphous and shapeless features.

"Question: why intruder is othering again? Question: why unhappy here?"

Othering. He had to hang on to that. And yet he felt a kindliness to the friendly gnome. He struggled to form words the gnome could understand.

"Happy here, certainly, enjoying sun and warmth and society of rock things. But—but not my own world. Afraid hairy things hurting friends, people in other worlds, people I love. Needing to go and fight against hairy things, tell other people they are coming . . ."

The gnome's rock body seemed to ripple and flow like water instead of its own earthy stuff. The thick voice grated, "Understanding. Other world living, must to other world moving, this one showing where. Be following."

The humanoid form rippled and was a rock again, a lump, a boulder . . . no; it was long and thick and crawling like a heavy-bodied lizard. And yet the voice was still the concerned, harsh, friendly voice of the gnome. Fenton understood; the sameness of the rock, the metamorphosis to be like Fenton, but not truly Fenton, was too tempting. At all costs he must preserve that sense of *otherness* or he could be trapped here. He followed along after the lizard, who now seemed a rocky dragon, coiling along across the sandy waste.

Something he had read, years ago, flickered across his mind; *elemental contacts are dangerous to mankind* . . . . .

It was hot again, and he felt sticky and uncomfortable, but he was glad of it; it meant he was less endangered, less likely to sink into the cozy awareness of the elemental rock. He slogged along behind the writhing coils of the gnome.

There was a faraway shimmer, colorless, rippling, unstable, like water on the face of the burning desert, like

the mirages he had seen in the Mohave. Water, here, or
mirage? Again and again it dissolved as they approached
it, then, as the gnome shot out his dragon-coils toward it,
it seemed somehow to solidify, become a pallid wall of
nothingness across the burning sand. The lizard-shape of
the gnome reared upright, put out arms and legs and the
stubby face.

"Question: not wanting entering place of hairy things?"

"Emphatically, not wanting," Fenton said. He didn't
know what the world of the ironfolk was like, but he was
also perfectly sure he didn't want to find out.

"Where wanting, sunworlds, world of water things,
which wanting?"

"The Alfar," Fenton said without much hope, and the
blobby rocky face of the gnome rippled into the sem-
blance of puzzlement, then understanding.

"World where dancing in light, tree-world shining, you
wanting, opening for going," it said, and again put out
its stubby hand. "Hairy things coming, take jewel-lights
from walls out of sun, hoping that when Gate opening for
them they finding in other world only root-rottings. Sor-
rowing now at separating but Gate opening and must going. Question: intruder will coming again to be rock in
sun with this one sharing?"

Fenton said, "I hope so." He barely felt the touch of
the gnome's warm hard fingers under his own when the
world rippled under him and *shifted,* with an indefinable
slurring of the light across his eyes. For a moment, dizzied, he thought that he saw a glimmering of walls,
houses, darkness; then the shifting slither of the world
under his feet came again and he was standing in dim,
hazy sunlight, in the midst of a ring of white, feathery
trees in the world of the Alfar.

The grove was deserted. He did not yet know the landmarks well enough to know if it were the same tree-ring
which, before, had corresponded to the eucalyptus grove
in his own world. But it certainly looked like it. The ring
of thorns which had been there, last time, to close the
gate to the ironfolk, was not there this time. It was the
first time he had seen the world of the Alfar in sunshine;
he had seen it in snow, darkness and moonlight, but now
it was filled with a misty brightness. Nevertheless, he

could not anywhere see the sun. The sky was all an even glowing haze, without a hint of blue anywhere, and though the light was not unlike sunlight, it was not the sun.

He had been here before; Irielle had brought him once, saying it was a good place. But here, also, he had struggled to get through the spell of thorns which had been laid to keep out the ironfolk.

At least there were no ironfolk here now. Fenton breathed relief, knowing he had unconsciously started expecting to see those gentry everywhere now. Evidently, when he encountered them in the gnome's world, they had been on their way somewhere else. What a pity the gnome hadn't simply shut them into the rock, and done away with them once and for all!

The grove lay deserted in the still and misty light. He might be able to find the palace from here . . . if the landscape hadn't shifted too much since the last time he was in the world of the Alfar. And if the palace wanted to be found. The palace . . . or was it Kerridis who determined whether or not he could find the palace? If it depended on Findhal, he was damned sure he'd never find it again!

At the far edge of the grove he heard soft voices. Not the high, singing trill of the Alfar, but voices which, though they were soft and musical, were unmistakably human. Fenton went softly toward them, limping, feeling in his legs the painful cramps which, last time, had been a warning of danger. He wondered how much time, all together, he had wasted in the gnome's world . . . though he supposed it was worth it; he had at least learned something about the unreliability of Antaril in pill form! Maybe the time hadn't been wasted at all. Fenton stooped, rubbed his calf until he could walk on the leg again, and went toward the voices.

He started, then, to back away; for in the depths of the grove he had surprised a pair of lovers; a man and a woman stood half hidden behind the bole of a tree, in an embrace so intense, so all-absorbing that neither heard, nor saw, Fenton approach.

Automatically, with the courtesy which was a part of his own world, he started to back quietly away; but softly as he had moved, they heard him, and the young man raised his head with a swift movement, displaying a dark, subtly familiar face. The woman turned, and Fenton drew a breath of dismay; for the woman was Irielle.

For a moment Fenton felt a surge of anger and actual betrayal, felt that he would drown in the rage that overcame him. Irielle was *his,* the main reason for visiting this world . . . then, tardily, sanity washed through him again. He had absolutely no reason to think that Irielle's feelings for him were anything but kindliness and human fellow-feeling.

Anyway, she's my great-aunt or something like that. . . .
The young man stepped away from Irielle, sweeping her behind him in an arrogant, protective movement.

"Why are you spying on us here?" he shouted. "Did you really think I wouldn't know you in that disguise, or in any other? You'll stop at nothing, will you? I don't want anything from you! Why won't you let me live my own life?"

It was the cry of the young in every age and in all worlds, and even as Fenton knew the mistake the youth was making, and who he must be, the youngster pulled a dagger from his waist and rushed at him.

"Get away! This is vrill, and it can put an end to your life in this world, or any other . . ."

Irielle caught him around the waist. "No, Joel," she cried out. "No, you're making a mistake, it's not Pentarn . . ."

The boy stopped with the dagger already on the downstroke, giving Fenton time to move out of the way with a sharp and undignified movement. He stood staring at the older man and finally said, "Chaos and iron! Who are you?"

"My name's Fenton. I met your father once," Fenton said. "He said I was his—" he stumbled over the word Pentarn had used. "His analogue. If it's any comfort to you," he added, "I don't like him any more than you do."

Joel Tarnsson nodded briefly. He said at last, "Of course. Nobody else you could be." There was, Fenton thought, a resemblance. The son's face was the face he had seen in his own mirror, fifteen years ago. Tarnsson put the dagger awkwardly back into its sheath.

"I owe you an apology, I suppose. Irielle told me about you, but when you surprised us like that, I couldn't think."

Irielle came toward him. Pale as she always was, he could see that she was blushing.

"But you are still a 'tweenman," she said in surprise. "I thought—you have the talisman—"

Fenton shook his head, and she asked anxiously, "You couldn't carry it between worlds?"

"Oh, I could, all right," Fenton said. "But it was taken away from me, by the one—by the man who sent me into this world to start with."

Irielle was indignant. "How did he dare? Did the fellow think he could use it for himself?"

Fenton thought: *I just wish Garnock would try it! It might convince him, when I can't.* How could he explain to Irielle that Garnock wanted only to put it on the wall for a display? It didn't make sense. He said, "I don't know *what* he thinks he can do with it."

Irielle said briskly, "The important thing is that you managed, somehow, to come here." She looked at him, shaking her head in dismay. "You look as if you had passed through the thorny wastes! Was it very difficult?"

Fenton didn't know where, or what, the thorny wastes were, but he was fairly sure they weren't much worse than the barren world of the rock-elemental. Though, remembering how for a time he had melted contentedly into the sun and warmth, he realized there were probably worse worlds. He hoped fervently he would never have to visit them. "I was lost for a while in a world where there was nothing but a rock and a wall. It doesn't matter."

"Why did you come here?" Joel asked, again suspicious, and Fenton realized he didn't know, he wasn't sure. He had wanted to prove to himself that there *was* such a place as here; but he couldn't tell Joel that.

"My foster-father will be angry," Irielle said. "He said he hoped we had seen the last of you; I cannot imagine why he does not trust you." Her face wrinkled in its pretty frown. She said, "Somehow, we must manage it so that you can come properly through the Worldhouse, and I know of no way to arrange that except through Kerridis. Come, you must go to Kerridis."

That suited Fenton perfectly well and he said so, but Joel was doubtful.

"The Lady has given orders not to be disturbed. She is making ready for the Council. I don't think you ought to disturb her, Irielle. Why not take him to Findhal and try to make your foster-father see reason?"

"He will be angry," Irielle said practically, "and he too is making ready for the Council. If I am going to risk angering one of them, I think I would rather anger the Lady, for she has said herself that she owes Fenton for his services to us. My father does, too, if he would only admit it, but he is far more stubborn than the Lady, and not half so ready to see good sense."

"He is more ready to see reason than *my* father," said Joel, but he said no more, and Irielle stretched out her small, slender fingers to Fenton.

"Come, then, we will take you to Kerridis."

Fenton watched closely, trying to assess some landmarks, now that he saw this land in sunlight. But the dim haze on it prevented seeing more than the most misty outlines, and the haze moved with them, not clearing. The air had a still, underwater sound, and when they passed through the great place with the pillarlike trees, although there was the faint sound of the Alfar singing, it was distant, and there was no one to be seen; the green and misty spaces were deserted.

Irielle looked compassionately at Fenton, who was bent over, rubbing his legs. "You are beginning to fade again," she said. "Shall I send you back so that you can come again, properly, through the Worldgate?" But Fenton shook his head in agonized determination. After this bummer, it was going to be a long, long time before he would risk taking that damned bootleg Antaril again. He'd stay while he could.

"You can't find Kerridis," Joel said, irritably. "I told you, Irielle, she is resting, making ready for the Great Council, and no doubt she has withdrawn under a spell and does not want to be found!"

"I know," Irielle said, frowning. "But I know I can

make her understand. I think I must risk it . . ." She turned round, looking, with narrowed eyes, at nothing Fenton could see. Then she shook her hand free of Joel Tarnsson's and said, "Stand away, Joel, I *must*—"

She cried out, a high musical phrase in the Alfar tongue, touched the ring on her finger, and turned round three times in her tracks where she stood. Again she cried out, and of the words, Fenton understood only "Kerridis."

There was a faint bright shimmering in the air, and all at once there was a little shifting under their feet. It seemed as if they were looking through shimmery light into a kind of room hung with green moss, filled with green light, underwater brightness. Kerridis' face seemed to waver in the brilliance, and for the first time Fenton was shocked and frightened at the bright sternness of that face.

"Irielle, child," she said, and she sounded displeased. "I gave orders! When I must face the Council this full moon—"

"I am sorry, Lady," Irielle murmured, "but I did not know what else to do. It is the 'tweenman, the one who came to the caves, and later bore us warning that the ironfolk had broken through in the flower-ring; he is here, and he is fading, and in pain."

"Dark and ruin!" Kerridis said, and sighed audibly. Then said, "Well, there is no help for it, child, so I am not angry, but I cannot manage to speak with Tarnsson now. He is your problem and not my own. As for the 'tweenman—" She raised her head and looked directly at Fenton as if they were standing face to face, and for the first time Fenton understood the legends of awe and terror surrounding the fairy-folk. Before this, though he had spoken of her in his own mind as the Faerie Queen, he had still somewhere inside sensed her as a woman, human, and therefore nothing to be afraid of. Now, as when he had faced Findhal with his great axe, he sensed a kind of raw power that his own world had not fitted him to face.

She said, " 'Tweenman, I am not angered with you. You have come at an inconvenient time, but I know you did not choose it, and the Powers beyond us all send things to us at their will and not ours. I accept it as mean-

ingful that you have come at this time, when I am beset
and know not where to turn, and even my dearest councillors seem more like enemies than friends. Irielle!"

"Lady—" Irielle whispered fearfully.

Always before Kerridis had spoken to Irielle as an indulgent mother to a favorite child; now there was, again,
raw power in her voice.

"Make certain that I am not disturbed again until the
Council, unless chaos and death are upon us! Make very
sure of it!"

The words were a cracked whip and Irielle whispered,
"I will obey."

" 'Tweenman, come." Kerridis stretched out her hand.
Fenton saw the glow of a great sparkling diadem, and her
face was shadowed by the high crown; the glow brightened, the ground under his feet reeled, and suddenly the
misty sunlight was gone and he stood enfolded in green
light filtered through mossy veils and a curtain that
looked like falling water, so that he felt the spray cool on
his parched forehead.

Kerridis sat on a bench of velvety mosses; the cur-
tained water seemed to reflect light on her face, so that
she was clothed in glowing light, and her eyes flared like
lightning. Fenton shrank away a little; she saw it with a
sad smile.

"I am gathering power for the Council, when I shall
need strength to face my friends and my foes," Kerridis
said. "But I do not need it for you and I should not have
shown myself like that to Irielle; she means me no harm."
Slowly, she lifted her hands, which seemed to flash with
jewels, to her forehead, and raised the great gemmed
crown from her head. The lights seemed to fade and dim
out in her face, as she set the crown aside, until she was
only a slender, sad-faced woman in a pale green robe
which fell in loose folds about her narrow body. Her hair,
no longer streaming with light, was pale and fell softly
around her face, shadowing it. She sighed and said,
"You are weary. Here. This is vrill, it will give you some
ease."

His fingers closed around the tiny cylinder and he felt
the cramping pains recede a little. She gestured to him to
sit; he sank down on what felt like a bed of soft moss.

"Findhal thinks you mean danger to us," she said, "for the ironfolk, it seems, follow where you go. But there were ironfolk before ever you came into this world, and if anyone brought them here it was Pentarn. I do not believe that you are in league with Pentarn to do us harm."

"No," Fenton said. "I am afraid because the ironfolk have come into my world, too, and I cannot make anyone believe in them."

Her smile was wan. "I think we would all like to disbelieve in the ironfolk, if only there were some virtue in disbelief that could make them go away. There may be worlds where they are welcome, and I wish they would stay there. Findhal is right this far, that we must muster all our defenses against them, and enlist the aid of any worlds we can reach. I think Pentarn has encouraged them to make us the prime point of attack, and they are not at all averse to the idea, for they find us and our beasts good prey." A shudder rippled over her mobile features. "They fear our vrillswords as we fear the very touch of the stuff of which they are made. But they are stronger and their numbers are greater; I do not know how we can hold out against them, we have lost so many."

Fenton asked, "How could Pentarn do this?"

"I am not sure," she said, "but I think he has opened his world for the ironfolk to come through without using the Worldhouse; those who keep the Worldhouse are sworn to keep the balance also. So that predators do not escape except at the appointed times when the Gates open normally. And if he opened that Gate, he could probably be persuaded to close it again, and I know what would persuade him; but I am not willing to do that."

"What would persuade him?" Fenton asked, but he already knew the answer, before Kerridis told him.

"He wants his son. He wants Joel Tarnsson back again. But I swore Joel could have sanctuary here; and I will not break my word. It is a byword in the Worldhouse that the Alfar cannot be trusted, and I fear sometimes it is true; we are never twice the same, but this is because our world changes and we must move as the tides of our time moves. We can protect ourselves and others a little with staying-spells, but still, we move, inexorably, and we change, and things in our world are never twice the same. But I will not knowingly cheat anyone of a bargain he has had, nor break an oath unless the tides of the world force me to do so, and I have sworn to Joel that he shall have sanctuary here so long as I have power to give it. Findhal would have me say to him that it is no longer in my power to allow him shelter in the woodlands of the Alfar. I will not say this unless I must, and so Findhal is angry with me and has said I am in league to destroy us all. Even though Joel Tarnsson is a fosterling here and has taken up sword against his own people, even though Irielle has sworn herself to Joel, Findhal has sworn that Joel shall be returned to Pentarn for the safety of our people."

She sat slumped on the mossy bench, sighing. "I do not know what I ought to do. I can appeal to the World-house, but I am afraid there is no way to help us. I have no friend now in the Worldhouse. I don't know where to turn. Look at me——" Her smile was strange, rueful. "Reduced to confiding in a 'tweenman!"

Fenton said, "I would help you if I could."

She stretched out her slender ringed hand to him. It seemed to glow faintly with light, even though she was not now wearing the crown that shimmered with power.

He was still holding the vrill, and for some reason it made her touch very palpable to him, her hand very soft like the petal of some unknown flower. She rose to her feet, gesturing to him to rise. She said, "I am weary of sitting here in my secret retreat, awaiting ill news and trying to gather to myself power enough to force my will upon my councilors who are determined to be my ene-mies. Come, Fenton, walk with me under the trees a little. I will be summoned soon enough to strife! Tell me how it goes with you in your world. How did you come here again as a 'tweenman?"

"I hardly know how to tell you," Fenton said, and was silent as they went out from the green-lighted bower of leaves. Here the trees outside in the glade were tall, with pale-ivory bark and great drooping branches laden with leaves and pale, silky-looking moss; they were like no trees Fenton had ever seen before and vaguely he wished he were naturalist enough to know whether they were some tree that might have grown in some unfamiliar part of his own globe or whether they were unknown trees, extra-terrestrial. He was beginning to have a considerable amount of sympathy, more than he had ever had as an ordinary parapsychologist, for people who had an extraordinary experience they were unable to share. Mythology and legend told of people who strayed into the realms of the fairy-folk and on returning could not make themselves understood or believed by those around them. Trained as he was in accepting what other people had been taught not to believe, Fenton for the first time was confronting the completely subjective nature of reality. The traditional advice about keeping an open mind was absolutely no help at all in a situation like this.

"What are you thinking, Fenn-ton?" The faint hesitation in her speech, the way she had never been quite able to pronounce his name, enchanted him, but at the same time reminded him of Pentarn—and Pentarn's son, and of his quest here.

"I was thinking," he said, "of the fact that nobody in my own world would believe this."

She smiled. Why was her smile so bewitching? Was it only strangeness, the lure of the bizarre, the faint, faint reminder that she was not human, not quite? "I find that hard to understand," she said. "I have not spent a great deal of time in the sunworlds; the light is dangerous for our people, after only a little time." Did she mean, he wondered, that the ultraviolet or actinic rays of ordinary sunlight would harm skin or eyes as they did with albinos and some few unfortunate mutants or sports in his world? Or was it some more mystical or subtle thing? He realized he wanted to know and at the same time was sure Kerridis could not explain in any way that would be meaningful in his world's terms.

"And yet," she mused, gazing up at him—for she was tall, but Fenton was taller still. "Over the years and the centuries, the people of our world and yours have come together many, many times. You are legends to us, yes, but more recently we know who and what you are, and we know a little, how to prevent your folk from suffering when they come to us; our changelings no longer die. Maybe Irielle has told you how Findhal insisted that she must spend some time under the sun of her own world, especially while she was still growing, so that the loss of her sun would not damage her growth. Surely your world has legends and tales of our people, of the days when the Gates between our worlds were closer together, and more accessible?"

"Yes," Fenton said, remembering. "But in these days people believe that to say a thing is a legend is only a way to say it is a lie, a—a story, a tale told to entertain."

She smiled. He knew then that he had been trying to make her smile; having once seen that smile he would never rest content till he had seen it again. "But that is foolishness," she said. "How could anyone be entertained, or how could anyone benefit, from being told anything which is not the truth? How can anyone speak a thing which has not happened? Pentarn was like that, a little. But we found out that he could say things which were not true, which had not happened, which he had not seen; it was a strange sickness we did not understand. Is it like that in your world, that people can say a thing which has not been seen or known?"

"They certainly can," Fenton said grimly, and Kerridis shook her head.

"How strange their minds must be! There was a time when our language had no word for anything which had not happened, which was not true; now we have come to believe that some people can say and do such things. Oh, I could say in jest that such or such a thing will come to pass when the snow rises from the earth to the sky, or when the leaves on that tree turn the color of violets, or when frogs sing in the Alfar speech; but I could not speak such a thing in seriousness. Our language has no way to say it."

That explained another old legend, Fenton thought; that the fairy-folk were full of tricks. If they could not imagine how to lie, they must find other clever ways to protect themselves. But it also explained the old belief that if you could—for instance—catch a leprechaun he could be compelled to tell you his secrets. Pragmatic knowledge: that although the fairy-folk could and would evade your questions, they could not tell a deliberate lie and were reluctant to give their word because they were incapable of breaking it.

And this would explain, perhaps, why they had become so wary of contacts with humans, who could lie and falsify the truth and invent things they had not seen. . . .

He said, "I will try never to lie to you, Kerridis." He discovered that his voice was not as steady as he had wanted.

"I know that," she said. "I know you are not Pentarn. I am a little afraid of you, because it is true that you look very much like him; but I know you are not he, nor even very much like him when I come to look closely at you." She stretched out her hand to him again, and he took it, but the magic of the moment had been disturbed with the thought of Pentarn. He found himself remembering the peacefulness of the mountains up at his Uncle Stan's place and how the ironman had suddenly burst out through the trees and made off with the axe.

"You said once that the Gates between our worlds were once more open than now, Kerridis—"

"That is true," she said. "I think as the seasons turn, our worlds are drifting further and further apart and it becomes more and more difficult to bridge the gap. There are fewer 'tweenmen who visit us simply in dream; only those who come legitimately through the Gates, being possessed of legitimate keys and talismans. Or those who, like Pentarn, have learned how to cross that gulf, and use the knowledge for their own purposes. There was a time, when I was young when many, many people walked in our world during their dreams, leaving their bodies behind and existing here as you do now, a shadow, existing to themselves and, in a sense, to us, but able to walk through walls and to drift like shadows in and out of solid things. And there have always been those who crossed the Gates when the sun and stars and moon were right, and wandered in our world as if in a dream, knowing they were awake but not believing what they see. Madmen, some of them, songmakers, those who knew where the Gates were and how to make the conditions for opening them—they have always come through. But it does not often happen now. Pentarn was the first in many, many generations, I think, of your people. Except for those we took as changelings."

"Pentarn is not of my world," Fenton said, "but his people seem to be like mine. Irielle is of my world. She told me how Findhal took her, because his own wife had no child. Did you take Pentarn's son like that?"

"No," Kerridis said. "He came to us, though we have treated him in all ways as if he were our changeling. He was sickly and weak and, I think, his father considered him not of much worth in his own world, whatever it is that they do there. But Pentarn was indulgent with his son—an indulgence that may cost us all a great deal!" She spoke vehemently, then added, with a faint smile, "I should not say that. I trust the lad. I think it happened like this. Pentarn taught him to open the Gates for amusement during a long illness, and when he came here we welcomed him as a playmate for Irielle—her foster-mother was my dearest friend. Sometimes he came as a 'tweenman, while his body lay resting and he was ill, but but he was always well and strong here, and at last he begged us to let him stay forever. We did not mind, for we loved him well, but Pentarn was beside himself with rage, and would have had us force the boy back into his own world, where he was sickly and always unhappy. We tried to make Pentarn see reason, but he could only see that we had his son, and that his son did not want to return. So he swore he could force us to give Joel back, as if Joel were a thing, a sword or a cup to be passed from hand to hand without choice in the matter. I think that is why he had me kidnapped and ill-used by the ironfolk, in the hope that they would give Joel back to him in exchange for me. As if the one thing had anything to do with the other!"

And Pentarn, Fenton thought grimly, was willing to destroy any world that got in the way of his own ambition and revenge. He said abruptly, "That is why I came here today. I don't know how the Gates you speak of work; I understood that conditions had to be exactly right, or the Gates couldn't open, except at certain places and times. But I saw ironfolk twice where they had no business to be. Do you think Pentarn had anything to do with that?"

Kerridis said, "I am sure of it. He has somehow discovered a way to make a Gate open where he wants it to be, and I am afraid this will weaken the fabric of space or time which lies between the worlds. You were there, in the caverns, when he opened a Gate around himself and disappeared. Where you saw these ironfolk—were they anywhere near the Worldhouse?"

"I don't know," Fenton said. "I've never seen the Worldhouse when I knew what it was. Only I saw it disappear once, when I tried to go into it—"

"—at the wrong time," Kerridis finished, as if it were nothing unusual. "Sometimes it simply does not want to be found, and unless you were carrying the proper talisman, you probably could not find it. But perhaps I should inquire into this matter myself. The others are preparing for the Council too, and I am reluctant to do what they want—to close the Gates, send back all our changelings so we will have no further link with your worlds, smash and destroy all the talismans and cut ourselves off from you entirely. I don't see how we can afford to do that. We are dependent on your world. There are bonds that go back into our prehistory. How can we turn against the wisdom of endless generations of the Alfar, which says that you are our children, even though our ways and our worlds have moved apart? But I am not sure I can prevail against my whole Council."

She looked at him in sudden sharp concern. "You are beginning to fade," she said sharply. "Hold tightly to the vrill; it will ease you a little."

Fenton stopped, trying to rub the agonizing cramps from his legs. Had he stayed long enough to damage his body? Was his body being carted off again to a hospital? But he could not return now, not when he was on the very edge of discovering the secret of the Worldhouse from the very lips of Kerridis! He clutched the small cylinder of vrill with agonized determination.

"Fenton, I am afraid for you. Perhaps I should send you back at once . . ."

"No," he said, "I'm all right."

She smiled, and the smile was very sweet and compassionate. Her small insubstantial fingers closed over his and though the grip was almost impalpable, he felt it warm and comforting. "I wish I could help you," she said, "but perhaps I can best help both our worlds by accepting that gallant untruth. For I think, like Pentarn, that you have spoken untruth to me, but now you have done it without malice, and from bravery. Fenton, come, I will take you to the Worldhouse."

He felt compelled to ask, "Is it very far?" He had no idea where he was in relation to his own world. But Kerridis looked confused.

"It is where it is, but you need not travel far to get there, if that is what you mean. I think—" She looked around, assessing, in that curious way some of the Alfar had. "I think I can make this path take us there. Come—" He felt her almost-impalpable finger-touch closing on his again. "You must remain very close to me, then, if I am to take you by this way."

He started to say: *that would be a pleasure.* But could he say that to the Lady of the Alfar, the Faerie Queen? He was silent, taking her hand in his.

They walked for a moment and it seemed to Fenton that the faintly-traced path between the trees grew more perceptible, as if travelled by more and stronger feet. Then, as they rounded a corner, he saw ahead of him the strangest thing he had seen in the world of the Alfar; stranger even than the Rockhold.

Ahead of him the trees cleared, opening on a grove of spacious proportions, carpeted with the greenest of grass, starred here and there with tiny golden flowers. Rising from the middle of the grove was a Gateway; twin golden pillars, delicately carven and chased with delicate filigree, rose up out of sight; he could not see their tops, for they were lost in a delicate mist.

"That is the Worldgate, and beyond it lies the Worldhouse," Kerridis said, but needlessly. Fenton could not imagine anything else it could possibly be.

Between the pillars was—emptiness. Nothingness. When Kerridis drew him between the pillars, for a moment he felt the brief shock of *falling*—the old nightmare terror, plunging downward without gravity, asprawl, loose-limbed without breath even to scream—and discovered that he was standing beside Kerridis, his feet solid on the grass, looking down the length of a great spacious hallway, rising overhead into vastness too enormous to be guessed.

Shadows moved at the far end of the hall, too distant for focus. But as happened so often in the world of the Alfar, they moved almost with thought-speed toward where, in the shadow of the overhead pillars, a grey-robed figure sat.

He was the first bearded Alfar Fenton had seen. And when the Alfar were bearded, Fenton thought, they went all the way, for hair white as snow streamed over his shoulders and down his face, below a pair of deep-set greenish eyes, a wrinkled thoughtful forehead.

He raised his head slowly and looked at them, and the forehead, already seamed and creased like a withered apple, wrinkled further.

"It is the Lady," he said, stating the obvious in a way that immediately annoyed Fenton. "We have not seen you here in the Worldhouse for many a day, Lady. Whither away are you bound, Kerridis?"

"I seldom travel beyond my own world," Kerridis said, her level brows drawing down in a faint frown that reminded Fenton of Sally, making him wonder if he had been attracted to Sally only because, in some faint and indefinable way, she reminded him of Kerridis.

Kerridis said, "How is it with the Gate, Myrill? You who keep Gates are sworn to keep the balance, yet here stands a man from the sunworlds who tells me that ironfolk are spilling into his world where they have no place and where they should not be. If those who keep the Gates cannot keep them from being misused—"

"They're not coming through this Gate, Lady, and that's all I have to say to you," the old man Myrill said in a truculent voice. "I've got nothing at all to do with the other Gates, or with folk who go meddling, making Gates where they've got no business being. That's nothing at all to do with me."

Kerridis frowned again and said, "But what are we to do, then, with those who allow the wrong things to come through?"

"It's nothing to do with me, Lady," the old man repeated stubbornly, while Fenton thought that this seemed to be the problem in all the worlds; how to keep the wrong Gates from opening and the wrong people or things from coming through.

"I should tell you," Kerridis said, tapping her foot in frustration, "that Erril and Findhal want to close the Gate for all time; close the Worldhouse from this direction, so that no one can go in or out."

"They can't do that, Lady," said the old man. "The Worldhouse exists for a good reason, believe me. If it closes, then you'll just have those who need to get through going through at the wrong place and time. Like that Pentarn. When Findhal closed the Worldhouse Gate here against him, he found his own way through; and those things he brought with him, he'd never have been able to get them through a proper gate or the Worldhouse."

Fenton looked past the old man, down the long room of the great hall. There were shadows, and shadowy forms, and doors, not ordinary doors with sills and frames and posts and lintels, but arches and strange gaps into nothingness. Through each door was shadowy emptiness; but as he stared at one of them, he realized he was looking into something like a computer center. Through another door he somehow could see outlines which reminded him of the little Dungeons and Dragons print-shop. Was this the central Worldhouse then, from which all the others opened? Or was this simply the way it looked from *here*, and would it appear different in every different world?

Somehow Pentarn—and he could believe it, from what he had seen of the technology of Pentarn's world—had managed to create movable Gates for himself. And from what Irielle had told him, there were times at which the Gates were naturally open between certain worlds. Was this why there were many legends of the dangers associated with full moon or eclipses, when the Gateways between different levels of reality somehow thinned and people could step from one world to another? The dreams, from which one awakened with the sudden shock of nightmare falling . . . was this the passage through a Worldgate in dream? Were dreams, too, on some concrete level of reality *elsewhere?*

What the hell is reality anyhow?

"Will you come and speak at the Council, then, Myrill, to give your opinion about the closing of the Gates?" Kerridis asked.

"Oh, Lady, such things are not for me . . . with all the great ones of the Alfar . . ." the old man protested.

"They will not believe me," Kerridis said. Fenton would never have believed that her lovely voice could hold so much bitterness. "They owe me homage and allegiance. But now I have no real power among them."

"You are our Lady," said Myrill stubbornly. "We do not obey you because we wish to obey or even because you command us rightly. We obey you because the Lady is to be obeyed."

She smiled rather sadly. "I wish they all felt as you do, old friend. Perhaps you had better come and remind them of that. If I command you to come, will you come?"

"You know I must do as you command," said the old man, grumbling.

Kerridis laughed this time and said, "Can you leave someone in charge of the Gate?"

"Let me see who is free to come and go," Myrill said. He walked slowly down the room of portals, while Kerridis turned to Fenton in deep concern.

"What can I do for you? Shall I send you back through a Gate? No, for you are not in the body, you can return from anywhere. No, keep the vrill," she said. "It will be a link between us if you choose to return."

Fenton opened his hand with difficulty and looked at the piece of flintlike pale stone, with lights within, the vrill from which the sword-blades were carved. It was roughly cylindrical, carved with Kerridis' seal, and he wondered if it was the same in all worlds. His fingers tightened again spasmodically. He looked down at his fingers and he saw, in sudden dread, that he could see the pale stone through his fingers. It was a terrifying sensation.

The old man Myrill came slowly back, along the long corridor of doors. Walking behind him was a young woman, the girl Fenton had seen in the little print-shop which had vanished so unaccountably. So it had been the Worldhouse after all. *I knew it,* Fenton thought with an odd sense of triumph.

"You want me to keep your Gate, Myrill?"

Myrill said, "As the Lady wishes." He was grumbling unhappily.

Kerridis said softly, "Will you do me this favor, to keep the Gateway here while Myrill is in Council with us?"

The girl from the print-shop dropped a deep curtsy, which startled Fenton—it seemed at variance with the modern dress she was now wearing—until he realized that the place was frequented by Anachronists, and she would certainly have been versed in courtly manners and customs.

Kerridis asked, "But what of your own Gate?"

"It is closed at the moment, and guarded otherwise," the young woman said with a smile. She glanced at Fenton and he saw her eyebrows go up in faint speculation; Fenton wondered if she recognized him, but he was in distress too acute at the moment to care whether she did or not. She said, "So be it, Myrill, I will keep your Gate." She went off toward the far end.

Kerridis said, "In the Council chamber, presently, Myrill." The words dismissed him. Kerridis led Fenton out into the hazy sun again.

"You are fading," she said in deep concern. "Somehow I must find a way to make it possible for you to come to us in the body. There is no reason you should not come and go as you please; if Pentarn can come unbidden, it is foolish to forbid you, who mean us no harm!"

"I do not know when I can come again," Fenton said. Then, with great bitterness, "Or how, or if I can come again at all." It was going to be a good long time before he would risk that bootleg Antaril again, if ever! And he was beginning to feel that coming, under these conditions, as a 'tweenman, was worse than not coming at all. Every separate inch of his body ached with agonizing cramps. How this could be, when his body was not here at all, he supposed he would never understand; the rules of this world were still confusing to him.

Kerridis stopped, lifted her face to his; the diffuse green treelight fell softly on her lovely features, making them seem more alien, further than ever from human, but for some perverse reason more appealing. She said in a whisper, "I should be very sad, not to see you again, Fenn-ton, even though my councillors would be shocked if they should hear me say so."

Suddenly she dropped her eyes and could not meet his,

but she touched his hand again. He could not feel the touch, and it frightened him. He wondered if he would ever again return to the world of the Alfar, if he would ever see her again.

He heard his own voice catch as he said, "If you are closing the Worldgates and the pathway is closed to the world of the Alfar . . ."

"No," she said. "We cannot do that. Whatever Findhal says, we cannot risk it. There may have been a time when the Alfar could survive without the crossing of worlds. But now I do not think we can stand alone, there are so many things we need from other worlds. Our world is old, exhausted. Our changelings would die if they could not come and go in the sunworlds, and yet they have no place any more, most of them, in the sunworlds and they could not live there. Unless we accept that the time has come for the Alfar to accept our fate and die, unless we accept that we are fated to be exterminated by the ironfolk, then I think we dare not close our Gates. We cannot close entry to our world without closing the exits also. Unless we give to other worlds what we have to give, we cannot take anything from them, whatever the need. There must be open exchange; we cannot live as raiders and scavengers on other worlds, or we should be worse than the ironfolk."

"No," Fenton said, "that does not seem right."

"And I am not sure we could close our Gates, even if we would. We would have to fight to defend them; and even so, there are those like Pentarn who have found ways to open the Gates whenever they wish, wherever they want. He can open Gates where there were never any Gates before. I am sure he would loose the ironfolk upon us, and there would be desperate carnage and death. We have many brave warriors, but I think that war with Pentarn's world would be worse than war against the ironfolk."

"It would." Fenton shuddered, whether from his own pain, or the thought of the Alfar at war with Pentarn's world, he was not sure. The ironfolk were repulsive but, like the Alfar, they fought hand-to-hand; insofar as any war could be fair, this was a fair and equitable battle. But Pentarn's world was geared to modern warfare, and the thought of those weapons turned against the Alfar made

Fenton physically sick. It would be senseless slaughter, massacre. And, he thought, the ironfolk would probably take to it like ducks to water.

Kerridis said, and he could see that she was trembling, "I wish you could come with me to the Council, Fenn-ton. They should know about it, if ironfolk are breaking through into your world as well."

"I would try to stay, if you think they will listen to me," Fenton said.

"If only you did not look so much like Pentarn," she said miserably. "I am not sure they could listen to you, if only for that. Still—" Again her hands closed on his. Her hands, touching his and touching the vrill in his hands, were the only real thing in his fading universe, the only real thing that had ever existed; his body felt aching, hollow, insubstantial, and he found himself wondering in dismay if he would somehow have to find his way back through the gnome's world to get back to his own. He wanted to stay here, beside Kerridis. He knew that somehow he had a very real stake in the world of the Alfar. If he let himself be thrust back, would he ever manage to return?

And yet even as his mind tried to find a way in which he could cling to the Alfar world, his body was one great physical ache to get back to where it really was, to stop being separated from his substantial self. He saw that her hand, lightly laid on his shoulder, seemed to go through his body, he was no longer in the world of the Alfar where natural objects were substantial to him. Her voice was shaking, but seemed to come to him across a very great distance.

"I wish you could stay. When you are here I do not feel so alone," she whispered. "Since the first time you came to me in the caves of the ironfolk, I have felt safe only when you were near. Fenn-ton, Fenn-ton, stay with me, don't go!"

"I wish I could stay," he said hoarsely. Her arms had gone out to him, and he caught her close, carefully, the horror being that he might reach through her body, find himself clasping emptiness. For the first time she was not remote, not the distant Faerie Queen, but a woman, despite her majesty and the shimmering crown of her power, a woman frail, vulnerable, shaken with pain and fear. She had always been like this, even when he first saw her captured by the ironfolk, but he had not realized it. He bent and her lips touched his, but it was like embracing a shadow, only the faintest touch, the distant thrill of the touch dreamlike, fading.

He cried out in despair, "I want to stay! Kerridis, Kerridis, I am fading, I don't want to go."

But even as he spoke she was gone from his arms and the trees and green light of the Alfar forest were gone, and he stood in a small room; four or five young men were seated around a table, shaking curiously-cut dice. On the table before them was a labyrinthine drawing, a strange gameboard covered with small figures that *glowed* somehow. Vrill—the figurines were made of vrill, and somehow the drawing of the labyrinth seemed not flat, but shimmering, moving, as if it had its own life, its own dimension of reality.

Fenton was out of his body, insubstantial, agonizingly pulled along by the cord, the silver-grey umbilicus of his spirit, and through all this he had the curious illusion that he was one of the pieces on the board, subject to the fall of the Dungeons and Dragons game dice.

One of the young players looked up. "There's a 'tweenman here. I can almost see him. Hey," he said, looking straight at Fenton, "are you lost? You shouldn't be, if you're carrying vrill."

"Guest of the management," said the young woman he had seen in the hallway of doors, the young woman from the print-shop. Somehow she was and was not there; he could see through her. "Kerridis of the Alfar let him through here."

The young man laughed rudely. "A friend of the Lady? I guess he gets VIP treatment, then, doesn't he, Jennifer?"

"No 'tweenman is a VIP," said Jennifer, looking over her granny glasses at Fenton. She said to him in a scolding voice, "You'd better get back to your body. Run along, now." She sounded exactly as if he were a small boy too young to be out after dark in a strange neighborhood. "If you're going to travel this way, you'd better learn the rules, hadn't you?"

Fenton started to protest that nothing would suit him

better, but the young man with the dice chuckled. "Oh, he's from the college parapsych project. They talk a lot and play with their cards and their computers and their probability math, but they don't know a damn thing and wouldn't believe it if you told them. Let them fool around, they won't bother anyone. Run along, professor."

Stung, Fenton opened his mouth to reply, but in the split second of speaking, he was pulled ignominiously out of the room behind the Worldhouse, jerked along by the cord. He clutched the vrill in an agonized grip—he wasn't going to lose *this!* He wasn't going to show it to Garnock either.

Abruptly, with an agonized wrench, a sharp shock like the shock of falling, he was in his own apartment, drifting over his body, which was slumped uncomfortably on the floor; then he was kneeling there, fallen half-forward against the couch, his fingers cramped and numb. As he stretched cautiously to ease them, shifting his weight and carefully straightening his back against the stabbing pain, the small cylinder of vrill fell from his stiff fingers and clattered to the floor. He clutched at it, fumbling, eager to see what it looked like in this world—lapis-lazuli, jade, gold, precious crystal?

Disbelieving, he clutched in his hand a small prism of transparent plastic.

Plastic!

Plastic? He didn't believe it!

CHAPTER FIFTEEN

His KNEES HURT, reminding him sharply that he had spent a very long time crouched in that unmoving position on the hard floor. He managed to stumble to his feet, aware of knife-edges of pain all through his body, pins and needles as his numbed feet began to move, a raging thirst. The first thing was to get a drink of water. He moved automatically through the apartment to the kitchenette, twisting the handle of the faucet and stooping to drink without even looking for a glass. When he could think of anything but the quenching of thirst, he straightened, in dismay.

For the place had been ransacked.

Cans and cartons of food were scattered over the counters and in the sink a package of spaghetti had burst open. Underfoot was the sticky crunch of a five-pound bag of sugar, overturned and spilled there on the floor. Already ants were crawling around the edges.

The kitchen window was a grey square, dimly flushed with the coming dawn. The face of the clock said five-thirty. But five-thirty of what morning? The next day? Or had he been there unconscious for two or even three days?

And who had trashed his apartment like this? Kitchen drawers and cabinets had been pulled out, dumped helter-skelter on the floor. Returning in shock to the living room, he saw desk drawers rummaged, papers in confusion, pillows and chair-cushions everywhere, bookshelves emptied. The table where the other Antaril pills had lain was empty, everything dumped in a heap on the rug. Fenton went back into the kitchen, fished a plastic glass out of the mess and ran it full of water, and drank again. He wondered if he would be thirsty for the rest of his life. He stared at the chaos and muddle of his possessions.

He had really been out of it, then, dead to the world. They, whoever they were—and Berkeley was full of sneak thieves—could have walked off with everything. But on his desk the electric typewriter stood silent and untouched, a paper in it still holding half of a report he had begun to write. The letter he had written, detailing precautions if he were found unconscious, was still on the couch beside which he had collapsed after taking the Antaril. His stereo player was intact, including his father's heirloom collection of Callas records and a few antique and valuable Beatles originals. Not robbery, then, not crude robbery of easily portable valuables, anyhow.

There was a sound inside the bedroom of the apartment and Fenton started; it had not occurred to him that the thieves might still be here. He thought briefly about hiding, stepped on a fallen cushion and stumbled over it. Amy Brittman came out of the bedroom. She had a gun in her hand.

"So you're back," she said. Her mouth twisted with contempt. "What did you learn this time, *Professor*? And do you think you'll have any better luck proving it than I did?"

His mouth and throat were still too dry to speak. Fenton wet his lips with his tongue.

"You'd better put that gun away, Amy," he said. "It might go off. Somebody might get hurt." He realized that the plastic hunk of what, in the other world, had been vrill, was still clenched in his hand. He slid it into the pocket of his bathrobe. He was sure, irrationally, that if Amy Brittman saw it, she would take it. With his stereo and typewriter intact, it was obvious that she wasn't here just to rob him. But what was she looking for? As far as he knew, there was only one link between Amy Brittman and himself; they had both been part of the Antaril project and had both been involved, one way or another, with the conflict between Pentarn and the Alfar.

He asked, "Did Pentarn send you?"

Her face contorted. "I ought to shoot you! It would save a lot of trouble for everybody, especially the Lord Leader!" Her knuckles were white on the trigger and

Fenton froze. He had done his share of therapy, in training; he knew a hysteric when he saw one, and it was clear that Pentarn had been playing on the girl's neurosis. He remained quiet for a moment, then said, in friendly fashion, "Why don't you tell me about it, Amy? What were you looking for?"

"I'm not going to tell you!" she blurted.

"All right." Fenton kept his voice soothing. "You don't have to."

"I don't have to do anything!" she cried. "Nothing's been right since you came through our world!"

"You've been through a lot, haven't you?" Fenton agreed, his voice still gentle and soothing, but he had begun to move stealthily. "Sometimes nothing goes right, does it? Why not sit down and tell me all about it? What's gone wrong this time?"

She started to relax and sink down toward a chair, and at that moment Fenton, with a swift movement, tackled her, football fashion. The gun went off, exploding harmlessly through the wall. Fenton thought, crazily, *What am I going to say to the landlord?* Gallantry forgotten, he grabbed Amy's wrist, wrestled the gun away from her, and shoved her into the chair.

"Sit down and stay there. And why not tell me all about it? You might feel better, at that."

Amy cursed him, in words Fenton hadn't even known when he was in college; then she collapsed in the chair and started to have screaming hysterics.

Fenton sat and listened while he looked at the gun. He didn't know all that much about guns. It wasn't anything like any weapon he'd had to learn to use in the army, and he had never been interested in handguns, considering them too expensive a hobby. But it was strange. The grip was made of a material which seemed neither wood nor plastic, but something like ceramic, glazed and elaborately chased; the barrel seemed longer in proportion to the length than was common for pistols Fenton had seen. What it really looked like, he thought, was some kind of toy blaster from a science-fiction space-war epic, but the bullet that had exploded through his wall had been a real enough projectile.

"One of Pentarn's little toys?" he asked. "Come on,

Amy, tell me what you're looking for and why, why don't you?"

She went on sobbing and snuffling. Fenton didn't make a move toward her. He was completely sure that if he did, she would get even more hysterical, and about all he needed now was some kind of accusation of rape. He didn't really think she was clever enough for that—any woman who could passively slip into the role Pentarn had designed for her, that of the Lord Leader's woman, couldn't be all that bright—but in case she did think of it, Cam Fenton didn't want to give her the slightest excuse.

"Maybe I ought to call the police," he mused aloud. "Show them my apartment, the mess it's in, and this little toy. I'm sure they'd be interested. Pentarn could try his hand at getting you out of the Women's House of Detention." He went toward the telephone, picked it up off the hook and started to dial.

"Berkeley police," a disinterested voice remarked on the other end of the line.

"I've surprised a prowler in my apartment," Fenton said, "I'm holding her here at the point of her own gun. Can you send somebody?"

"Oh, God!" Amy cried. "No! No! They mustn't get the gun! Please! Please, Professor Fenton, please—"

Ignoring the cries, Fenton gave the police his name and the number of his apartment. The policeman at the other end promised to send a car around right away; Fenton hung up and Amy flung herself at him, so violently that he had to hold her up or she would have fallen.

"Please, oh God, please give me the gun, let me go, I promise—I promise—I'll do anything, anything you want me to—"

"Don't be a fool, Amy," he said, holding her with distaste at arm's length. There must be more difference between himself and Pentarn than either of them realized, if this was what Pentarn wanted in a woman. "The police won't hurt you, if you haven't taken anything. Why not tell me, to start with, why Pentarn sent you here, and what he wanted?"

"I can't. I can't. He'd kill me. If the police have the gun—" She was babbling now, in sheer terror. She grabbed him and grappled for the gun, but Fenton was on his guard and managed to hold her off easily, with one hand.

"Sit down, I said, and behave yourself."

She began to swear again, atrociously. Then, tripping over a pile of clothes, she stumbled against the door, flung it open and bolted out and down the stairs. Fenton stepped to the door to watch her go, taking one step after her, then stopped. People from the other apartments had stuck out their heads to see what all the noise was about, and he decided there was no sense in trying to catch her. He went back and stared at the mess, deciding he had better leave it until the police got there. He changed into a suit, then went into the kitchen, found the coffeepot in the dumped pile of junk from the cabinet, and put on a pot of coffee. He was hungry too.

By the time the police got there he was finishing a third piece of toast and a third cup of coffee. He had found only one unbroken egg in the mess. He let them in and told them the story as he had decided to tell it, that he had been out all night—*it was true enough that he'd been out, damn it, out of this world, as the saying went*—and on returning had found his apartment in this mess and had surprised a female prowler, who had shot at him, then escaped down the stairs because he hadn't wanted to shoot her.

"You'd better let us keep the gun," one of the policemen said, examining it with brief interest. "Don't think I ever saw one just like it before."

"I have," the other policeman said, bored. "You get a lot of those foreign handguns in here now. Some kind of Korean outfit, I wouldn't be surprised. Maybe Japanese."

Fenton concealed a grin. Amy had been agitated at the thought of Pentarn's gun falling into the hands of the police, but she obviously overestimated the interest, or curiosity, of the ordinary policeman. No policeman was ever going to admit that there was anything so extraordinary he hadn't seen it before. The very concept of a weapon not made on Earth wouldn't occur to them. Fenton had been there once when a group of ordinary scientists was checking out a very well-authenticated poltergeist report in an old house in San Francisco. They had it thoroughly determined before they ever entered the house that the phenomena were caused by the couple's fourteen-year-old son. And so they had been; but the scientists were convinced that if they had only been a little more clever, they could have caught young Stuart Maynes physically throwing the dishes and breaking the windowpanes. The fact that their cameras, mounted on hidden swivels, had shown that he was at the opposite end of the room, sleeping, when the windows broke, simply convinced them that he had been too clever and too fast for them . . . not, of course, that there could be anything parapsychological about the occurrence. After that, Cameron Fenton had been convinced that the average investigator would sooner reject the evidences of his own sanity than admit there was anything he couldn't understand. If they had seen Pentarn and a dozen ironfolk bringing that gun into his apartment, they would still be convinced there was nothing unusual about it.

One of the police asked, "Did you get a good look at this female prowler? Can you tell us her age, coloring, height, that sort of thing? Would you know her if you saw her again, perhaps in a lineup?"

"White female, about thirty pounds overweight, brown hair, I'm not sure about her eyes," Fenton said, "but I can do better than that. I know who she is. She's a student in the Department of Parapsychology at the university."

"You teach at the university? And this girl is a student of yours?"

"No," Fenton said patiently. "I'm not teaching now. I'm working with Doctor Garnock—or I was until recently—on a special research project, and Amy Brittman is also associated with the experiment."

It took them a while to get that straight, and they had to ask him how to spell *parapsychology*. Finally one of the cops said, "Oh, I saw about that on TV, you're the ghost research people. Say, professor, is that for real? They're all fakes, aren't they, and you guys go around exposing phony fortune tellers and stuff like that, don't you?"

Fenton didn't feel like explaining parapsychological research to a uniformed policeman at this hour of the morning. There were, no doubt, a few educated officers on the force who knew almost as much about it as he did, but they wouldn't be the ones who had to ask him how to spell it.

So he agreed that yes indeed, dishonest psychics were the curse of the parapsychologist, and gave them Amy Brittman's address as he had found it in the student service. He had a certain number of qualms about turning her in to the police—after all, she hadn't stolen anything he wanted to report missing, and as for the bootleg Antaril, she was welcome to the stuff and he wished her, or Pentarn, joy of it. But she had trashed his apartment, and she deserved at least a damn bad quarter of an hour trying to explain away the possession of the gun. He'd have bet his Ph.D. that she didn't have anything remotely resembling a permit for it. And if they never gave it back to her, and Pentarn had to struggle along without it, he wasn't going to lose any sleep over Pentarn's plight either.

"And she didn't steal anything that you know about?"

Fenton said, "Let me just check the bedroom." But his portable tape recorder and his father's gold railroad watch were intact, as were his discharge and other personal papers, though the file had been dumped on the floor; so, too, were his checkbook, wallet, and credit cards.

"I don't think she took anything; I may have surprised her before she found whatever she was looking for," he said. He wished he knew what that had been. They agreed to question her, and he signed a formal complaint, listened to their eternal comments about students, and when they had gone away, settled dismally down to the job of clearing up the mess Amy had made in his apartment. It was hard to realize that a few hours ago he had been walking with Kerridis in a sunlit elfin glade.

He was taking his third sackful of garbage down to the downstairs pickup area and contemplating the necessity of getting in groceries, too, when the phone rang. Silently he cursed whoever would call him right now, picked up the phone and barked, "Fenton."

"What's the matter, Cam?" Sally's voice sounded concerned. "Did I wake you up? Had you forgotten? Isn't this the day we were going to drive up into the Sierras to visit your uncle?"

Fenton blinked at the wall. After a minute he said,

"I'm sorry, love. I thought that was tomorrow. I must have lost count of the days." At least now he knew how long he had been in the alien world this time.

"You can't make it?"

"Sure I can make it," Fenton said. "Only you'll have to drive." He still ached in every muscle. "I had—sort of a bad night."

And that, he thought, was the understatement of all time.

"I'll pick you up in an hour, then," Sally said. "I have to get some alcohol for the car; and I'll bring along something for lunch."

"Fine. And I'll call Uncle Stan and tell him when we'll get there. All right?"

When Sally showed up, she looked briefly around the apartment, and asked, "What was it, a tornado?"

He laughed. "You should have seen it two hours ago."

"Burglars, Cam?"

"Burglar. Female, singular. By the name of Amy Brittman. I suspect by now she's in police custody, and I certainly hope they scare the hell out of her. I don't wish her any real harm," he added, patting the still-stinging scratch she had left as a result of their struggle for the gun. "But I think she ought to be spanked and sent home to her mama, or something."

"Amy?" Sally stared in dismay. "I always knew the girl was unstable, but she must be stark raving mad! Did she put that bullet hole in your wall, too?"

"If it was a bullet," Cam said. "She fired some kind of gun. The police have it." As he spoke, he wondered if they would find her at her apartment, or if she had popped through one of Pentarn's Gates and would never be seen again in this world.

"Let's not talk about her," he said, carrying the lunch out to Sally's car. "Let's just think about us, today."

She said softly, raising her face to him, "That suits me perfectly."

The gesture once again struck him with its resemblance to Kerridis. So, in the other world, Kerridis, Lady of the Alfar, was an analogue of Sally? It must be that. He was struck with strangeness, remembering that only a few hours ago, by the time of *this* world, he had kissed Ker-

ridis under the trees near the Worldhouse, and he wondered, in dismay, how she fared with her Council, among
her councillors and those she now thought of as her ene-
mies. He had abandoned her to them; it was not his fault
but he had had to abandon her to the troubles that beset
her, and he felt guilty.

"Cam, you do look tired," she said. "Maybe you'd better just try to sleep while we drive up." She brushed aside
his objections with a curt, "Don't be silly, Cam! While my
knee was bad you put yourself to all kinds of trouble for
me. Now it's my turn to look after you, for a change. Put
your head back and take a nap."

Fenton didn't argue. The big breakfast had put some
life back into him, but he still felt exhausted and worn,
and Sally's logic struck him as reasonable. He climbed
into the car, put his head back and almost immediately
dropped off to sleep.

He slept for hours, and when he woke the car was
climbing slowly into the Sierras. He did not stir for a moment, looking across at Sally's sunlit profile. Yes, the
physical resemblance to Kerridis was there, but without
the fragile vulnerability that he had seen first in the Lady
of the Alfar. He supposed it said something about him
psychologically, that he was attracted to timid, fragile
women in distress. Sally was tough and self-sufficient; but
he had seen her, too, with her defenses down. And now
Sally was ready to admit that he, too, had a right to admit
weakness, and to be looked after and cared for.

But this brought his thoughts back to Kerridis and her
plight. How was he going to help her? What made him
think he could do anything to help, anyhow? He thought,
in a gust of anger and self-pity, that he was just a
damned fool of a 'tweenman, blundering into the world of
the Alfar as a shadow, unable to take a hand in the
events which were going on around him. Did he enjoy
this kind of powerlessness, did he have a streak of mas-
ochism after all? If Sally were right after all, and the
world of the Alfar and his experiments with Antaril were
all part of a singularly self-consistent fantasy formed from
his own neurotic needs, he couldn't blame Garnock for

coming to the conclusion that he wasn't sufficiently stable
to take part in such experiments.

But that line of thinking was a dead end, and brought
him back to the memory of Amy Brittman in the hands
of the police. That had been real enough, and the bullet
hole in his wall was real enough, as was the alien gun in
the hands of the Berkeley police. And this led him back
to what he had known all along, that Kerridis and the
Alfar were real, and Pentarn and the ironfolk, and for
that matter, the world where he had been content to veg-
etate as a rock in the sunlight.

Now somehow he would have to explain it all to Sally.
He sighed, and she turned her face from the road ahead,
briefly, smiling.

"Awake? I was just going to try and wake you up; I
don't know the way from here, and you'll have to tell me
what turnoff we want."

"Why not let me drive a while? Your bad knee must be
getting cramped," he said, glad of a chance to avoid the
inevitable confrontation; he was sure that she would
quarrel with him again about it. Shifting places, he thrust
his hand for a moment into his pocket, where the small
plastic prism rested, the prism which, in Kerridis' world
was a bit of precious vrill. Plastic, of all things whose
form it could have taken in this world! Common, ubiq-
uitous, *cheap* plastic! What was the connection? Was
there any connection at all, would all plastic be vrill in
the Alfar world? Or was it chance that vrill took the form
of something commonplace and undetectable, as the exquisitely filigreed talisman seemed to have become a common, very ordinary rock?

One thing was absolutely certain. He was going to get
that talisman back from Garnock, if he had to burglarize
Garnock's office the way Amy Brittman had done with
his apartment!

"I envy your uncle," Sally said, smiling at him, her
hair windblown from the open windows of the car. "Living in this lovely countryside. Are we nearly there,
Cam?"

"Just up this road. It's the house with the gray slates
on the roof. You can just see it—the road's pretty steep

along here. And look, there's Uncle Stan in the backyard feeding his goats."

He turned into the drive, parked there, and they scrambled out of the car and up along the drive to the goat shed.

Stan Cameron was effusive, grinning, taking Sally's hand with a smile.

"This the girl you told me about, Cam? Good to meet you," he said. "Come along and help me feed the goats and put them in for the night." They followed him into the shed, and Fenton, watching Sally smiling at the goats, scratching their wiry polls, pushing them gently away from her skirts, saw again that glimpse of a happy, unbothered Sally, at peace with herself, which he had seen only briefly and for moments. This, he realized, was the real Sally, which he had seen through her sharp, defensive toughness. Even the good-natured way she slapped one of the kids away when he started to nibble on her clothes, delighted him. She asked Uncle Stan intelligent questions about the animals and about his work taking students on backpacking trips, and ate the good meal he had cooked, complete with homemade bread, with relish and delight.

"More coffee?" he asked, at the end of the meal, tilting the pot over her cup.

She laughed and shook her head. "Goodness, no, I wouldn't sleep a wink."

"I wouldn't argue with a psychologist," Stan Cameron said. "That's your business, but I always figured that was all in people's minds. Every day of his life, my dad drank a cup of strong coffee, with sugar and milk, last thing before he went to bed. Said it helped him sleep. And considering that he never had any trouble sleeping in his life, except three weeks when he was in a hospital for some trouble with his back and they wouldn't give coffee to him, I'm inclined to believe him. The human mind is a funny thing."

Sally laughed and nodded. "I forget which scientist it was who said that the universe is not only queerer than we imagine, but queerer than we *can* imagine," she said.

"That's so," Uncle Stan agreed. "In your business— Cam told me you were working in parapsychology too—

you ought to know that, if anybody does. You must get awfully tired of skeptics who don't believe what's right under their noses. And almost as tired, I'd imagine, of people who believe all kinds of hogwash without a shred of proof. You folks really have to walk a chalk line, in that business, don't you? Skepticism on one side and credulity on the other, and both of them completely blind to logic and rational proof, either way."

"Oh, you're so right," Sally said. "That's why we try to make sure the people we take in the department are fairly stable to start with. Accept an ignorant and logic-proof skeptic, breach his skepticism, and he turns into an equally ignorant and logic-proof True Believer."

"I can see where that would happen," Uncle Stan admitted. "Let's face it, what most people want most is just to feel secure, to trust what somebody *they* trust tells them, not to have to make up their own minds, or get their brains rusty thinking. You've only got to turn on the television and see what they watch most of the time—anything they can watch without having to think. Comedies. Cop shows. Political speeches. Cute animals. So when they have to stop trusting what they believed all along, they're scared and hurry to fix up a nice safe belief in something else, even if it's exactly the opposite of what they were brought up believing. I think open-minded skepticism and rational examination of facts is probably the rarest thing in the world, and that's why the open education programs they had some years ago didn't work. For a while, there was this notion that giving some ignorant and culturally deprived yahoo a college education, a *chance* at a college education, would make an educated, cultured, rational thinker out of him, whatever his background and childhood experience had been. Instead, out of five thousand ignorant culturally deprived yahoos, they got maybe a hundred or so who were exposed for the first time to thinking for themselves, and took to it like a goat to alfalfa, and four thousand nine hundred ignorant culturally deprived yahoos with a whole new load of prejudices and new jargon labels to stick on them. I got into a lot of trouble when I was a young man, teaching in college, telling people that you couldn't make a silk purse out of a sow's ear. They called me a racist and worse for saying that all you could do was discover a few silk purses hiding out in disguise as sow's ears to keep from being bullied to death by the grunters all around them."

Sally grinned out of one side of her mouth. "That's so right," she said. "I grew up on a farm outside Fresno, trying to pretend I was a sow's ear in the middle of a class of high school girls who couldn't imagine why the end of every girl's ambition wasn't to marry the guy on the next farm who'd make a hundred thousand a year by the time he was thirty, win a few ribbons at the country fair—oh, yes, they still have them out there—make quilts and jellies, raise a batch of good Christian citizens, and never rock the boat. They thought *they* were the silk purses and I was the rotten sow's ear who wanted something freaky, like a life of my own. So I pretended, until my kid died and my husband and I split up. Now I've quit pretending. Only there's more of them than there is of me, so who's right?"

Uncle Stan nodded. "Maybe nobody's right," he said. "Maybe people just have to go different ways, and the crime is to try and make the silk purse out of the sow's ear—or, for that matter, try to make a sow's ear out of a silk purse even if he happens to be born into a family of sow's ears. Living up here with the goats wasn't exactly what my family wanted for me, either. They thought I ought to be a doctor or a lawyer or something intelligent like that. Only I like goats better than most people." He smiled to take the sting from the words.

Sally promptly retorted, "Baa-aa-aa."

As the laughter subsided, Stan Cameron, setting a plate of fresh cookies on the table before them, asked, "Speaking of ignorant believers and skeptics, Cam, have you had any more trouble with that business you were telling me about?"

Fenton felt the brief respite subside. Now he would have to tell Uncle Stan about it and face Sally's scorn or hostility. Well, he wasn't going to put Stan Cameron off with evasive answers.

"Things are just about the same," he said. "Only something happened last night that bothered me. Sally said that we must have our failures in the department—unstable people. It seems that one of them is a girl named

Amy Brittman." He told Stan all about it, starting with his first sight of Amy Brittman—he had not known, then, who she was—in Pentarn's world as the Lord Leader's woman, and ending with how he had discovered her in his apartment and attempted to turn her over to the police.

The coffee stood cooling in the cups, and the cookies were untouched, while Stan Cameron listened. Sally stared from one to the other, but she made no comment.

"Sounds like what you said about the universe being queerer than we can imagine was right on target, Sally," Stan said, smiling across the table at her. "How does it feel to be right at the knife edge between what people know and what they're just starting to discover?"

"I'm not sure—now," she answered. She hesitated, studying the old man. "Mr. Cameron, do *you* believe it—really believe all of it?"

Uncle Stan nodded. "No reason not to. Cam never lied to me."

"And you saw the footprints of the—the ironfolk monster?"

"I saw them. I've got photos of them, too, though the prints don't show much. They weren't bear prints, and no animal smaller than that could run off with an axe. What's this all about?"

Sally ignored the question, frowning down at her hands. "But it's all so . . . it's against all the laws we know for the universe."

"It won't be the first time our laws didn't fit," Stan Cameron told her. "Used to be a law that the sun went round the earth. And Newton's laws were supposed to be universal until a fellow named Einstein came along. If we find the laws we have don't fit, I guess we'll just have to figure out new ones that do."

"Which is the scientific attitude—the attitude I should have learned by now," Sally said ruefully. She leaned on her elbows across the table; she reached her hand to Fenton and clasped his. "Cam, I'm sorry. I've been guilty of just what I accused others of—judging without evidence. I should have assumed you were telling the truth until I had reason to think otherwise. Or at least, I should have reserved judgment."

"What made you change your mind, Sally?" Fenton asked.

She said, smiling across the table at Stan Cameron. "The relationship you have with your uncle and the way you talk with him. You might, for some unguessable reason, lie to me or con me. But I can't imagine you saying anything to your uncle that wasn't the truth, and I can't imagine him not sensing it if you were deluding yourself when you were talking to him."

"I think," Stan Cameron said, "that I've just had a compliment of some kind."

"However it happened, I'm grateful, Sally," Fenton said. "But the question is—what are we going to do about it?"

"I wish I knew," she said. "It will all take some getting used to. I've got to rearrange all my thinking. I still can't believe everything, Cam. But I don't disbelieve now, and I'll try to accept what you say—to assume what you've told me really did happen."

She looked up at him, and again, in that indefinable way, he thought of Kerridis. That was the one thing about which he had said nothing—his feeling for Kerridis. He had no reason to speak about it with Uncle Stan; and he was not yet ready to confess it to Sally.

And now again all his feelings were in revolt, for again he was aware of the hopelessness of any real relationship with Kerridis. She was, after all, Lady of the Alfar, his Faerie Queen, distant, untouchable. Sally was close at hand and real and dear, and he had just had proof that she cared enough about him to look, with an open mind, at things which had profoundly disturbed her.

Sally had poured herself another cup of coffee. She said, "I think you'd better tell me all about it again, Cam, tell me the whole story. I have the feeling that when I heard it before, I didn't really *listen;* I had a fixed notion that I was dealing with a hallucination."

"I'd like to hear the whole thing from the beginning, too," Stan Cameron said, and Fenton leaned back and started telling the whole story from the beginning, when he had first moved into the world of the Alfar.

When he came to his first mention of Pentarn, in the volcanic caves under the Alfar world, Sally stirred as if she wanted to say something; but when he stopped, looking at her expectantly, she shook her head.

"No, go on, Cam, I'll tell you all about it later."

Fenton went on with his story, ending with the policemen who had taken Amy Brittman's name and address, and the gun which he suspected had come from the arsenal in Pentarn's world. This time he left out nothing—except for embracing Kerridis, like a woman in a dream. *That* he did not tell; that, he suspected, he would never tell anyone.

"I wonder," Stan Cameron said, "what the police will do with the gun?"

"God knows," Sally said, "I'm not concerned about the gun. I'm more concerned what Pentarn might do with Amy when he finds out that she failed. The girl is a fool, but she's a student of mine, and I do somehow feel responsible for her; I recommended her to Garnock for the Antaril experiment. And I feel that I failed her because when she came to me, worried about what Pentarn might be planning, I treated her the same way I treated you, Cam; I had her removed from the experiment, saying she was psychologically dependent on the drug. She's obsessed with Pentarn; emotionally, sexually, every other way; and while I believed Pentarn was imaginary, it seemed to me that this was an unhealthy state of affairs. The demon-lover syndrome."

Stan Cameron tightened his mouth. "I don't know," he said, "but if this Amy Brittman girl were my sister or my daughter, I'd a lot rather have her obsessed with an imaginary Pentarn than a real one. At least an imaginary demon-lover couldn't do the girl any physical harm."

Sally nodded. "There's something to that. She's obsessed with Pentarn, yes. But she's also terrified of him."

"He doesn't call her the Lord Leader's woman for nothing," Fenton pointed out. "I don't think he'll hurt her. The obsession, if that's what you call it, seems to be mutual."

"I'm not so sure," Sally said doubtfully.

"I wouldn't worry about it," Uncle Stan said. "Pentarn can't hurt her if she's safely locked up for burglarizing your apartment, Cam. He could probably get inside her cell as a—what was your word—'tweenman, but if he was a 'tweenman and not solid, he couldn't even beat her black and blue, let alone harm her any other way. And if he came in his solid body, he couldn't get into the cell—I'll bet on the Berkeley cops to keep anything they want locked up, safely locked up. Call it protective custody."

"I guess that's something," Sally said, relieved, but Fenton was not so sure. He realized, with irritation, that now he had another worry; not only must he fear for Kerridis and Irielle, but he must now feel responsible for the fate of Amy Brittman. Well, would he want Sally to be callous about a student? Certainly not.

Stan Cameron glanced at the clock.

"Midnight," he said, "and a considerable day tomorrow; I've got a group of backpackers coming. We'd better get to bed." He glanced at them straightforwardly. "One bed or two? I don't know what kind of terms you two are on. You can have the spare room, Sally, and Cam can crash on the floor down here if you want it that way. But if you want to be comfortable, the bed's big enough for two and I'm not interested in regulating other people's private lives."

Sally did not hesitate. She smiled across the table, then straight at Cam.

"One bed," she said, "I've been a fool, Cam, and I don't want to waste any more time."

The next morning, Stan Cameron left early with his hikers; Fenton and Sally fed the goats and put them in their outdoor pen, enjoying the chance for simple work, far away from the preoccupations of the city. Fenton took her to the place where he had seen the ironfolk with his uncle's axe. The footprint, of course, had vanished long ago, but Sally, studying the ground with a frown, said, "I suppose the axe didn't turn up anywhere?"

"I think he would have told me if it had, and I haven't seen one in his toolshed," Fenton answered.

On the way back to the house, Sally was deep in thought. "Can you remember exactly what Kerridis said to you—or was it Findhal?—about there having been a time when the ironfolk could come through only when the full moons were synchronized? I wonder if that could be one reason for the ancient belief in astrology—the idea that one had to keep track of cycles, because there

were times where Gates could open between the worlds
and let the wrong things through?"

Fenton repeated it as well as he could.

"So the Gates are open more often now, and Kerridis
thinks it is because of Pentarn's meddling," Sally mused.
"I wonder, if in that arsenal of his, he has a weapon
which will force the Worldgates open? That could explain—" She was silent, carrying her overnight bag out to
the car. "Do you think you can get into the Worldhouse
now?"

Fenton grinned without mirth. "If I can find it."

He had repeated to her what the people in the Worldhouse, the young men playing Dungeons and Dragons,
had said about the parapsychology department. She said,
with a faint shrug, that there were always differences between theoretical research and people working in practi-
cal fields. "Ask a therapist in a home for retarded
children, what he thinks of research in educational psychology! Or ask a classroom teacher in a ghetto school,
better yet!"

"The difference is," Fenton said, "that until recently
there hasn't been any kind of field work in applied parapsychology. Except perhaps those peculiar people who go
out and try to quiet down haunted houses by getting in
touch with the ghosts that supposedly haunt them and
try to psychoanalyze them and make them realize that
they're dead and have no business bothering the living."
He chuckled, stowing his kitbag in the back of the car.
"Listen to me. I sound like Garnock talking about the
Worldhouse."

Sally climbed in behind the wheel of the car. She said,
"You've got to face it, Cam. Acceptance of these things
is slow. I've just had my nose rubbed in the fact that,
scientific objectivity or no, I believe what I was brought
up to believe. The fact *I* am beginning to believe you
isn't going to cut any ice with Garnock. He'll just
think—" She turned and smiled again, that breathtaking
smile that made her beautiful "—that I'm like Amy Brittman—a victim of a sexual obsession that's warped my
mature scientific judgment."

He took her hand, closing his fingers over hers as she
put her own to the key of the ignition switch. He said,

"That's all right with me, darling, and the hell with Garnock."

But it was not going to be that easy, and they both knew it. All the long drive home, they argued about ways of convincing Garnock. They both knew that the first step was going to have to be finding the Worldhouse again, and, although Sally risked the heavy traffic of cars and pedestrians on upper Telegraph Avenue, nothing was there except the dry-cleaner's shop. Sally looked dissatisfied; Fenton knew she had hoped for a look at it. It would have been more proof.

She wanted him to come home with her, but Fenton insisted he had still some work to do, cleaning up his apartment. "I'll come over later," he promised.

She said, a trace of color in her cheeks, "Maybe you were right, Cam. Maybe we ought to think about one of us moving in with the other. Just think. I don't know yet if I'm ready."

He asked when he should come over.

"I have to prepare a class for tomorrow. I'll call you when I'm finished, shall I?" She leaned over and kissed him before she dropped him off in front of his apartment building.

Fenton went up the stairs, drearily contemplating the remainder of the cleaning to be done. He would have to buy a new mop, and perhaps a bottle of detergent. And some sponges, certainly some sponges. And rubber gloves; he thought there was broken glass somewhere on the floor.

But the door of his apartment was standing open. Adrenaline spurted in him as he wondered: *What now? Pentarn? Amy Brittman on a return visit? Ironfolk?* He tensed, wary, ready to defend himself, grateful for the few karate lessons he had had—though he didn't know whether they would be any good against those hairy little horrors!

He stepped through, with quick, wary glances about the living room.

"All right," said a tight, controlled voice. "Hold it right there, Fenton. Hands against the wall, and bend over."

It was a uniformed Berkeley policeman. And he held a drawn gun, pointing straight at Fenton's heart.

CHAPTER SIXTEEN

THERE WERE two policemen. A third person, identically garbed, was technically a policewoman, short and sturdy, looking, if anything, considerably tougher than her male counterpart. Stunned, but automatically cooperating, Fenton put his hands up, moved over against the wall and leaned there, submitting as the policeman patted him down for weapons and turned out his pockets.

"Not armed," said the policeman. "No weapons, except maybe—what's this little thing?"

He held it out on his open palm to Fenton, and Fenton said, "It's a veterinary needle. I was sewing up a wound in one of my Uncle Stan's goats this morning." Dazed by the sudden change, he thought of Sally, milking a nanny-goat, pushing a playful kid out of the way. "Look, what's this all about, officer?"

"Sit down, Fenton," said the policewoman, not bothering to answer his question. "You are Cameron Fenton?"

"Yes, but what—"

"This is your apartment, you are the legal resident of this place?" She read off the address.

Fenton admitted it, confused. He was beginning to suspect that something was very, very wrong. It didn't take much brains, he thought bleakly, to suspect *that*. The Berkeley police were overworked, and it wasn't likely they would make a second visit to recheck on a routine burglary where nothing important had been taken. Not unless they wanted him to swear out another complaint against Amy Brittman, and he found it hard to believe they wouldn't simply call him to come down to the station for that.

The policewoman said, "Cameron Fenton, you are under arrest on suspicion of wilful murder. It is my duty un-

der the laws of the state of California to tell you that you
are not obliged to answer any of our questions but that if
you do answer any questions, your answers will be re-
corded and may be used in evidence against you at any
future legal proceeding. You have the right to call a lawyer, and if you are unable to afford a lawyer, one will be
provided for you by legal aid. Do you understand all that?
You don't have to answer any questions and you can have
a lawyer, now or any time you ask us for one. That
clear?"

"Sure," he said, "but I wish you'd tell me what's the
matter. I don't mind answering your questions. I haven't
done anything."

"No?" said the policeman. "And I suppose you'll
change your story and tell us you never heard of the girl,
that she didn't come here and tear up your apartment?
That you didn't come and bail her out of jail and leave
her in her apartment dead and mutilated?"

"Oh, God," he said. "Amy Brittman?"

"He knows the name. Write that down, Sergeant," the
policeman said to the policewoman. She wrote it down.

"Sure, she trashed my apartment," Fenton said, "and I
called the cops and handed her over to you people. I
didn't bail her out, though. And I've never been near her
apartment." He corrected himself. "No. I went there once,
but I didn't get inside. She opened the door, saw it was me
and slammed it in my face."

"And your story is that you never saw her since?"

"It's not a story. It's what happened. I never saw her
since she ran down the stairs out there." He pointed. "I
gave the police her gun, and I never saw or heard of her
again. Is she dead?"

"She's dead, all right," the policeman said. "And we
have a dozen witnesses saying a man answering your description in every particular, but dressed up in some idiotic stupid Anachronist costume, complete with a false
beard, came and bailed her out, giving your name. Want
to change your story, Fenton?"

Fenton shook his head. But it was a blow to the pit of
his stomach. Pentarn! "No," he said. "I told you the truth.
I left town three hours after I called the police, and I've
been up in the Sierras with my uncle, up on his goat

ranch. I was with a colleague from the University—Miss Lobeck of the parapsychology department. You can call her and check that."

The policeman said, "Don't worry, we will. We need her to identify the body. The Brittman girl had no local relatives, so we checked with the University and found that Miss Lobeck was her advisor. If your stories check, you've probably got nothing to worry about."

"Maybe they were in it together," the policewoman said.

"How could I have killed her?" Fenton asked reasonably. "I gave the police her gun."

"What makes you think she was shot? Listen," the policeman said, "we're asking the questions."

"Can I make a phone call?"

"You get to make a phone call down at the station after we book you. Unless you want to give us your lawyer's name, and then we have to call him for you right away."

"I don't know any lawyers," Fenton said. "Hell, I never needed a lawyer."

"Looks like you need one now, buddy," said the policeman, without any malice, but dead serious.

"After you book me, I'll call Doctor Garnock and he can tell me if there's a lawyer for the department," Fenton said; but afterward, riding down town in the police car, he wondered drearily if Garnock would want the department involved in a murder.

They took him downtown, and booked him. They let him call Garnock, who was shocked and insisted on coming down right away with a lawyer and a representative of the department to provide bail if he needed it. Fenton wondered if Garnock thought that he, Fenton, had become so deranged from the Antaril experiment that he was actually capable of murder. After booking him, they asked if he had any objection to medical tests; after which they took samples of his body hair, head hair, took scrapings from under his fingernails, examined his body carefully for scratches and contusions, and asked for a sample of semen, asking when he had last had sexual relations. He told them, knowing that in a situation as serious as this, Sally would certainly not mind backing him up. But had Amy Brittman been raped, too? If it was Pentarn, he thought with ironic detachment, rape would hardly be necessary.

Then he sat in a cell, wondering, dreading what was ahead. Murder was not a bailable offense. He left the cell once that day when they escorted him down to the morgue and pulled open a drawer to identify the body of Amy Brittman as that of the looter he had reported.

She was still clad in a few tatters of clothing, much stained and bedraggled, pulled tight around her neck. Her face was twisted into a grimace of frozen horror; her body was mottled and livid with bruises. But the real horror was the marks of claws, or teeth, or some brutal hacking weapon, which had half severed one of her hands from her body and left deep torn wounds in the throat. One breast had been severed, and something had *chewed*— there was no other way to describe it—at the top of her thigh near her groin.

"Good God," Fenton said, and hid his face in his hands. "Good *God!* That doesn't look as if anything human had done it! I could have killed the girl, maybe, though God knows I'd have no reason to. But—she's been raped—and strangled—and *hacked. Mangled!* What do you think I am, Jack the Ripper, or something?"

Nobody answered. He hadn't expected them to answer. They just took him back to jail and to his cell, where they fed him something which was supposed to be stew made with hydrolized protein, and something even more distantly related to coffee, and left him in a cell with a dim bulb that burned all night.

For a long time he did not sleep; the mangled body of Amy Brittman floated before his eyes, hideously twisted and torn. He should have held on to her for the police. He should have given her the gun and let her go, so Pentarn would not have revenged himself this way for her failure—if it had been Pentarn. No more than Fenton himself could Pentarn have managed to make those terrible ripping wounds in the girl's body. God help us, he thought, the poor girl was half eaten! And then, on a nightmarish edge of sleep, he saw the remembered picture of ironfolk, slicing up the horses of the Alfar living, and cramming the dripping flesh into their mouths with both fists.

Ironfolk! Had the ironfolk somehow come through and murdered poor Amy? He remembered their fangs, their crude machetelike weapons, their long claws. Would they have left so much of her?

This meant that the ironfolk could come through into this world—but then he had known it, since he had seen one of them run off with his uncle's axe! Why had he not warned anybody? Well, he had tried. But somehow, somehow, he should have managed to make them believe it.

Was it too much of a coincidence that the first victim of the ironfolk in this world—so far as he knew, of course; there were unsolved psycho murders which might perhaps be laid at that door—should be a woman so closely connected with Pentarn, who somehow managed to control the ironfolk?

I knew he was a bad man. His own son believed him so bad a man that he gave up his place as Pentarn's heir. But would even Pentarn turn the ironfolk loose on a woman he had loved, or professed to love?

Pentarn had turned the ironfolk loose on Kerridis and Irielle. Wasn't that enough answer?

Restlessly, he turned over so the light was not in his eyes and hunched the thin jail blanket over his head. He realized that he felt guilty. Somehow, somehow, he should have managed to warn someone about the menace of the ironfolk.

Yeah. I can just see it now. I go to the Berkeley police station and warn them that little hairy horrors from another dimension are going around eating people. He hoped that Amy Brittman had been dead when they did whatever-it-was they did to her, but he didn't really have too much hope of it. He hadn't liked the girl, hadn't had any reason to like her, but she shouldn't have met a horrible death like that. He wondered if her actual murderers were nearly as tormented with dread as he was. That wasn't likely either.

Finally he fell into an uneasy sleep, riddled with dreams in which Irielle stared at him mournfully from behind a barricade and Joel Tarnsson caught up a vrillsword and went charging off in a patricidal fury, while Pentarn stood in the center of a ring of ironfolk trying vainly to quiet their gobbling cries, and Kerridis led Fenton to the door of the Worldhouse. Kerridis. How did she fare with the Council? In the affairs of this world it seemed almost that he had deserted or abandoned her.

But what could he do for her?

Again and again these dreams repeated themselves, or something very similar, so that when morning came, with more of what the jail people laughingly called coffee and something with a faint resemblance to oatmeal, he could not manage to swallow, but sat, sick and shaken, on his bunk, waiting for something to happen.

Midmorning, it happened.

They gave him back his belt, shoes, tie and wallet, made him sign a receipt for his money and keys and his Uncle Stan's veterinary needle, and took him in to the precinct room where Garnock, Sally, and Stan Cameron were waiting for him.

"Okay, Fenton," the desk sergeant said. "Your story checks out; you can go. I guess you couldn't have killed the girl." He looked unhappy, and Fenton wasn't surprised; his manner said, as plainly as if he had spoken, that now he would have to find out who *had* killed Amy Brittman. Now he had the unpleasant task of looking for the kind of psychopath who would rape, strangle and mutilate a young woman that way. Fenton felt guilty again that he couldn't warn the desk sergeant that there were likely, if ironfolk were around, to be a couple more murders just like that, but he was in enough trouble already. He had just gotten out of it by the skin of his teeth and he wasn't going to jump right back from the frying pan into the fire.

He didn't envy the desk sergeant, either. The police weren't going to find any psychopath. He was sure they could hunt till hell froze over for the tall Anachronist in beard and boots who had bailed Amy out of jail, and they'd never find him.

And if they ever did, Pentarn could always jump into that handy portable hole he carried around with him and pull it in after him and disappear!

It sounded crazy even to Fenton, who knew it was true. He could just imagine what it would sound like to an ordinary desk sergeant of police. And so he didn't say anything at all.

"It seems to me that we have a very clear duty," said Stan Cameron. They had gone back to Garnock's office, where Fenton had told the whole story over again. He wasn't sure Garnock believed him completely, but Garnock had been badly shaken up by what had happened to Amy; he hadn't, like Sally had, to look at her mangled corpse to identify the body, but he had seen the lurid account in the newspapers. Now he was willing to listen to what Fenton had to say about the ironfolk.

"A clear duty," Uncle Stan repeated, "to warn people about the ironfolk."

"They won't believe it," Garnock said. "Believe me, Mr. Cameron. I'm head of the parapsychology department, I'm committed to believing what people think is impossible, and it took the horrible death of one of my students to make me even halfway believe it. If I don't believe it," Garnock said, "how the *hell* do you expect that anyone else will?"

"Whether they believe it or not," Stan Cameron said inflexibly, "my duty is to warn them."

Sally's eyes glinted at him. "What good do you think you can possibly do anyone when you are locked up in a psycho ward?"

"Just the same," he said, "I've got to try. That's my responsibility. Whether to believe it or not, that's theirs."

Nothing they said would deter him, and finally he went off alone toward the police station. "If they do hold me, as a psycho," he called back to Cam, "send somebody to take care of my goats. All right?"

Garnock shook his head as the old man walked out of the office. "I admire his guts," he said, "but I don't think he's going to get anywhere. It doesn't make any sense, Cam. I have enough trouble keeping up with the power struggles in this world, and how are we supposed to keep up with a dozen worlds all around us?"

"I think that must be what the Worldhouse is for," Fenton said. "To make sure that the internal affairs of one dimension don't come through to the others. But something seems to have slipped. The people in the Worldhouse aren't doing their thing properly." He remembered the old man, Myrill, who kept repeating that nothing had come through *his* Gate and that the others had nothing to do with him. If this was the kind of person Kerridis—or her agents—put in charge of the Worldhouse, they had only themselves to blame for what came through.

What kind of person, then, *should* be placed in charge of the Worldhouse? The only person he had ever seen on this end of the Worldhouse was the young woman, Jennifer, and the young people gathered around the gameboard playing Dungeons and Dragons. How did the people in charge of the Worldhouse qualify for that high responsibility?

"There used to be legends," Sally said thoughtfully, "of secret societies who had the keys to other worlds. Maybe the Worldhouse was always in charge of them—" The sight of Amy Brittman's body seemed to have removed the last of her doubts.

"But most so-called secret societies now are mostly tax dodges," Fenton said. "Maybe they lost track of what they were *supposed* to be doing. Lost the secret of managing the Worldhouse properly."

"That could happen in one world, maybe," Garnock demurred. "Hardly in all of them at once. And there seems to be something pretty badly wrong with it on all levels, from what you tell me."

"The problem seems to be," Fenton said, "that most of the intruders who are troubling the Alfar world—and this one, too—aren't coming through the Worldhouse, or even at the proper times when the Gates are supposed to be open. It all seems to come from Pentarn's world. Maybe there was so little trouble, for so long, that the people who guard the Gates got careless, and when somebody like Pentarn started trying to make mischief, they weren't prepared for it, and had no defense for it. It's Pentarn who has been letting things like the ironfolk into the Alfar world."

"Are they from his own world, do you think?" Sally asked.

"I think not. The way the gnome spoke, I would say definitely not. I think Pentarn found a way to open up a Gate through the gnome's world and let the ironfolk directly through, even when the normal Gates into the Alfar world were shut."

"Why did the gnome let him do it?" Sally asked.

"I don't think he really knew, until I came along, what was happening," Fenton said. "I told you that he seemed only to sense two kinds of things, himself and *others,* and if he couldn't convert whatever it was into himself, he only wanted to get rid of it as fast as possible—so without any malice at all toward the Alfar, he opened up a Gate into their world just to get rid of the ironfolk."

Sally suggested, "You could try to get back to the gnome's world with that special lot of bootleg Antaril that took you there—"

Garnock and Fenton protested with one voice.

"Anyway," Fenton added, "Amy stole it. She probably turned it over to Pentarn, if she lived long enough; I haven't got it. I might be able to find the dealer again, but they come and go and I could never be sure it was the same lot. It might send me anywhere, not the gnome's world."

"But if the gnome knew what he was doing," Sally asked, "wouldn't he be willing to help?"

"How do I know? Did you ever try to talk to a gnome?" Fenton asked, remembering the frustration of that particular experience. "It seems to me that the only thing to do is try and find the Worldhouse and try and talk to whoever's really in charge of the place. Not the people who tend the Gates, but the higher-ups, if there are any."

Garnock frowned. "It goes against the grain to give you Antaril for anything like this, but if it will send you directly to the world of the Alfar—" he began.

Fenton shook his head and demurred, "It's useless for me to go as a 'tweenman. I've had enough of this, being a helpless victim of circumstances, and if I go as a 'tweenman that's all I'll ever be."

Whatever happened, he resolved, he was *not* going again into the world of the Alfar—or any other—helpless and flung about by the winds of chance, without substance, a shadow, walking through walls, without any force to affect the events going on around him! "Give me the talisman I brought back, Doc." And as Garnock stared at him without comprehension he added, "The rock. The apport. Whatever you call it. I'm going back in the body, this time, as a worldwalker, or I'm not going at all."

Garnock started to demur. Fenton hardened his jaw and said, "Look here, Doc. Like Uncle Stan said, whether other people believe it or not, that's their responsibility. This is *mine*. I'm going, and I'm going with the talisman, so I can go as a worldwalker. Get it for me, right now." And as Garnock still hesitated, he rose to his feet and loomed, menacing, over the older man.

"Doc, I mean it. I don't like to argue with you, but I'm going to have it, and that's all there is to it. Go and get it for me, or I'll go and smash that damned glass case and *take* it. Or I'll stand here and call it—and find out whether I have enough telekinesis to teleport it out. Take your choice. But I'd rather you'd give it to me."

Garnock did not move. For a moment he sat and looked up at his student. Then he said, slowly, "All right, Cam. On your own head. It's yours." He went to the glass display case, took a key from his ring, and unlocked it. He took out the rock, holding it reluctantly between his hands.

"You really want to do it this way?"

"I don't have any choice, Doc."

"What are you going to do?"

"I'm going to walk down Telegraph Avenue until I find the Worldhouse, or at least the little print-shop which is one of the doors of the Worldhouse, and I'm going in with this in my hand, and demand to go through to the world of the Alfar. The girl there, Jennifer, saw me with Kerridis. But I saw what they thought of 'tweenmen; I can't insist on anything, as a 'tweenman. I've got to go with a talisman to enter as a worldwalker."

Garnock handed him the rock. He said, "All right, then. I'll gamble on you this far; I guess I owe you that, after letting the Brittman girl get murdered. Here's your talisman—and I'll walk down to Telegraph with you. I'd like a good look at the Worldhouse."

"And so will I," Sally said but Garnock turned on her with a scowl.

"Oh no you don't. Two lunatics in the parapsychology department are enough, at one time. You've got to stay here and take my class on scientific validation in parapsychology!"

CHAPTER SEVENTEEN

THEY DIDN'T TALK at all as they crossed the campus to the Sather Gate and walked out on Telegraph Avenue. Fenton found that he was shaking with eagerness, and the talisman in his trouser pocket felt hard and cold. It was flat and featureless, a piece of grey rock, but he fancied that under his fingers he could feel the fine filigree carvings. He pulled it out and looked at it. No, just a piece of rock, but could he faintly see the line of carvings?

Down one block and the next. He realized that he felt sick and faint. Suppose the Worldhouse was not there, suppose the little print-shop had been replaced by the dry-cleaner's shop again? He saw it across the street and his heart sank, for it seemed at that moment to be the flat white sterile facade that said DRY CLEANING . . .

"Is that the print-shop you meant, Cam?" Garnock asked.

Fenton blinked, and it was there, the print-shop with the Rackham illustrations in the window, the small pile of games and books and fantasy art books and Dungeons and Dragons many-sided dice. The Worldhouse. There was a strange thickness in his throat. He grasped the talisman between his fingers, as they stepped across the threshold; under his fingers he felt the ridgings, the carvings . . .

"Doc! Look at this!"

In his hand the talisman *changed*—a small writhing and stirring in his fingers. It was not, now, a round rock. It was flat, hard, a piece of green soapy stone, perhaps even jade, carved elegantly with runes. As he looked at it, it changed again, glittering, golden filigree, as Irielle had given it to him. Garnock's eyes seemed to be starting from his head.

"Let me see it. Cam, I don't believe this!"

The young woman with long hair and granny glasses came slowly toward them.

"May I help you gentlemen, please?"

Fenton started to take the talisman from Garnock; the older man clutched at it spasmodically, still studying it, so Fenton caught Garnock's wrist and held it out toward the woman. Now he remembered her name.

"Jennifer. You know what this is."

She did. He could see that in her face. She said, "Right this way, please. Come through here."

The floor tilted under Fenton's feet. With a yell, Garnock disappeared, still clutching the talisman. Fenton, dizzy and disoriented, grabbed at him, clutched only empty air. He shouted, spun through a dizzying glimpse of a great bare room, of the long hall of doors, of something strange and faraway that looked like a crystal cavern, heard someone say in the far distance, "No. Kerridis has said it. Pentarn is not to come through this Gate to the Alfar." Space reeled dizzyingly again around him, while Fenton tried to shout that it was all a stupid mistake, that he was *not* Pentarn, but he knew no one heard.

Fenton's mind cleared at last. He was standing on firm ground in darkness. He had not the slightest idea *where* he was. Had Garnock, with the Alfar talisman, fallen through into the Alfar world? And had he, mistaken for Pentarn because of that foolish resemblance, been sent elsewhere? And if so, where was he?

One thing was certain. He was not in the little print shop which was the Telegraph Avenue terminal, or station, or end, of the Worldhouse in his part of the world. He was somewhere out of doors. It was cold; he was not in the gnome's world. He strained his eyes through the darkness to see some kind of light through the gloom, but without success; the darkness was so intense that for a panicky moment Fenton wondered if he were blind, or in a lightless underground cavern. He said, tentatively, "Hello?" There were no close echoes; he was not in a cave and, from the quality of the sound, he had the impression that he was in the open air.

Slowly, as his eyes accustomed themselves to the intense blackness, he began to see again. Dim shapes around him, darker than the rest of the darkness, the flat sides of distant buildings or hills—it was hard to see which, but something cut off his view of the horizon. High and far in the sky was a faint sprinkle of stars. Well, that settled one thing; he had never seen stars in the Alfar world, and he was therefore somewhere else.

But where? He could pick a direction and walk until he saw a light, but that would be random. He could stay here until he fell through somewhere else, or whatever spell had brought him here took him back again. That seemed almost equally hopeless.

He couldn't just *stand* here. On the other hand, why couldn't he? It seemed almost as profitable as walking in some unknown direction—for there was neither sun nor moon to tell him in which direction he was oriented—toward some equally unknown destination. And having thought it all out carefully—that there was no reason to go anywhere or do anything—he studied what seemed to be the nearest of the distant shapes in the darkness, and started walking.

As he walked he had plenty of time to make nightmares for himself. He had not, this time, come under the influence of Antaril, so there was no assurance that if he waited it out and kept out of trouble, he would materialize somewhere, tied by the silver cord to wherever he had left his body. It was possible that if they had mistaken him for Pentarn and refused him entrance to the Alfar world, they had sent him into some unknown world to which Pentarn presumably had free entry and egress. He might be anywhere; he was certainly no closer to warning Kerridis or the Alfar. Not that they needed warning. They already knew about the dangers of the ironfolk, and they knew more than he could about Pentarn's treachery.

What happened to anyone who went as a worldwalker, unheralded, unwanted and ungreeted, into a strange world, any world? What could be lurking here in this world? Anything, he thought gloomily, up to and including man-eating dragons. In a cosmos which suddenly included ironfolk, gnomes and the Lord Leader, who could say that dragons were impossible or even unlikely? Sally had been right; the universe was not only queerer than Fenton imagined but queerer than he *could* imagine. Despondent, and aware that most of what he felt was quite simply self-pity, he plodded along from nowhere to nowhere. So much for his brave resolve to take matters into his own hands, to be no longer the helpless tool of circumstances! Now he was considerably worse off than before, and Kerridis and the Alfar were no better off.

Then he saw a light.

It flared out of nowhere, into brilliance. Then there were two lights, then more, coming slowly toward him, and he could hear voices, rough men's voices, but human, not the singing bell-like tones of the Alfar, nor yet the harsh growling of ironfolk.

"Around here someplace, I thought. Something patched through. A disturbance. One of those cursed Alfar, I shouldn't wonder, come to steal what they can."

"What's happened to the Gates, anyway, that things are coming through?"

"If you ask me," said one voice, circumspectly lowered, "not intending any disrespect to the Lord Leader, all this mucking around with the Gates could be dangerous. A Gate is one thing, but to make patches in the very stuff of space, just to go and come without having to bother with a Gate, I say it's dangerous and I wish he'd find some other way to do his business, hear?"

"It ain't for the likes of you or me to criticize the Lord Leader," said the first voice, and Fenton suddenly knew he was in Pentarn's world, and these people must be in the service of their Lord Leader—in other words, Pentarn's men.

Then the lights were in his eyes, and the torches—they were not open flame but more like electric lanterns—flashing on him.

The men bowed and one of them said, "We didn't know it was you, Lord Leader." The man gestured him ceremoniously forward. But even as Fenton recognized the mistake they were making, and before he could figure out any way to take advantage of it, one of the men stepped closer to him and grimaced.

"Save your bows, mates. It's not the Lord Leader, it's that wretched 'tweenman he brought through a while back. We ought to kick him right back the way he came, through the patch."

That, Fenton thought, would save him a lot of trouble.

And so of course they didn't. One of them pushed forward, looking directly into Fenton's face. "This one's the Lord Leader's analogue. He gave orders that if this one turned up again he wanted to see him, on the minute! Brisk, now, all of you!"

Then they had him between them, pushing him along by torchlight. Fenton was partly relieved to know he wasn't in an unknown part of an unknown world, to linger there until he starved or died; but turning up in Pentarn's world didn't seem very preferable. After a time they began to walk through big buildings, some of which looked like warehouses or crowded apartment buildings without a soul awake; they were enormous many-windowed structures, but Fenton hadn't the faintest notion of their function. Gradually the dirt roads underfoot turned to smooth-laid roadways. The men talked among themselves in low tones but none of them bothered to address a word to Fenton. After a long time they approached a larger building than the others, with light flooding out from an open door.

"In there, please," one of them said, and shoved him into what looked like an open guardroom, with benches, and notices on the walls, and some uniformed men sitting around waiting to go on duty. It looked rather like a police station at a slack time, but instead of reading newspapers, working on paperwork and drinking coffee, one of them was taking a weapon apart and oiling it, another was working at some sort of string puzzle that made Fenton think of a solitaire version of cat's-cradle, and a third was forthrightly napping, his head down on a bare wooden table. Another was cracking some oddly-shaped kind of nuts and chewing them with a loud crunching noise.

This one got up and asked, "Well, well, what did you bring in this time, friend?"

The man who had taken Fenton into custody said, "One of the Lord Leader's analogues, looks like. The Big Man said if this one came through he wanted to see him."

"That so? I suppose that was what patched through a while ago? What are those people with the Gate thinking of?"

"The Gate had nothing to do with it, and you know it as well as I do," said the other, in a gloomy tone. "It's all these stray patches. Mark my words, one of these days the space around the Gate's going to give way, and then what's going to be coming through? I ask you now! The Alfar, that's one thing. They don't do any harm, and if they start chucking their big swords around, well, while I've got this I'm not worrying." He put his hand on his gun, which, Fenton noted without surprise, was an exact duplicate of the one Amy Brittman had brandished at him. "But those ironfolk, they give me the creeps, and there's worse things on the other sides of those Gates and patches! When just anything can go in and out, I don't like it."

"Hold your noise," said the other. "You were as glad as anybody to get plunder in some of those places the Lord Leader took us. I remember some of the women in that city with the red rocks—"

"I'm a soldier, sure, I take what comes my way. But enough's enough, and I don't like to think what's happening to the Gates."

"The Lord Leader can handle them," a third one said with confidence. "Better than the old Kings ever did. It was a good day for our people when he married the old king's daughter, and better the way things are now than when the Kings were on the throne. The Lord Leader, he knows how to look after the army."

"And he doesn't give a grin for anybody else," said the first speaker gloomily. "Ask the city folk what they think. And where's the boy? That's what I ask you, where's Prince Joel that he promised us on the throne again when the big troubles were over? I think myself the boy's dead and the Lord Leader isn't daring to tell us for fear the old King's supporters get up and riot!"

"I heard the boy was promised an Alfar princess, as a bond between the worlds," another one suggested, but this was greeted with hoots of derision.

The man cracking nuts said, "Enough gabble; let's try and get through to the Lord Leader—supposing he's in the palace and not out gallivanting somewhere on the other side of the Gates."

He used some kind of intercom device, then turned back to his fellows.

"I couldn't get the Lord Leader, but one of his aides

told me that he's in the palace. I heard he has a new woman, he's probably with her, but if we send the analogue, he'll probably make time for him sometime tonight." He looked at Fenton with a certain amount of concern, not at all unfriendly.

"You look like you'd had a long march," he said. "Hungry?"

"Don't be an idiot," said one of the others. " 'Tweenmen don't eat."

"Can't you tell a worldwalker when you see one? Look at his shadow. If he made a break for it, we could put him in cuffs, and he knows it," said the man who had used the intercom. "But no point treating him rough till we have to. Give him a block of rations. If he's the Lord Leader's analogue, probably the Big Man has some use for him and he ought to turn up in good condition. Here," he said, handing Fenton a moist chunk of something. "It's only gump, but it'll keep your belly from sticking to your backbone. And fetch him a mug of beer from the storeroom, Jem."

The man addressed went through a door and came back with a bent tin cup of something which Fenton, when he sampled it, found to be a strong and rather bitter beer, somewhat like bock beer. He drank it down and, at the advice of the giver, chewed on the "gump" as he walked along from the guardroom and through the quiet street. It was quite tangible food and, unlike the much more palatable drink he had had in the Alfar country, quenched his thirst and hunger adequately. The "gump" was a semi-moist, hard-pressed chunk of something that tasted like cold fatty corned beef mixed with breadcrumbs and dried raisins; a form of pemmican. Definitely iron rations of a kind. It was filling and doubtless nourishing; but the taste definitely was nothing to write home about.

The walk through the streets this time would not have been more than a few blocks; and he recognized the place where he ended as the arsenal where Pentarn had brought him before, coated with the immense pictures of the Lord Leader on the wall. Again Fenton noticed the faint resemblance. If he grew a beard, he would be Pentarn's double. He thought, with revulsion, *I shall be very careful not to grow a beard.*

"Lord Leader's too busy to see anybody just now," said another uniformed officer at the barrier near the back. "Gave orders not to be disturbed. Sit down there and wait, why don't you, young fellow?"

Fenton sat in the indicated place, finishing the last crumbs of the "gump" and rather glad he had had it. It looked like being a long wait. All things considered, he thought he had learned something by coming here. Pentarn's men—bodyguard, army, special police, whatever he called them—had treated him humanely and now he knew that he and Garnock were not the only people concerned about what was happening to the careful structure built up to protect the Gates.

How long had the Worldhouse been in operation? Probably, he thought, from time immemorial—if time had any meaning in the new picture of the cosmos which the very existence of the Worldhouse had given him. And somewhere along that line, control of the Gates had slipped. In Pentarn's world they had fallen under control of a power-mad dictator who was using them recklessly for his own purposes, without realizing what this might do to the Gates. And in Fenton's world, their existence had been forgotten, kept secret, eventually fallen into the hands of amateurs and volunteers because the scientific establishment was less and less ready to accept anything like that. The time could be measured in millennia here, too. Certainly the Worldgates had not been known in historical times. But historical time, according to some new theories, was only a fraction of the time man had lived on this planet . . . unless you wanted to stick to the exploded theory that history had begun with 4004 B.C. when God created the world in seven days, fossils and all, to confuse the ungodly.

The night crawled by. He wondered if Pentarn was already consoling himself for Amy's death with his new woman. He wondered what Sally was doing, waiting, holding down Garnock's classes. He wondered how Garnock was getting along wherever he had been sent, and if it had been the world of the Alfar. He wondered if Irielle and Kerridis were safe, or if ironfolk were even now breaking through Pentarn's "patches," bent on extorting Pentarn's revenge for his defector son. And he wondered, angrily, why he was wondering about all these things when he couldn't do a single thing about them.

It was never easy to gauge time in any alien dimension, though it was easier, Fenton thought, as a worldwalker than as a 'tweenman; at least he had his own body's internal rhythms to help him judge. It was getting on toward the small hours of the morning—the sky was flushing pale with incipient sunrise—and Fenton was beginning to feel that the mug of beer and block of "gump" had been a good long time ago and that he wouldn't mind another good substantial meal, when finally the door to Pentarn's private apartments opened.

Pentarn stood in the door. He looked drawn and tired. He raised his eyes curiously at Fenton and asked, "What are you doing here?"

"He patched through, Lord Leader," his guard said. "We thought *you* sent for him."

Pentarn shook his head. "Unauthorized things do sometimes get through the patches. Well, since you're here, you may as well come in," he said to Fenton, and gestured him inside. When the door was shut, he motioned him to a seat, and once again Fenton was struck by the spartan aspect of the small private rooms. Whatever Pentarn sought from being Lord Leader, it certainly was not personal luxury. The chairs and bed were hardly as comfortable as those in Fenton's own apartment, and not noticeably finer than the benches in the barracks guardroom.

The Lord Leader looked older than when Fenton had last seen him. Had he genuinely aged—was time so different in this world? Or was it the burden of some worry or great grief weighing on him? He looked for a minute at Fenton without speaking, then asked, "How'd you get here?"

Fenton shrugged. He had no intention of explaining that he had started out with a talisman which would have sent him into the Alfar world. But Pentarn's question he could answer precisely, because he didn't have the faintest idea how he had gotten *here* instead. "I haven't any idea."

"I see this time you managed to get here as worldwalker," Pentarn said. "Easier, isn't it? I've spent time as a 'tweenman, but not willingly, I assure you. Well, did you manage to bring me some of the drug? A good sample, and my chemists could analyze it."

Fenton said, "It only sends people between the worlds as 'tweenmen."

" 'Tweenmen are useful to me," Pentarn said. "They can spy for me, and they can't be killed unless someone happens to have a piece of vrill handy and knows just how to use it. I could use the drug, and I could offer you something for it. I could use a double; and you're close enough to me that a little hair on your face will make up for it. I pay my accomplices well, and will do better when I finally make my way clear between worlds."

Fenton couldn't resist it. He asked, "Would I get the same pay as Amy Brittman—being torn to pieces by iron-folk? Thanks, I've seen how your friends end up."

Pentarn's face looked worn, exhausted. He said "What are you talking about? Amy? I went and got her out of jail—I borrowed your name; it did you no harm to lend it —and punished her only by refusing to bring her back to me for a small space of time. She wept and wailed, as women do, but it was only a small punishment. What makes you think she is dead? Did she tell you I would kill her? I wouldn't kill even a woman for so small a failure."

"I know she's dead," Fenton said bluntly, "because I saw her corpse."

Pentarn stared at him in horror. He said, "No!" And again, "No!" His frown was angry, suspicious. "You'd better tell me what you know about it!"

"More than I want to know, believe me," Fenton said, and explained that he had spent a night in jail for Amy's murder.

"It was just dumb luck that I happened to be out of the city and more than two hundred kilometers north," he said, "or I'd still be trying to convince them I wasn't a raving madman who could rape a woman, strangle her and chew her corpse to mangled bits!" Deliberately he made his words harsh. He wasn't going to mince words with Pentarn.

"But this is horrible, horrible," Pentarn said, and Fenton realized with shock that the man was in tears. "Poor little Amalie, poor child. If only I had allowed her to come back to me. I should not have punished her so severely!"

Crocodile tears, Fenton thought in sudden rage. Pentarn let the ironfolk into our world. It was dumb luck that it had been his own woman who was murdered by iron-folk. Otherwise it would have been some other harmless student and Pentarn wouldn't care a damn.

"Can't you control your allies?" he asked, angrily. "If you have no control over the ironfolk, you're not likely to have many friends, even if you have any now, which I doubt. Anyone who would let the ironfolk loose on inno-cent bystanders—"

"You don't understand," Pentarn said. "They are the only weapon I have against the Alfar, and somehow or other, I must destroy the Alfar . . . all of them, every miserable last one of them!"

"And because of a private grudge, you'd turn the iron-folk loose on the Alfar?"

"You don't know a damned thing about the Alfar," Pentarn said viciously. "They deserve worse than that—far worse! Or have they hoodwinked you too, with their music and their dancing and their beauty and their gold?"

Nothing was to be gained by making Pentarn angry. Fenton reminded himself, with a brief shudder, that this time he was a worldwalker and could be injured physi-cally by any captors. He said, "That's what you said be-fore."

"Believe me," Pentarn said. "I'm horrified by what you tell me about poor Amalie; horrified, shocked, overcome. I'll make certain that the ones who did it are strictly held to account. But nothing can bring the poor girl back, and we must simply go on from where we are. I wish you'd see this thing reasonably. I can send you back, and pro-vide you with a talisman so that you can return at will, without going through my bodyguard; you could come straight to my private apartments. Only a few of my guard would know I had a double—the others would be told I had disposed of an intruder who tried to impersonate me. You would live in luxury, if that is what you care for, have what women you want. But I must have some of the Antaril drug and full instructions about how to use it safely. I don't want to deal with street pushers in your world; the impurities in the stuff make it unreliable. And some is so strong that it takes a user to worlds so far away, in the timeline, that they're no use to me. But if you can find me some of the pure pharmaceutical, I can have it synthesized."

Fenton nodded as if he were considering it. If he could get out of here alive; and with a talisman that would bring him back, he might somehow manage to make Pentarn accountable for Amy Brittman's death. The rest of Pentarn's promises he tuned out. Live in luxury, access to women . . . not likely. He supposed he would meet exactly the fate the bodyguard expected—that an intruder, trying to impersonate the Lord Leader, would be summarily executed.

Fenton said, "I could probably get you some of the drug, the pure injectible from the parapsychology lab." He didn't think he could do any such thing, even if he wanted to, which he didn't.

Pentarn smiled, and the smile reminded Fenton of a hungry tiger.

"Good! Good! When?"

"Perhaps in three days," Fenton said at random. "How do I let you know when I have it, so that I can bring it to you?"

Pentarn took up, from a small, bare desk, a small strip of metal. He said, "Put this on your wrist; see this stud? Press it when you want to patch through and it will bring you directly here. You look tired; I suppose I ought to send you back. Besides, the sooner you go back, the sooner you will return with the drug; and since there is some talk that they will close the Gates entirely into the Alfar world, I must have 'tweenmen there who can come and go unseen and slip out again without being harmed." Fenton wondered if Pentarn knew of the Rockhold, which would imprison even a 'tweenman. He fervently hoped not.

"Haste is fairly important. I think—" He broke off, turned, swiftly as a prowling animal. "What is this, Malar? I gave orders I was not to be disturbed—"

It was not Malar. At the corner of the apartment where Pentarn had spoken of a Gate—Fenton supposed it was what the man in Pentarn's guard had called a "patch" instead—there was a thinning and swirling of the air, a darkening like thick cloud. Then there was a harsh gabbling noise and a growling voice shouted, "Pentarn!"

A good dozen of the ironfolk burst through into the private room.

Pentarn turned around, his face drawn with displeasure.

"How did you get in here?" he demanded. "You know what we have agreed; you wait on my convenience and you never, never come directly here. We meet only in the Middle World."

"We're tired of waiting on your convenience, Pentarn," growled one of them. "We made a bargain and we want it now. What have we got so far? Two raids on the Alfar and a few horses! We want more—a lot more—than that!"

"What more do you want?"

"We want women and plunder," one of the ironfolk yelled. "And we're going to have it. We want talismans like you gave the other folk, so we can get into the Alfar world on our own! Not just when you think you need us! We'll get your precious youngster for you, if you give us a free hand, but in return we want the Alfar, and we want them now! We told you we were going to get it—"

Pentarn held up his hand. "Look, look, all promises will be honored in good time, but you must wait till the time comes—"

"The time is *now*," one of the ironfolk yelled, and then they were all honking and gabbling and croaking, surrounding Pentarn in a tight ring. Fenton could not make out all the words, but the gist of the howling, honking yells was, "Women and plunder! We want the Alfar!"

"Wait, wait—" Pentarn demanded.

He was fully occupied. Fenton took a quick step, unobserved, toward the desk where Pentarn, when they were interrupted, had laid the bright-metal strip which, he had said, would bring Fenton back here. Another step; and the metal strip was fastened on his wrist. Now was the dangerous part; if they saw him, he could imagine what steps they might take to get it off him again. Fenton whirled and ran like hell toward the "patch."

Pentarn saw him; he yelled, over the shouts of the ironfolk, "Get him! Stop him! Two iron axes to the one who brings him to me!"

The ironfolk broke off their screeching demands and pelted after Fenton, howling. Fenton shivered with reflex terror, knowing that if he had been mistaken about the Gate, or patch, he would die a very nasty and slow death, and this time he was not an invulnerable 'tweenman, but was in the body. For a moment it seemed that he would run right into the wall, be cornered there, but with the claws of an ironfolk already reached out to seize him, the stinking breath on his neck, the ground swirled under his feet and he fell, reeled, stepped *through* with one mighty leap, and fell headlong on hard ground.

And behind him the patch fizzled faintly and was gone. He stood safe, breathing hard, from a vantage point high above the Greek Theatre on the Berkeley campus. The sun was just setting. He was tired of trying to keep up with time-changes between the various worlds. He looked down at the lights of Berkeley going on below him, at the bay shining like wet hot metal from a forge far, far below. And this time there was no silver cord to help him. He would just have to hike all the way down to the main campus again.

He glanced at his wrist. The strip of bright metal he had fastened around it in Pentarn's rooms was still there. It was no longer bright metal, but a strange, rusty, greenish substance—he was not even sure it was metal. But in the middle of it was a small thing like a white rubber button, which would, Fenton knew, if pressed, take him directly into the private rooms of Pentarn, the Lord Leader.

He didn't know what use he was going to make of it. Not yet. But it struck him, that in their present troubles, it was a very good thing to have.

CHAPTER EIGHTEEN

HE STOPPED off at the campus, but Garnock's office—and the parapsychology building—was dark and deserted. The campanile clock told him that it was well past two in the morning. He wondered if Garnock was somewhere in the Alfar world, or caught unimaginably between dimensions. Well, he couldn't waste much sympathy on Garnock, who, after all, had Irielle's talisman and should get along all right. He debated going back to his own apartment for some food and a shower and some sleep, but the place was still in chaos after the raids, first of Amy Brittman, poor kid, and then of the police. He found an all-night restaurant still open and consumed a hasty hamburger and two cups of dubious coffee, then headed for Sally's apartment.

When he arrived there, he almost thought better of it. Would she open the door at three in the morning? But when he pressed the button her voice came immediately. "Who is it? Is that you, Doc?"

So she had been waiting up for one of them; which told him that Garnock was not back, either, for Sally, if he could not be reached at Smythe Hall, would certainly know his home number. "It's Cam," he said.

"Oh, thank God." She pressed the buzzer. When he climbed the stairs to her apartment she fell into his arms, holding him tight.

"Where were you? What happened?"

He gave her a brief rundown. Halfway through, she said, "You must be starved." She began to move around in the kitchenette, cracking eggs.

He started to say that he had had a hamburger, but realized that she was too restless to sit still and probably hadn't eaten, herself, while she was waiting for him. He said that would be wonderful and he hadn't eaten anything worth mentioning for days; which was true, for nothing they had fed him in jail, nor the block of "gump" in Pentarn's world, nor the fast-food burger, was worth mentioning, and one of Sally's omelettes was worth waiting for. When she set it in front of him, he said, "I hope you'll never neglect your work because you think you have to cook for me, darling. But will you call me an exploiting male if I say I'm going to be holding my breath and saving up my appetite for the times when you really feel like cooking?"

She leaned over and hugged him till he was breathless. She said, "I don't feel like cooking very often. But it's nice to be appreciated when I do."

She put away a substantial portion of the omelette herself and poured herself a glass of milk to go with it. When they had cleaned the plates, she sat across from him, frowning.

"Then Pentarn's tampering with the Gates is starting to come home to roost, you'd say?"

"I think so." He remembered the frightening glimpse he had had of Pentarn, surrounded by the honking, shouting ironfolk, yelling demands at him. "I'd say he was losing control of the ironfolk, too. I can't work up much sympathy for him; he deserves anything he gets now. But what I'm afraid of is that he may try to keep the loyalty of the ironfolk by turning them loose on the Alfar—and I honestly don't believe the Alfar can stand up against a full-scale onslaught from ironfolk, any more than they could stand up against Pentarn's war machine. You don't know the Alfar, Sally, but they're good people, harmless people. I feel as if I were watching Nazi storm troopers walk all over a group of tribesmen on a coconut island in Polynesia. I can't just stand by and see their whole world brutalized this way!"

"Of course you can't," she agreed instantly. "No decent person could, if there was any way to stop it. I really feel guilty about this, Cam. If I'd taken both of you seriously, and put together what you said about the Alfar with what Amy said about Pentarn, maybe I could have convinced Garnock. I think even he would have called it independent verification."

"Don't feel guilty," he comforted her. "You couldn't know; you were thinking in terms of the collective unconscious, and who could blame you? The universe is queerer than we *can* imagine; don't blame yourself because you weren't superhuman."

"You're right; guilt is useless. What's done is done. And even Garnock—good heavens, he thought he was experimenting with a new method of getting perfect runs of ESP cards, not getting entangled in the politics of half a dozen alien dimensions!" Sally said, "I wonder where he is? Do you suppose *he* has a chance to warn the Alfar?"

"He might," Penton said soberly, "but he doesn't have the background I do. He hasn't *seen* the ironfolk; he doesn't know what they're like. He didn't even have to see Amy Brittman's body." Looking at Sally's slender hand, lying on the table before him, he thought of Kerridis' fingers, crisped and blackened; later, permanently scarred by the very touch of the ironfolk's claw-hands. And what would come to Kerridis, if Pentarn was forced to relax his iron demand that Kerridis should not be harmed, if he no longer wanted Kerridis alive and well for exchange in return for his son? What the ironfolk had done to Amy Brittman, what they could do to Irielle— for he did not think Pentarn would have her protected just because she was Joel's beloved, and in any case the ironfolk cared nothing for that—was terrible enough. But what they could inflict on Kerridis, whose hand had blackened as if with fire at their very touch—*that* was horror beyond horror. Fenton found that the very thought turned him sick, faint, exhausted. He shut his eyes, in a spasm of horror.

"Cam—darling, what is it?"

"Kerridis. Somehow, we must warn them, we must get through and tell them that—that Pentarn is no longer able to control the ironfolk, that even if they make peace with him, even if Joel should agree to go back, he can't stop the ironfolk. I can't think of what could happen to Kerridis, if she falls into the hands of the ironfolk—"

Sally nodded. "I saw Amy Brittman when they got through with her. And if nobody stops the ironfolk it could happen to any woman in this world," she said, while Fenton was remembering the screeching of the ironfolk for *women and plunder!* "Somehow, we have to warn the Alfar. But how?"

He asked, "Can you get Antaril from the parapsych Lab?"

"Yes, if it comes to that," she said. "I have Garnock's keys. I could go into that world and try to warn them. But they don't know me and they have no reason to trust me; to them I am simply a woman from what could be Pentarn's world—didn't you say they were all human there?"

He nodded gloomily. "Pentarn's human enough, God knows; more shame to the human race! And you might be caught by ironfolk too—"

She quailed, but then she said, recovering her courage, "I'd be a—what did you call it—a 'tweenman, my body here, so they couldn't do me any *serious* harm."

"I'm not so sure of that," he said, remembering the marks the banewolves had left on his leg, painful and lasting, even though it had only been repercussion from injuries to whatever body it was that moved in the alien dimension.

"I'll take the chance if you want me to, Cam. Or we could go together."

"I'd rather keep that as absolutely the last resort," he said. "But we shouldn't waste too much time." He stared grimly at the strangely colored bracelet on his wrist. "As a last resort I could push this stud, go into Pentarn's private apartments and shoot him. That would help, maybe."

"But it wouldn't stop the ironfolk," she pointed out. "If they can patch through uninvited into Pentarn's private apartments, they must have learned to go almost anywhere. And even if we warn the Alfar, I don't know if we could stop an ironfolk invasion. As you said, even fully prepared, the Alfar probably couldn't stand against a full-scale ironfolk invasion, or against Pentarn's war machine. Warn the Alfar, yes; but mostly we have to find a way to stop the ironfolk. And Pentarn, too; but mainly the ironfolk."

"I think perhaps the trouble lies in the Worldhouse," Fenton said, "with unauthorized use of the Gates, and Pentarn's tampering, his 'patching.'"

"If the people at the Worldhouse could stop it, wouldn't

they already have done so?" Sally asked, and Fenton nodded, gloomily. It would be too easy to say they could report him at the Worldhouse, and 'they'—some super-powerful all-encompassing 'they,' some Secret Masters or Guardians of mankind—would reach out and slap Pentarn down for breaking the rules. But it was still a chance. Who was he to say there *wasn't* some great superpower like that guarding mankind? After what he'd seen in the last few days, who was he to say *anything* was impossible?

But having seen the people who seemed to be in charge at the Worldhouse, he didn't believe it. If there were any important higher-ups, they would hardly have left it to hostile, incompetent old Myrill for the Alfar!

Sally glanced at the chiming clock on her mantel-piece. She said, "Four o'clock. I suppose we could try and see if the Worldhouse is there. But if the print-shop is open, wouldn't that attract the kind of attention they don't want? Don't they have to keep something like regular hours?"

Fenton realized, grimly, that what they were most likely to find, at the Worldhouse site, was a closed and locked dry-cleaning shop. But if they waited until the normal hour for Telegraph Avenue businesses to open, so that the print-shop could be open without attracting notice, they would have to waste at least half a day. He yawned and said, "I guess we'd better go out and try to hunt up an open Worldhouse."

It wasn't much of a joke, but at that hour it made Sally grin faintly as she fetched her scarf.

The one good thing at this hour was that they did find a parking place within ten blocks of the crowded campus area. Her hand stole into his as they walked down the street. It was good to have her this way, close to him, sympathetic.

"At least," Sally said, moving closer to him, "it's not the dry-cleaning shop. Cam, it's scary. I believed you, I believed every word you said this time, but still, down deep, I *knew* that dry-cleaning shop would be there, would *have* to be there, and it isn't, and I don't know if—" Her voice wavered. "—if I can live with the fact that it isn't."

"It's closed," he said, staring at the locked door, the Rackham prints in the window. "Closed up tight."

"But there's a light inside," she pointed out.

"Half the shops on this street have lights inside, Sally. Light, just plain old electric light, is still the cheapest burglar insurance there is, to keep sneak thieves away."

"That's true," she said, pressing her nose to the pane, "but I still think there's somebody inside there."

"I don't see anybody."

"Neither do I," she insisted, "but I have a hunch about it, Cam. I just can't believe that any place as important as this would be closed so nobody could reach it. There *has* to be a way to get in touch with the Worldhouse when you need it."

He frowned slightly. Of course he took her hunches seriously; Sally was a trained parapsychologist and she could certainly tell the difference between a valid hunch and wishful thinking. But he remembered and repeated what Irielle had said to him. He had not understood it then.

"The Worldhouse shifts about; you cannot find it unless it wants to be found. Otherwise, your thoughts cause it to hide itself. I don't think Irielle had the technical vocabulary, but I also think she had the idea. What do you want to bet that right now, that place is a completely ordinary print-and-art shop, and the Worldhouse is somewhere else, hiding itself because it doesn't want to be found?"

"I can't buy that, Cam. That would mean that nobody outside would have any discretion—it would all be at the discretion of the people *inside*, whether to be accessible or not." Fenton had to admit that what Sally was saying made sense. But he still felt pessimistic about it.

"I'll bet you anything that the people outside who have business here have an emergency telephone number to call, or something like Irielle's talisman," he argued. "Or they may know where the Worldhouse is when it isn't here; probably some place that can stay open all night like a service station or all-night restaurant."

"Cam, we can't just give up now. We have to *try*," she demanded, and hammered on the door. There was no response. She knocked hard, again. "Cam, you try too!"

"And the next thing is that the police come along and arrest us for disturbing the peace," Fenton grumbled. Then he blinked, seeing what he had not seen before. Had it been there at all? Under a very tiny light, no more than a faintly glowing light-switch, there was a small printed card; he had to bend close to read it.

NIGHTS AND EMERGENCIES
RING BELL

"Here. I didn't see that bell; did you, Sally?"

"I didn't see it because it wasn't there," she asserted, very quietly, but with a positiveness that made his skin prickle. "Do what it says, Cam. It's night *and* an emergency."

He pressed the bell—once, again. Nothing moved in the lighted, deserted shop; but in the room behind something stirred, and though Fenton did not see any lights going on, it seemed to him that the lights there were brighter.

Then the door opened, and the young woman Jennifer looked out at him; she frowned as she saw Fenton and Sally. "Well?" she said sharply.

"Jennifer, you have to let us in; we have to talk to someone in charge," Fenton said quietly. "Pentarn has been tampering with the Gates; unauthorized people have been getting through."

"I don't—"

"For heaven's sake, don't say it's nothing to do with you!" he said fiercely. "I heard that from old Myrill, and how Kerridis ever came to put that incompetent in a position of power—"

Jennifer shook her head. "He's not in a position of power," she said. "There is no true Guardian in the Alfar world; there has not been for centuries. Come along in here." She led them through the deserted shop and into the room behind. There were no young men there now playing Dungeons and Dragons; only the glowing labyrinth of the gameboard, a few faintly glowing pieces placed there, motionless. Jennifer cast a practiced glance over them and said, "As nearly as I can tell, everything seems peaceful. What's the matter, Professor Fenton?"

"I'm not a professor," he said irritably. Jennifer shrugged.

"I don't suppose you called us up in the middle of the night to argue about that. You said that Pentarn had been tampering with the Gates," she said, and gestured to the table. "Sit down, but don't touch anything; that one isn't a game. Sometimes it's just a gameboard, but at night we set up the monitor. There don't seem to be any unauthorized patches," she said, "but it's hard to tell; Pentarn discovered most of the patches, and we can't keep track of them all. Most of them don't open into our world at all, and even if we sealed off the ones that do, there's nothing we can do about what goes into other worlds." She scanned the table carefully again. "Nothing is open just now, certainly nothing on this continent."

"Can you let us through to warn the Alfar about what Pentarn is doing?"

Jennifer shook her head. "Can't be done. That would rank as interference in internal affairs of another dimension. If someone in *this* world was interfering, I could report it . . . not that there's really anyone to report it to, but I could have the Gate closed where the interference was taking place, and the people manning the other Gates would close their Gates too, and try to make sure no patches were opening. But I can't take sides between Pentarn and the Alfar, much as I'd like to—or even between Pentarn and the ironfolk."

"That's a ghastly miscarriage of justice!" Sally snapped. "Do you mean to say you will stand there without moving, and let the ironfolk destroy the Alfar? Do you know there was a murder yesterday, that the ironfolk killed and mutilated a student of mine, here in *this* world?"

Jennifer's face hardened. "I know," she said. "We closed that patch and they're still sitting on it. Look." She pointed at the gameboard she had called the monitor. Bending close, Fenton saw a group of small figures —painted figures—seated around a glowing blue crystal stone. "I give you my word, by the Oath of the Guardians," Jennifer said. "No ironfolk will get through that patch again. Look." Following her finger, Fenton saw, dimly sketched, on the board, the Greek Theatre where he had come through a few hours ago. "We saw you come through that patch; though we didn't know it was you. We knew it was from Pentarn's world; but nothing is going to get through *that* patch again; not ironfolk, not nothing. It's been closed. How did you get through? Did Pentarn send you with one of his damnable gadgets?"

"No," Fenton said, "I sent myself with one of his damnable gadgets. With ironfolk howling right behind me, I ought to add."

She nodded. "We saw the ironfolk and closed it behind you. You belonged here; you had a right to come in, even through a patch, but they didn't. Give me that," she added, holding out her hand, pointing at the band around Fenton's wrist. "As long as it exists, that patch can be opened again. We can close it for good, if we have the gadget."

Fenton hesitated, reluctant to surrender it. As long as he had it, he had the last-resort option of going into that world and killing Pentarn, putting an end to Pentarn's tampering with the Gates. Jennifer scowled at him angrily behind her granny glasses and said, "You want to keep it? You're as bad as Pentarn! You want power to break all the rules, don't you, power to play God!"

"Aren't you playing God yourself, saying I don't have the right to go through and stop Pentarn from doing what he's doing that's wrong?"

She shook her head. She looked very young, but the way she spoke made Fenton wonder how old she was. She said quietly, "It's not the same. We want to lock up Pentarn in his own world, not to interfere with what he does in any other. We have the absolute right to keep him out of our world. It is for others to say what they want in their worlds."

"But the Alfar are helpless against him—"

"You don't understand," she said, "and I honestly don't know how I can explain it to you; you don't have the training. The Alfar can keep him out of their own world, if they have the courage. If they come to us for help we will close any access through our world. But we must not interfere. Do you understand that? We must not in-

terfere. If we interfere in a small thing we will interfere
in great ones. Power is addictive. We don't have the right
to step in and protect, any more than we have the right
to step in and punish. *We do not interfere.* All of Pentarn's evil came from the fact that he thought he could
interfere; he did not take his son back, or allow him to
stay with the Alfar; instead he brought a third party into
it; he used the ironfolk. And the balance began to get
out of hand."

"You will stand here and watch the Alfar die at the
hands of the ironfolk?"

"It would break my heart if that happened," she said,
and he could not doubt her sincerity. "I, too, love the Alfar and I fear the ironfolk. But I am sworn, and I will
keep my oath, to do nothing—*nothing*—that can interfere in any world but my own. That is my responsibility.
What the Alfar do, and the ironfolk, is theirs." For some
reason what she said made him think of Uncle Stan.
This woman had the same kind of inflexible integrity
and there was no way he could move it. He lowered his
head and unclasped the metal band Pentarn had shown
him. He laid it in her hand.

Sally said bitterly, "I hope you realize what you've
just done!"

Jennifer looked at her. Despite her youth, Fenton suddenly had the impression that she was years older than
Sally. She said, very softly, "Yes, I know what I have
done. I have made it impossible for the ironfolk, or Pentarn, to use that patch into our world again. Look."

She laid the bracelet down on the monitor board,
picked up something that looked like a glass rod. She
said a few words in a language Fenton could not identify;
they seemed to ring and echo in the quiet room, and Fenton, a chill of strangeness creeping down his spine, saw
the little carved crystal figures on the glowing board begin to stir and move about. It seemed that they clustered,
moving slowly and inexorably toward the metal bracelet.

The metal bracelet began to glow; red-hot, white-hot,
blue-white; so bright Fenton put his hands over his eyes.
When he peered through his fingers, it was gone; only a
little powdery stuff like broken glass remained on the

board, and the board was quiet again, glowing sluggishly.
The figures were immovable, carved lifeless figurines.

Jennifer said gently, "No one will use that patch again.
The fabric of space there is healed. Now if Pentarn
wishes to come through, he will have to come through
here."

"But he still has patches into other worlds," Fenton
said bitterly.

She reached out and touched his hand for a moment.
There was a strange note in her voice; shocked, he
recognized it as pity.

"You still have much to learn, Professor Fenton. I am
sorry I mistook you for Pentarn; I am not perfect,
either, or superhuman. But I try to keep my oath as best
I can; no one, not you or anyone else, can do more."

Sally said, "Is this the only access to other worlds in
this planet?"

Jennifer shook her head. "No," she said, "this one was
discovered only a few years ago, and so we built a
Worldhouse to cover it; which is what we do whenever
there is an unguarded Gate or patch which comes and
does not close of itself within a very few days. The
Gates—drift. There are abandoned Worldhouses, too.
Sooner or later, they simply take on a mundane purpose.
Stonehenge, for instance. It's closed; no tourist has fallen
through there for a hundred years. There isn't even a
Watcher, let alone a Guardian. Most ancient temples are
the sites of Worldhouses, or were once. We don't really
have enough people to staff them." She smiled faintly at
Sally and said, "I heard you lecture once in a parapsychology department. You spoke of the difficulty of getting people who aren't either skeptics or True Believers.
Believe me, Miss Lobeck, I can relate to that. I talked,
once, to Amy Brittman. Before she took up with Pentarn." Her voice was hard, but Fenton could see the mus-
cles moving in her throat as she swallowed. "She
shouldn't have died that way. And it happened because
some people were careless about interference. Or because there weren't enough people who would do their
job right. I—" her voice shook. "I'm not everywhere, and
I'm only one Watcher. We're understaffed, and so some
ironfolk got through."

"I should think you'd have no trouble getting volunteers—"

"Not in getting volunteers, no. But people who can be trusted to keep their oath, never to interfere no matter what the provocation—*that's* hard," she said, and there were tears in her eyes. "And so Amy died. And the—the Alfar may not be able to stand against the ironfolk. But if we step in to try and change it, we don't know what we may be doing to the balance somewhere else. The only safe thing is to guard our own Gates, make sure no one comes through here to harm the Alfar—and wait." She sobbed. Just once. "That's what's hard. The waiting part."

"Are you saying that all we can do is to go home and wait—not knowing if the Alfar will survive or not? Not warning them about what the ironfolk may be doing?"

"I'm not saying that at all," she said. "Someone from the Alfar may come through to you. I can tell the Alfar to close their own Gates against unauthorized entry. There may be something for you to do; I can't tell. If there is, you will know. But I can't take it on myself to interfere in a third world's affairs, or to mediate. When I took this post, I swore never to interfere; and I will not. I'm sorry, Professor Fenton," she added. On a curious impulse, he reached out and hugged her briefly. She clung to him for a moment, then let him go.

"You'll have to go," she said, with a quick look at the monitor board. "The tides are rotating. You don't want to be locked up inside the dry-cleaning shop, do you? You've got about ten seconds to get outside."

And then she was hustling them through the doorway, and as they crossed the threshold, space reeled dizzily under their feet and they were standing on the sidewalk outside a locked, shuttered facade that said

LAUNDRY AND DRY-CLEANING

And the place was closed, without the glimmer of a light inside.

Sally was dejected as they drove home. "We might as well have saved our time," she said. "We got nowhere. Nowhere!"

"I'm not so sure. She said she is going to send warning to the Alfar to close their own Gates. And she said—" He frowned, knowing that what she said was important, even if he didn't understand it. "—that there might still be something for us to do. Or that—that someone from the Alfar might come through to me. To us. That if there were something for us to do, we'd know."

"I wonder what she meant by that?"

"I don't know, any more than you do," Fenton said, putting his arm around Sally, "but I think she meant we'd know when the time came."

"That's absolutely idiotic! Do you believe in that mystical tosh?"

"Sally," Fenton said, wearily, not even intending a reproof, just speaking the precise literal truth, as it came to him, "after all I've been through tonight, I'm never going to rule out believing *anything* until I prove it one way or the other. Right now, I am going to assume that Jennifer knew what she was talking about. She knew enough to destroy Pentarn's patch, didn't she? Well, then, I'm going to assume that if there's anything more for me to do, I'll know. And until I know, I'm not going to do anything."

Her answering smile was faint. "Well, I am," she said. "What I'm going to do, while we're waiting to know whatever it is that we have to do, is to get some sleep. And I suggest you join me."

They turned in together, on the opened-out couch in her living room, without even taking off their shoes.

CHAPTER NINETEEN

Somewhere an alarm was jangling, an earsplitting sound. The sun was in his eyes, and there was a crick in his neck. Fenton, turning over, heard Sally mumbling, "Turn off the alarm, I don't have a class—" Then suddenly she was wide awake. "Cam! It's the phone!" She jumped for it.

"Miss Lobeck, parapsychology," she said; then: "Oh, my God! Doc, what—yes, he's right here!" She passed him the phone, whispering, her face white. "Garnock. For you. He sounds terrible!"

"Cam—" Garnock's voice was hoarse and terrible. "Over here—Sally—I'll—cover. Say it was a—a lab experiment. Right away. Have to hold together until—"

"Where are you?"

"Smythe Hall, lab. Hurry—" His voice, agonized, cracking, went silent.

Fenton said, "Doc—Doctor Garnock—" a time or two, then dropped the phone, not bothering to hang up. "Sally! Your car keys, right away! We've got to get over there! Doc's hurt!" His mind was in a tangle of ironfolk, Pentarn, the Alfar, vrillswords, any of the things that could have happened to Garnock as a worldwalker. "You drive. You know the fastest way to get to the lab." He was conscious that he had slept in his rumpled clothes. It didn't matter.

The way Sally took led them on to the campus, in a parking lot behind Dwinelle Hall. Sally glanced at the sign which marked *parking restricted,* said violently that she'd pay the fine if she got ticketed and the hell with it, and ran, Fenton right behind her. He took the steps of Smythe Hall at a dead run, Sally at his heels. They burst into the lab, and found Garnock lying on the floor. He had obviously fallen out of the swivel chair behind his desk, and Fenton felt his breath catch as he bent over the older man.

Garnock's clothes were torn and cut and charred, one shoe half burnt off and burned flesh showing through. He let out a faint cry as Fenton touched him.

"What happened? Doc, what happened?" Fenton pleaded. A long singed mark, not a serious burn but probably hellishly painful, ran down the side of Garnocks' head; his hair was scorched.

"Fire—in the rock," Garnock muttered. "Under the caves, the Alfar. Ironfolk—a trap for the ironfolk. Alfar —ready to make a suicide stand there." And Fenton remembered the caves into which the ironfolk had dragged Kerridis.

"Through a world of rock," Garnock whispered. "Close —the rock. Can't close the rock. Irielle—I had her talisman. Take it to her. She says she will meet you where the—where the trees are in a ring. Said you would know. A good place in both worlds. Where she wrote her name. Take her the talisman. She—she sent me back because I had been burned, trying to get through to close the rock—" He opened his scorched fingers, with a cry of pain as something fell from the singed flesh. Fenton had expected it; it was the talisman, the piece of rock, in this world only a piece of flat featureless rock, which in Irielle's world was the talisman between the worlds.

"Doc," Sally pleaded, "you're hurt. Let me call the ambulance!"

"Call—the ambulance," he whispered. "Tell them— lab accident."

His eyes fell shut. Cam leaped for the phone; Sally took it from his hand.

"This is what Jennifer said you must do," she said urgently. "She said you would know when the time came. Go and do it, Cam! I'll look after Garnock!"

"Is he going to be all right?"

"I think so. His heart's beating." And as Fenton still hesitated, she said, "Cam! Doc risked his life to bring you that talisman! He waited till you got here to call any help —he could have had an ambulance here ten minutes ago! Doesn't that show you what it meant to him?" She started dialing the emergency number, ignoring him.

"Right." Sobered, Fenton rose to his feet, looking down with shock and dismay at the unconscious Garnock, but knowing Sally, too, was right. This was what he must do; he *knew* it, with a sense of rightness stronger than any hunch in his life. "I know the place Irielle means. I'll go there right now."

He took the rock-talisman in his hands, stopped, looking at Sally. He had a strange, shocking premonition that he would not see her again for a long, long time, and the thought was frightening; but there was nothing he could say. This was something he *must* do, and he knew it, as Sally knew it. He said, "Sally, I love you." He turned without a backward look and ran; ran down the stairs of Smythe Hall; ran across Sproul Plaza. Even before he passed through the inner gates, he heard the wailing scream of an ambulance, coming up along the avenue, but he paid it no heed. He ran across the campus, disregarding students on their way to eight o'clock classes, political activists setting up card tables distributing Young Conservative and Young Socialist and Libertarian literature, a group of Anachronists clustered on a lawn around two masked and gauntleted men with their wooden battle-swords, striking at one another while their referee or marshall or whatever they called him circled slowly around the fighters. He ran full tilt into a jogger, knocked him off his feet, apologized hastily and ran on while the jogger yelled after him in righteous indignation. He was almost run down by a bicyclist coming along a path, and the bicyclist yelled at him, too, demanding what the hell he thought he was doing barging along like that, but Fenton ignored him.

At last! The eucalyptus grove. It lay deserted in the early morning sunlight. He remembered the Dungeons and Dragons players who had clustered here, months ago, when he was new at interworld travel. They had probably been real Dungeons and Dragons players, not the people of the Worldhouse, with their game that was sometimes a gameboard and sometimes a mystical monitor for Worldgates.

Was the game of Dungeons and Dragons a training device for helping people to visualize other worlds, to play roles in other worlds? A concept introduced into the culture, like the Anachronists, to allow a mundane society some practice in the idea of shifting worlds and cultures? Fenton didn't know; he realized with unusual humility that he might never know. Why should he assume that he could know everything?

He walked into the open space of the eucalyptus grove; dropped to a seat on one of the redwood logs laid in a circle there. In his hand he held the rock-talisman. He felt it stir a little in his hand, as if the filigree carvings of the Alfar world lay just under the surface of the rock, but it did not change. Yet Irielle had said it would take him into the world of the Alfar.

"No," said a soft, almost ghostly voice. "It cannot take you into our world, not this time; the Gates have been closed. I have come through to you—I have been able to come through to you—because this was once my own world and even Findhal cannot gainsay that right. Joel—" he looked up and saw Irielle walking toward him. Her face was pale and tear-stained. "Joel has gone into his father's world. He said—he said he had no right to stay here when it meant war; he swore he would come back to me, if he could, but he would sacrifice even my love when the alternative was war and chaos."

She was sobbing helplessly. Fenton held out his arms and Irielle fell into them. She felt insubstantial, like a ghost. She had come as a 'tweenman, risking all that danger, to beg for his help; he knew it, and wondered what he could possibly do.

"Oh, Fenn-ton, Fenn-ton, I know he is right, but I cannot bear it! He has done what he must do, I know it, but I know he will kill himself before he becomes the leader of Pentarn's army of death and ruin! He has sworn that he will die first, and I know he speaks the truth!"

He held her, gently; put the talisman into her hand. She clasped it, and strangely he felt her solidify, turn warm and woman in his arms, and even as she sensed it she drew a little away from him, shy and sensitive again.

"Why have you come here, Irielle?"

"For the talisman," she said. "Somehow I must get through the Worldhouse and ask them to help me close a Gate they have not closed; the Gate into the rocks. Somehow, the ironfolk are still coming through the rock below the caves, where no Gate should be. All of the Gates they know, in the Worldhouse, have been closed; old Myrill swears it; but there is a Gate that is none of ours and somehow I must find a way to close it."

Fenton knew, immediately, that this was the Gate from the gnome's world. No one from Earth could interfere; but the Alfar wished to close their Gates, and Irielle, an Alfar changeling, had the right to go into the gnome's world and demand that he close this gate.

The gnome bore the Alfar no ill-will. And he hated the ironfolk. Surely he would be amenable to such a request. Fenton asked, "Irielle, can't you go through the Worldhouse there?"

"The Gates have been closed," she said, shaking. "Lebbrin and Erril and my foster-father forced Kerridis to close them all; and Myrill would not make an exception, even to send me into the unlawful Gate through the rocks. We tried to go down and force the Gate closed ourselves, the brave man from your world, and I; but he was burned when the rocks opened and spewed fire, and I made him keep the talisman so that he could reach your world alive. Findhal could have healed him as he healed my leg; but he would not, he said he would never again trust any man of your kind," Irielle said, and she was crying again, trying to control herself. "Oh, he was so hurt, the doctor, I thought he would die then and there, I made him use the talisman to go through, but I could not come with him, I tried to hold to him and come through, but his burns were so bad I could not hold to him, it gave him too much pain—"

So Irielle had risked the permanent loss of the talisman, and perhaps the last chance of the Alfar, because she would not see a brave man die. She went on, helplessly, "Findhal is angry with me; he has cast me off, he said my loyalty was to the sunworlds and not to the Alfar, because I would not let the doctor die. But he did not come willingly into our world. There was no reason he should die for our quarrels." She looked up at Fenton and pleaded, "Will you take me to the Worldhouse?"

"Of course. Of course, my dear." Fenton took her hands; they were solid, now, but cold and shaking. "Come."

As they walked along, past the buildings of the college, a few early students stared at the young man in rumpled clothing and the girl in the long heavy dress, wrapped in scarves and shawls. She took off her fur-lined russet cloak and carried it over her arm, and Fenton realized as they passed the group of Anachronists that she simply looked like one more of them. She clutched at his arm, hearing the ring of swords.

"Oh, what is it—"

"A game. A mock-battle," he said.

She shivered and said, "I think I have seen so many battles, I will never again be able to watch a mock one with any pleasure!" She turned her eyes away. "Even, sometimes, the mock-battles of the dragon-game on the board!"

So the Alfar had boardgame battles, too, and he wondered if it were some form of Dungeons and Dragons. Irielle shrank from the crowds as they walked down Telegraph Avenue. He caught a glimpse of the shaven hippie who had sold him the bootleg Antaril and wondered if he, too, was a part of this unfolding drama, told himself firmly not to be paranoid; there *must* be some innocent bystanders, after all.

They passed the Rathskeller, and the bookshop and the Greek restaurant, and the dry-cleaning shop—damn! The dry-cleaning shop was still there.

He said aloud, "A watched pot never boils."

"What, Fenn-ton?"

There was no need to take out his frustration on Irielle. "What do you do when you can't find the Worldhouse?" he asked.

"I can usually find it," she said innocently. "At least in the world of the Alfar. Here I do not know."

"Well, you'd better start looking," he said, "because that's where the Worldhouse ought to be. Only it isn't."

"There? The—the white place?"

He remembered that she probably could not read more than a few words; she had been able to print her name, but no more skillfully than a kindergarten child. "Yes. There. Sometimes it is a little shop which sells pictures. And then it is the Worldhouse. Only now it isn't."

She clutched at his arm. "What are we going to do?"

"I don't know," he said grimly. "Pray, maybe. Or try to locate it somewhere." He remembered the little card on the door that said, NIGHTS AND EMERGENCIES, RING BELL. Only this was even more of an emergency and he couldn't find any bell to ring. He went to the door of the dry-cleaning shop, carefully inspecting the frame for any sign of the small emergency bell. There ought to be some way to force the Worldhouse to come back when it was so badly needed, damn it! Only it worked on its own laws, and he didn't know all of them yet.

No sign. No night bell. No emergency bell. Nothing. He stared at it, fiercely willing it to be there, remembering that when he and Sally had come here this morning, it hadn't been there, either, the first time he looked. But ten minutes later he had to admit that it just wasn't there, and the little old man inside the dry-cleaning shop was beginning to look at them very strangely.

The best thing to do, Fenton resolved, was to get the hell out of there before somebody called the cops and turned them in for loitering or something.

Now what? Accept defeat and say that there was nothing he could do, if the Worldhouse wasn't where he expected it to be?

No, damn it. Irielle had said that the Worldhouse could hide itself when someone sought for it when he had no business to be there. By the same token, then, a genuine need for the Worldhouse could make it be there. Fenton was riding on one of the strongest hunches of his entire life. He said, "Come on, Irielle, I think I know where to go now."

He led her along the avenue to the turnoff for his apartment; but he did not go inside, simply fished his car keys from his pocket and handed Irielle inside.

She hung back a little, frightened. "I have not been inside a—a carriage since my leg was hurt," she said.

Thinking of her scars, he reassured her gently. "I'll make sure you won't get hurt this time. Get in, Irielle." He leaned across and fastened the seat belt across her lap and shoulders. "That's to make sure you won't get hurt, see?"

He checked the alcohol level, briefly. Then he started

up the car and broke all existing speed laws getting to the
Bay Bridge. He saw Irielle staring open-mouthed at the
San Francisco skyline, and realized that the girl was probably in shock—if she had ever been in San Francisco,
which seemed unlikely, it had probably been well before
the earthquake in 1906—but, coping with the traffic, he
had no time to reassure her further.

He had to park well outside the North Beach area, but
fortunately the rush-to-work was over and it was not yet
time for the lunchtime crush. Thousands upon thousands
of people on the streets would blur, he supposed, whatever ESP facility he would have to use to send out the
kind of message he was going to send out. However, he
thought, forcing himself to positiveness, if he could do
ESP experiments on the crowded conditions of the University campus, where there were more students than in
most middle-sized cities, he could do them anywhere.
But this was the most important one of his life.

Now. Where had he seen that little bookshop, years
ago, two or three times, when it was closed and shuttered? Not on upper Grant Street, but on one of the little cul-de-sac streets that ran off it at an angle, where the
main streets ran down to Broadway and the garish, tour-
isty Fisherman's Wharf area. He said, "Take the talisman
in your hand, Irielle. And think hard about finding the
Worldhouse."

She looked at him, troubled, but did as he said; he
could tell she had done as he said, though thought-
reading was not really among Fenton's talents. But he
was still riding the crest of the tremendous hunch he had
been following. *When you have something to do, you
will know.* That was what Jennifer had said. And he was
absolutely sure she had been right.

A momentary trouble flickered across his mind, that it
was ridiculous to go around strange streets trying to
broadcast, calling as if it were a lost dog. *Here, Worldhouse; come, Worldhouse.* . . . He had to restrain a gig-
gle. But of course it sounded silly when you put it that
way. Was it any sillier than the idea of a little print-shop
that was sometimes a dry-cleaning shop, or a girl torn to
pieces by little hairy uglies out of a Rackham illustration
for *Goblin Market?* Yet they were real, dreadfully real,

and so was the Worldhouse, and so was the power which
would bring the Worldhouse to him. He formed the
thought firmly in his mind.

*There is a great need. I must get through to the World-
house. Lives are at stake, lost in ignorance.*

He kept repeating it, in his mind, allowing nothing to
distract him. Irielle walked at his side as if in a trance,
holding to the talisman.

Up one small street and down the other side. Once he
thought he saw it, but it was a fruit market. The trouble
was that he couldn't remember precisely what it looked
like. Though he was sure he would know it when he saw
it. Up another street, and down, and another.

"Fenn-ton—"

"What is it, Irielle?"

"The talisman. It moved in my hand."

He thought with a touch of elation, *we're getting warm*.
But it was too soon for elation. He said in a low voice,
"Good. Let me know if it happens again."

A bookshop, open, books in a basket, shopworn and
soiled and fourth-hand, marked $1. A spaghetti parlor,
grubby, a skinny teenager mopping it out and a fat
woman chalking prices on the blackboard for lunch.
Good smells. A small market, hung outside with strings of
garlic and long phallic salami in bunches. A storefront
painted in sloppy poster-paint letters, CHURCH OF
THE GOLDEN LIGHT, SERVICES SUNDAY NIGHT,
PRAYER, ALL WELCOME. Another used-magazine
shop.

*We are in search of the Worldhouse. There is great
need, lives are being lost in ignorance because there has
been tampering with the Gates, we must get through
to the Worldhouse . . .*

"The talisman," Irielle whispered, "it glows . . ."

She held it hidden in her hands, but he could see it
through her fingers. The Worldhouse, then, to be an ef-
fective Gate between the worlds, must be at the center of
some incredibly powerful force. How did the local citizens live their lives so close to a pivot between worlds,
and never know it was there? Or did they, were they like
the young Dungeons and Dragons players in the back
room of the print-shop which was also the Worldhouse?

He felt warmth in his pants pocket; he reached in and pulled out what looked like a cylinder of cheap plastic, the vrill Kerridis had given him. He whispered to Irielle, "Are you carrying any vrill?"

"My dagger. In case I meet with ironfolk," she murmured.

"Take it out. We may need it."

The moment she took the vrill dagger from its sheath Fenton began to feel the pull of force—or had he simply been sensitized to it? He did not need to look up; he simply walked hastily down the next street, and only on the threshold did he raise his head to see the sign, the books in the window; an old, probably priceless copy of Chambers' *The King in Yellow*, a shopworn copy of Leiber's *Our Lady of Darkness*, Anderson's *The Queen of Air and Darkness*, half a dozen odd volumes lying on their sides. Inside he felt the tingle of power in the air, but he saw the thin tall old man, with a face like an intelligent camel, and knew that he was in the presence of what Jennifer had called a Guardian.

He didn't waste time; simply held out the cylinder of vrill and the talisman.

"You know what these are. We need to get through."

"This way," the old man said and drew them through into the back of the shop. He looked sharply at Irielle and said, "You belong to this world but you are an Alfar changeling. Do you want to go back? The Gates into the Alfar world are closed, but you have a right to be there."

She shook her head. "I must get through to the rock world. A Gate has been opened where there should be no Gate and ironfolk are being let into the Alfar world. Somehow I must persuade them in the rock world to close the Gate against the Alfar world."

The old man looked troubled. He said, "You know the law, child. I am Guardian; we in the Worldhouse cannot interfere or even intercede."

"You're right," said Fenton, surprising himself. "But you also say no third party can be allowed to interfere, and the gnome is doing it, in ignorance. He is letting things go through his world to the Alfar, not even knowing that he is contributing to the death of the Alfar. He has a right to choose; to act freely, knowing what he is doing. He has a right to *know*. Then if he still chooses to help the ironfolk against the Alfar, that will be his choice. But he has a right to know the truth."

The old man said, troubled still, "What you say is true. But I have no right to go uninvited into the gnome's world—"

"I don't know anything about that," Fenton said, "but I was invited. The gnome asked me to come back." With his whole soul he dreaded returning to that world of rock, where he had lost his identity, been content to turn to rock in the sun, a rock of rock society, with no desire to be other than he was. And yet, for the Alfar, and for the harmless gnome, he would go back. This was what he knew he must do; everything that had happened to him since he chose to take the bootleg Antaril had been moving him inexorably in this direction. *If there is something more you must do, you will know.* He was still riding on the surging crest of that knowledge. Irielle's eyes were wide and frightened. They met his, but he smiled reassuringly, ignoring her frightened eyes.

The old man asked, "You are aware of the risks?"

Fenton nodded.

"That world is dangerous for humans. I myself ventured there only once, when I was learning the Gates, and I have never dared to return."

"All the same," Fenton said, "I have the right to choose what risks I will take." He had been taking risks, knowingly, ever since he choose parapsychology as a field —first, the risk of abandoning a respectable psychologist's profession, then the risks of strange talents, experimentation with drugs that could loosen the inner girders of the mind. He wondered if all those risks had been run to prepare him for this moment of choice.

"I am not sure you know all the risks. One of my functions is to keep out the ignorant."

Fenton said, with absolute sure knowledge, "You have no authority to keep an invited guest from crossing into any world of his own free choice, if he goes with no intention of doing any harm." He did not know if he was reading the old man's thoughts, or whether it was intuition or clairvoyance. Maybe, in the universe he was now inhabiting, there was no difference between them. He simply *knew*. Jennifer had somehow known that he was ready for that knowledge. Cameron Fenton had been a parapsychologist for ten years. And he knew, now, that he was only beginning to learn the very first thing about parapsychology. It was an opening door, a new world he was entering, a new universe.

The old man nodded in recognition. He said a strange thing; he said, "I recognize you." Then he took up a glass rod like the one Jennifer had used this morning to destroy the patch.

"This way. The Gate isn't easy to find."

"But Irielle—"

But before the old man spoke, Fenton knew the answer. "Irielle has two choices: to remain here or to return to the world of the Alfar. I cannot let her into the rock world. She is not ready."

"Fenn-ton—" Her hands clutched at him; her eyes were frightened.

He held her briefly for a moment, in an embrace almost fatherly, before he let her gently go. He said, "Don't be frightened, Emma." He didn't know why he used her Earth name. "I will handle it. Wait here, or go back to Kerridis; she needs you, I think. You have done what you can here. I'll do what I can, and if I can't—well, then it is not possible. If this doesn't work, we'll have to take whatever comes, I guess." Gently, for the first and last time, he kissed her soft lips. "If—if anything happens, if I don't make it, tell Kerridis—" *No*, he thought, *hell with that. Not yet, not now*. "Tell Kerridis —tell her I did what I could. I'll see you if I can, kid." He turned, moved after the old man, resolutely, without looking back, knowing that she was crying.

CHAPTER TWENTY

THE SUN BURNED, orange and hot. He stood in the center of the rock, the low wall stretching into infinity in either direction, as far as the eye could see, with the rustle of small things beneath his feet. But these were the gnome too. *One is rock. Also one is small beings.*

"Gnome," he said aloud, and before his eyes the rock moved, writhed, heaved slowly upward and put out stubby head, small hard stumpy fingers.

"One is rejoicing in return, togethering. Warm is sun, joyous under brightness. One greets in happiness."

Fenton thought, *I'm glad to see you too, gnome.*

"Other is troubled," remarked the voice. "Be saying cause of othering, not rejoicing."

In his mind Fenton formed a clear picture of the ironfolk; and even as it formed, the gnome's mind seemed to open into his so that he saw the Gate where the ironfolk had penetrated into the rock world, unsought, uninvited, a shortcut to the Alfar world which the ironfolk could normally enter only at the proper time.

"Seeing as intrusion. Not wanting."

And they seemed to move with the speed of thought through the world, so that Fenton saw the yawning Gate, with ironfolk galumphing through from their world, in full howling cry. The gnome's revulsion and dismay held it paralyzed, filling Fenton's mind too, so that he felt his very identity sink into the gnome's, into the peace of the rock, with disgust and horror at these intruders who had thrust themselves into this world, violating it, fouling it! A yawning hole opened and vomited them forth, and Fenton saw the cold snow-filled hills of the Alfar country, the cave-mouths from which the ironfolk could fall upon

the Alfar and ambush them, the caves below filling with
ironfolk—

"*No!*" It was an anguished cry, splitting the rock with
dismay, and he saw the gnome's stumpy form waver with
the pain of it, dissolve into the shapeless wall. Then very
slowly the gnome began to re-form, first thrusting up
the small bullet-head, finally struggling upward and form-
ing a small stumpy hand which it held toward Fenton in
bewilderment.

"Friend fellow is grieving/othering?"

"Don't you even know what you are doing with those
ironfolk? Do you know you are turning them loose on the
Alfar, letting them loose in the Alfar world to kill, burn,
ravage . . ." Fenton's mind formed an anguished picture
of the ironfolk swarming out of the caves, falling on the
Alfar in spite of their vrillswords, hacking them living,
slicing up the horses and cramming fistfuls of living flesh
into their dripping maws, dragging Kerridis with her
flesh blackening at their touch. . . .

He felt the gnome's dismay through his whole mind,
an agony of awareness he could not shut out or close
down, so that his whole body was one ache of agony. "Not
knowing. How stopping?"

Fenton said fiercely, "Send them back where they
came from! Better still, don't let them come in at all! But
don't throw them out on the Alfar! The Alfar never did
you any harm!"

It was a convulsion of pain through the gnome and
through Fenton, closely attuned to it. "Not knowing.
Stopping. Meaning no harm to dance-world, light-world,
tree-world." And again it seemed that the world yawned
and gaped around them, that the whole world was filled
with the howling and honking of the ironfolk, a frenzied
hunger and pain, an insatiable savage blood-lust, so that
Fenton felt his eyes bulging and his loins swelling with
the lust of it, as if he ran and honked and screeched with
their cries, *Plunder and women!* Time telescoped and
he fell into the cry, he was one with it, and at the same
time he felt the total sickness of revulsion at these others,
these horrible intruders . . .

A voice—the gnome's voice—croaked through his total awareness and horror of the ironfolk, "Stopping."

And then the world upheaved in convulsion, searing fire, flow of scalding fire and molten rock. It surged over the ironfolk, scalding, searing, swallowing them up, engulfing them in a vast chaotic ruin. Numberless screams of agony quivered inside him, tearing his own throat with the howling agony of their deaths; he felt them die, he felt them all swallowed up alive.

And he died with them.

A long, long time later Fenton became aware that he was lying in silence, lying quiet, bathed in peace and sun, curled relaxed and sleeping against the soft warmth of the rock wall. Somewhere, very far away, his mind felt bruised, with the memory of agony and many, many deaths, but at the moment there was nothing except peace and sun and rock and warmed by sunfire and the wall in whose shadow he lay. But as memory came slowly back, the rock stirred at his side and began again, slowly, to heave itself into the vaguely human form it had taken before: the gnome.

Stumpy bullet-head; clumsy small hands, and somehow a hint of something else, different *form*—somehow, now, in the gnome, there was a hint of the shape of the ironfolk.

"Surely," the gnome said. "Hairy intruders now part of self-substance, where made harmless, changing self somewhat. Changing in much pain and death and rock never now so peaceful, but never coming those again. Closing, stopping forever, never those to come through again. Closing forever. Others having forgotten that all life is one, and meaning harm to dance-world, tree-world, light-world. So making them, in pain, one with self-substance, showing them once that all life is one."

Fenton reached out for the gnome's small horny warm hand. He felt shaken, inadequate to take it all in. The gnome had taken the ironfolk into itself—as a way of making them aware that all life was one. Fenton, too, had felt that monstrous apocalypse in his own substance.

All life is one.

"And now returning," the gnome said. "Knowing only one way to send you, and closing Gate after so afterward no intruder be disturbing peace of rock. Knowing all life

is one always." Its hard little hand clasped Fenton's
tightly, there was a shimmer of the rock, and . . .

. . . and Fenton stood in the high hilltop road, his
boots crunching on snow, where he had first come into
the Alfar world and seen the ironfolk come swarming out
of the caves to carry Kerridis away. At the cave-mouth
he could see two tall Alfar sentries.

One of them turned, saw him, recognized him.

"Chaos and iron," he said. "It's that 'tweenman who
keeps turning up, like stones in a dance-ring! Here, you,
what are you doing here? Didn't Findhal give orders that
no one from the sunworlds was to be let in? You'll
answer for this, 'tweenman."

"I'm not a 'tweenman," Fenton said, conscious that he
was solid in this world this time, a worldwalker, seeing
his shadow black and real against the dim light of the
snow. "And I have good news for Kerridis. Take me to
her."

"Take me to Kerridis," mocked the Alfar warrior, angrily. "Do you think the Lady of the Alfar is at your beck
and call, whoever you are?"

"No, I sent for him," Kerridis said. She came out
slowly from the cave-mouth. He had no time to be surprised that she was there, waiting for him. Nothing surprised Fenton now. He knew that he had only to move
along the lines decreed for him. She came and for the
first time in his solid body he felt the touch of her hand,
firm and delicate, in his own.

"Fenn-ton. Tell me what has happened."

"The gates in the rock are closed," he said, and
swayed, suddenly conscious of great weariness. How
long had it been since he had stood there, one with the
rock, and known the screaming death of the ironfolk?
"No more ironfolk will come through *that* Gate. Never."

"They came into our world, screaming for women and
plunder," Kerridis said, "and then suddenly there were
no more. Our warriors have gathered to make a final
stand against them. Come." She reached out to him
and led him down into the caves. Far below he heard the
sound of battle, where the war-cries of Alfar and ironfolk resounded. They stood on a ledge above the great

cavern where Kerridis had been imprisoned and watched the battle raging; with their vrillswords, the Alfar warriors were slaughtering the ironfolk.

"It is no longer the suicide battle Irielle foresaw," Kerridis said, leaning against him. "Since the ironfolk did not come in numberless hordes, we can stand against them—ah, look! Look! They are defeated, they are in rout—ruin and death! There is Pentarn, Pentarn among them—"

And Fenton could see where he stood, the figure of Pentarn, surrounded by ironfolk. He was too far above them to hear; the voices were lost, but he heard fragments of speech, Pentarn urging them back to the attack, to charge again. But the ironfolk no longer heard. Turning on Pentarn, they forced him back, back to the very lip of the rock, raging, evidently demanding an accounting for leading them into this battle they could not win, as they had always won before.

The air around Pentarn shimmered; once again he would escape into his handy portable spacewarp, the hole in space, the patch he could make where he chose. And suddenly, with that knowledge which had been rising in him ever since he went through the Worldhouse that day, Fenton knew what he must do. The cylinder of vrill was still in his pocket. The Alfar used their vrill as a simple weapon. But vrill, which belonged in all worlds, was more than a weapon, more even than a healing stone which could heal the hurt of the ironfolk against those of other planes. It could heal the Gates themselves. He snatched it out, as Jennifer had done with the glass rod which, he now knew had also been vrill, and concentrated on it fiercely.

The shimmer in space was gone; the patch fizzled and died. Pentarn, his escape cut off, turned hopelessly to face the ironfolk he had led, first to ignoble conquest and then to massacre under the Alfar swords. He was drowned in their cries; he went down under their claws; he vanished, trampled under their feet. Kerridis cried out in horror and hid her face in Fenton's chest; he held her close, crooning to her, and when he raised his own head nothing was left but red stains on the floor, where the Alfar warriors had moved in and were killing off the

last of the marauding ironfolk. Of Pentarn there was no
sign; only blood, mingled with the blood of the dead and
dying ironfolk.

Fenton could not control a shudder. But he realized it
had been a quicker and more merciful death than Pentarn had meted out to other victims; a quicker death than
Amy Brittman's.

He looked, dazed, at the vrill in his hands. It had
trapped Pentarn here, to face his fate, by abolishing the
unlawful patches in space that he had made; now only
the genuine Gates remained.

Kerridis took his hand and led him out of the caves of
death, into the light of the Alfar world.

"I would like to stay with the Alfar forever," said Joel
Tarnsson. "My only happiness is here. But I shall be
needed in my father's world. My mother was the old
King's daughter; it is my duty to rule there in her name,
for a time at least, until the army my father built for conquest can be put back to a better use." He looked at
Findhal, his head raised in defiance; but in supplication
too.

"I cannot do it without Irielle at my side. For the good
of both our worlds, will you let her come back to my
world as my wife?"

The giant Alfar sighed, then reached out and clapped
both his hands on the slender youth's shoulders. He said,
"So be it, lad. I will miss her, but any father who rears a
beloved daughter knows he does it to yield her some day
to another. You are both from the sunworlds. I think
she will be happy there." He smiled and said, "Take her
with my blessing, Joel Tarnsson; but let her come to us
sometimes, when the moon is full and the Gates are
open, to dance with us in the Alfar forests."

Joel smiled and drew Irielle to him. He said, "If I may
come too."

Kerridis drew Irielle to her and kissed her on the forehead. She said, "And my blessing too, dearest child.
Come and sing to us now and then. Be happy with your
lover in the sunworlds."

Turning to Fenton with a smile, she said, "I thought at

first it was you who would take Irielle from me, back into the sunworlds where her destiny lay."

He shook his head, smiling. He said, "Maybe I thought so too, for a little while." And he thought how strange it was that Irielle, who was his great-aunt, or maybe his great-great-aunt, had in a curious way become his daughter.

"And your destiny too lies in the sunworlds," Kerridis said with a sad smile. "Come, I will take you back to the Worldhouse. But you, too, will come again?"

She raised her face to his; and suddenly he knew, even though she was the Lady of the Alfar, what she wanted of him. He drew her close to him and kissed her; a long and lingering kiss, that was, by the time they drew apart, a promise and a beginning. She smiled up at him and they walked on, hand in hand.

As they moved into the shadow of the grove where, he knew, the great hall of doors opened, she said, hesitantly, "I can command all things from my own people; but of you I can only ask this as a friend. You know how I am served in the Worldhouse. Findhal has commanded my armies too long, unrewarded; I intend to send him there as Guardian. But I feel I need a friend there, too. I have no right to ask this; but, Fenn-ton, will you petition in the Worldhouse to become a Watcher there, and perhaps, some day, Guardian?" She looked up at him, her small hands resting on his shoulders. "When you are there, Fenn-ton, I shall feel safe. I shall know that no evil can come to us from your world, at least . . ."

"I should like it above all things," Fenton said softly, holding her hands clasped in his, as they went into the Worldhouse.

"And you will be near us, in the Worldhouse; and you will come back to us, sometimes . . ."

"I will," he promised.

Inside the Worldhouse the old man Myrill was there; at a word from Kerridis he summoned Jennifer, who came and glanced at Fenton.

He said, almost defiantly, "When the time came, I knew."

"Of course," she said, almost carelessly. "Well, are you going to be a Watcher for us? We're always understaffed, you know, and it's hard work. And all the pay you'll get is the kind of salary you'd get working in a print-shop, and you'll have to sell books and prints on the side to people who wander in, not knowing; so that you'll be there when people really need the World-house. What about it? I understand Lady Kerridis wants you there."

"I—" Suddenly Fenton knew he had to do this; that it was what he had been born to do, that the long road of parapsychology had been only a preparation bringing him here, to the appointed place.

The place of his destiny, the House between the Worlds, the place where the real nature of the universe was defined.

"I will," he said.

"You'll have to take the Watcher's oath, you know," Jennifer said. Fenton realized that she had been guiding him along as they spoke and now he realized that, this time without the dizzying sense of reeling worlds, he was back in the back room of the print-shop, standing beside the game-table which was also a monitor of shift-ing universes. "And, some day, the Guardian's oath."

The young men sitting around the table were shifting their small figures. "What have you got there, Jenny?"

"Professor Fenton," she said, and Fenton corrected her.

"Cam."

The young man shrugged. "The names are all tradi-tional," he said. "Whatever your name is, your name in the Worldhouse has to be a Guardian name. I'm Lance. This is Arthur. That's Kay, and this is Gareth, and this—" He pointed across the table. "—is Morgan. She's new to us, too, but she's an analogue and we knew she belonged right away."

Dazed, he looked into Sally's eyes, and she smiled, a dazzling smile.

"Welcome—or welcome back, Cam," she whispered.

He looked down at the table. It was only a gameboard now; but he knew that when the proper time came, the worlds would shift and it would be a monitor screen, keeping watch over the multiplex universes which came and went, shifting from place to place in space and time.

He looked at the place where the Alfar hall of doors had vanished. He had had no opportunity to say goodbye to Kerridis. But he knew he was not saying goodbye; he would change worlds again, many, many times, and the promise was there, waiting for the proper time. Meanwhile, here was Sally, whom he loved, and he had to find out how it was with Garnock and Uncle Stan, and what had brought Sally back here. But there was time for that too.

"Your move, Cam," said Gareth, across the game-table from him, and Fenton looked down at the little glowing game-figures on the table before him. "Now that you know us. And you've met Jenny; sometimes we call her Gwen. Name your universe."

Cameron Fenton smiled across the table at Sally, and at his new associates, and accepted his destiny. There was plenty of time to learn a Watcher's duties. And while he was waiting, he might as well learn to play Dungeons and Dragons.

It was what they all did, he supposed, while they were waiting. And they had been doing it, in one form or another, since the days of King Arthur—and before.

He took his place at the Round Table and shook the dice Gareth handed to him. Soon they would tell him his new name.

About the Author

Marion Zimmer Bradley has been a professional writer for more than twenty-five year. She is best known for her novels of exotic fantasy adventure, particularly her best-selling DARKOVER series.

Ms. Bradley lives in Berkeley, California, with her husband Walter Breen, a celebrated authority on American coins, and their two children.

She has just completed a major historical fantasy dealing with the incredible women of the King Arthur legend.